The jump light turned green. *"Go!"*

Brandon stepped into a flying exit and spread arms and legs to create drag and slow his descent. Those at the rear of the stick went head down and arms alongside in order to barrel down at speed to catch up with those who jumped first. Brandon hesitated a second or two to make sure everyone was with him, then stabilized and pulled.

His square popped open on heading. His parachute buffeted about across the sky. Swinging underneath it made freeing his night vision goggles and getting them on a challenge.

Finally, he got them on and looked around for the others. Looked good. Glow strips shone all around him like neon lights. Below lay nothing but the corrugated darkness of rain clouds.

Brandon took a reading on his Global Position System and calculated they were southeast of Checkpoint Mobile and traveling faster than anticipated. He set his course. "Hold the wind to your one-eighty," he advised through his voice-activated helmet mike. "Guide on me."

A voice jumped out of airspace and into his helmet with chilling presence.

"Somebody's going down!"

One of the glow strips, far below, streaked toward earth like a falling star and vanished into the black cloud cover . . .

Books by Charles W. Sasser

DETACHMENT DELTA
OPERATION COLD DAWN
OPERATION ACES WILD
OPERATION DEEP STEEL
OPERATION IRON WEED
PUNITIVE STRIKE

DETACHMENT DELTA

OPERATION COLD DAWN

CHARLES W. SASSER

AVON BOOKS
An Imprint of HarperCollinsPublishers

This is a work of fiction. Names, characters, places, and incidents are products of the author's imagination or are used fictitiously and are not to be construed as real. Any resemblance to actual events, locales, organizations, or persons, living or dead, is entirely coincidental.

AVON BOOKS
An Imprint of HarperCollins*Publishers*
10 East 53rd Street
New York, New York 10022-5299

Copyright © 2006 by Bill Fawcett & Associates
ISBN-13: 978-0-06-059236-3
ISBN-10: 0-06-059236-2
www.avonbooks.com

First Avon Books paperback printing: January 2006

Avon Trademark Reg. U.S. Pat. Off. and in Other Countries, Marca Registrada, Hecho en U.S.A.
HarperCollins® is a registered trademark of HarperCollins Publishers Inc.

Printed in the U.S.A.

10 9 8 7 6 5 4 3 2 1

**This book is dedicated to
the American Armed Forces**

"Never in the history of the world has any soldier sacrificed more for the freedom and liberty of total strangers than the American soldier."

SENATOR ZELL MILLER, GEORGIA

Author's Note

While this novel is a work of fiction, with no intended references to real people either dead or alive other than the obvious ones, discerning readers will undoubtedly make connections between recent history and events in this book. These are intended. For example, I have used the tragic terrorist attacks of 9/11, the War on Terror, and subsequent expansion of the war into other areas, specifically Iraq and Russia in this instance, for the adventures described.

In this volume, as in previous ones, I have emphasized that the War on Terror encompasses many fronts and that politics, both international and national, is one of them. While I use fictionalized accounts of political figures and political events, even changing the names of major political parties, I do so with the understanding that these are used in a fictionalized context. These figures and events are shown through the eyes of soldiers in a way that I know from personal military experience reflects upon a certain reality commonly accepted by our armed forces.

This is the fifth book in the series. A comment made by Jennifer Fisher, my editor at HarperCollins, applies as well to this current saga as it did to previous ones: "There was an eerie sense of wondering what was fact and what was fiction . . ."

For thirteen years I was a member of the U.S. Army Special Forces (the Green Berets), and therefore have some understanding of covert and SpecOps missions. I hope to continue this merging of fact and fiction to create stories that may very well reflect the *real* stories behind counterterrorist operations by the United States.

Finally, I want to make clear that my rendering of certain high-profile characters in both politics and the military are largely creations of my own imagination or are interpretations necessary to the plot.

DETACHMENT
DELTA
OPERATION COLD DAWN

CHAPTER 1

Earth's Atmosphere

". . . ballistic descent!"

Final static-garbled words erupting from the Russian *Soyuz* space capsule returning to earth from the International Space Station. Two full hours before scheduled reentry. Three spacemen aboard—two American astronauts and a Russian cosmonaut. Houston Space Center had heard nothing since. NASA assumed this last message meant a malfunction in the guidance computer had switched the *Soyuz* from a normal to a premature ballistic descent. This was the first time in twenty-eight years that U.S. astronauts had returned to earth in a capsule, and their first time ever to land in a capsule on the ground.

It was going to land only God knew where. Certainly it would miss its targeted landing zone in Kazakhstan by hundreds of miles. Or it would break up and burn in the earth's atmosphere.

The first sixteen minutes of atmospheric reentry were the most brutal. Riding it was like being stuffed into the core of a bullet and shot at the earth from a giant pistol. Friction sparked flickering tongues of flame from the outer skin. The inner skin glowed.

Tremendous heat sucked sweat from the pores of the three riders aboard the *Soyuz*. Eight G's, twice the normal amount, molded them to their seats. Pressure made breathing laborious, even though the spacemen wore G-suits.

Eyes bulged. Tongues slipped back in their heads and into their throats. Skulls felt like they might explode.

The only thing they could do was ride the ship in—and pray that it held together.

By some miracle, it remained intact, earth's cushion of air finally slowing it enough to allow the main parachute to open normally. The capsule dangled below the huge multicolored parachute like a silver bullet in the high intense sunlight. Slowly it drifted downward into heavy cloud cover, into a monstrous blister of thunderstorms that gave the frightened spacemen a second wild ride, albeit comparatively tamer than the first.

"Vomit comet . . . !" someone gasped, already suffering from the motion sickness common to travelers returning from long space flights.

Blown about like a dandelion seed in wind, the *Soyuz* finally spurted from the clouds and swept at dizzying speeds above a soaked and dreary landscape so rugged a giant might have mauled it with his fingernails, a terrain so alien the capsule might be landing on a planet other than earth. It skimmed over a flood-swollen river and barely cleared a rocky promontory that clawed at it with one horny finger.

It hit hard on a mountainside meadow. The inflated parachute dragged it tumbling downhill for more than fifty feet. It finally came to rest among a field of boulders with one hatch lodged solidly against the ground, all its exterior antennas having been ripped off. The deflating parachute continued to whip and pop in the wind and driving rain.

The three spacemen, sick, weak, and shook up, remained buckled in their seats to recuperate from the rough reentry and even rougher landing. What was another hour or so after their having spent the last five months in the International Space Station? Communications were out and they had no idea where on the globe they might have landed. For the time being, all they could do was wait for someone to come.

Smoke from the pyrotechnic bolts that automatically opened the parachute oozed into the capsule and finally compelled the spacemen to pop the clear hatch. Although the rain had slackened, it still slashed through the opening and into their faces. No one minded. They smelled the rich earth odors of soil and grass for the first time in months. There had been a time when they thought they might never feel rain or sunshine or *anything* again.

The travelers solemnly shook hands all around. Then, curious about their surroundings, they pulled themselves out of the capsule. Their legs would not support their weight. Returning spacemen had to crawl around on hands and knees until their bodies made the transition back to gravity from prolonged weightlessness. They sought shelter from the rain where the nose of the ship rested against a boulder, forming a relatively protected hollow underneath.

Soon, a group of men came into sight, hurrying over a ridgeline and downhill across the meadow toward the boulder field and the space wreck. The parachute by this time had collapsed like a used condom. Expecting rescue, the spacemen waved and shouted.

They stopped waving and shouting. The ratty-looking men, armed with assault rifles and pistols, surrounded the capsule and stood in the rain, heads lowered, black beards and mustaches beaded with rainwater, eyes sharp and hostile. Their leader barked a command in Russian. He repeated the order, followed by an impatient jabbing gesture with his AK-47.

"He's telling us to get up," the cosmonaut interpreted. "We are their prisoners."

CHAPTER 2

SPACE CAPSULE FEARED LOST

Houston (CPI)—NASA announced today that a malfunction aboard the *Soyuz* space capsule returning from the International Space Station caused it to make a premature reentry. Communications with the capsule ceased at 10:00 a.m. local when it apparently entered the earth's atmosphere two hours ahead of schedule and at a too-steep angle that may have caused it to catch fire and explode.

Search and rescue efforts have been initiated in the Pacific from Japan and Sakhalin Island to China, Korea and eastern Russia. North Korea has already protested violation of its air space should the *Soyuz* land on its sovereign territory.

"We have no idea where it is at this point," said NASA ground mission commander Alan Cunningham. "There is no indication that the craft exploded on reentry. We think it landed. We just don't know where yet."

Aboard the ship were returning U.S. space station commander Roger Callison, astronaut Larry Williams and Russian cosmonaut Alexei Minsky . . .

CHAPTER 3

Sacramento, California

As a young captain during the Vietnam War, U.S. Army general Darren E. Kragle, commander of USSOCOM (United States Special Operations Command), led the only successful POW escape from North Vietnam's notorious Hanoi Hilton. U.S. senator (Alabama) Denton Fullbright had also been a prisoner of war. It was he who, while being interviewed by North Vietnamese television in Hanoi after the third degree to get him to "respond correctly," used his eyes to blink out in Morse code the word T-O-R-T-U-R-E. For their courage, both soldiers received the nation's highest medal for valor—the Congressional Medal of Honor.

The two tall men in Army Class A Dress Green uniforms stood together outside the highly polished double doors of the California State Assembly in Sacramento. General Kragle took another look at his watch. They had been waiting for quite some time. A few minutes before, Assemblyman Richard McGlothin of San Diego stepped out to say there had been a hitch. He didn't say what kind of hitch.

"There's been a . . . Well, there's a problem," he blurted out. He looked apoplectic with rage—his cheeks florid, his eyes sharp and angry, his tie disheveled and loosened. Sounds of debate from the assembly floor escaped around him when he opened the door and went back inside.

Annoyed at the delay, General Kragle swept off his gold-braided bill cap with one hand and ran the other across a military buzz cut that had turned almost silver within the past few years; the thick brush of his trimmed mustache matched his hair. The lean, permanently weathered face looked more tired and worn than usual, but the hardness remained. The graying hair might have been hammered like nails into the solid oak of his skull. Almost everyone called him *the General*, including his three sons attached to U.S. Army 1st Special Forces Operational Detachment-Delta, otherwise known as the Army's crack counterterrorist unit Delta Force.

General Kragle had not wanted to fly to Sacramento in the first place when Assemblyman McGlothin telephoned him at USSOCOM headquarters in Tampa, Florida.

"General Kragle," he petitioned, "I've been a minority member of the California State Assembly for four years. Party of the People controls the House. They have sponsored many so-called celebrations on the assembly floor, including Cinco de Mayo, St. Patrick's Day, Ramadan, and Kwanzaa. Not once have we celebrated America's Independence Day. I would like Colonel Fullbright and you to represent patriotism at this year's first celebration of Patriots Day. We would be honored if you appeared to speak. In your careers, Colonel Fullbright and you have demonstrated the highest qualities of courage, commitment, and integrity to our nation."

The General demurred. Party of the People indeed dominated the California House and was outspoken in its support for presidential candidate Senator Lowell Rutherford Harris and in its opposition to President Woodrow Tyler and the War on Terror. In General Kragle's opinion, which he was never loathe to proffer, the Party of the People was no longer the party of Jefferson, Jackson, and

Cleveland; it had turned into the party of Marx and Lenin. Some members of that august body booed the Boy Scouts, the *Boy Scouts of America,* for God's sake, because they refused to take "God" out of their pledge and declined to accept gay Scoutmasters. They'd likely as not throw rotten tomatoes and pies if the military showed up.

McGlothin went over the General's head to General Abraham Morrison, Chairman of the Joint Chiefs of Staff.

"I can't order you to go, Darren," General Morrison said, "but I think it's a good idea."

"What will I tell them?" the General hedged. "That our Jihad junkie enemies don't fear the United States for its diplomatic skills or for its compassion and sensitivity? That our enemies are irrational, even outright insane, and that the only thing they respect is the firepower of our tanks, planes, and helicopter gunships? I'd be lucky if they didn't tar and feather me and ride me out of the state on a rail."

"Your visit is not political," General Morrison countered.

"*Everything* is political to a politician."

"The Left Coast needs a dose of old-fashioned patriotism. Assemblyman McGlothin says it needs to see heroes."

"Then why doesn't he invite Barbra Streisand and Michael Moore?"

The General finally acquiesced, against his instincts and better judgment. Now, cooling his heels outside the State Assembly, he knew he should have stayed in Florida.

McGlothin reappeared within a few minutes, this time looking as embarrassed as he did furious. "A . . . a problem," he reiterated.

"Which means?" Colonel Fullbright prompted.

Assemblyman McGlothin passed him a memo from the

Party of the People leadership. Fullbright read it, his eyes narrowing, and passed it on to General Kragle.

> *After due consideration, there will be no Patriots Day celebration. Problems have arisen both with regards to the spirit, content and participation of various individuals with regard to the ceremony. We do not feel it appropriate for military men to speak who do not believe in separation of church and state and who support policies that allow an unjust and illegal war to continue being waged against the Muslim populations of the world . . .*

General Kragle executed a stiff about-face. He and Colonel Fullbright marched out of the California assembly, which then opted to celebrate the career of a *Los Angeles Times* reporter who had written a series of articles critical of President Tyler and the War on Terror.

CHAPTER 4

Fayetteville, North Carolina

Lying naked in bed, only a sheet pulled over his midsection, Cassidy Kragle listened to water running in the bathroom as Margo Foster washed her frustration down the shower drain. Ordinarily, he would have gotten up and gone home—except he *was* home. His off-base apartment at Fort Bragg, home of U.S. Army Special Forces, the elite Delta Force, and the 82nd Airborne Division, flaunted the macho masculine touch of a bachelor's pad. A basketball rested in the doorway to the living room. The bedroom itself accommodated a stack of old Army FM manuals in one corner, a sweaty karate gi thrown over them; a Kevlar paratrooper's helmet in another corner; a pair of well-scuffed running shoes on a bearskin rug next to the bed; and a SOG SK 2000 sheathed combat knife, an empty beer can, pizza crust, and a pager on the nightstand. Delta Force required each soldier to keep a pager with him twenty-four hours a day.

Margo had dropped her blue bikini panties, bra, and Army BDU uniform on the bedroom carpet as she fled the battlefield. The garments lent the room an incongruous feminine touch. Cassidy's own BDUs were tossed carelessly over a chair, his green beret caught jauntily on its back, one boot next to the basketball and the other partly underneath the bed. He grinned ruefully. *His* and *Hers*, matching combat uniforms. Therein lay the root of most of their quarrels.

He turned over on his side to face the bathroom's closed door. In his late twenties, the younger of the three Kragle brothers was tall and lanky and slab-sided with toned muscle, much like the other Kragles. He was clean-shaven with a dark military buzz cut and piercing blue eyes clouded a bit from his own frustration.

The angry cascade of the shower continued behind the door. Margo was one stubborn piece of female. A center-fold when she dropped her BDUs, all curves, long dark hair and big brown eyes. But *stubborn*.

Sergeant Margo Foster filled a slot in Delta Force's Intelligence Section, a member of the "Funny Platoon," so-called because it accepted a limited number of women. Like the other Kragles in his extended military family, Sergeant Cassidy Kragle made no bones about his conviction that females did not belong in either combat or combat support outfits. Women should not be sent to war where they could get good men killed trying to protect them.

Kathryn, Cassidy's first wife, had gotten out of the navy so they could get married. She was pregnant with their child when she died from anthrax poisoning following the terrorist attacks of 9/11.

Cassidy and Margo had jumped laughing into his Miata convertible as soon as they went off-duty at six and raced from the Delta compound to his apartment for a passionate roll before they went out clubbing with Bobby Goose Pony, Goose Pony's girlfriend, and some of the other Delta couples. Things got serious when they arrived at his place. Margo gasped at the sight of the clutter—discarded pizza boxes, Coke and beer cans, dirty dishes, soiled clothing . . .

"You are a slob, Kragle," she scolded. "I just went through here with Tide and Borax the last time I was here.

We're going to have to clean up your act the same way when we get married."

He should have kept his mouth shut. Instead, he said, "Name a date—after you get out of the army."

That set her off; he should have known it would. "I'm not getting out of the army."

He tried to shrug it off before things went too far, as they always did whenever the subject was broached. He grabbed her hand playfully and headed for the bedroom. She jerked free.

"Maybe Summer got out of the CIA so Brandon would marry her, but that doesn't mean I'll give up the army so I can marry you, Cassidy Kragle."

"That's your choice," he rejoined.

"My God, Kragle! Listen to you!" she flared. "Your way or the highway, is that what you're saying? Brandon and you are just alike, and you're both carbon copies of the General. Is this what you all expect of your women—waiting around to spit out kids while you men run off to war every few months?"

"Summer knew what she was getting into when she married my brother. It's your choice to make."

"Well, Summer can just *stay* pregnant. I won't. You Kragles! You . . . You . . . You *Kragles!*"

At least she hadn't stormed out of the apartment; she locked herself in the shower.

Cassidy inhaled deeply, drawing in her lingering scent left in the bedroom. Faint and sweet and musky. He supposed he really was in love with her. At least he was as much in love with her as a warrior Kragle had a right to be.

"The Kragles are good men," Brown Sugar Mama forthrightly informed the women who aspired to become her "sons'" wives. Gloria—dear Brown Sugar Mama—

was the only mother Cassidy or his older brothers Brandon and Cameron remembered. The General hired the black woman while Rita was still alive. She stayed on to take over the household and the rearing of the Kragle brothers after their mother died.

"You ain't never gonna put chains on 'em unless they wants it," she said. "So don't you try or you just runs them off. They is hard-headed too. They got they principles and they got they beliefs, just like they daddy. The Kragles got core. I raised my sons with core. You got to accept that or you don't accept them. If you wants something else than that, go out and find yourself one of them sissy boys that get his hair styled, wear earrings, and sit down to pee."

Cassidy heard the shower cut off. Maybe it had cooled Margo down. The bathroom door opened after a minute and she stood there, still wet and fresh and wearing nothing but the look of a contrite little girl prepared to make up.

"Will you make love to me?" she asked.

He threw the sheet off his body and vaulted to the floor, intent on sweeping her into bed with him. The pager on the nightstand buzzed. The only time it ever went off was to signal an alert. Margo stiffened.

"Damn!" Cassidy muttered.

The display face printed out a code number that, translated, meant *Report immediately.*

Cassidy said, "We have time for a quickie if we hurry."

"I don't do quickies," she snapped. "Go on, Kragle. Get out of here. Damn you."

CHAPTER 5

Tampa, Florida

General Kragle was in one shitty mood. The abortion that was the California State Assembly hadn't improved it any. Back during the years when Colonel Charlie Beckwith and he were forming Delta Force, the nation's strike counterterrorist unit, Charlie referred to such moods as "the shit-blahs." The General had the shit-blahs, had them bad.

He flinched as he leaned against the door frame to his home study. The recent bullet scar on his arm remained tender to the touch. He ducked his head to avoid knocking his cap off on the overhead—he sometimes failed to appreciate how his six-six frame would not fit through ordinary doorways—before he realized he wasn't wearing his uniform. The military no longer traveled commercial air in uniform for fear of being targeted by terrorists.

The General had telephoned General Abraham Morrison, Joint Chiefs of Staff chairman, on the way back from California to inform him that he was going to take a couple of days leave.

"I heard what happened, Darren. Bastards. If this were World War II, they'd all be strung up for treason."

"I'm due in Washington to testify before the 9/11 hearings," the General said. "I'll be there after I take my days off."

"You need it, Darren. The War on Terror will keep on keeping on with or without you."

The General thought he and his father might spend his days off resting up in Tennessee at the Farm, the Kragle homestead that had been in the family for nearly three hundred years. He would call his father's nurse Dolores in D.C. and have her fly with the old man to Memphis, where he would meet them and motor over to Collierville.

Much as he felt obligated to his father, however, he wasn't sure his mood made him mentally equipped for watching the ailing old man degenerate right in front of his eyes for two days. Children, he supposed, were never really prepared for replacing the generation ahead of them.

First, his mother Little Nana had had Alzheimer's. She failed to recognize her own husband the morning he put her aboard the ill-fated United Flight 175 that terrorists were about to crash into the South Tower of the World Trade Center at 9:03 a.m. on 9/11. She and her nurse were on their way to California for yet another treatment against the frustrating disease.

Now, Jordan Kragle, the family patriarch known as "the Ambassador" for the years he occupied that position in Egypt, was fighting his own bout with Alzheimer's. His mood and memory were going fast, as had Little Nana's and Ronald Reagan's. Sooner than the General cared to think about, his father was bound to go the way of Little Nana, first in the loss of memory and awareness, then in loss of life itself.

Life wasn't always fair.

The General took the chair behind his great oaken desk and swiveled it so he could look out the wide window of his second-floor study toward the bright sheen of Tampa Bay. A boat crawled across the water, leaving a wake. The wake soon vanished.

Life was like that. You left your wake. Then the wake was gone.

God, where had all the time gone? Sometimes it was hard for the General to imagine himself sixty years old and about to be a grandfather when Brandon's wife Summer delivered in another few months. In spite of himself, in spite of a nature he had trained to always look directly ahead, he felt his thoughts creeping back through the years. To Vietnam, to the days of the Iran Hostage Crisis when Delta was first deployed against terrorism, to Grenada and Panama and Bosnia . . .

The boat in Tampa Bay disappeared, leaving behind not even its wake.

The General had to get rid of the shit-blahs. He turned from the window and dialed Claude Thornton's number. Claude was director of the FBI's National Domestic Preparedness Office and a close friend from the days when he ran the FBI field office in Cairo and helped rescue Cassidy from al Qaeda in Afghanistan.

Claude's assistant Della Street answered. The General tried to sound cheerful.

"Della? This is Darren. Is Perry Mason in?"

"Claude's in San Diego, General. I thought you knew. Something about terrorists JTTF caught coming across the border."

"Claude told me, but I must have forgotten. I wanted to invite him down to the Farm. You're invited if you can stomach my cooking."

She laughed. "It sounds tempting, but you're just wanting *me* to cook. I know how you bachelors are. Rain check? Who's going to keep Claude out of trouble if I don't pull a tight rein on him?"

The General forced himself to chat a few minutes, even though he didn't feel like it. He hung up the phone and slumped forward over his desk, chin wrapped in his big hands. The grandfather clock against the other wall *tick-tocked* a booming echo.

The old house was so *damned* quiet, almost spooky quiet, since Brown Sugar Mama married Raymond and moved out. Gloria had been a part of the Kragle family since before Rita died, first as housekeeper and then as surrogate mother for the three Kragle sons. Memories and shadows reminded the General how much he missed her. He looked up, half-expecting to see her breeze through the door with coffee, her dyed-red hair bound in that ste- reotypical Aunt Jemima's rag, forefinger ready to scold him for some perceived misbehavior while they sat down for coffee together and talked through some domestic challenge.

"Lawdy, Darren," the fat black woman had said as she prepared to move out, displaying the warmth, dry humor, and open affection that so endeared her to the Kragle men, "my job here is did. Our sons is done grown up and left the nest. It be about time they old daddy learn to take care of himself too. Maybe even get married again."

"I'm too old for that, Gloria."

"Ain't nobody too old for Cupid's arrow. Ain't I proof of that? I always said I think Rita would want you to get married again."

"There isn't anyone else who can take her place— except you, Brown Sugar," he teased.

"Pshaw and hog dumplings. Folks is *talking* about an important white man living in this big ol' house with a colored lady."

"I feed the rumors as much as possible. I've almost de- stroyed your reputation while enhancing mine. Then you had to go and get married."

"Raymond be a good, decent man, same as you be, Darren. You don't need me no more."

Out came that terrible finger wagging in his face. "But you ain't about to get rid of me till the Lawd call me home on that Last Judgment Day, which might not be long in the coming the way this old world is. You take care of my sons, Darren, you hear? Or I'll ha'nt you till the day you dies."

Tears flooded her dark eyes.

"Take care of yourself too, Darren. I loves all'a you. You been my fambly—and you still my fambly."

He should have told her how much he would miss her. There were always things you *should* have told other people. You rarely did, though, if you were a Kragle who constrained his emotions.

He turned on the TV and jacked up the volume to chase back the silence. Immediately, he regretted it. He rarely watched anything except the History Channel, FOX News, or CNN when he felt the need to see what the other side was carping about. Today, CNN had Party of the People's national committee chairman Russell Pope on to extol the virtues of presidential candidate Senator Lowell Rutherford Harris. While Pope spoke, answering some softball question by a sympathetic talking head, a frame-in showed Harris pressing the flesh at a whistle stop.

Harris was shortish with a long, aristocratic face dominated by lips stretched permanently into distaste and disapproval. General Kragle experienced that old familiar rush of anger that jolted him every time he saw Harris, or even thought about him. The scar on his arm was a constant reminder of how he had been shot in Arlington by thugs from the George Coalgate Geis corrupt political organization known as the Committed—a bunch of wealthy avowed socialists who used blackmailers, extortionists, and even foreign terrorists in a desperate attempt to unseat President Tyler by any means possible and replace him with Senator Harris during the upcoming November elections. While Geis and most of his cohorts went to jail, Senator Harris managed to dodge the scandal fallout. Polls showed him in a dead heat with President Tyler, an unsettling indictment, in the General's opinion, on modern American society.

Claude Thornton had put it this way: "If Harris and POP gain power, the nation's Terror Alert system will have to include *Hide, Run, Collaborate*, and *Surrender*."

"We are dealing with a basically unstable president," Chairman Pope charged from the TV set. "We are dealing with a messianic militarist. How does Mr. Tyler explain to the American people how he got it so wrong about weapons of mass destruction in Iraq, and how does he answer to how he took the nation to war on the basis of what turned out to be a series of false premises? There is an important movement in this country suggesting the United Nations should consider sanctions against the United States . . ."

"Asshole," General Kragle muttered. He got up and turned off the TV. Better the silence than this.

The dedicated phone on his desk rang; it was an extension from his USSOCOM office.

"Kragle," he answered it. "This is a secure phone."

"General Kragle. Mac here," replied, MacArthur Thornbrew, director of the National Homeland Security Agency (NHSA), which was responsible for coordinating all national and international counterterrorism efforts. "We have a situation. The President has issued a finding."

Special Operations Forces were prohibited by law from acting without a specific finding of cause by the President of the United States.

Thornbrew got right to the point. "NASA calculated the *Soyuz* space capsule may not have broken up on reentry after all," he said. "It could have survived and landed somewhere in the vicinity of North Korea, in which case we may be witnessing the start of an international incident. Papa Kim Il Sung would like nothing better than to snatch high-profile Americans and turn them over to terrorists."

General Kragle digested that.

"The secretary of defense wants the entire counterterrorism leadership in Washington tonight," Thornbrew continued. "Darren, I know you're on leave, but we have to move fast. The space capsule contains nuclear materials involved in Star Wars research."

The General gave a start. "The *Soyuz* is a *Russian* ship."

"It's also the only transportation to and from the International Space Station. I'll explain when you get here."

"I'm on my way to the airport in fifteen minutes."

At least he could put off watching his father's slow decay for another day or so.

CHAPTER 6

Camp Peary, Virginia

Camp Peary, a secure twenty-four-square-mile compound used by the CIA for training in covert and unconventional warfare, was often used by the nation's SpecOps troops when they were in a hurry to get into isolation, get briefed, and get the hell out on mission. The Agency referred to it as "the Farm."

The camp had the look of government all over it—landscaped grounds, neutral-colored buildings, unmarked sedans and pickup trucks so alike they may as well have been stamped U.S. GOVERNMENT. Operations occupied a square, flat-roofed building with beige metal siding. Neatly stacked on the sidewalk out front, dress right dress—First Sergeant Alik Sculdiron saw to it—were the combat rucks, weapons, and equipment needed to supply a Delta Force detachment about to deploy on mission.

A large conference room inside Ops was equipped for a mission briefing. Before each of nine places arranged on two long tables lay pens, note pads, area studies, and other materials dominated by thick red folders stamped with dual notations: OPERATION COLD DAWN and TOP SECRET. Up front, drop cloths covered maps and charts, pencil boards, globes, and other aids. As newly designated Detachment 3A filed into the room—nine young, fit-looking warriors in camouflage BDUs and green berets—chairs up front facing the table were already settled by a collection of high-ranking brass that detachment commander Major Brandon Kragle hadn't seen in one place since Operation Deep Steel. It appeared the entire top crust of the War on Terror had assembled at the CIA training camp.

"Fu-uck!" rumbled commo sergeant John "Mad Dog" Carson underneath his breath. "Our pooch is done screwed—again."

"Second that motion," Master Sergeant Gloomy Davis agreed.

Top Sergeant Sculdiron growled, "At ease!"

Detachment 3A took seats. Older warriors on stage faced young warriors at the tables—older warriors planning and directing war, younger ones carrying out the operations. That was the way it had always been.

General Darren Kragle of USSOCOM stood at the lectern. Brandon Kragle at the front table turned his head slightly to catch the eye of his brother Sergeant Cassidy Kragle at the table behind him. Cassidy responded with a single nod. He had also noticed how worn their father looked, how tired and brittle. For the first time in his life, Brandon thought his father looked *old*.

Seated behind USSOCOM were: Delta commander Colonel Buck Thompson, a tall, broad-shouldered man in uniform wearing glasses; General Carl Spencer, JSOC (Joint Special Operations Command); General Paul Etheridge, CENTCOM (Central Command); deputy director of CIA operations Thomas Hinds, a former college halfback gone a little to seed in his forties; MacArthur Thornbrew from NHSA, a rugged-faced man from General Kragle's generation who had been on TV all week testifying before the congressional committee investigating the causes of the 9/11 terrorist attacks; and Carlton Horn, an assistant to National Security Advisor Condoleeza Rice. Lower-ranking ops, intel, commo, and logistic officers stood in a rigid collection to one side, briefcases at their feet, ready to spring into action to point, highlight, and display upon demand once the briefing began.

Major Brandon Kragle concentrated on the folder in front of him. His brows lifted in astonishment as he thumbed through the pages. The target selection confirmed his initial impression about the high priority being placed upon this as-yet-unspecified mission. For it, he had selected a detachment of what he considered the best men from his Troop One, no easy task since Delta was made up of "best" men, all capable of diving into the pits of hell should it be required of them. Limited to eight men, not including himself, he selected three regulars who had accompanied him on CT (counterterrorist) missions since before 9/11; the other five were either new to Troop One or had proven themselves on one or two previous actions. The "old-timers" were: Sergeant First Class John "Mad Dog" Carson, communications; Master Sergeant Gloomy Davis, sniper; and Sergeant First Class Theodore "Ice Man" Thompson, weapons specialist, and no kin to Delta commander Buck Thompson.

Of deceptively average height, Mad Dog Carson was thickly built and gloweringly dark with abnormally long arms and lots of hair growing on shoulders so wide he had to turn sideways to enter narrow doorways. To the Troop he had contributed the epithet "fu-uck," spoken in two nasty, distinct syllables, and a legend of how he had once picked up the front of a Humvee so Thumbs Jones (killed in the Philippines) could change a flat tire.

Sniper Gloomy Davis had been with Major Kragle almost from the beginning and had assumed personal responsibility for the boss's safety. He was a wiry little man with great blond drooping mustaches and merry blue eyes that turned to chips of ice whenever they peered through the scope of the .300 Winchester rifle he called "Mr. Blunderbuss." From Hooker, Oklahoma, a former cowboy, Gloomy entertained the troops with tales of the Hooker Hogettes cheerleaders, the bowling league known as "the Holy Rollers," the high school girls' basketball team called "Hooker's Hookers," and his old girlfriend Arachna Phoebe. Around his neck he wore a bullet called a "Hog's Tooth," the symbol of his sniper profession.

Ice Man Thompson might have gone unnoticed in a NASCAR crowd of average-looking men, except for the scars on his left cheekbone left there by a bullet he took during Operation Punitive Strike. He was also shot in the torso during Iron Weed. Reticent and soft-spoken, Ice, as he was commonly called, spent words the way a miser spent pennies. Gloomy once counted the words the weapons specialist used in a normal day: thirty-three. Only those closest to him, mainly his teammates, knew that in addition to being a gourmet cook he had recently won back the North Carolina middleweight kickboxing championship.

Of the five other operators Major Kragle selected for the mission, four were returnees who had proven themselves on at least one previous ops. First Sergeant Alik Sculdiron, ops sergeant; Staff Sergeant Corky "Perverse" Sanchez, heavy weapons specialist; Sergeant First Class Mozee "Diverse" Dade, engineer and demolitions; and Sergeant Cassidy Kragle, assistant engineer and demolitions.

Top Sergeant Sculdiron was a hard chunk of a man, hard as woodpecker lips, with a face reflecting Tartar blood from the armies of the Khans—broad face, high cheekbones, wide-set eyes that disappeared into slits whenever he laughed, infrequently, or scowled, more frequently. A Polish Jew, he'd fled the Russian army a decade earlier to come to America and, with the blessing of the

CIA, enlisted in the U.S. Army. Major Kragle and he had butted heads initially over the running of Troop One, but after Operation Aces Wild into Algeria and Morocco they had settled into a comfortable relationship of mutual trust and respect.

Perverse Sanchez and Diverse Dade replaced men killed during Operation Deep Steel. Aces Wild had been their first mission. Mad Dog, who dubbed all new meat with appropriate monikers, referred to Dade as the Troop's "black token," a contribution to the unit's "diversity." Sanchez, by the same reason, was a "brown token." But since "Diverse" was already taken, he became "Perverse." Collectively, they were Diverse and Perverse, the "Dynamic Duo of Multiculturalism." The nicknames stuck.

From the *barrios* of East L.A., Perverse Sanchez, who spoke in explosive, accented Chicano, was short and muscular with a shock of black Mexican hair, a nose like a raptor's beak, and an axed-out jaw line. He had broken his arm when the detachment's helicopter crashed during Aces Wild in Morocco.

Diverse Dade was long and slender with the finely chiseled midnight-black face of a Zulu warrior and the startling amber eyes of a lion. Engineer and demolitioneer, he possessed equal skills in cooking up homemade explosives or fine sauces in the kitchen. Gourmets of a feather in refined tastes, Diverse and Ice Man hit it off and were often seen around Bragg attending ballet or the opera together with their girlfriends.

The mission alert included a specific requirement for an additional demolitions man to expand the normal eight-soldier deploying detachment to nine. Brandon tapped his brother Cassidy, who was otherwise assigned to Major Dare Russell's Troop Two. Dare bitched about it.

His Troop was on alert about a possible clandestine WMD facility, but so far no movement had been undertaken. Brandon's mission took priority.

"You're robbing me of my best engineer," Dare protested.

"I need another demo. You have three, I have one. Besides, I want to run my last mission with my brother."

Major Russell blinked. "*Last* mission? What are you talking about?"

"I'm putting in my papers to go back to Group. My wife is pregnant."

Dare had two kids of his own. He failed to understand what children had to do with Delta Force. Brandon left it that way, not explaining further. He had already gone through it when he dropped long-time medic Doc TB Blackburn from the Troop. Doc TB's wife had given birth to a son following Aces Wild.

"I'm sorry it has to be this way, Doc," Brandon had apologized. "I don't want fathers of small children in the Troop. Sons need their fathers at home with them, not wandering all over the globe and taking chances on never coming back."

Brandon's Troop One had already suffered seven KIA in the war against terrorists.

"I understand, sir," Doc TB said. "But . . . but Delta is all I've ever wanted in the army. It's . . . been my life . . ."

Misted eyes made the huge teddy bear of a young man appear exceptionally vulnerable. Brandon would not be moved.

"This is not a selective thing, Doc. I'm also transferring out as soon as Summer has our baby."

Staff Sergeant Steve "Doc Red" Mancino took Doc TB's slot. Doc Red was a gaunt young soldier from Georgia, with hair so red it looked orange, a slow drawl, and a bagful of "Southernisms" like "Only a true Southerner knows that *booger* can be a resident of the nose, your neighbor's first name, or something that jumps out of the dark and scares the peewaddley out of you." Doc Red had no steady girlfriend.

Major Brandon Kragle himself, commander of Troop One and therefore of any detachment peeled from it, rounded out Det 3A. In appearance, he might have been his own father a war's generation ago in Vietnam. Only an inch shorter than the General, he had matured in his early thirties to a healthy, muscular bulk similar to his sire's. He also had the General's dark, lean face and piercing gray eyes. Whereas the General's hair and bush of a mustache were turning silver, Brandon's retained the darkness of his Iroquois and Black Irish ancestry.

From the front of the room, General Kragle allowed Det 3A to settle in at the two tables and take a look at their Cold Dawn folders before he spoke.

"Gentlemen, welcome to Operation Cold Dawn," he finally began. "You are now officially known as Delta Detachment 3-Alpha. Your government is sending you on an all-expenses-paid vacation—to Siberia."

CHAPTER 7

General Kragle's attempt at levity came out sounding weary. His voice lacked its customary resoluteness and optimism. He seemed to realize it and lifted his tone to compensate.

"It's not exactly Siberia," he corrected himself, "but it's so close you can hear the ghosts of the gulags. You may open your folders if you haven't already done so. Director MacArthur Thornbrew, National Homeland Security Agency, will provide the *Situation* portion of the operations order."

Thornbrew stood up. He was all business.

"The situation is grim enough," he began. "Two days ago, the Russian space capsule *Soyuz* returning from the International Space Station with two U.S. astronauts and a Russian cosmonaut aboard made a premature reentry and missed its designated landing zone. First reports indicated it may have incinerated. We have since learned it landed intact in southeastern Russia near the borders of China and North Korea—and that the passengers have been captured by either Muslim terrorists or the Russian mafia. Either way, they will likely end up in the hands of Jihadia."

He paused to let the gravity sink in. He had the Delta detachment's attention. A sigh echoed.

"This mission might be better handled by Russian *Spetznaz*," the director continued, "except for complications. Since shortly after 2001, Americans aboard the space station have been conducting carefully guarded experiments with Star Wars nuclear technology designed to locate and strike, from space, targets identified as either terrorist sites or rogue state WMD locations. Naturally, this technology is not being shared with other allied nations because of a variety of complicated diplomatic issues."

This was a lot to digest at one sitting. Silence in the conference room deepened. Director Thornbrew took a long breath before going on.

"Commander Callison and astronaut Williams were bringing back sensitive results of those experiments, including very small amounts of isotopes and nuclear wastes, when *Soyuz* went down. Had the capsule landed normally, Commander Callison would have handed all this over to American ground reception and that would have ended it. I don't have to tell you what it means if this data falls into terrorist hands and from there into the hands of nations like North Korea or Iran who may be able to use it against us. That brings us to your mission, Detachment Cold Dawn, and why you and not the Russians must clean it up and, if feasible, recover our spacemen."

General Carl Spencer, JSOC's no-nonsense commander with an iron-gray buzz cut, stepped to the lectern to provide the *Mission* portion. He got right to the point.

"Gentlemen, Operation Cold Dawn's mission is to infiltrate Russia, locate *Soyuz*, recover all documents and research from it, then destroy the capsule and whatever amounts of radioactive product it contains to prevent its coming into unfriendly hands. Target photos, maps, area studies, weather patterns, and other EEI (Essential Elements of Information) are included in your mission folders. Video and satellite footage is available of the Partizanskaya River Basin and the Russian city of Partizansk near which *Soyuz* went down. Our ops, intel, commo, and other specialists will remain with you during your isolation phase to answer questions. Any questions for me at this point?"

Top Sculdiron stood up, at rigid attention. "Sir? What about the astronauts?"

"We have intelligence on the ground in Partizansk providing us with information. That was how *Soyuz* was located, then verified by satellite. However, there is still no word on who took the men or where they are being held. Their recovery remains a secondary mission, as your primary mission is the space capsule. You will be updated while you are on the ground as to any intel we may receive on the spacemen—at which time you may or may not be cleared to extend your mission to them."

"Sir?"

"Major Kragle."

"Why don't we simply smart-bomb the capsule? That seems the obvious solution."

"It isn't that simple, Major. As we're seeing in our own nation, politics is one of the fronts of the War on Terror. Russia, Germany, and France opposed military action against Iraq by claiming there was insufficient proof that Saddam was attempting to build the bomb. That's not the complete truth. France is 20 percent Muslim at this point and wants to pacify its Islamics. Russia has its own Islamic problems in Chechnya and elsewhere. Russian public opinion seems to be against any military cooperation with the United States. President Putin doesn't want to complicate his problems by officially allowing the U.S. entry into Russian airspace. At the same time, unable to recover the capsule himself because of the political situation there, he realizes it cannot be allowed to be recovered by China or North Korea."

"Then why doesn't Putin take it out?"

"Other than the fact that the White House considers it

vital that the U.S. itself recover Star Wars research from *Soyuz*, one word describes the Partizansk region: corruption. Partizansk, Nakodka, Vladivostok—that entire region—is run by the Russian mafia. The crime rate there is the highest in Russia, in the entire world for that matter. The province is virtually lawless and the Russian government is too weak to regain control. Any action Putin takes there could easily result in a rebellion. Putin won't chance that."

Major Kragle sat down. "Politics!" he murmured scornfully under his breath.

The deputy CIA director of operations, Thomas Hinds, stood up. He was fighting one of his periodic bouts to kick the habit and looked like he needed a cigarette.

"Do you want to add something, Tom?" General Spencer asked him.

"Just a couple of points," Hinds said in his gravelly smoker's voice, taking the JSOC's place at the lectern. "The Russian mafia doesn't run Primorye Province; it *owns* it. Former state duma deputy Viktor Cherepov, the don of the mafia in eastern Russia, is now mayor of Vladivostok. Since the mafia owes allegiance only to the mafia, it sells its services to the highest bidder. Among its underground clientele willing to spend big money for protection are al-Qaeda and other terrorist organizations and Jihad fugitives.

"For example, do you recollect the deck of fifty-two playing cards, each of which presented the photo of a high-ranking Iraqi official wanted for war crimes? The Ace of Spades was Saddam Hussein, the Ace of Hearts his son Uday, and so forth. The Queen of Hearts is nuclear scientist Huda Ammash, the woman in charge of Saddam's nuclear development program. She's better known as 'Dr. Death.' She escaped from Iraq after the U.S. invaded. All indications are that she and other scientists and engineers from Iraq, Iran, and North Korea are in Primorye Province now and, shielded by the mafia, may be working on efforts to build nuclear WMD devices."

Director Hinds permitted himself a sour smile. "It's a nest of vipers and rats you men will be dropping into," he said.

He sat down. Delta Force commander Buck Thompson, a big man in Class A Greens, stepped forward. He adjusted his glasses.

"I'll deliver the *Execution* portion," he said, paused, then plunged on. "President Tyler has made it clear that the nation is tired of being surprised by our enemies over and over again. The Tyler Doctrine of preemption says we are no longer going to wait around and turn the other cheek when it comes to national security. If other nations don't have the balls to police their own, then the U.S. will do it for them."

"Hoo-ya!" the detachment concurred.

"My concept of this mission is this: You will be inserted by HAHO parachute at 0000 hours two nights from tonight midnight with sufficient explosives to do the job. Control will be through CENTCOM with an operations base aboard the carrier *Abraham Lincoln*. The CIA has a man in Partizansk, code name *Cage*. Cage is crucial to the mission. He will receive you on the drop zone to guide you to the *Soyuz* location. Trust him. Trust no one else. In that part of the world, you need a score card to tell the bad guys apart—and there aren't many good guys.

"This is another sheep dip, men. You must not be identified as U.S. Naturally, your presence will be disavowed if you are compromised. You will have three days incountry to complete the mission. Extraction will be by submarine. All the intel and information you require to formulate your mission plan is included in your mission folders. There is no need to stress how crucial this operation is. The formal brief back is at 0800 hours tomorrow before movement begins."

He looked the detachment over. Nine fierce-looking warriors adjusting to the reality of another foray into harm's way.

Light colonels from JSOC, CENTCOM, and USSO-COM presented *Service and Support* and *Command and Signal* portions of the five-paragraph ops order, after which General Paul Etheridge, CENTCOM, delivered a final morale booster. The men of Operation Cold Dawn then broke up into ones and twos with support staff officers for more detailed preparations pertaining to insertion, extraction, aircraft, communications, logistics, and other support. Things were about to get hectic. Major Brandon Kragle couldn't help considering how Murphy's Law applied. The law stated that anything that could go wrong *would*.

General Kragle went around to shake hands with each member of the detachment. "Come back safely," he said. His voice sounded dry and thin and dusty with fatigue. A sadness, almost a listlessness, dominated his manner.

"I understand how critical the mission is, sir," Brandon said to his father. "Sir, will you look in on Summer?"

"I've already phoned Gloria. She's driving up to Fort Bragg to stay with Summer while you're gone."

"Sir, are you all right?" Brandon couldn't help asking.

"Why would you think otherwise?"

The General looked at his sons, shook hands again, clasping their hands longer than necessary, then turned and walked slowly away.

CHAPTER 8

San Diego, California

FBI senior agent Claude Thornton, director of the FBI's National Domestic Preparedness Office, always dreaded flying commercial air. Getting through airport security these days required at least two hours. Deputy director Fred Whiteman dropped him off at San Diego International at 9:20 a.m. Fred and Claude had attended the FBI Academy together over two decades before. Thornton slung his carry-on over a shoulder and bent down to the sedan's open passenger window.

"See you back in Washington, white man," Thornton said.

"You got it, black man." Black man/white man was part of their repartee. "I'll wrap up the details and catch a flight back tomorrow."

The Border Patrol working with an FBI JTTF (Joint Terrorism Task Force) had nabbed seventy-one illegals being smuggled across the Mexican border east of the Sanders Ranch near the foothills of the Chiricauha Mountains. Forty-three of them were of Middle Eastern descent, mainly from Syria, Saudi Arabia, and Iran, reinforcements for the growing army of Jihadia terrorist sleeper cells already nested inside the United States. Eight were, puzzling enough, Russian Muslims from Siberia.

"Knock 'em dead at the hearings," Whiteman said.

"Politicians don't hold hearings. They hold lynchings."

Thornton was scheduled to testify before the Second Congressional 9/11 Commission hearings the next day. He executed a mock salute and strode off, a big, solidly built man as black as his African heritage with a shaved head slicker than a bowling ball, and about the same color. Now in his late forties, he had been considering retirement when 9/11 happened and he was tapped to head Domestic Preparedness, the function of which was to combat terrorists within the borders of the U.S. where the CIA was proscribed. He had been working terrorism almost from the day he graduated from the Academy, mostly in the Muslim countries of the Middle East and North Africa where he learned to speak Arabic fluently. As a result, he possessed almost a sixth sense when it came to spotting what Whiteman called "a hinky situation."

His sixth sense sounded an alarm when he noticed six Arab-looking young men hanging around the waiting area preparing to pass through security for the loading gates. Although they were scattered among the other passengers and pointedly ignoring each other, it soon became obvious to Thornton that they were acquainted. They made eye contact with each other, as though they shared a secret. One nodded at another, a single slight bobbing of the head.

Several other passengers in the waiting area also noticed and appeared nervous. Thornton casually made his way to a nearby open-fronted newstand and gift shop where he could watch while he pretended to browse for reading material. He selected a *Los Angeles Times* and opened it.

Two of the Middle Easterners carried musical instrument cases—thin, flat, about a foot and a half long, of the sort in which Al Capone's gangsters lugged around Thompson machine guns during Prohibition. A third wore a blue tracksuit with Arabic writing across the back. How much more obvious could he be? The fourth wore jeans, a plain green sweatshirt, and a video camera around his neck. Another in a yellow T-shirt carried a McDonald's Happy Meal, while the sixth limped in a built-up orthopedic shoe. This lame one appeared uncertain. He sighed repeatedly, as though about to hyperventilate.

The six got up with other passengers when a flight was called and moved toward the security check line. The musicians got together, but the others dispersed themselves separately in the line. Thornton slapped the *Times* on the checkout counter and hurried out.

"Sir, don't you want the newspaper?" the clerk called after him.

"I never read yellow journalism."

He fell into line behind the Middle Easterners. Security personnel ushered away the first two, the musicians, for further questioning after looking inside their instrument cases. The others removed their shoes and were patted down but still allowed to pass through. Instead, guards selected a middle-aged, balding white man for further questioning. Claude's brows jumped high on his forehead. The balding white guy was *suspicious* while the orthopedic shoe *wasn't*!

Thornton bent toward a security guard, a chunky black woman in a blue uniform. He kept his voice low.

"FBI," he identified himself, showing his credentials while keeping them concealed from those around him. "I'm armed, so don't get your panty hose in a bunch. I need to talk to a supervisor, right now."

The supervisor was a young white man in a business

suit. He directed Thornton to an empty room where passengers were sometimes interrogated.

"My office issued a warning to the airline industry," Thornton said after establishing his bona fides, "to be wary of groups of five men or more who might either be trying to build bombs in in-flight bathrooms, or at least be testing airline security. Shouldn't a group of six Middle Eastern men acting strangely be screened before boarding a flight?"

"I agree with you, sir," the supervisor said. "But it can't be done due to our rule against discrimination."

Thornton stared.

"Don't you know, sir?" said the supervisor, whose name tag identified him as Lourdes. "It's federal policy to fine airlines if they have more than two young Muslim males in secondary questioning. That's considered racial profiling and the ACLU will file a lawsuit. Screening must be done at random."

The FBI agent shook his head. "Whatever happened to common sense?"

"Congress passed a law against common sense," Lourdes said.

Thornton liked this kid. "You're probably right. What flight are they taking?"

"Northwest 427 to Washington, D.C."

"Are there federal air marshals aboard?"

"Yes, sir."

"I need to contact them."

"We're not privileged with the information of who they are. The flight crew will know."

"I see. I'm on a later flight, but I need you to transfer me to Flight 427. Can you arrange it promptly?"

Lourdes brightened. "You bet."

"Let me ask you something. Considering that I'm packing a gun, would I have been singled out of line for further screening?"

Lourdes half-smiled. "Assuredly not. We've already screened our quota of two black males."

CHAPTER 9

The six suspicious-looking Middle Easterners took seats in coach. The musicians sat in 17A and 17B. The Shoe, as Thornton branded him, occupied 8E. Yellow T-shirt and his Mickey D bag moved to 27C. Tracksuit stopped at 11D while Cameraman slipped into 31A. Thornton's seat was about halfway between the first Arab up front and the last—18C on the aisle.

He thought about grounding the flight and seizing all six. He had the authority. But he knew if by some slim chance he was wrong about this one, the news media would be all over him for racial profiling. A lot of irony there, considering that Claude was black. The nation's antiwar mobs incited by the President's "peace at any cost" political enemies would attempt to crucify him, the FBI, President Tyler, and the entire War on Terror leadership.

On the other hand, if he waited too long to stop suspected terrorists and they crashed the plane, the same bunch would still be out to string him up, posthumously, of course, for doing nothing to stop it. Damned if you did something, damned if you did nothing. America these politically correct days, he thought, was one weird place.

He waited.

Cameraman in 31A attempted to videotape out the window as the plane taxied out for takeoff. A flight attendant told him it was not permitted. He glared at her and stopped taping.

The aircraft reached altitude and the seatbelt lights went off.

Yellow T-shirt got out of his seat and walked to the front lavatory, taking his McDonald's bag with him. He still had it with him when he came out of the john, but it now looked almost empty. He sent a covert thumbs-up sign to the Shoe and continued down the aisle to the back of the plane, passing his own seat. The Shoe's face tightened into a brittle mask and his hands trembled. Thornton thought of Richard Reid, the al-Qaeda "shoe bomber" who attempted to blow up a U.S. airliner with plastic explosives concealed in his shoe. He had no way of knowing whether he was witnessing a real attempt to take over the plane or whether it was merely another probe to test airline security for later actions.

He couldn't afford to take a chance and wait much longer. He adjusted himself in his seat and reached inside his tan sport coat to release the holster safety snap on his Glock 9mm.

Tracksuit in 11D stood up and took something from his carry-on in the overhead bin. It was about a foot long and rolled up in cloth. He headed toward the back of the cabin, pushing past a flight attendant's drink cart. He threw Claude a hard mind-your-own-business look.

Cameraman in 31A got up and followed Tracksuit. Yellow T-shirt went into the aft lavatory. Now it was the musicians' turn. They stood up in unison and walked to the front lavatory. The attendant had to maneuver her drinks cart to let them by. She looked so scared she had tears in her eyes.

Claude caught her eye and motioned urgently, keeping his hands low and in his lap. She looked back at the musicians heading for the front, then at Thornton. She started down the aisle toward him, pushing the cart.

By this time, other passengers were starting to notice.

A young couple across the aisle from Claude whispered anxiously to each other. The woman looked frightened. Her husband patted her hand.

A middle-aged businessman leaned out into the aisle and looked toward the rear lavatory. Other flight attendants seemed stressed and were passing notes to each other. Thornton hoped the sky marshal, whoever he was, was equally observant. Things could get real nasty in a place as enclosed and crowded as an airliner cabin. They could get nasty real quick.

The drinks cart stopped next to Thornton. He flipped open his ID case for the attendant. The young woman passenger next to him sighed in relief and gripped his arm.

"Everything will be all right," he reassured her. "Sit quietly and don't look at them."

To the attendant he continued in a low voice. "I'm with the FBI. How do I contact the air marshal?"

She bent down with the presence of mind to have a Pepsi can in one hand, as though serving him. She also looked relieved. Thornton liked her perfume.

"We have only one," she whispered. "He's sitting in 38A."

The agent took the Pepsi and turned his head to look. A beefy young man in jeans, boots, and a Western-cut sport jacket to conceal his firearm returned the look.

"Advise him who I am," Claude said, "and tell him to watch for my cue. The three suspects at the rear are his. I'll take the two at the front lavatory and the clubfoot in 8E. Clear?"

"I'll help him," the attendant volunteered.

"Brave girl. Now move."

Claude's seatmate continued the death grip on his arm. "Are . . . are they going to blow us up?" she whispered on the verge of hysteria.

"No."

He gently removed her hand from his arm, patted it, got up and hurried toward the front. One musician was inside the lavatory. The other stood watch at the door, pretending to be waiting his turn. He pointed at the OCCUPIED sign.

"What is he doing—paying homage to Allah?" Claude asked sarcastically in perfect Arabic.

Being spoken to in his own tongue by a big black American surprised the musician. Before he recovered, the agent expertly tossed him to the deck, frisked him, and used his only pair of handcuffs. The man was clean of obvious weapons, but he immediately began howling *"Allahu Akbar"* at the top of his lungs.

The Shoe half-rose from his seat. Claude wheeled and drew, pointing his gun. Shoe froze partly out of his seat.

"Move from there and I'll kill you!" Claude shouted. Like maybe the guy really cared. He and his Jihad comrades probably intended to kill themselves anyhow in the name of Allah, taking a few "enemy" men, women, old people, and children with them.

A commotion at the rear lavatory told Thornton that the air marshal had gone into action.

Momentum building, Thornton took a little hop back from the lavatory and in the same motion kicked the door hard enough to snap the lock. The door sprang outward. The Middle Easterner inside was also a big man, nearly as big as the agent, but there was no room in the cramped compartment for him to fight back or evade the huge fist that caught him flush between his eyes.

As the Arab sprawled out into the aisle, Claude saw that the mirror had been removed and the guy was attempting to break through the wall into the pilots' cockpit. He grabbed the unconscious Jihadia and jerked him the rest of the way out of the toilet and threw him on top of his partner and fellow musician.

Passengers were beginning to react; no longer would Americans placidly sit by and ride to their deaths.

"Beat this sonofabitch if he comes to and starts moving," Claude ordered a pair of college jocks.

They didn't wait. They pounced and began kicking and stomping the pair of would-be hijackers. Claude had no time to intervene. The assholes were only getting what they deserved anyhow.

The Shoe was Thornton's next target. He proved amazingly spry for someone with a clubfoot. He started running down the aisle toward the back. Several passengers cut him off. Other passengers had joined the sky marshal and everything at the rear seemed to be under control.

Shoe's eyes widened as he stared into the muzzle of the agent's handgun. The flash of terror in his eyes gave Thornton a quick jolt of satisfaction. *Now you know what it's like, you bastard!*

"I don't want to die! I don't want to die!" Shoe shrieked.

Claude seized the man and slammed him on his back in the narrow aisle. He pinned him to the deck with a knee and shoved the barrel of his Glock into the cavity of his open screaming mouth. All the way to *Add Oil.*

"Allahu Akbar!" Thornton taunted. "Now we're going to have a long talk, isn't that right?"

The Shoe gagged and retched around the barrel, but Thornton understood his response. "Yes, yes, *yes!*"

CHAPTER 10

Washington, D.C.

The nervous one, the Shoe, whose hands trembled aboard the plane, turned out to be the most exploitable for interrogation, as Director Claude Thornton expected. The other five merely glowered with deep inner hatred whenever questioned. The Shoe, true name Abdul-Rahim Hamden, from Egypt, had the shakes for hours after Northwest 427 landed safely at Ronald Reagan in D.C.

Hamden was a small, insipid man with a weak chin, watery eyes, and a meaty lower lip that seemed disconnected to the rest of his thin face. Like a leech. There was nothing wrong with his foot; his shoe sole had been built up to give him a limp. A cup of good Starbucks coffee Thornton brought to the interrogation room at D.C. police headquarters soon had him chattering up the agent in Arabic.

In spite of himself, despite warnings from his sleeper cell commander, the little man had been seduced by American culture during his four years' sojourn as an al-Qaeda sleeper member of a Kansas City mosque. He began having second thoughts about martyrdom. Initially tapped as one of those to hijack airliners on 9/11, he had feigned serious illness and temporarily avoided claiming his virgins in the afterlife. He was unable to avoid his current assignment.

"I mean, you are a sick, godless nation of pornography, homosexual marriage, nudeness . . ." he charged. "We do not want our daughters to become harlots, our wives jezebels, nor our nephews to become nieces and gangsta rappers. But . . ." He hung his head and blushed, looking guilty at the admission. "But life is very good in America."

Claude understood. There were times when he looked around and thought modern society had gone insane, that, as Chaplain Cameron Kragle once said, if God didn't do something soon He owed Sodom and Gomorrah an apology. Still, life in America *was* good.

The agent probed Hamden's brain for three hours, hoping to mine something useful. Sleeper cells in the U.S. were isolated and insulated from each other to avoid compromise of the structure. A member of a cell might know only one other member of his unit, would probably never see the others until the day he was selected for a mission. Before that day, Hamden had had no contact with his comrades aboard the airliner. He had heard, however, that Islamics were attempting to recruit operators from American dissidents, especially from the ranks of common criminals and prisoners where Islam made rapid inroads.

"Ordinary-looking Americans, Christians, will be selected for future martyrdom because they do not look like . . . *us*," he explained. "Therefore, they will not be scrutinized."

Thornton sat on the other side of the table from the Shoe, nursing a plain coffee. Black, no sugar.

"Today was not a martyrdom," Hamden said. "At first I thought it was. Massi—he is the team leader—told us that it was too difficult to secret explosives aboard an American airplane since the first time with the towers. Therefore, what we will do is *pretend* we were hijacking it once we got aboard to show the infidels that we cannot be stopped. We would crash it into a city if we *could* get control, but either way it would spread terror. Massi said the

U.S. was a toothless tiger and that the only thing that would happen if we were caught was that we would be deported. We could always come back across your border with Mexico."

"It's not quite that simple," Claude advised him. "Have you heard of the Patriot Act? You're going to prison."

Tears welled in Hamden's eyes. "My comrades will have me executed if they find out I betrayed my blood and spoke with you."

"Then we won't tell them—as long as you continue to cooperate."

He was about to give up pulling anything useful from the nervous little Egyptian when a chance remark opened up another avenue.

"I had wanted to see New York again," Hamden said with an air of regret. "That was where I was supposed to go at first. It is an exciting city."

Claude looked up sharply. "Why were you going to New York?"

"I was to assemble there with others for a mission. At the last moment my orders were changed to the airliner."

"What kind of mission?"

Hamden shrugged. "I assume it was to do with the Federalist National Convention at Madison Square Garden since it begins this week. I know only an address. We were to be briefed when we assembled."

The Cross Directory listed Hamden's rendezvous address to Patsy Koehler, attorney-at-law. How was a lawyer mixed up in all this? Claude's sixth sense told him that something cataclysmic was being planned for the Federalist convention during which Woodrow Tyler would be renominated for the presidency.

CHAPTER 11

Sea of Okhotsk

The aircraft carrier USS *Abraham Lincoln* rolled with the white mares' tails that stampeded relentlessly across the roiling blue-gray surface of the sea. Fog, wet and cold and persistent, restricted vision. Stiff breezes snatched cold spray from the ocean's surface and slashed it and a thin rain into Major Brandon Kragle's face. He rocked with the ship on the rain-slick outer gangway that ran just below the flight deck on the island side of the carrier. He cast a long and apprehensive appraisal of the lowering morning sky.

According to ship meteorologists, the weather *might* clear some in the afternoon, making insertion into Russia possible by that night. Operation Cold Dawn had already postponed operations for one twenty-four-hour period. Murphy's Law again: anything that could go wrong would.

Brandon had been reading *My Three Years With General Eisenhower* prior to alert. He now understood how Ike must have felt when weather became the principal concern affecting D-day schedules.

He gripped the wet railing with both hands and leaned forward into the motion of the big warship, his eyes narrowed against rain pelting his navy foul-weather clothing. Fog enveloped the ship like the hand of a giant ghost, causing him to fret even more. He had time on his hands, and time on his hands was not a good thing for a man keyed up for action, whether anticipating D-day or a CT mission. A man got to thinking . . .

This was likely his last mission with Delta Force. His resignation would become effective when Summer gave birth to their child in the fall. He dreaded the day, but it was a promise he intended to keep. A mother and child deserved some security in knowing their husband and father had a better chance of returning home safely if he were in a conventional army unit rather than in SpecOps.

"I won't make you keep your promise if you want to break it," Summer had said, but her voice told him how disappointed she would be. Brandon wasn't cut out for a desk job—but that was what he might come down to.

The steel watertight door behind Brandon opened and First Sergeant Sculdiron stepped onto the gangway. He pulled a hood over his Ranger patrol cap and stuck his hands deep into the pockets of his foul-weather jacket. He squinted into the fog.

"Major," he greeted.

"Top."

"Nasty. More of the same. We will scrub it again."

Brandon grunted, in no mood for long negative conversations.

"Do you want me to reveille the men, sir?"

"Let them sleep in if they will."

There were no better men in any armed forces in the world than those of Delta. Hard, tough men, thoroughly professional when the situation required it. Back in the 1980s, Colonel Beckwith and then-major Darren Kragle promised to create a CT unit that could go anywhere in the world and do any damned thing required of it—and they had. Terrorists feared Delta more than they did Allah, for they never knew where, when, how, nor with what bag of tricks the deadly clandestine warriors might appear.

Tightly wound and battle-honed soldiers got restless, got the jitters, when they had to wait around. They were rough-talking, direct-action men prone to get into mischief and minor misdemeanors if they remained too long inactive. The previous night's delay in the ops gave them an opportunity to discover that *women* served aboard the carrier.

"Major, do ya'all know they *issue* swabbies their own camp followers?" young Doc Red Mancino had drawled in amazement.

"*¿Mujeres! ¿Chicas?*" Perverse exclaimed.

Mad Dog corrected him. "No, you dumb spic. *Women.*"

"Well, I caught myself looking 'em over," Doc Red confessed.

Because of integration of the sexes—male, female, and *other*, as Mad Dog wryly observed—sailors now called the carrier "the Babe" rather than "the Abe."

"This is no man of war," Top Sculdiron noted, his Slavic eyes nearly disappearing into grim slits. "It is a floating whorehouse."

Brandon collected the detachment in the cubicle belowdecks that had been issued to him as a ready room.

"Stay away from the women," he warned. "Consider yourselves still in isolation and steer clear of everybody."

"Loose lips sink ships," Top Sculdiron added.

"Speaking of loose lips," Mad Dog rumbled, "any of you seen that yeoman in ops? She could suck the brass chrome off a—"

Sculdiron glared at him.

"Yes, Top," Mad Dog said. "No pussy, Top. No pussy here, no pussy there, no pussy anywhere."

"Chew are an animal," Perverse Sanchez said in his explosive Chicano.

Mad Dog grabbed his crotch. "Chew on this, wetback."

Brandon shook his head and turned to walk away with Top Sculdiron.

"Keep away from the natives," he shot back over his shoulder. "Get some sleep. Pre-mission inspection tomorrow and mission drill. All day."

Troops had to be kept busy.

That was the previous night. The next day, weatherwise, looked to be a repeat of the day before. Cold Dawn was put on hold until further notice. Brandon glared into the fog and rain as the *Abe Lincoln* steamed south across the choppy sea of Okhotsk, passing through mist and fog to the eastern reach of Sakhalin Island. So far, it looked like another "no go."

CHAPTER 12

Due to OPSEC blackout, the *Abe* was conducting no air ops of its own during the period it served as an operations base for Cold Dawn. The hangar was closed off to all hands to allow Det 3A to drill and handle its pre-mission functions. Two Air Force CV-22 Ospreys were parked in the hangar hold, one to insert Cold Dawn, the other to serve as backup. The CV-22 variant of the Osprey was designed specifically to provide USSOCOM with long-range VSTOL (vertical /short takeoff and landing) insertion and extraction capability. The tilt rotor propeller design combined the vertical flight capabilities of a helicopter with the speed and range of a turboprop airplane.

Major Kragle ran the detachment through loading and exiting procedures. Men took positions inside the fuselage, wearing their 'chutes, weapons, and bags, and repeatedly went out the door in prearranged sequence, jumping out onto the steel deck. Even Sergeant Sculdiron finally groaned in protest.

"Major, I think we got this one down, sir."

"Good." Brandon consulted his watch. "We'll have a full field equipment inspection at 1600 hours here on the hangar deck."

Busy hands is happy hands, as Brown Sugar Mama always said.

An inspection this late in the game was unnecessary. Brandon trusted his men implicitly to have all their gear and for it to be repaired and ready. The weather had not

settled since early in the morning when Brandon stood on
the outer gangway willing it to change. That meant another possible abort that night. All the more reason to
keep the detachment occupied.

As a prank, the men showed up for the 1600 inspection
wearing jump helmets and night vision goggles. They resembled a row of giant grasshoppers or bug-eyed green
frogs in their unmarked forest BDU camouflage. The major and Top Sculdiron ignored the frolic. They moved in
formal inspection mode from man-to-man down the
short rank.

"Ri-vet! Ri-vet!" Mad Dog chorused, sounding exactly
like a bullfrog on a pond bank.

"You are at the position of attention," Top Sculdiron
sternly reminded him. "If you have forgot what the position is, perhaps a week or two with a drill instructor will
refresh your feeble memory when we return to Fort
Bragg."

It was chicken-shit army. Everyone acknowledged it
was chicken-shit army and therefore accepted it in good
humor.

The men laid out their rucks, equipment, and weapons
on the deck at their feet. For uniformity and easy exchange of ammo, each operator except Ice Man Thompson and Gloomy Davis carried a Colt M4A1 carbine,
adopted by USSOCOM as SpecOps's weapon of choice
in the CQB/CT (close quarter battle/counterterrorism)
role of Delta shooters. The M4 was a smaller, more compact version of the full-sized 5.56mm M16A2 rifle. Designed lightweight for speed, it had a retractable buttstock
and a barrel shortened to 14.5 inches.

Each rifle came with accessories: the ACOG 4X dry
optical scope with ballistic compensating reticle that allowed the weapon to be used at its maximum effective

range of six hundred meters; an Infrared Target Pointer/Illuminator/Aiming Laser (ITPIAL), which could be used with night vision goggles for shooting out to three hundred meters in darkened buildings, tunnels, jungle, or under other low-sight conditions; and a Trijicon reflex collimator sight designed for close quarter battle.

Sculdiron attached an M203 40mm grenade launcher to his weapon, and Perverse Sanchez carried a short-tubed 60mm mortar in addition to his M4.

"Do not fear the night," Special Operators said. "Fear is what hunts in the night—and *we* are what hunts."

As his weapon of choice, Ice Man chose an M249 Squad Automatic Weapon (SAW), a lightweight machine gun that fired 600-round linked belts or, in a pinch, the same 5.56 magazines as the carbines. Gloomy Davis never went anywhere without Mr. Blunderbuss, his .300 Winchester sniper rifle.

Travel light, freeze at night. Even light, no ruck weighed less than forty pounds, the weight depending upon the military occupational specialty of its owner.

Mad Dog Carson, communications specialist, generally humped the heaviest pack, stuffed as it was with an AN/PSC-5 "Shadowfire" long-range radio; a SATCOM UHF/VHF radio equipped with field computer and the technology to transmit and receive hard copy in the field; and spare batteries and antennas.

In addition to his sleeping bag, MREs (Meal, Ready to Eat), ammo, water, and an extra pair of socks, SOP for a Delta detachment, Doc Red Mancino carried a full aid bag complete with IV fluids and a compact field surgical kit.

The two demolitions specialists, engineers Diverse Dade and Cassidy Kragle, filled their ALICE rucks with block charges of C4 plastic explosives and plastic bonded explosive (PBX) sheets of RDX, the most powerful non-nuclear explosive known to science. The amount may have seemed an overkill to any soldier not familiar with Delta Force; however, in Delta a detachment on mission inserted with equipment and weapons to handle any eventuality. Besides, as previous engineer Thumbs Jones, who was killed in a firefight in the Philippines, always used to say, "There are very few of the world's problems that can't be solved with a good stick of TNT."

Handguns of choice and combat knives rounded out the detachment's gear. Brandon preferred the new USP Tactical .45 caliber semiauto pistol and the Ka-Bar blade his grandfather, Ambassador Jordan Kragle, had used while with the Alamo Scouts in the South Pacific during World War II. Cassidy used a special-built SOG SK 2000 combat knife that he had learned to throw almost as accurately at short range as he could fire a .45 pistol.

Two pocket-sized Geiger counters, digital cameras, and four two-man deflated rubber rafts dispersed among the team members completed the basic list of equipment. The rafts would be used to transport the operators out to sea for submarine exfiltration once the detachment completed its mission. Due to the bulk of equipment being jumped, the team decided against wearing Mae West PFDs, which were normally required for operations over water.

Brandon left the rest of the inspection to Sculdiron and went topside to check the weather one last time before nightfall. The rain had stopped and fog banks seemed to be lifting. The watertight door behind him on the gangway opened and closed with a steel clang.

"Major Kragle?"

Something about the tone of the voice caused him to turn promptly.

"You're needed in ops right away," said the second class meteorologist. "There might be a brief break in the weather over land about midnight. Right now, it looks like you're a go."

CHAPTER 13

PROTESTORS PLAN TO DISRUPT CONVENTION

New York (CPI)—The potential for explosive confrontation between protestors and police is increasing as the Federalist National Convention draws near. Antiwar radicals are reportedly planning to "shut down" New York City and the Madison Square Garden convention by creating "maximum disruption." Organizers of the protest—Peace and Justice International, Not My Name, BUCKUS Alliance and World RSPONSE—say they expect to draw 250,000 people.

Sources say BUCKUS Alliance is running training camps to teach radicals how to block doorways, disarm arresting officers, throw pies at public figures, trick bomb-sniffing dogs on subways and bring traffic to a halt. The BUCKUS "call for action" states: "We'll take over the streets, transform them into theaters, stages for resistance and forums for debate . . ."

Some officials fear a repeat of the rally against the Iraq War in February 2003 when demonstrators and police clashed, leading to hundreds of arrests, or the attempt by BUCKUS to close down Seattle during the NAFTA Conference. Some organizers promise a return to the "Days of Rage" when radicals ran wild through the streets of Chicago during the 1968 Convention, burning and looting at will.

At the same time that radicals are planning protests,

Homeland Security Director MacArthur Thornbrew warns that a steady stream of intelligence indicates al-Qaeda wants to attack the United States to disrupt the upcoming elections . . .

CHAPTER 14

Washington, D.C.

General Darren Kragle stayed on in Washington following the Cold Dawn briefing that threw two of his three
sons back into the maw; the third son, Chaplain Cameron
Kragle, was in Iraq on a temporary assignment to the U.S.
Army 1st Infantry Division. The General was subpoened
to testify before Congress in what was termed around
D.C. as "the Second 9/11 Commission Hearings" on what
had gone wrong in government to allow 9/11 terrorists to
crash airliners into the Twin Towers and the Pentagon.
The hearings gave him a few days to visit his father, conduct some Pentagon business, and keep a lunch date with
his old friend Claude Thornton, all of which in his present
state of mind he viewed as obligations.

Claude, as it turned out, was in a hurry. He flew in
from New York to catch up at his office, then had to fly
right back out again. General Kragle met him at an airport deli.

"I believe it may have been a diversion to take the light
off something else being planned," Claude speculated
about the six would-be hijackers of Flight 427. "We're
getting all kinds of chatter that we're going to be hit again
before the November elections, and hit hard. In this business, I've learned not to believe in coincidences."

Claude informed the General about the illegals caught
sneaking across the border near the Sanders Ranch in Ari-

zona, many of whom were not Mexicans at all. Eight were even from Siberia.

"There's a connection here," he pondered, "between the attempted hijacking, if that's what it was, and the border crossing. I'm just not smart enough to put it together. Russians! That's a twist."

Although the General saw no obvious link to the newly launched Operation Cold Dawn other than the Russian angle, he and Claude had long ago established an informal exchange of information between their two departments. He summarized the *Soyuz* incident and the mission to insert a detachment in-country.

"A second detachment was alerted by JSOC concerning intel about a possible clandestine WMD facility, also believed to be somewhere along the Russian-Chinese border," he added.

Claude thought it over. "I don't believe in coincidences," he said again. "Keep me posted?"

General Kragle nodded. He seemed disengaged, restless, distracted, almost indifferent. Claude was concerned, but understood from experience not to pry. The Kragles, all of them, were closed and private when it came to their personal lives.

Lunch ended in uncharacteristic silence. They soberly shook hands before Claude got up to catch his flight. General Kragle walked stooped as he turned away. His blue sport shirt and khaki trousers hung loosely on his frame, making it obvious that he was losing weight.

"How about that weekend invitation to the Farm when everything calms down again?" Claude called after him. "Maybe we can drown some worms?"

General Kragle nodded absently and kept walking.

He drove his rental from the airport out to the Pleas-

ant Valley Retirement Community where his father was
under constant nursing care to prevent him from wandering off and getting lost. God, how the name repulsed
him—*Pleasant Valley*. It was neither a valley nor, in his
opinion, was it a particularly pleasant place. It was more
like an upscale old folks' home, an intermediary stop
between this world and a final resting place a short piece
farther down the road. Depressing. Nonetheless, brother
Mike and he had settled on Pleasant Valley as the best
alternative for their father's final years. What a screwed-
up way to end an otherwise successful and productive
life. Maybe Little Nana's flying into the World Trade
Center hadn't been a bad way to go after all. At least it
was fast.

Darren supposed every man had to follow this road
sooner or later, if he lived long enough. Old age, infir-
mities, and, as with both the Ambassador and Little
Nana, Alzheimer's to rob him of a knowledge and
awareness of his past life. President Ronald Reagan
hadn't even recognized Nancy for the last ten years he
lived.

Darren wondered if Alzheimer's was genetic.

"How is the Ambassador today?" the General asked
Dolores when she answered his knock. She was a plump,
motherly RN with a wistful smile and dark hair growing
on her upper lip.

"Bless his heart," she said and left it at that. "He's sitting out back on the veranda."

The veranda was about ten feet long and four wide, surrounded by a high redwood railing to keep "residents"
from falling off or walking away. Potted flowers and plants
hung around the eaves—wisteria and pansies and petunias
of various colors. Darren faltered a moment, stunned all

over again by his father's withered appearance.

The old man sat stiffly in a chair staring out over carefully groomed grounds dotted by late summer trees and pretty little cottages occupied by other human relics. Dolores had spread a blanket over his legs, even though it was a warm day. His big hands clenched together tightly on the outside of the cover so that the liver spots popped out in relief. It was like he was trying to hold on desperately to whatever remained of his life.

Like all Kragles, he was a big man, or had been at one time. There wasn't much left of him now—the large bony frame that made him look frailer than his size might indicate, thin white hair, mustache also thin and bleached against a gnarled face of angles and squares, and pale gray eyes with a new vacancy in them. His health had deteriorated so suddenly after Little Nana's death.

The Ambassador flinched but did not look around when Darren lay a hand on his shoulder.

"Ambassador? Pops? It's Darren."

The General sat down in the other chair. He looked at his father until he could bear it no longer. Then he also stared out across the grounds. How he missed the lively conversations he and his father had once enjoyed—about world affairs and politics and soldiering and . . . Two soldiers getting together for an afternoon or evening.

Now, there was nothing but silence.

The Ambassador turned his head slightly. "Now, who did you say you are?" he asked, trying to concentrate.

"It's Darren, Pops. Your son Darren."

The Ambassador nodded as though he understood, but clearly he didn't. How, the General wondered, did you talk to a stranger who had withdrawn inside himself? After another ten minutes, the General got up.

"I'll go get us a couple of cups of coffee," he volunteered. "Yours black with sugar, right?"

The Ambassador seemed not to hear. Dolores offered to brew up a pot, but Darren needed to get out. He couldn't help himself; a visit with his father was always a trying event. Lately more so than ever. He strode out onto the landscaped grounds and looked back. His father appeared small and alone on the veranda, a man diminishing right before his eyes. How could God let good men end their days like this?

Was this all he, Darren, had to look forward to?

At the cafeteria he took a table near the front windows to fortify himself with a cup before returning to his father's apartment. He selected a table where he couldn't see the Ambassador. He hunched deep in reverie, withdrawn into his own dark thoughts.

It was a minute or so before he realized someone had approached his table and was speaking to him in a soft voice. He finally looked up into large brown eyes as open and expressive as a deer's. He remembered his manners and stood, finding that he towered by a good foot and a half over a nice-looking woman in her fifties. She kept smiling at him, a smile that immediately made him think of Rita.

Her dark hair was slightly tinged with gray and done into a stylish French bun. Petite and attractive with full lips, she wore a plain black shift and a red apron with PLEASANT VALLEY stenciled on the bib. Darren felt both shy and a bit resentful of the intrusion.

"I didn't think you were ever going to come back from wherever you were," she said. "Would you like a paper to go with your coffee?"

"You work here?" It wasn't much of a response.

"I'm a volunteer. It keeps a young—well, *youngish*—widow from walking the streets. Besides, my mother is a resident here. If you'll pardon my saying so, you look as though a Mack truck whopped you a good one, then turned around and ran over you again."

"Something like that."

"I can always tell when a new resident is admitted. Visitors come and stare out the window."

"Yes." The General reached for one of her newspapers. Maybe that would get rid of her.

"I suspect you're the kind of man who prefers the *Washington Times*," she said cheerfully, giving him a paper. "My name is Vanda. You look as though you could use some company. I'll get a coffee and be right back."

She was gone before he had time to protest. He remained standing until she returned, balancing a cup in a saucer.

"Please sit down," she invited. They sat across from each other. "You have the advantage," she added.

"Pardon?"

"I've told you my name . . ."

"I didn't mean to be rude."

She arched her brows inquiringly and waited.

"Darren Kragle," he offered. "Is this part of your volunteer job—cheering up distraught visitors?"

"Only those who look like they need it. Pleasant Valley is actually a wonderful little community—"

"I've read the brochures."

Her attractive features sobered. To his surprise, the General suddenly feared she might get up and leave.

"It seems all I'm doing is apologizing," he said, softening his voice.

She remained, chatting about whatever topic happened to enter her mind. Children, world affairs, parents, ageing . . . One of her hobbies was photographing old barns. The General's mood lifted somewhat, in spite of himself. By the time she got up to go, Darren felt he knew her entire life story. Her mother's name was Mollie Belle; she lived in Cottage 17 with *her* private nurse. Her husband's name was Jim; he had died in an auto accident the week after 9/11. She had two daughters, Patricia and Jennifer. Jennifer attended grad school at Harvard, studying political science, and there had been some trouble with her. Patricia was married and had a four-year-old son.

Vanda laid a hand on the General's arm. "We all get old if we live long enough," she said. "It's better than the alternative. And we all have to watch our parents grow old, unless we're orphans."

"Yes," he said.

"My mama always said I was forward. Do you think so?"

"Yes."

She laughed merrily. "Good. Then it won't damage my reputation further if I suggest we have dinner together tonight? You seem like a fine man, and you're not wearing a wedding band."

"My wife Rita . . . She died years ago."

He looked at her for a long moment. He *wanted* to, but he was not skilled in the social graces of dating. It had been too long. Besides, he wasn't sure he'd make good company. His attitude needed adjustment.

"I'd rather not . . ." he said. "Dinner, I mean."

She squeezed his arm. "It's okay. I just thought you might need the company."

She picked up her papers and cup and moved off, looking vibrant and alive. He watched her approach a middle-

aged couple staring out the window and offer a paper.
Within a minute or two she had them laughing with her.
She glanced back over her shoulder at the General and
smiled Rita's smile.

CHAPTER 15

Sea of Okhotsk

Sleep was a commodity a combat soldier took wherever and whenever he could get it. Although Major Kragle provided the detachment an opportunity to grab a few hours' rack time before H-hour, the men were too keyed up to avail themselves of it.

"I figure to have plenty of sleep when I'm dead," opined Gloomy Davis, who as Brandon's self-appointed guardian, positioned himself next to the boss on the loading-and-insertion plan aboard the Osprey.

"It's too hot to sleep in hell," Mad Dog advised.

The Osprey lifted chopper-like from the deck of the USS *Abe Lincoln* at 0000 hours, midnight, for the Cold Dawn jump into Russia, shooting into the unsettled night and quickly clawing for altitude. It was almost as cramped inside the aircraft as in a Blackhawk helicopter, the cabin merely a tube with facing rows of web seats. The nine operators of Det 3A sat shoulder to shoulder, jostled by rough air. The red night vision light above the closed jump door glared at them like a malevolent eye. Military aircraft were too noisy for easy communications. The men sat quietly, dozing off for the one-hour-and-ten-minute flight. Brandon listened on earphones to the pilots' business-like exchange about headings, altitudes and weather.

Mad Dog, sitting across from Brandon, opened one

eye. His pupil caught the glint of the nightlight. He repositioned his ruck on the vibrating deck between his knees. He closed his eye again and his face returned to shadows.

These men . . . Brandon's appraisal took in the two facing rows, the men helmeted, their parachutes, weapons, and rucks prepared for exiting. Their unassuming appearances when they were out of uniform, out of combat gear, would not have singled them out in a crowd, with the possible exception of the lion-like Diverse Dade with his blue-black skin and amber eyes and Top Sculdiron with his thick neck and Tartar countenance. Outward appearances, however, could be deceiving. These men to an individual possessed an inner power that could be felt like a jolt of electricity when they approached.

God, how Brandon was going to miss them.

A half hour into the flight, the pilot came up on Brandon's earphone: "Sir, weather is marginal again and closing in."

Ten minutes later he was back: "Major, the window is closing fast. Meteorology informs us we have a half hour. After that we'll have to abort."

Brandon asked, "How much time until TOT?" Time over target.

"Twenty minutes if we push it."

"Push it."

Brandon nudged Gloomy, who in turn passed it down the row and back up the facing line. The men came alert and began making last-minute checks of their gear. Gloomy Davis had Mr. Blunderbuss's case taped and strapped to his left shoulder, Ice Man likewise with his SAW. The others rigged their shorter M4 carbines to their parachute waistbands and upper parachute harnesses for quick access. Operators never knew what they might encounter on a DZ; they survived by being prepared.

The jump would be a HAHO—high altitude, high opening—using the MC-5 canopy. To avoid Russian airspace and therefore a coast radar alert, the Osprey must release jumpers at an altitude of fifteen thousand feet ten miles offshore over international waters. Radar might paint the aircraft, but it would never see the flyers. The detachment had to depend upon a stiff breeze from seaward in order to fly fifteen miles horizontally while falling fifteen thousand feet to land on their drop zone five miles into Russia's black interior.

Delta Force drilled in precision air work and other infiltration techniques almost as much as it practiced shooting. Brandon wore two strips of glow tape, one on each leg, while the rest of the team taped only one leg each. Once in the air "flying" and stabilized, the detachment members would don their infrared NVGs (night vision goggles) and guide on Brandon. He would lase the drop zone and the DIP (desired insertion point) with his PEQ-4 infrared pointing device and lead the detachment to a landing in which no jumper hit earth more than fifty feet away from any other. That was precision flying at its best. That was precision flying without Murphy.

"Major, Meteorology reports we have ten minutes at best," the pilot warned.

"We have to make it. Put us out sooner if you need to."

The cabin depressurized. At fifteen thousand feet, the air was thin. Anyone working in that environment for long required oxygen. The Air Force crew chief got up from his seat near the pilots' compartment and, dragging his O2 line and commo cable, worked his way down the aisle between knees and rucks resting between knees. He slid up the jump door to reveal the awful black abyss of the world outside, then stepped back out of the way. Invisible wind howled past like a freight train through a tunnel. Brandon smelled rain and cloud. The red jump light above the door blinked twice. *Get ready!*

Brandon unbuckled and shot to his feet, spread-legged to maintain his balance on the unsteady deck. He moved to stand in the open doorway, gripping the edged steel of the opening with one hand and turning back to face the detachment. He listened through the intercom for a moment, then ripped off the earphones and replaced them with his black skydiver's helmet with the built-in radio mike and O2 mask. He buckled the helmet tightly, checked for NVGs attached to his battle harness for easy access and the PEQ-4 in a holster strapped to his leg.

The jump light kept blinking red.

Brandon thrust a stiff arm toward the paratrooper stick and immediately began the jumpmaster commands: *Stand up! Equipment check! Sound off for equipment check! Stand in the door!* There were no static lines; each jumper would pull as soon as he stabilized in the air.

Men reached across the aisle and mutually pulled each other to their feet, laden as they were with 'chutes and equipment. Mad Dog punched Perverse Sanchez lightly on the shoulder, a gesture of human contact he and his buddy Rock Taylor always exchanged before Taylor was killed in Afghanistan.

In a rush, the detachment lined up front reserve 'chute to back main 'chute, Major Kragle ready to lead the stick, Top Sculdiron pushing it. Brandon stood in the awful yawning door, nothing but blackness beyond and below, gripping either side to keep his balance, legs spread, his heavy ruck hanging down from his waistband. It would be released on its fifteen-foot lowering line before he landed to relieve some of the shock on his legs.

He looked back into the interior. The men stared back at him, wearing oxygen masks, their eyes through goggles

set and expressionless, hands clasped across their reserve
belly 'chutes. Cassidy nodded *Ready* at his big brother.
Brandon nodded back.

The jump light turned green.

"Go!"

The Air Force crew chief blinked in amazement as the
entire stick of nine disappeared out the door in a single
explosion.

Brandon stepped into a flying exit and spread arms and
legs to create drag and slow his descent. Those at the rear
of the stick went head down and arms alongside in order
to barrel down at speed to catch up with those who
jumped first. Brandon hesitated a second or two to make
sure everyone was with him, then stabilized and pulled.

His square popped open on heading. He couldn't see
shit. Nothing but a blackness with distant stars. The wind
felt stronger than anticipated at this high altitude. His
parachute buffeted about across the sky. Swinging underneath it made freeing his night vision goggles and getting
them on a challenge.

Finally, he got them on and looked around for the others. Glow strips were more visible through NVGs. Pulling
his right steering line, he made a three-sixty to survey
through his NVGs the mushrooms blossoming around
him as parachutes opened. Looked good. Glow strips
shone like neon lights. There was no moon, but, through
NVGs that high above the earth's cloud cover, stars
blazed at him as in some great magnificent planetarium.
Below lay nothing but the corrugated darkness of rain
clouds.

He discovered his left steering line had not snapped
free from its finger trap, thereby necessitating that he ex-
ert constant pressure on the right line to counter the left
turn. While he was busy with that, he broke the retaining

bands securing his GPS (global positioning system) in order to run a quick fix on their location and guide the detachment to its DZ. Somehow the dummy cord that held the GPS to his harness jerked free when he tugged on it.

Damn! What a clusterfuck!

He had a malfunctioning parachute and a GPS in his free hand that was no longer dummy-corded. That meant he had to keep one hand on the parachute at all times to counter a left turn while using the GPS with the other hand, careful not to drop that vital aid.

He managed to get a reading. He calculated they were southeast of Checkpoint Mobile and traveling faster than anticipated. He set his course.

"Hold the wind to your one-eighty," he advised through his voice-activated helmet mike. "Guide on me."

Murphy wasn't through yet.

A voice jumped out of airspace and into his helmet with chilling presence.

"Somebody's going down!"

One of the glow strips, far below, streaked toward earth like a falling star and vanished into earth's black cloud cover.

CHAPTER 16

Partizanskaya River Valley

Helmet mikes went into overuse as startled flyers attempted to sort out who might have disappeared into the clouds. Bad air overcharged the resulting confusion. Gusts of wind bounced parachutes all over the sky, making navigation difficult. Brandon watched through the liquid cast of his NVGs as two parachute canopies collided and ricocheted apart. One of the troopers exclaimed, *"Damn!"* Brandon couldn't tell who it was.

"Can the chatter. You sound like a flock of geese." The rough accented voice of Top Sculdiron. At least he remained in the air and functioning.

"Headcount!" Brandon ordered.

Each man had been assigned a number for brevity. The headcount began, the men radioing in their numbers in sequence. Brandon went first. "One . . ."

". . . Two . . . Three . . ."

A long hesitation . . . *"Five . . ."*

Number Four was missing. Perverse Sanchez!

". . . Six . . . Seven . . ."

". . . Nine . . ."

Another vacancy. Who was Eight?

Cassidy Kragle!

"Say again the headcount," Top Sculdiron insisted.

"One . . . Two . . . Three . . . —Five . . . Six . . . Seven . . . —Nine."

Brandon counted seven parachutes other than his own in a cluster. Only one man was gone; that meant the second must be having radio trouble and couldn't respond to the headcount. Which one was therefore missing— Sanchez or Cassidy? Everyone was naturally concerned about which of his comrades might be in trouble, but Brandon dared not let the clusterfuck continue. Mission always came first. In this weather, the detachment had all it could do to maintain heading and fly safely and in a group to a landing. Malfunctioning of a main didn't necessarily mean the jumper was lost—unless he dropped into the sea. He could always cut away the bad canopy, go for his reserve, and fly it to dry land.

"Get your minds back on the job!" Brandon snapped, covering the anxiety in his voice. He experienced a sudden sinking feeling that it was his brother who went down; he wouldn't know for certain until the detachment assembled on the DZ.

The tight cluster of mushrooms descended into lower clouds after ten minutes of flying through air silence. Clouds enveloped the detachment in an amorphous blanket so thick Brandon could not see the lighted dial of his GPS, even through NVGs. Thin rain blasted his goggles. Blinded and isolated, he held right brake to compensate for his stuck left steering line and kept the wind behind him. He felt rather than saw another parachute glide by. He could only hope the team did not become scattered in the murk.

The detachment broke out below the clouds in pretty good shape at twenty-five hundred feet. Moisture remained confined to the clouds and it was not raining, although wet earth smells said it had been when Brandon dropped his O2 mask from his face. Night vision narrowed and darkened without stars and other ambient light, not a single pinprick of light in all that landscape. Rugged terrain ripped apart by streams and canyons, crusted with rain forest and corroded with mountains to the west, spread out below 3A's dangling feet.

Brandon picked out the landmark he most recognized by its lighter glow—the narrow Partizanskaya River that serpentined out of the Lasaya Mountains on its way to emptying into the Sea of Japan. It looked exactly like the mockup and aerial photos supplied the detachment during mission briefing. Using that as a guide, he quickly located the DZ clearing snugged against hills about a half mile northeast of the river. Brandon assumed their contact, the CIA spook code-named Cage, was already waiting and watching them through his own NVGs.

Winds were calmer than those aloft. The detachment still had plenty of altitude to reach the DZ, no problem. Brandon confirmed the DZ with his GPS, broke out his infrared PEQ and lased it for the rest of the stick. Parachutes glided silently toward it. Two flew directly behind and below Brandon. There were other small clusters to both his left and right. Brandon counted them, hoping somehow that his eyes had deceived him regarding the plummeting jumper and *two* men instead of one were having radio trouble.

Eight parachutes, counting his. He scanned the airspace below. Hopeless. Even if the missing jumper went to his reserve, he could never reach the DZ. If he had streamered in . . . Well . . . Either way, one member of Cold Dawn—either Sanchez or Cassidy, dead or alive—was now on his own.

Mad Dog, heaviest man on the detachment, especially loaded as he was with commo gear, landed first. Brandon loosened his ruck. It hit the end of his lowering line with a jolt. He turned into the wind and experienced ground rush before he executed his PLF (parachute landing fall).

The rest of the detachment came in like silent night-flying predators, touching down within a circle no more than forty meters wide. After PLF and release, they got their weapons out and stayed still for a minute, listening, watching. Everything was markedly still and suddenly calm after the excitement of the jump.

Sergeant Sculdiron conducted another headcount, going from man to man, then dropped a knee next to the commander. He hesitated. Brandon drew in a breath.

"Sir," Sculdiron reported, "Sanchez is accounted for."

It took Brandon a moment to get it out: "It's my brother then."

Gloomy Davis moved in on the other side and gripped his CO's shoulder. The three men remained like that for an extended minute while the major digested developments and regained his composure. He dropped his chin to his chest and closed his eyes.

Why hadn't he chosen some other demo from Dare Russell's Troop? Why did he have to select Cassidy? But then, on the other hand, *all* these men were his brothers.

Mission came first.

"Have Dog radio in a SITREP," Brandon instructed presently, his emotions under control. "Insertion successful. One man . . . One man MIA."

"Cassidy will have gone to his reserve, Boss," Gloomy Davis commiserated. "He's cool-headed. He'll be recovered on his E&E corridor."

Every mission plan included an escape and evasion contingency.

Brandon stood and methodically surveyed a three-sixty, still wearing his NVGs. He mustn't think of Cassidy now; there was plenty of time for recriminations later.

They were surrounded by forest on two sides of the

clearing and rolling, lightly timbered hills to the north. The river sheened dimly below them between its high banks.

"Top, send out a two-man perimeter patrol to locate Cage," Brandon ordered.

The contact should already have spotted them. Brandon's GPS said the detachment was exactly where it ought to be. One way or the other, 3A would have to vacate the DZ promptly. Hostiles in the vicinity might have witnessed the drop.

While Perverse Sanchez and Ice Man scouted the perimeter for Cage, Brandon and Top Sculdiron mulled over the situation. Cassidy's loss left the team short one rubber boat and half its explosives. It affected the mission, but it was by no means a fatal blow. Sergeant Dade assured the CO that he had sufficient demo remaining to blow up a small town. A detachment's essential items of equipment were never packed solely in one man's ruck, in anticipation of just such an occasion as this.

Ice Man and Perverse returned to the perimeter hustling a small figure between them. To Brandon's astonishment, the figure turned into a *woman*, a young female with loose dark hair. She wore jeans and a plaid woolen jacket open in front to reveal a flannel shirt well filled out in the breasts. She wore a small day pack on her back, as though ready for a hike. Mad Dog looked up from breaking down his radio after sending the SITREP.

"Camp followers already?" he quipped. "Ask her if she's from *the Babe*."

"We found her out there, Major," Ice Man said, typically supplying only essentials in as few words as possible.

"Che rode up on a motorbike," Perverse added. "Che was looking for us."

Brandon's eyes narrowed. Cage was supposed to be a *man*. The woman stood unmoving between her captors, her head tossed back defiantly. Quiet.

"Who are you?" Brandon demanded.

"Cage is sending me."

Brandon didn't believe it. It was against all OPSEC. But how else would she know the spook's code name.

"Where is Cage?"

"He is being dead. He is being murder earlier in Partizansk by the Russian mafia."

Her voice was accented; certainly English wasn't her primary language.

"I am coming in place of Cage," she offered. "I am helping. I know these mountains. You must be trusting me."

CHAPTER 17

New York City

Claude Thornton's lunch the previous day with General Kragle at the airport preyed on the agent's mind as he drove the Verrazano Narrows Bridge that connected Brooklyn to Staten Island. Midday traffic was horrific, primarily due to antiwar, anti-Tyler demonstrations beginning all over Manhattan. Stop-and-go traffic sometimes reached dizzying speeds of up to ten miles per hour. Impatient, Thornton kept up a steady finger tapping on the steering wheel.

The General had looked totally worn out, used up, almost depressed. He looked *old*. Claude had never seen his friend like that. But, hell, Claude reconsidered, he looked into the mirror some mornings to shave and *he* looked old and burned out. The War on Terror, both domestically and internationally, quickly wore down men and resources. He suspected if he didn't keep his head shaved, his hair would come in startlingly white and kinky against his black skull.

The War on Terror was being literally fought around the globe, from Afghanistan and Iraq, Israel and Chechnya, Korea and Japan, to the Philippines and Australia, London, New York, Washington, and Los Angeles. The FBI, Homeland Security, Joint Terrorism Task Forces, and Thornton's own National Domestic Preparedness conducted SpecOps missions within the boundaries of the United States. The worst part was that while they fought the war, a large portion of the American public, who never heard about the skirmishes that thwarted dozens of planned attacks each month, who even denied that there *was* a war, actively participated in efforts to stop it. The centerpiece of Senator Lowell Rutherford Harris's campaign for the presidency was his allegations that government measures to protect America from terrorists and terrorist supporters were unnecessary, unconstitutional, and perhaps even evil.

Just that morning, Senator Rowen Johnston, chairman of the Second 9/11 Commission, threatened to have Claude arrested and brought to the hearings if he didn't show up himself to testify by the afternoon. Only personal intervention by MacArthur Thornbrew saved him. Thornton had more vital matters to attend to than satisfying a bunch of self-centered politicians intent on mugging for cameras. To Claude, *politics* seemed an appropriate word to describe this election year. In Latin, *poli* meant "many" and *tics* meant "blood-sucking creatures."

Any other cabinet-level or subcabinet-level director of a law enforcement or counterterrorist agency would have been either coordinating operations from his office or delegating it to subordinates. Not Claude Thornton. He was a hands-on type who liked to be out in the field with his men. He had initiated this particular action anyhow with his arrests of the six Jihadia aboard Northwest 427. He was determined to see it through.

Time was wasting.

He checked in by radio with the JTTF agent he had assigned to pull surveillance on lawyer Patsy Koehler's Staten Island residence until a search warrant came through. He was a rookie Chinese American named Ching.

"There's been a lot of traffic in and out all morning," Ching reported. *"You know the type—long-haired, dope-smoking radical maggots. There have also been several Middle Easterners. Three or four are in the house right now. I don't know if your subject is home or not. I haven't seen her."*

"I have the warrant," Claude replied. "I should be there in a quarter hour or so. Damned traffic! Everybody copy?"

"Copy that: damned traffic!"

Two JTTF cars full of lawmen had been on standby at Staten Island's Clove Park since early that morning.

It had taken Claude more than twenty-four hours to push Abdul-Rahim Hamden's, the Shoe's, signed affidavit through the court system in order to obtain a search warrant for Koehler's house. The sixty-three-year-old radical lawyer had attained some notoriety over the years, especially among socialists and left wingers, who protected her through the media from the "vast right-wing conspiracy." The first federal district judge Thornton approached passed the warrant request on up to a federal appeals judge.

"The national press will crucify you and the administration and turn her into a martyr if you're wrong," the appeals judge predicted.

"I go by the evidence, not by *who* the evidence is against," Claude countered. "An admitted terrorist, who confessed against his own self-interest, has signed the affidavit stating he was to meet at this address to receive a briefing on a terrorist mission within CONUS."

The agent feared the delay may have already cost him

the element of surprise, that if Koehler *was* running a safe house and command center for terrorists she had already heard of the Shoe's apprehension and cleaned up her act. On the other hand, Claude was counting on the sleeper cells' proclivity for secrecy and limited interaction with each other to keep in the dark those not directly involved.

Like a number of other native-born, non-Muslim Americans Thornton had encountered in his investigations since 9/11, Koehler fit the profile of what he called "the useful idiot." He had accumulated a file three inches thick on her.

A graduate of Harvard Law School, she turned political in the 1960s and started a criminal practice defending such underground groups as the Black Panthers, the Black Liberation Army, the Chicago Seven, and assorted cop killers, drug dealers, and counterculture leftist radicals who had been "betrayed" by the system. In her words, "defending the people against our poisonous government." Again, like most useful idiots, she turned to socialism as a cure for all of society's perceived ills, as a panacea against American capitalism and American politics. The more she came to hate her own country, the more extreme her views became.

In one interview, she said, "I believe that entrenched institutions will not be changed except by violence. I believe in the politics that lead to violence being exerted by people on their behalf to effectuate change . . . I believe in a people's revolution to fight entrenched ferocious capitalism that is in this country today . . . We must come out and confront the Tyler effort to destroy human rights and scare the country into lurching to the right . . ."

She was one of the lawyers who defended Sheikh Omar Abdel Rahman, the so-called blind cleric who masterminded the first bombing of the World Trade Center in

1993. Currently, she was on retainer by BUCKUS Alliance and Peace and Justice International to defend New York "protestors" expected to be arrested during the Federalist National Convention. It appeared she may have gone from defending terrorists in court to joining them in the streets, helping to cement what Thornton believed to be an "unholy alliance" between the American radical left and radical Islam.

After much hedging, the appeals judge had finally signed the search warrant an hour earlier. Claude departed Manhattan promptly, his raid team having already collected on Staten Island. He noticed in astonishment how signs in hotels, restaurants, and clothing stores were offering discounts to the quarter-million demonstrators expected to arrive within the next day or so to cause, in their own words, "maximum disruption."

Only in America!

CHAPTER 18

Staten Island

Anyone who willingly strapped a bomb to himself to blow up an airliner in hopes of winning seventy-two virgins in the Happy Hereafter wasn't playing with a full deck. Extremists and what they were capable of must never be underestimated. Claude Thornton planned the raid against Koehler relying on the experience and confidence he had gained from numerous such actions since the War on Terror began. The key to success lay in surprise and in swift, determined movement. Get inside, secure the occupants before they could resist, get down to business.

The appeals judge, however, had built complications into the search warrant, adding certain restrictive conditions because of the status the radical attorney commanded in her profession, especially among the bar's left wing. He feared fallout from a chronically critical media in case something went wrong. He stipulated that the warrant must be served during daylight hours only and that it must be return-filed within twenty-four hours. Plus, he refused to authorize a "no-knock" entry. There went the element of surprise.

Patsy Koehler's house took up a corner of a street in a neighborhood that, in contrast to similar suburbs in Manhattan and Brooklyn, might have been transported from a small town somewhere in Illinois or Kansas. Twin one-hundred-year-old oaks in the unfenced front yard shaded a wide lawn freshly mowed. The house itself—brick with cedar trim—*looked* like a house that belonged to someone's grandmother. It certainly seemed unconventional for housing a nest of suspected Islamic fanatics.

A few curious neighbors paused in their lawn work or in watering their gardens to watch unmarked government sedans speed down the quiet street and spew out armed plainclothesmen. Agents raced across the corner lawn to surround the house. Thornton, Ching, and an FBI resident agent named Jonathan Barnes rushed the front door with its narrow entryway porch. The warrant required them to knock, announce their presence, and request entry. Ching pounded on the door. He stood to one side with Thornton. Barnes stood on the other side, handgun undrawn but palm on the grip. Any good cop knew never to stand in front of a closed door where he couldn't see a threat on the other side.

"FBI! Open up!" Ching called out.

Nothing happened. Claude waited a minute, then nodded. Ching rapped again.

This second announcement initiated a flurry of action. Claude's earpiece filled with excited reports from the team leader at the rear of the house. Someone was attempting to flee.

"We got movement! They're coming out . . . ! No . . . ! They're back inside . . . !"

"Hit it!" Claude said to Ching. The warrant's formalities had been observed. Now it was time to get serious.

Ching hopped away from the wall and cocked a leg ahead of his solid two-hundred-pound body. Thornton snatched his 9mm Glock semiauto from its holster and crouched in a two-handed combat stance. Barnes followed his example on the other side of the door.

Ching hurled all his weight behind a kick. The hollow-core door crashed in, splintering and banging back against the inside wall, breaching the house. Everything after that went into slow-motion mode caused by accelerated adrenaline flow.

"Look out!" Barnes shouted.

Movement inside caught Claude's eye. A blur, punctuated by the blossom-splash and deafening banging of automatic-weapons fire in a confined space. Slugs striking Ching made jarring, meaty *smack-smack* sounds. The agent cried out in pain and shock. The impact knocked him off the small porch. He landed hard on his back on the manicured grass.

More slugs clapped past Thornton's head, whizzing and stealing the air. He and Barnes returned fire simultaneously. Thornton tapped off a volley of three quick shots. The gunman inside screamed and staggered away from the door, crashing over a straight-backed chair and falling to the floor. Claude knew the bastard was dead. He aimed for the heart and rarely missed. Barnes had also drilled him.

Claude glanced back and saw Ching lying motionless on the ground.

"Sons of bitches!" Claude roared before launching himself through the open door into the acrid haze of gun smoke. He took the heavy side of the room. Barnes crossed the X to the other side.

Two additional suspects were already halfway across the living room, fleeing in terror. They appeared unarmed. Both feds began yelling.

"Get down! Get down! On the floor! *Now,* you fuckheads!"

One screamed at the top of his lungs as he dropped. "Don't shoot! God! Please don't shoot me!"

The other blubbered with his face flat against the floor,

his eyes wide and staring horrified into the face of his deceased comrade.

"Stretch out your arms! Don't move or you're dead!"

"Please, please, please don't shoot us . . ."

The room seemed secured—one dead, two apprehended. The stench of freshly spilled blood, thick and coppery to the palate, made one of the prisoners retch. Sobbing, he vomited all over the floor and himself. That added to the stink.

Barnes assumed a stance to cover all approach entrances with his service weapon. Claude held the prisoners at gunpoint. His heart raced but he remained outwardly calm as he issued orders via his voice mike.

A second team busted through the back door. Thornton and Barnes, alert for the appearance of a further threat, listened to the agents' rapid footfalls and their calling out to each other—*"Go . . . ! Clear . . . !"*—as they searched room to room.

"All clear!" someone called out shortly. "Don't shoot. We're coming front."

Three agents entered the front room, guns drawn but hanging at their sides. They looked at the dead man and the two captives. Claude kicked the dead man's Uzi submachinegun to the other side of the room so the prisoners wouldn't be tempted.

"Koehler's not here," an agent reported.

Claude had been afraid of that, but he felt it important to strike as quickly as possible. Sometimes what a fugitive left behind was more valuable than the suspect.

Burnt gunpowder pinched Claude's nostrils. "Check on Ching," he said, picking up a phone on a long table in a corner of the living room. He dialed 911 and requested EMTs, police, and an ambulance.

Bracing himself with both hands splayed on the table,

head lowered to compose himself, Claude gradually became aware of what was on the table. He straightened slowly, staring. The lawyer's front room, he suddenly realized, had been converted into a conference room, a war room of sorts dominated by the table upon which sat two computers, one at either end. Piles of books, papers, manuals, and other materials overflowed the space in between.

"What have we got here?" an agent asked, curious.

"I don't know yet," Claude said. "Get these assholes out of here."

Two agents frisked and handcuffed the prisoners, jerking them to their feet. One appeared to be of Arab extract, a scrawny little sucker who had quickly recovered from fright to glare back at his captors. Claude guessed he was likely another Jihadia sleeper.

The second was American, about twenty or so with earrings and a matching diamond stud stuck through his lower lip. He wore a dirty tie-dyed T-shirt with vomit still steaming across FUCK AMERIKA emblazoned on its front. He couldn't seem to shut up. Words, tears, slobber, and his lunch poured out at an amazing rate. "Didn't know they had guns . . . just here . . . not know them . . . not part of this . . ."

The third man was stone dead. "Five shots through the Ten-Ring," an agent confirmed.

Barnes appeared in the outer doorway, standing there, his face pale, shoulders slumped forward. "It's too late for Ching," he said. "He's gone."

Silence flushed the room like a blast of frigid air. Everyone stared at the bearer of bad tidings as though he were personally responsible. Claude sucked a long, tired breath, picked up the phone again and dialed.

"Cancel EMTs and the ambulance. Send Homicide instead."

Claude had hardly known Ching. Yet, he was a fellow agent and it was always tough when a lawman went down in the line of duty, another casualty to the War on Terror whom hardly anyone outside his immediate circle would ever hear about.

The prisoners were led away. Thornton riffled through the stacks of papers on the long table while he waited for local police, who would assume jurisdiction over the crime scene. His eyebrows lifted higher and higher onto his forehead.

"My God!" he whispered. He may have struck the jackpot.

Many documents mentioned BUCKUS and Not My Name, Peace and Justice International, and Americans Standing Up For People, all organizational sponsors of the protests intended to shut down New York City during the convention. Piles of flyers, obviously intended for distribution to protestors, listed lawyers and their telephone numbers. Claude recognized some of the names—American Civil Liberties Union attorneys and others involved in lawsuits on behalf of "victims" such as Islamic terrorists held by the government in Guantánamo.

What really caught his eye, however, and stunned him to the core, were catalogues and manuals on building and using IEDs, improvised explosive devices, both nuclear and conventional. One paper seemed to calculate how many people would be killed if a nuclear device were detonated downtown of a large undesignated city. There were also photos and schematics on power plants, dams, public buildings, train stations, airports . . . Prospective targets. A blow-up map showed central Manhattan and Madison Square Garden where the Federalist National Convention would open that week. Another depicted the U.S. Capitol in Washington, D.C. A big red *X* had been drawn across it, out of which emanated a mushroom cloud and repeated doodling of a single phrase: *Boom-a-boom, boom-a-boom, boom-a-boom . . .*

CHAPTER 19

Russian Coast

Any number of factors might contribute to a parachute's malfunctioning—winds, faulty equipment, poor body position, plain bad luck . . . The RAM-air MC-5 military square parachute was a good piece of equipment, reliable under most conditions. However, no 'chute was intended to fly in winds like those that unexpectedly buffeted Sergeant Cassidy Kragle a moment after he exited the Osprey behind Doc Red Mancino. He knew he was in trouble when he attempted to stabilize in freefall in order to pull his main canopy. He must have hit some kind of freak downdraft, a hole in the sky through which ground weather sucked air. Stars streaked in and out of his vision as he tumbled through the darkness like a bug caught in the draft of a speeding car. Air shrieking around his helmet told him he was falling too fast, even for the altitude and its thin atmosphere.

He finally stabilized. He figured he must be far below the other jumpers at this stage. He had to pull immediately if he intended to remain with the stick, if he hoped to retain enough altitude to make the DZ.

Movement in the bad air flipped him forward and upside down when he reached for the ripcord handle. Nylon streamered from his pack. He kept flipping, entangling himself in his deploying lines. Instead of experiencing the tug and sudden arrest of his fall when the canopy opened, he felt instead only a slight reduction in his rate of descent. Above, chillingly, he heard the canopy's thin fabric popping and snapping as it resisted opening. A cigarette roll! The damned thing was not inflating!

On top of that, one boot was ensnared in his shroud lines. He fell toward earth head down. He couldn't cut away and go for his reserve until he first disentangled himself. Otherwise, his reserve would wrap itself around the malfunction—and that would effectively seal his doom. He plunged face toward earth at a dizzying one hundred miles per hour, the speed of his fall only slightly reduced by his streamer.

Although he knew of jumpers who had streamered in, some of whom had even survived, this was his first malfunction after hundreds of parachute training exits and one previous combat jump into Algeria. Incongruously, the beat of an old airborne fighting chant flashed through his mind:

> *Gory, gory, what a helluva way to die.*
> *Gory, gory, what a helluva way to die.*
> *There was blood upon the risers,*
> *There was brains upon the ground.*
> *And he ain't gonna jump no more.*

He figured he had a minute left, maybe slightly more, at his rate of descent before he collided with earth. Struggling to remain calm and stave off desperation and therefore inevitable disaster, he ripped open the quick releases to his ruck and let it plummet on its own. Freeing the additional weight might buy him another second or two. But there went all his gear, including a team rubber raft and his share of the team's explosives. He continued to nosedive toward impact.

Panic welled in his throat. He swallowed it and fumbled for his combat knife. It came free of its scabbard. He almost dropped it.

He had it now, firmly clinched in his fist. He *felt* the ground rushing at him.

Desperation was setting in. He buckled himself into an upside-down situp and knife-hacked at the lines that trapped his foot.

He fell loose suddenly and dangled right-side up below the streamer. He immediately released into another brief freefall and pulled his reserve handle just as he plunged into the total blindness of clouds hovering above the earth. Wet air whistled around his face.

Nylon from his belly reserve pack hissed past his head. His feet kicked up in the welcome pendulum effect of a properly inflating parachute. It was then he realized he had been holding his breath the entire while.

He scabbered his knife and fumbled to get his NVGs on and operating. Barely had he time to congratulate himself on avoiding one close call than he confronted another. He glided out below the clouds; his blood froze in the sudden realization that he was now drifting down into the sea.

Through NVGs, which often affected a wearer's depth perception, he made out the faint pale drift of whitecaps. He heard waves crashing angrily against rocky shoresides. Their roaring filled his entire being with dread and, for one of the few times in his young life, with raw, unadulterated terror. He was a dead man if he landed in the shoals. No way in those savage waters would he be able to cut loose from his parachute and swim in full combat uniform and boots. This was one time he wished the team had gone for safety, Mae Wests, over convenience.

One damned thing after another. It seemed when things

started going wrong, they went wrong all the way. Brandon called it Murphy's Law.

His only hope lay in reaching and landing on dry earth. He toggled with the wind, riding it toward landfall. At first he descended in agonizing slow motion, seeming to pick up speed the nearer he came to the sea. He began experiencing ground rush early through his NVGs. The 'chute skimmed him swiftly above the roiling surface of the water. He drew in his legs to delay the inevitable. He clutched his quick-release wells, ready to jettison the canopy the moment he felt his boots strike the drink. Otherwise, the parachute would fill with water and drag him under.

It was going to be one hell of a fight for his life, but that was the way he intended going out—fighting. It was the Kragle way.

He saw land below his feet. *Land!*

His relief proved short-lived. A rock wall loomed directly in his face. And then everything went black.

CHAPTER 20

Partizanskaya River Valley

The mystery woman on the DZ said her name was Katya Sokolov. She claimed to be Russian. Even with the distorted view provided by his NVGs, Brandon saw she was gorgeous by any man's measure. He couldn't determine her complexion, whether dark or light, but her long hair was dark, almost black, Brandon thought, and she bore the aquiline, haughty features of a Russian princess. Full, pouty lips that any movie starlet would die for, wide dark eyes that dominated her face, a thin nose with flaring high-bred nostrils, and a tiny, pointed teacup chin completed the picture.

"How thoughtful of ol' Hugh to send us a *Playboy* bunny," Mad Dog declared.

Taking no chances on *who* might have sent her, Brandon went through her day pack, but hurriedly, finding only extra jeans, underwear and shirt, a First Aid kit, and two apples. The girl traveled light.

"Turn around," he said. When she hesitated, Brandon turned her physically so that her back was to him.

"Oh!"

"Sorry. I'm in a hurry."

He frisked her quickly for weapons, running hands down her back, up her braless front, massaging her slim waist at the beltline, and checking the legs of her jeans. She protested when he would have checked her crotch.

"Do you always taking liberties such as these with strange women you are meeting?" she asked, sounding more amused than offended.

"Only when I meet them in the middle of the night in places they shouldn't be."

"Oh, but you are misunderstanding. I am where I should be. How else should I be knowing about such handsome strangers arriving in so manner a dramatic?"

"Turn off the sex, lady. I won't shoot you—yet."

Top Sculdiron made up his mind about her. "She is a spy."

"You are Russian?" Katya said, catching Top's accent.

Top turned away. "I am *American*."

"How did you know Cage?" Brandon asked her.

"Mikhail. His name is being . . . *was* Mikhail. Michael. Lovers we were."

Brandon started to challenge a CIA agent getting romantically involved with an indigent, until it dawned on him that something similar developed between Summer and him in Afghanistan during Operation Iron Weed. Summer had been a CIA plant with the Northern Alliance. Now she was his wife.

All right, it could have happened, Brandon conceded. Whatever, Cage clearly wasn't going to show up. This girl had arrived somehow in his place. Losing the contact was a major blow to the mission. Cage knew these mountains and any accesses to the target. But his loss was not a fatal blow.

There wasn't time now to continue the interrogation, not when the insertion may have been compromised and this woman sent to either hold up the detachment or set it up for a fall. Cold Dawn's first order of business was to get the hell off the DZ and into a safe place from which to continue the operation. Under the det's time constraints, there was no room for delay—not even to search for Cassidy, or, more likely, his body. Delta never left a man behind, but Cassidy's recovery would have to wait.

"Cuff her," Brandon ordered.

"Chew mean—tie her up?" Perverse exclaimed.

Top Sculdiron's scalding voice cut into him. "That is what the man said. Do it."

Mad Dog produced a plastic cuff link he used in securing radio gear. He twisted Katya's arms behind her back and bound her wrists. She tossed her head, chin up, defiantly regarding the giant goggle-eyed insects gathered around her.

"Sorry about this, baby doll," Mad Dog apologized. "You really got a nice ass."

"An ass *you* are," she retorted.

Doc Red snickered. "Watch out, Dog. She's fixin' to pitch a hissie fit."

"I thought you Southern rednecks called 'em conniptions."

Cage's mysterious absence compelled Brandon to dust off his contingency plan. A contingency was what you turned to when Murphy stepped in and screwed up the original.

"Move out in five minutes," he said. "Ice, get rid of the woman's motorbike. The rest of you cache the air gear so it can't be easily found."

Brandon and Top Sculdiron huddled together underneath a spread poncho to contain light while they pored over a map. They selected a line of march through particularly rough-looking terrain in the direction of the downed capsule.

"We'll be moving fast," Brandon warned the girl when he came out from underneath the poncho.

She seemed to be pouting over having her hands tied.

Ice Man and Diverse Dade took point with a map, the

GPS, and a compass. Perverse brought up Tailend Charlie to keep an eye on their back trail. Brandon set a brisk pace in order to put as much distance as possible between the detachment and the DZ before daylight.

The route climbed through a thick entanglement of rain forest at first. Once or twice they startled large animals, deer perhaps, or even a tiger or a bear that supposedly inhabited the region. Forest turned to even rougher country—rock scree in landslides, steep grades across boulder fields, brush-choked gulches and washouts clawed into mountainsides. It was a cool night with a mist of rain now and again, but soon the men were breathing hard and sweating. Brandon marveled at what good shape the prisoner—Katya—must be in to keep up without being prodded or urged, even with her hands tied behind her back and without benefit of NVGs.

She stumbled occasionally and fell face down, unable to catch herself with her hands. Traveling a few paces behind her, Brandon helped her to her feet. She jerked away from him without a word and continued trudging along behind Mad Dog immediately ahead with his heavy radio pack.

During a rest break, Brandon had Dog release her hands and retie them in front where she could at least break her falls. He offered her a drink from his canteen. She accepted in resentful silence. In Brandon's opinion, she appeared remarkably self-controlled for someone who had just lost a lover. But then again, an observer might look upon him the same way, considering he had lost his brother that very night.

"What happened to Cage?" he asked her.

She sat on a rock resting. He knelt next to her in the dark.

"To you I am not talking," she puffed. "You tie me up."

"Have it your way." Brandon rose to his feet.

"Wait!"

He waited, taking a knee. After another minute, she finally explained in a husky, strained voice how Cage, or Mikhail, or whatever the hell his name was, had stumbled up to her bungalow on the outskirts of Partizansk shortly after nightfall. He had a bullet in his chest.

"Who shot him?" Brandon asked.

"Oleg Kopylov."

"Cage told you that?"

"I am knowing it, but, yes, he tell me."

"Who is this Kopylov?"

"He is being the mayor of Partizansk and is heading the Freedom and People's Power Party. In American he is being known as the Don, but he is being just a *little* don. Viktor Cherepov is being the Don of dons."

"As in mafia?"

"I am seeing the movie *The Godfather* too. Yes. Organized crime is what we producing most of in Partizansk and Vlodivostok."

"Why did the mafia shoot Cage?"

She cast him a quick side look. "You are knowing that already."

"I'm asking you."

"The astronauts," she said, as though it should be obvious. "Is that not being your purpose—to rescue them?"

Her revelation that she knew the mission gave Brandon a jolt.

"Is that what Cage told you?"

"But, of course. Why else am I being here? Mikhail is telling me before he die that the mafia is capture the American astronauts and the Russian cosmonaut and is holding them for money. He is saying that I must come to you and assisting you in finding the spaceship and them. That is why I am coming here tonight. Mikhail ask me before he is die."

She held up her bound hands. "Maybe I am foolish and am making the mistake. You are not trusting me."

You're right, lady. I don't trust you.

That she even knew of the detachment's presence was suspicious enough, much less that she knew its mission. A spook would *never* reveal the details of an ongoing operation in which he and other Americans were involved— unless he was tortured, or unless he was careless. A good piece of ass sometimes made even the best of men careless, while torture skillfully applied could make the best of men talk.

But what was in it for Katya? Why had she met the detachment on the DZ if not out of loyalty to Cage and a willingness to carry out the final request of a dying lover?

Brandon studied her face through his NVGs. Her features were liquid and dim through them and he failed to read her expression. It seemed neutral.

"I am knowing where the spaceship is being," she offered suddenly. "You are on a most difficult route in getting to it through the mountains, and it is taking you another day. I am knowing a trail that is being very fast. You must trusting me in this matter. I am helping. It is what my Mikhail is asking of me before he is dying. I am helping."

Right.

Brandon pulled Top Sculdiron aside and they pored over the topo map again. The girl was right. The most direct route to the space capsule led across a rugged mountain range. If, by chance, she did know a faster way, a trail . . .

"I do not trust her," Top grumbled.

"We could waste two days in those mountains," Brandon countered. "We don't have two days to waste unless we want the sub to leave without us. Cage *was* going to guide us."

Top Sculdiron nodded, but said nothing further. Brandon returned to Katya.

"All right," he said to her. "I'm listening. If you pull anything, lady, if I so much as suspect you of pulling anything, I will personally put a bullet right between your pretty eyes."

Something flickering through those pretty eyes said she believed him.

CHAPTER 21

Russian Coast

Sergeant Cassidy Kragle awoke with the lingering impression that he and Margo were quarreling again. At first, still in a haze, he thought he lay in Margo's bed back in Fayetteville. The faint smell of woman surrounded him . . . but of *stale* woman. Certainly not Margo's clean, crisp scent that he liked to absorb through his pores whenever he lay with his head between her bare breasts.

Gradually, he became aware of pain. Every part of his body felt stricken with it. Even his eyelids ached.

He blinked. This wasn't Margo's . . . This wasn't . . . This wasn't *what*?

Things slowly came back to him. He recalled pulling up his legs while trying to avoid parachuting into the sea. The rock wall . . . Oblivion. Until now. Waking here. Wherever the hell *here* was.

Weak, cloudy daylight filtered through a window veiled in what Brown Sugar Mama called chintzy curtains. Cassidy looked around the single small room, his eyes and head turning carefully to avoid pain lashing out from behind his eyes with every quick movement. He took in an austere room with crude rock walls, only the one window, and a single closed door that apparently led into other parts of the house. Mold or gray-green lichen—some kind of foreign growth—crusted the corner he could see behind a crude wooden table upon which rested a kerosene lamp with a blackened globe and no flame, an ashtray filled with home-rolled cigarette butts, and a heavy book that might be a Bible.

The thick quilt that covered him and the feather bed, he determined, explained the source of the female scent. The bed was not filthy, at least not *really* filthy, but it was not clean either. Someone had used it a long time between washings. *Who's been sleeping in my bed?*

Other than the bed and the table, the only additional furnishings in the tiny cell were a straight-backed country chair and, incongruously, a crude wooden wheelbarrow that, except for the rubber wheel, might have been a century old. The bed was wide but too short for Cassidy's six-four frame. One bare foot hung over the end. Bandages encased the other foot; it occurred to him while attempting to move it why a wheelbarrow might be in the bedroom. He had to bite his lip to keep from crying out in agony as pain shot all the way up to his groin. Someone, some improbable individual, must have wheelbarrowed him up here from the seashore.

The crowing of a rooster outside and the thin bleating of a sheep or goat completed his inventory of his immediate environment. He was in someone's farmhouse. He then conducted a practical assessment of his condition.

His left leg appeared broken above the ankle. Someone had splinted it with old barrel staves while he slept. That same someone had also capped his head with bandages perhaps ripped from chintzy curtains somewhere else in the house. He must have suffered a serious concussion, perhaps even a skull fracture, judging from how long he seemed to have been unconscious.

He was naked except for his undershorts. Where was his clothing, his equipment, his weapon? He especially needed the Motorola radio to contact Brandon and Detachment 3A. He looked around the room again. None of his belongings were in sight.

Having learned all he could through his own senses, he called out, "Hey! Hey? Is anybody out there?"

The rooster crowed.

"Who's out there?" he shouted, louder this time.

He started to get out of bed to go take a look, but the broken leg flattened him. He gritted his teeth and felt sweat popping out of his forehead. The torment finally subsided.

After a short while during which he lay quietly, listening, not daring to move again, he heard a door open and close in an outer room. He again cried out.

Almost immediately the door flung open. Cassidy's eyes popped wide with surprise and disbelief. In the doorway stood a curious creature barely five feet tall, broad and strong-looking in the shoulders, legs stubby and thick and slightly crooked sticking out the bottom of a faded old house dress, bare feet wide and calloused and dirty. Her hair was the color of molded hay, unkempt, and of the same texture as hay. Her eyes, brown and green, like mold and decay, were sunken far back into the dark caves of their sockets. They regarded the invalid with sudden eager glee.

The wide mouth split her face in a tremendous grin. Rapidly batting eyelashes splattered tears of joy all over her face. Cassidy thought she looked exactly like a little green Smurf doll, ugly as unadulterated sin, even a bit off-putting, while at the same time disturbingly appealing.

She rushed to his side, dropped to her knees at the bedside, and snatched Cassidy's hand in both of hers. Cassidy was too stunned to resist. Drooling with relief and happiness, the creature rubbed his palm against her cheek and drowned it with wet, soaking kisses. Upon closer inspection, Cassidy saw that something was wrong with her other than the obviously physical. He detected a certain off-kilter look in her eyes, the look of a retarded child surprised at Christmas.

"Mine," she blubbered. *"Mine!"*

She chanted it, this the only English she apparently understood, perhaps even the only word she understood, running it together while she gripped his hand in both hers and clutched it possessively to her breast.

"Mine mine mine mine mine *mine*!"

CHAPTER 22

Manhattan

Agent Claude Thornton nursed this gut feeling that fugitive lawyer Patsy Koehler was the key to something big about to go down during the Federalist National Convention. Materials seized during the bloody raid on her Staten Island home introduced a broad spectrum of possibilities but no specifics. Claude counted on the FBI lab's breaking into her computer hard drives to provide more intelligence. The pressure was on to come up with particulars, and *fast*, if the FBI hoped to thwart whatever the hell was about to happen. They had to find Patsy Koehler.

"Name me one thing the Islam world makes that the rest of the world needs or wants," Agent Jonathan Barnes challenged as Thornton pulled out of traffic and parked on a side street a block away from the rising minarets of the al-Mukhaiyam Mosque on Manhattan's Upper East Side.

"Persian rugs," Claude offered.

"Name one other thing."

"Oil."

"I'll grant you Persian rugs." The previous day's murder of Agent Ching laced Barnes's voice with a tint of acrimony he hadn't yet shaken off. "They don't make oil. They just pump it."

The magnified warbling of the muezzin calling the faithful to prayer reminded Claude of the years he spent as

FBI resident agent in Cairo. These days, the muezzin seemed a mocking reminder that Islam, *radical Islam*, was invading America's heart in an effort to either convert or destroy the nation.

"Every convenience store in the city shuts down for prayer five times a day," Barnes said. "What do you suppose they pray for? More airliners to crash?"

Claude claimed many Muslim friends. After all, he had lived and worked in Muslim countries for decades before being recalled to the States to head Domestic Preparedness. Nonetheless, these troubled days, he sometimes had difficulty controlling his own sense of outrage and distrust.

The two feds from their stakeout position watched Muslim women covered in black from head to toe march to the mosque as though summoned against their will. Men joined them, most of whom had been Americanized insofar as dress was concerned.

"We'll never recognize Koehler in those black sheets," Barnes said. He was short and wiry, about forty, with a perpetual frown worn into features cops often developed from years of peering into society's seedy underbelly.

"Look closely at the old fat ones," Claude suggested. Patsy Koehler reportedly weighed about two hundred fifty pounds of fat slopped onto a five-four frame.

The Arab arrested at Koehler's house, the scrawny little sucker who looked as though he dreamed of taking the controls of an airliner aimed at the White House, had refused to provide even his name. The long-haired dope smoker with earrings *wanted* to spill his guts but knew little enough to divulge. About all he passed on was that Patsy was converting to Islam and that her mentor and teacher was a mullah in a mosque on the Upper East Side. He thought Patsy might hide out there, at least initially.

Information from the raid disclosed a number of references to Mullah Akhmed Maskhadov of al-Mukhaiyam Mosque, including quotes from his teachings: "True American blood brothers, why don't you get your guns loaded and kill un-arrested Tyler proudly. Then offer autographs at your legal preliminary hearing. Better yet, die a martyr by rightly sacrificing an enemy fighting with the lawless, godless devils of creation who will ultimately fail to enslave universal values."

So much for this mullah and his religion of peace.

The same appeals judge who reluctantly issued a search warrant for Koehler's house denied a similar warrant to search the mosque for the renegade lawyer.

"That's a holy site," he argued. "How would it appear to American Muslims, and to Islam worldwide, if the police stormed a holy site?"

"That holy site may be hatching plans for another 9/11," Claude patiently countered. "A reliable informant states the fugitive may be hiding there."

"That's not good enough," the judge said. "You're going to require a lot more probable cause to obtain a warrant for a mosque."

"What if this were a Baptist minister scheming in his church to bomb an abortion mill?" Claude asked.

"Well . . . That's different."

"Is it?" Claude had a tough time suppressing his sarcasm.

Staking out the mosque in hopes of catching Patsy Koehler coming or going was soldier work and not a task for the head of Domestic Preparedness. However, Claude wanted to look at the mosque before turning it over to a JTTF or New York Police stakeout team. Besides, there were few other leads to follow at the present time.

Islam prayers ended shortly. Black-clad women as alike

as penguins and their Americanized male counterparts departed the mosque. The agents studied them through binoculars, finding no exceptionally obese women among them. Barnes sighed, stretched, and offered to trot down the street to a deli. He brought back two sandwiches and cups of coffee in large Styrofoam cups.

"Black for you, no sugar," he said.

"Black is beautiful."

Claude began feeling they were wasting their time. His cell phone went off, playing "Dock of the Bay" by Otis Redding. Barnes chuckled.

Claude answered. "Thornton here. This is a secure phone."

It was the FBI lab. "We have some results from the computer scans," the agent at the lab volunteered.

"Give me the *Reader's Digest* version. I'll pick up the full report later."

"Two things stood out when we restored the computer hard drives."

"Go on."

"We discovered a big bunch of photos and building layouts of the U.S. Capitol. We thought that looked suspicious."

It *was* suspicious.

"It also seems that at least some New York agitators are being specifically funded to disrupt the Federalist Convention by a nonprofit group registered under the title Americans Standing Up For People."

That was interesting, considering that terrorists were obviously mixing with protestors and either working with home-grown radicals to cause mayhem or using them as cover.

"Did you come up with a CEO name for the group?" Claude asked.

"I did."

The agent had an annoying habit of pausing after each statement to wait for a prompt.

"And . . . ?"

"Ronald McDonald."

"Pardon."

"That's the signature on the nonprofit registration."

"You're shitting me?"

"No, sir. I wouldn't do that. Ronald McDonald."

CHAPTER 23

Partizanskaya River Valley

Major Brandon Kragle pushed the detachment hard, even though the going proved easier and faster with Katya's guidance. She seemed to know these mountains well. She selected a narrow valley that led upward in a gentle grade to an even narrower pass across the mountain range. Brandon cross-checked her constantly with map and GPS, still suspicious but willing to give her the benefit of the doubt. So far, so good. They covered ground that would have taken at least twenty-four hours longer for someone unfamiliar with the terrain. By 0400 local they were within a few hours of the capsule's crash site.

Even Top Sculdiron seemed relieved and found little to carp about when Ice Man and Diverse Dade on point stumbled upon the narrow, fissure-like opening to a cave and Brandon called a halt to check it out as a possible secure site to catch a couple of hours' sleep before dawn. He calculated they had gone about ten klicks from the compromised DZ and could not be easily tracked. It had rained in a weeping drizzle most of the night.

The cave proved big enough to accommodate the entire Cold Dawn team. Katya the mystery woman appeared wrung out. She barely protested when Brandon gave her his sleeping bag and deposited her inside near the cave's rear wall. She coughed against the raw disturbed odors of shuffling men in the darkness kicking up decades of accumulated bat guano.

"Ugh!" she protested. "Bat droppings."

"That means *bat shit* for all you Polacks," Mad Dog interpreted for Top Sculdiron's edification.

"Chew has slept in worst, *Perro*," Perverse Sanchez noted.

"Name one," Dog challenged.

"In Arachna Phoebe's bed."

"Unsubstantiated rumors."

The detachment sprawled out in their sleeping bags on the soft guano floor, using their packs for pillows, and soon began breathing deeply. No man slept soundly enough on mission to snore.

"Are you please untying my hands?" Katya requested of Brandon. "Where am I going with all you big nasty men around? Am I not earning your trust? I am bringing you already to the spaceship."

That she had done. Brandon illuminated her with a red-lensed flashlight and released her hands. She rustled around with her pack in the total night after he turned out the light. The drip-drip of water somewhere echoed, but the cave felt dry. Brandon wrapped himself in his poncho and stretched out across the narrow entrance to the cave. Gloomy Davis spread his sleeping bag next to the commander, their bodies creating an effective barrier and alarm against anyone coming or going.

"I still don't think she's what she claims to be," Gloomy whispered.

"Why otherwise is she doing this?" Brandon demanded.

Gloomy didn't know either.

Bats returned to the cave at dawn. The whisper and whir of their leathery wings awoke Brandon with a start. He was still wet from the rain; the chill of sleeping on the ground with only a poncho left him stiff and out of sorts. He turned over on his belly so he could see outside through the narrow fissure that formed the cave's door. While the others slept, he thought about the mission and watched day replace night, seeping like a gray mist into his limited view of the landscape.

A combat plan was an animal in a constant state of metamorphosis, under continuous revision right up until the first shot was fired. The detachment had already lost half its explosives and one man—two if you counted Cage—and the mission had barely started. The girl really tossed a monkey wrench into things. Ponder it as he might, useful though she had been, Brandon failed to figure out why she would have thrown herself into their hands the way she had—unless she was really who she said she was, improbably, and indeed had been sent by Cage, even more improbably. Either way, as far as Brandon could see, his choices concerning her were limited. He couldn't turn her loose, and he couldn't execute her. The only thing he could do was hold on to her, whether he trusted her or not, until he completed the Cold Dawn mission.

Damn you, Murphy!

He got up and went outside to get a lay of the land in daylight. The cave, he saw, its mouth almost invisible from more than twenty feet away, occupied one wall of a ravine-like valley, the opposite wall being a sheer granite cliff. A stream cut through the bottom of the valley among conifer timber so green it appeared black in the early morning light. The rain had ceased, but the world was still sodden and smelled fresh and clean-washed. The top of the cliff snagged some of the clouds. They were tired clouds, however, and seemed to be dissipating already at threat of the coming sun. Perhaps weather would provide Cold Dawn at least one break.

Katya emerged sleepy-eyed from the cave. She looked around, yawned like a waking lioness, and, spotting Brandon, percolated across the wet grass toward him. Brandon sat on a boulder and watched her approach.

Despite the gray dusting of guano on her clothing and in her hair, she was immensely more beautiful—*sexy* was a better word, a *hottie*—in the light than anyone could have imagined the night before. Her skin was a rich golden brown, her hair silky black and hanging loose around her shoulders. She was small, petite even, but filled out her jeans and flannel shirt in all the right places. Her face, even more than Brandon recalled from the previous night, had a classic sculpted beauty come alive out of a Renaissance painting. She had eyes like the Madonna. In spite of the previous night's grueling march and less than two hours' sleep, she looked rested except for a slight puffiness around her eyes.

Mad Dog, Diverse Dade, and Doc Red shot out of the cave entrance behind her, their admiring eyes glued to her sway. Her smile said she knew she had their attention and that she enjoyed it.

"Exquisite!" exclaimed Diverse, a connoisseur of music, food, fine art, and women.

Katya laughed with delight and stopped directly in front of Brandon, hip upshot, still smiling in a way that made him uncomfortable. She smelled of bat guano, but Mad Dog at the cave was already observing that she could roll in shit and *still* come up smelling like Christmas morning.

"You can turn off the sex," Brandon growled.

She returned an innocent little-girl look, really pouring it on. "Sex is part of who I am being," she said. Husky, accented, pure sex in sound. "You are looking like you are beating me. The whip and the rack? I am thinking should I be knowing your name if you are to beating me?"

She batted her eyes for her audience. Even Top Sculdiron and Ice Man came out to see what was going on.

"Knock it off," Brandon snapped.

"Ooooh! You are having a temper, *Americanski*. I am wanting to thank you for giving to me your sleeping bag for the night. I am sleeping most comfortable. Also you?"

"I'm all right."

Her voice lowered, teasing. "But I am most willing to have shared it with you. We could together be sleeping most comfortable."

"I said, knock it off." Couldn't he do better than that? She could.

"If we are sleeping together and rising, if we *are* sleeping, I will preparing for you eggs and steak and gravy and biscuits. Is that being an American hearty breakfast for a man being so handsome as you, *Americanski*?"

"Did you make breakfast for Cage?"

She sobered. Sadness entered her eyes as though in consideration of her former lover. Brandon couldn't tell if the emotion was affected or not.

"Mikhail is never wanting breakfast." She reached toward him. "You are giving me your canteen cup?" She wagged her hand impatiently. "Coming, coming."

He handed her his canteen and cup. She knelt with it next to the boulder at his feet and quickly built a little fire ring of stones, after which she darted into a nearby grove of trees and soon returned with a handful of pine tar and some dry bark collected from the underside of a deadfall.

"I am making coffee," she explained. "Perhaps it is turning you in better mood."

"No smoke," Brandon warned.

"But of course."

The entire team gathered outside the cave by now, watching with amusement as she poured water into the canteen cup and got it started boiling over a tiny, smokeless blaze. Brandon stomped over to the cave, irritated at being the focus of this little domestic scene.

"How's the little woman, sir?" Mad Dog heckled, straight-faced. His dark eyes twinkled. "Dining with the enemy, are we?"

"That's exactly what I'm doing. Don't anyone forget that she may well be the enemy. I'm trying to get some answers. The rest of you might be better eating while you can rather than entertaining yourself watching me."

"We are watching *her*, Major," Perverse corrected.

"This is not Club Med. Top, get things moving."

"You heard the boss. He is working hard. So will we."

Everyone, even the top sergeant, was getting in his licks and having a good time of it at Brandon's expense.

The team broke out MREs and lined up to eat around the cave mouth where they could observe Brandon and Katya. Although they were too far away to overhear, it was still the best show in town. "Cheap seats," Dog complained. Brandon shared his MRE with the girl, she shared her apple. They passed the hot canteen cup of coffee back and forth. She sat on the boulder next to him; he stood up immediately.

"How did Cage find out about the space capsule?" Brandon asked her. "A lot of people must have known about it?"

"I am thinking not many saw it landing. The men from space are being capture by Oleg Kopylov. Mikhail is saying so. But you are knowing this or you will not be coming, is that correctly said?"

Brandon had a feeling she was pumping him for information at the same time he was questioning her. Either she knew little about Cage or she was deliberately playing ignorant.

"Mikhail is a stranger in Partizansk," she said. "He is speaking Russian and saying he is from St. Petersburg. But Oleg Kopylov is being from St. Petersburg as well, and he is thinking that Mikhail is not having the correct accent. It is being common in town that Mikhail is under suspicion. Oleg's men are asking questions. They are to thinking that Mikhail is being an American spy. When the astro-men are landing, Oleg is shooting Mikhail because he is fearing Mikhail is being in contact with outsiders."

"Where are the spacemen being held?" Brandon asked her.

"I am being not knowing," she replied. "Mikhail is saying I am to find out for you."

CHAPTER 24

Russian Coast

The appearance of his unusual savior stunned Cassidy Kragle as much as his transition from a healthy, self-assured, eager young warrior to a battered cripple confined to a strange bed. He had no idea where he was, other than assuming he must be somewhere near the coast since no such tiny creature, no matter how extraordinarily strong, could have pushed a large man very far in a wheelbarrow. He guessed the Smurf lived alone and on a farm in relative isolation. Otherwise, her pushing a big stranger in a wheelbarrow through a village or settlement would have surely attracted the curious by now.

She let go of his hand and pulled the straight-backed chair to his bedside where she perched beaming good-naturedly over him while tears cut clean swaths through the grime on her cheeks. He concluded the only English word she knew was *mine*, which she had somehow acquired and which she employed at every opportunity. Of course, he couldn't ask questions of someone whose entire English vocabulary consisted of one word.

She must have his clothing and, more important, his other equipment stored somewhere in the house. He had air-dropped his pack somewhere over the sea, but retained his NVGs, GPS, compass, map, Motorola radio, knife, and pistol on his battle harness. His carbine was still attached to his parachute harness when he landed. There was no sign of any of it now. All he had left was his Fruit O' Looms.

"My clothes?" he asked. "Where are my clothes?"

She radiated upon him while he pulled on a pretend shirt and buttoned it, completing the pantomime by shrugging his shoulders and throwing up his hands and brows in a question. When at long last he made her understand that he wanted his clothing, her smile turned into an ugly scowl. She indicated by gesture and expression that he was to remain in bed. She pointed to his leg and bandaged head and shook her head vigorously while she scolded him in Russian.

"You don't understand," he argued, futilely. "I can't stay in bed."

He had to at least get his hands on his Motorola and contact Cold Dawn. He simulated using a telephone. Maybe he could make her comprehend. She shook her head until he hung up the make-believe phone. Then she beamed again.

He turned his head away in frustration. Thin sunlight shone through the chintzy curtains covering the single window.

"Where am I?" he wondered.

"Mine!" she chirped back.

He threw off the bedcover with the idea of making his way to the window so he could look out. He wore only his briefs, but now was no time for modesty. She had, after all, undressed him. Electric pain ignited nerve endings from the sole of his foot to the top of his skull when he moved his left leg. He collapsed on his pillow, sweat popping out on his forehead.

The girl jumped up and re-covered him. She hovered to wipe sweat from his face with a corner of the quilt. The attempt to get out of bed left him weak and dizzy. He took a few deep breaths to stabilize his equilibrium, then took the Smurf's shoulders and pushed her away from him and toward the chair. She understood and sat again, grinning happily. They stared at each other.

"Let's start from the beginning," he proposed. He tapped his chest. "My name is Cass. Cass. Understand? Cass."

Me Tarzan, you Jane.

The E&E survival kit on his combat harness included a rudimentary Russian vocabulary, but that did him little good now. He continued to tap his chest and repeat his name until she caught on.

"Cass!" she said. "Cass Cass Cass Cass!"

Okay. So she knew two words. He waited until her excitement abated before he pointed at her. "Your name?" he asked. "Name?"

"Cass Cass Cass Cass."

"No. *I'm* Cass." He patted his chest. "Cass."

He pointed at her. "You?"

She suddenly giggled with understanding after his third or fourth attempt.

"Cass Cass Cass Cass!" she chanted, pointing at Cassidy. She reversed her finger. "Lina Lina Lina *Lina*!"

He smiled his approval. "Lina it is. Now we're getting somewhere. Lina, I need my clothes. Understand?" He mimed again putting on his shirt.

She stopped laughing and shook her head stubbornly. Tired of the game, she rose and tucked covers up to his chin, then quickly padded out of the room on her bare feet, taking her slightly feminine, slightly stale scent with her. She locked the bedroom door behind her, although Cassidy couldn't figure why she bothered. He wasn't going far anyhow on a broken leg unless he had help.

It smelled like she was cooking. Stew of some kind, he

thought. It smelled delicious and reminded Cassidy that he was ravenous. Lina had rescued him, doctored him, and put him to bed. Now she was cooking for him.

Clearly she wanted him to stay in bed—but for his own welfare or because of *Mine*? He couldn't simply lie there as helplessly as a sick child and depend upon the good nature of a strange woman to look after him. Despite the pain, he had to get out of bed and start working on a plan to either rejoin the detachment or insert into his E&E corridor. The first thing he required was a look out the window to orient himself. Afterward, he could search for his clothing and equipment.

He looked around the sparsely furnished room for something to serve as a crutch. He had a choice of either the crude wooden table with the kerosene lamp on it or the chair. He chose the chair; it was nearest.

Excruciating pain flared up his leg. It was bearable, he thought. Gritting his teeth, sweat dripping down his forehead from under the bandage and stinging his eyes, he swung both feet over the side of the bed and sat up. Lightheadedness almost dropped him again. He caught himself and held on to consciousness with a will. He rested, panting softly, smelling stew from the other room and listening for Lina. He heard the clinking of glassware.

He felt better after he rested. He drew the chair close to bedside and used it as a makeshift crutch to lift himself to his one good leg, stifling a cry of agony when his injured foot struck the stone floor. His entire body trembled from the effort. He feared he would pass out. He caught his balance and rested heavily on the chair until he recovered.

The window seemed at least a mile away. He hobbled toward it a few inches at a time by balancing on his good leg, thrusting the chair out ahead as far as he could, then hopping up to it.

He was almost halfway there when the door flew open, Lina blocking it with a thick walking stick from the branch of a tree. She glowered at him and pounded the end of the stick on the floor like a petulant child about to throw a tantrum. She charged and jerked the chair away from him. He screamed in pain as, trying to save himself from a fall, he put his weight on both legs. The bad leg gave way and dumped him sprawling.

Lina towered over him, pointing to the bed while she pounded the butt of the stick against the floor in outraged rhythm. Veins popped out on her forehead and neck. She trembled all over from fury and kept pointing for him to get back in bed.

CHAPTER 25

Washington, D.C.

General Darren E. Kragle stayed at the Washingtonian Hotel in D.C. while he waited to testify before the Second 9/11 Hearing about the role USSOCOM might have played in the U.S. failure to anticipate September 11, 2001. He sat at his ninth-floor window overlooking Pennsylvania Avenue and the White House down the way, sitting there staring out since early that morning when CENTCOM's General Paul Etheridge informed him that his son, Sergeant Cassidy Kragle, was MIA during the insertion phase of Operation Cold Dawn. His rugged features remained stoic, belying the turmoil that racked his guts.

Noisy antiwar protestors were already collecting at the police barricades near the White House. A gaggle of women stripped off all their clothing and lay down in the street. News media swarmed the naked biddies while cops remained behind their barricades and looked disgusted.

"Damn them all!" the General muttered in exasperation and anger. His son was missing in Russia, possibly killed in the line of duty protecting the liberties of people like those protestors who seemed intent on surrendering them to a bunch of mad bombers and suicidal hijackers.

He got up wearily, shaved and showered and changed into fresh Class A Greens with ribbons in a bright flash concealing his left breast and shoulder. He could have worn only his Medal of Honor, but refrained, considering it ostentatious. He took a taxi to the Congressional Building and by nine a.m. found himself stiff-backed and impatient sitting in the witness chair waiting to be grilled by Senator Rowen Johnston, chairman, and the six other members of the commission.

Johnston, a pompous little man with red-veined asshole eyes and a Ben Nighthorse Campbell ponytail, took the floor and held it, setting the stage for the day's televised skewering of witnesses for the edification and entertainment of the public in an election year. The restless gallery of spectators, mostly other politicians and members of the media chattering classes, waited for something to happen. *For God's sake, cut out the bullshit and crucify the poor sonofabitch.* In the General's opinion, it was the 95 percent of politicians like Senator Johnston and presidential candidate Lowell Rutherford Harris who gave the other 5 percent a bad name.

General Kragle sat outwardly expressionless but inwardly boiling while Senator Johnston raged against President Tyler, the War on Terror, and everyone in the administration associated with the war effort. It wasn't enough that American soldiers had to fight terrorists, schemers, despots, and fanatics around the globe, they also had to fight pols, opportunists, and assorted backbiters and backstabbers within their own country.

The General barely listened until Johnston began to wind down. ". . . Is it not true that if we act in the same manner as our enemies, we imprison ourselves in their rage, their evil? General Kragle . . . ?"

"Is that the question you want me to answer?" the General responded, his expression wooden.

Someone in the gallery sniggered. Senator Johnston reddened. "That was merely rhetorical, General Kragle," he snapped.

"And a fine big pile of . . . *rhetoric* it was too, Senator."

"My question for you, General Kragle," Johnston said, biting off his words, "is a broad one. Considering that 9/11 *could* have been prevented, and therefore this unpopular war that followed, I think this commission needs to hear from someone in the trenches, so to speak, as to when our Special Operations community first became aware that we might be attacked on our homeland—and yet failed to act?"

General Kragle rose slowly to his feet.

"You may remain seated," Johnston said.

"I'll stand." The ageing warrior squared his shoulders and the old fire returned, at least for a time. "If straight talk offends you, or if you think there's an acceptable gray area between good and evil, or if you take the position that all we have to do is bring our troops home and sit back on our bulbous behinds to which our brains have drained and no one will ever bother us again, then you had better stifle me now . . ."

Senator Johnston looked as though he wished he had never asked the old soldier *anything*. "General Kragle, there is no need to be offensive—"

"The truth is often offensive to those who don't want to hear it, Senator."

Johnston harrumphed, coughed delicately into his palm, and reddened even more. General Kragle took a deep breath, but before he could proceed, spectator murmuring introduced a uniformed young army major who burst into the chamber and hurried forward, expressing his repeated apologies for the interruption.

"Please forgive me, gentlemen, but this concerns a matter of utmost importance."

General Kragle recognized Major Mosby, aid to General Abraham Morrison, chairman of the Joint Chiefs of Staff. The first thing he thought of was his missing son. Mosby whispered into his ear. The General's lips tightened.

"You'll have to excuse me and proceed with this later,"
he said crisply. He gathered his papers and uniform cap
off the table.

"General Kragle, this body has not finished—" Johnston sputtered.

The General turned and walked out of the hearing.

CHAPTER 26

Partizanskaya River Valley

Major Brandon Kragle snapped a digital photo of Katya without her being aware of it and had radioman Mad Dog Carson include it with the morning's satellite relay SITREP, with a request to run her through the government's intelligence service files. He and Top Sculdiron shared the opinion that she seemed too good to be true.

After a quick breakfast, Katya lay out the fastest route on the map to where the *Soyuz* lay on a rocky hillside some five hours' march away. A long ten-hour hump there and back, during which the Star Wars research would be recovered and the capsule destroyed, and Brandon could have Cold Dawn back to the river and preparing to float downriver in plenty of time to rendezvous with the submarine. He experienced bouts of hollowness in the gut over Cassidy's loss, but his brother's recovery was a job for SAR and not Det 3A. Likewise, rescue of the spacemen, if they were not with the capsule, which appeared unlikely, would have to be handled by another detachment. Cold Dawn's mission was to find *Soyuz*'s sensitive contents and then bug out of the AO, area of operations.

"I hear the navy feeds its submariners good," Mad Dog speculated, finishing up a packet of MRE ham and eggs with a loud disgusted burp.

"Where chew hear that?" Perverse Sanchez demanded.

"What else you gonna do in one of them sardine cans *except* eat?"

"Maybe they got *señoritas* too."

Mad Dog's eyes brightened. "Sanchez, maybe we oughta join the navy."

Perverse stared at Katya bent over a map on the ground with Major Brandon and Top Sculdiron, her jeans stretched and rounded over her tight bottom, which was turned toward them.

"I didn't see no ass on that carrier with a USDA rating better than that," he said.

Top Sculdiron nodded at some remark by Major Kragle, then rose straightforward and strode toward the cave where the team was assembled. "All right, listen up, shit-birds. Carson, keep Sanchez and the Doc here with you to secure the area for our return. The rest of you, saddle up. Leave everything behind except your weapons and survival packs. We're traveling light and fast. Dade, you'll need explosives. Move out in ten. Any questions? Good."

Since Katya still appeared to know where they were going, Brandon placed her on point with Ice Man while he and Top double-checked her on the map. The cloud cover soon burned off to leave a sky so clear and blue and deep that the view from the high country took away the breath. Brandon preferred rain and fog to cover their movement and wash out any trail sign, but he had to admit that it was a gorgeous day and a fine morning for a hike. He scanned the terrain with binoculars for other activity, but saw nothing other than an infrequent deer and once a bear.

They traveled hard and fast without rucks, stopping only to fill up canteens from clean, fast-moving mountain streams and take an occasional five-minute break. Katya sat on the ground next to Brandon and looked out over the panorama of forest and meadows spread out before them, her open-capped canteen poised halfway to her lips.

"I am in loving this country," she whispered.

Brandon said nothing. She looked at him.

"Are you being married, *Americanski?*" she asked. Deltas on mission wore nothing personal that might identify them, not even wedding rings.

Brandon thought of Summer and of how he would quit this business when the baby arrived. He forced himself not to think about it.

"How do you know this country so well?" he asked her.

"I am hiking it since . . ." She broke off.

"Since you were a little girl?" Brandon probed.

She smiled and dropped it at that.

"Is that how you knew about the space capsule, Katya?"

"I am telling you already. Mikhail is being informing me where it is crashing. I am not knowing how he is finding out."

She got up and moved away to top off her canteen from the stream and, Brandon suspected, prevent further interrogation. Top Sculdiron dropped down next to him. They both watched the girl. The rest of the detachment had spread into a small defensive perimeter in the shade of conifers.

"She has been helpful," Top said. "What are we going to do with her?"

"Put her ashore downstream somewhere. She's like a cat. I suspect you can throw her anywhere and she'll still land on her feet."

They topped a jagged sawtooth ridge via a trail Katya knew about and overlooked a downward sloping meadow cluttered with boulders at its lower end. A glint of sunlight reflected off the capsule, its red-and-white parachute deflated and spread out like a shed reptile's skin. Brandon glassed the area for signs of life. Finding none, he handed the binoculars to Top, who scrutinized it in turn. Gloomy Davis looked up at Brandon from his sniper's spotting scope.

"Boss, there ain't even a mouse moving."

"So it seems." With a pointed glance at Katya, Brandon made sure he had a round chambered in his carbine. "You lead the way," he told her. "I'll be right behind you."

She appeared unconcerned.

The detachment moved off the ridge, across the spring-greening meadow and through boulders, some of which were the size of Nissans. Brandon halted again before the final approach. This was just too easy. He couldn't help feeling Murphy was watching and sniggering up his sleeve.

Ice and Gloomy posted themselves on outer security while Brandon, Katya, Top, and Diverse Dade with his fireworks pack moved up to the capsule. Its top hatch hung ajar. One of the former occupant's helmets lay on the grass underneath where the nose was lodged against a boulder. The craft was much smaller and more flimsy-looking than Brandon imagined. An air of abandonment settled over it, like a wrecked auto left in a junkyard.

Brandon climbed inside while the others kept watch. Rain had driven in through the open hatch. The interior was cold and damp. There was barely enough room to seat space travelers at their work stations. If the International Space Station was as cramped as the capsule, Brandon wondered, how could the Americans have conducted re-search without the Russian and others of the nine interna-tionals living aboard being aware of it? That wasn't his job to wonder.

He had been informed during mission briefing on what

to look for. It didn't take him long to determine that whoever snatched the *Soyuz* crew had ransacked the cabin,
smashing the electronics and controls and taking whatever they could break off or that was already loose. Any
research documents or radioactive materials were already
gone. Brandon's Geiger counter let out not a single defi-
nite tick.

Disappointed, he climbed out and let Top conduct a
follow-up search to make sure he had overlooked nothing.
Top stuck his head back out the hatch and shook it. Negative. Mafia, terrorists, whoever, had taken not only the
passengers but also research results vital to U.S. national
security. Cold Dawn had arrived too late. As Gloomy la-
conically observed, the barn door was open and the horses
were gone, along with all their tack.

Brandon studied Katya's face for a hint that she not
only knew in advance what they were after but also knew
that it had already been stripped from the capsule. She returned his inspection without comment.

"Burn out the insides with thermite," Brandon instructed
Dade the demolitioneer. "I don't want a big bang."

Operation Cold Dawn had drilled a dry hole. Major
Brandon's last Delta mission was a failure.

CHAPTER 27

New York

Detective work consisted mainly of leg work, as Domestic Preparedness director Claude Thornton had learned during his many years pounding an FBI beat. Running down snippets of information, tracing connections, interrogating suspects or witnesses who may or may not have anything to contribute, who may or may not be cooperative. Hours and hours, even days and days, prowling cities and asking questions, hunting for the missing pieces to put the puzzle together. Not always recognizing the pieces when you saw them.

Chasing terrorists was nothing but detective work with a twist—and a bigger bang at the end if you failed.

Homeland Security director MacArthur Thornbrew ordered threat levels in New York and Washington raised to Orange, the second-highest level, in response to intelligence developing from the case of fugitive lawyer Patsy Koehler. Heavy security surrounded sites known to have been reconnoitered by al-Qaeda, such as the U.S. Capitol, the New York Stock Exchange, the World Bank, International Monetary Fund, and Madison Square Garden, where the Federalists were meeting in convention.

Israel had stood up for decades against terrorists who assassinated her officials and routinely suicide-bombed her citizens. Claude had often mulled over how America might cope with similar circumstances, with other attacks even bigger and more horrific than 9/11. He was not overly optimistic about the country's will to resist.

Claude called in his deputy director, Agent Fred Whiteman, to take some of the administrative load of running Domestic Preparedness off his shoulders while he personally retained command of the Joint Terrorism Task Force dedicated to running down Patsy Koehler and her circle of Islamic Jihadia. He was in too deep now to relinquish control of the investigation to a subordinate. Agents of the FBI and JTTF kept the pressure on by staking out the fugitive's known haunts, questioning her friends and associates, and delving into her dealings with Jihad sleeper cells.

Of all the bizarre clues arising out of the case, perhaps the most astounding was that of "Ronald McDonald" who organized and registered the nonprofit "Americans Standing Up For People," one of the groups affiliated with Koehler and her efforts to shut down New York—and perhaps to also fund and conceal her activities on behalf of terrorists.

The CEO of a Manhattan bank through which the organization was registered, a Mr. Dumfy, remembered Ronald McDonald as a middle-aged man with a substantial middle and insubstantial hair. He was accompanied by a tall, older man with bushy gray hair and a five thousand dollar suit. This one did not identify himself.

"Are you sure Ronald McDonald didn't have red hair, a bulb nose, big shoes, a ten-dollar clown suit, and Big Mac on his breath?" Claude asked, unable to contain his sarcasm.

Mr. Dumfy ducked his head in embarrassment. "I thought the name most unusual at the time," he admitted. "But he had identification to prove it."

"I'm sure he did. How long ago was the nonprofit registered?"

"About three months ago. I can get you the exact date."

"I'll also need papers pertaining to the organization, including a list of contributors."

"I can't let you see confidential papers, sir."

"Sure you can. This is a *nonprofit*, which means everything is open to the public. Mr. Dumfy, I can get a warrant if I have to. This could be a matter of urgent national importance."

Mr. Dumfy's eyes bulged. "Terrorism?"

Claude left with a thick folder stuffed with documents. That evening in the Washington offices of Domestic Preparedness, he, Della Street, and Fred Whiteman went through the file, cross-checking contributors, contributor groups, and beneficiaries of Americans Standing Up For People. BUCKUS Alliance, Not My Name, MoveOn.org, and other leftist groups seemed to get most of the corporation's donations. While the organizational hierarchy seemed to have used subterfuge to cover itself and prevent exposure, everything else appeared legitimate.

Whiteman glanced up from his desk and gave a whistle of surprise. "Well, I'll be a ruptured one-eyed mule. Claude, take a look."

Thornton and Della Street looked over his shoulder. Whiteman's thick forefinger jabbed at a contributor's name. *Marjorie Goodfellow Rawlings Harris.*

"You don't forget a blueblood moniker like that," Whiteman said. "Heiress to the Goodfellow steel billions, widow of the late POP senator Rawlings and—"

"—current wife of presidential candidate Senator Lowell Rutherford Harris," Della finished for him.

CHAPTER 28

Washington, D.C.

Each of the several times General Kragle had attended meetings in the War Situation Room in the basement of the White House portended a national crisis associated with the War on Terror. This time proved no different. The army officer, Major Mosby, who ushered him out of the Second 9/11 hearing escorted him directly to the White House, telling him only that he was being summoned to a top-secret emergency meeting. The General didn't know whether he should be relieved or not that the interruption of his testimony had nothing to do with his son's being missing in Russia.

Other officials of the State and Defense establishment involved in either the War on Terror, the Iraqi War, or both, were also being shown hurriedly to the War Room. The General exchanged greetings with Secretary of Defense Donald Keating, Homeland Security director MacArthur Thornbrew, CENTCOM's and JSOC's generals Paul Etheridge and Carl Spencer, CIA deputy director Tom Hinds, and other top-level acquaintances of the CIA, FBI, NSA, and related alphabet agencies. That so many big names were being drawn in attested to the urgency of the occasion. Little conversation was possible, as the meeting was getting under way immediately. The General managed to exchange a quick word with Fred Whiteman, deputy director of the National Domestic Preparedness Office run by Claude Thornton.

"Where's Claude?"

"Chasing terrorists in New York."

The War Situation Room was huge, with sturdy mahogany-paneled walls and a great polished table bearing cups and pots of hot coffee. Barely had attendees found seats around the table than a Marine in dress blues announced the President of the United States. The room of dignitaries snapped to its feet as Woodrow Tyler entered briskly. He was a lean, homespun, blunt-speaking Texan with a rugged face, a military haircut and cowboy boots that somehow seemed to match his dark blue suit and red power tie. With him, in full uniform, came General Abraham Morrison, chairman of JCS. President Tyler wasted no time in getting to the point.

"On the advice of secretary of state and secretary of defense," he began, "I wanted to personally inform the War on Terror leadership that I am issuing a finding for the immediate use of Special Operations forces on urgent priority. America's enemies are plotting at this moment to kill as many of us as they can—in our homes and in our places of employment. Intelligence estimates are that al-Qaeda and associated clusters have regrouped and are planning a spectacular nuclear attack against U.S. cities before this year's election. Their goal, as stated in radical Islamic Internet sites, is to kill four million Americans at one time. We conclude that the most likely means of attack will come in the form of so-called suitcase tactical nuclear bombs, each of approximately ten kilotons and weighing about thirty-five pounds. A single one of these devils could level Manhattan. Radiation fallout would render the city unlivable for hundreds of years, not to mention the economic and social fallout to the nation."

He paused dramatically. His blue eyes traced the grim faces of the men and women gathered around the table.

"General Morrison briefed me earlier," he continued. "Gentlemen and ladies, the CIA has located a terrorist uranium enrichment plant with the capability to produce nuclear bombs. That plant is operational even as we speak. Action must be taken promptly before nukes are smuggled into the U.S. across our borders. General Morrison will now brief you. I challenge you to come up with a plan before the day is over to destroy the plant—before it is used to destroy us. General Morrison?"

The JCS chairman stepped forward. Having demonstrated his concern, the President promptly left, taking his cabinet-level members with him to conduct further international political strategy, leaving the various military and counterterrorist experts alone in the room to hammer out a plan to deal with the looming crisis. General Morrison cleared his throat. An aide behind him erected a tripod and uncovered a large field map of eastern Russia. Another aide passed out folders with the covers marked TOP SECRET.

"The folders contain a synopsis of the current political situation in eastern Russia that makes it unfeasible for the U.S. to act openly in this matter," General Morrison said. "Other documents outline what all is required for terrorists to manufacture weapons of mass destruction. You can read these on your own."

He paused. Folders remained closed.

"Both the International Atomic Energy Agency and United Nations inspectors suspected Saddam Hussein of continuing a clandestine nuclear program after the Gulf War of 1991," he continued. "No facilities, however, were discovered when U.S. forces invaded Iraq in 2003. American and British intelligence think Iraq may have transported its research secretly to other nations prior to the invasion. Most of the hundreds of Iraqi nuclear scientists and engineers have also disappeared. Many sought refuge in Syria, Iran, and North Korea, where they are believed to still be conducting nuclear research.

"The CIA traced Iraqi WMD materials, including uranium, from Syria and other parts of Africa where they had been secreted before Iraqi Freedom began, to Russia's Primorye Province in the southeast near the borders of China and North Korea. Several CIA operatives were implanted in the area, whose task was to locate the WMD facility. Our satellites were unable to do so because of the plant's being built inside a mountain.

"Three days ago, an implant code-named Cage was assassinated after the *Soyuz* space capsule on its way to landing in Kazakhstan made a premature reentry over southeastern Russia. Cage managed to report the location of the downed capsule before his death. Cage's handler was injured, but he escaped. This morning the handler got through with a report that he had located the WMD facilities. Satellites have confirmed it."

The JCS chairman had General Kragle's riveted attention, not only because of the dire nature of his pronouncement and its potential consequences, but also because Operation Cold Dawn and two of his sons had already inserted into the region. General Paul Etheridge of CENTCOM caught General Kragle's eye.

"The uranium enrichment plant with the capability of producing nuclear devices is located in caves inland from the mountain town of Partizansk," General Morrison continued. That plant, under the control of al-Qaeda and related extremist Muslim groups, is being run by Saddam's primary research scientist, Dr. Huda Ammash, also known as 'Dr. Death.' It is operational even as we speak.

In fact, the urgency of this meeting is that WMDs may already have been produced and are in the process of being introduced into the United States. Six Russians were recently apprehended attempting to cross the Mexican border into Arizona."

General Morrison's gaze fell in turn upon General Kragle and General Etheridge, who maintained operational responsibility for that sector of the globe.

"The crew of *Soyuz* apparently had the misfortune of coming down in a nest of wasps and has been seized by terrorists," he said. "Operation Cold Dawn is already working in Primorye Province. It would seem that we have two choices regarding a SpecOps mission: we can either deploy a second detachment into the AO, which will require at least three days of preparation, likely more; or we can divert Cold Dawn to the WMD plant. WMDs, as the President points out, hold priority. We may not have three days left to prevent an attack. General Etheridge?"

Etheridge cast General Kragle a long look. General Kragle returned it and took a deep breath before nodding his assent. General Etheridge stood up.

"Cold Dawn can handle it, sir."

CHAPTER 29

Partizanskaya River Valley

Delta detachments, whether pre-mission or actually on-ground in the middle of a mission, had to remain versatile, adaptable. After all, old Colonel Charlie Beckwith and then-major Darren Kragle, now the General, had built Delta Force in the 1980s with the capability, as Charlie put it, "to go anywhere in the world and do any damned thing." Major Brandon Kragle wasn't particularly surprised to discover upon his element's return from the downed space capsule that Det 3A's objective had been modified; this had happened to him on other occasions. Central Command had learned of a clandestine terrorist uranium enrichment plant in the same AO that had to be destroyed, top priority. Apparently, the CIA had been trying to locate the plant when *Soyuz* came down where it did and Cage was assassinated, throwing a monkey wrench into the works.

Although Brandon felt bummed-out by his failure at the capsule site, change of mission provided him new hope. After all, the WMD plant and the raping of the capsule and seizure of its occupants must be somehow connected. The plant might still lead the detachment to the spacemen and the capsule's contents.

Brandon and the detachment's leadership erected a poncho hooch in the woods outside the cave and got to work on a new operations plan, laboring over it much of the night. Katya was kept under guard inside the cave out of sight and hearing of what was going on.

At dawn, Brandon dispatched Ice Man Thompson and the Zulu warrior to pull surveillance on the target. Provided a camera to record their observations, they were cautioned to pay particular attention to the layout of the site and potential avenues of approach and withdrawal, areas in which the slain CIA agent might have proved most valuable. As the enrichment plant was constructed underground completely out of sight of satellites and aircraft, CENTCOM had been unable to supply pictures.

Ice and Diverse, especially Ice Man, were old hands at the game and knew the drill.

Ice Man consulted both his GPS and compass before taking a last look at his map, folding it and stuffing it inside a cargo pocket of his unmarked cammies. He and Diverse shouldered their much-lightened rucks, stripped of everything except food, water, ponchos, Motorola radios, and a few personal comfort items. Katya loitered nearby, watching them intently. Ice tugged the bill of his patrol cap low over his eyes. The scars on his cheek flawed the side of his lean face. The weapons man rarely spoke, but when he did his assessments required respect.

"Major, that broad is trouble," he said.

He tightened the shoulder straps on his ruck, picked up Mad Dog's M4 carbine, having traded out his heavier SAW for it, and, after a second disapproving look at Katya, led Diverse down into the dark forest, crossed the stream, and came out on the other side where they followed the cliff wall to where the terrain fell off in the direction of the river.

"They are going where?" Katya asked Brandon.

"For a walk."

"There is being nothing in that direction in which they

are going," she said, watching the two-man patrol until it disappeared in undergrowth.

Brandon looked at her. "Do you know that for a fact?"

"Yes," she said. "There is being nothing for them to see."

She was lying—and doing so, Brandon surmised, because she knew about the nuclear plant, had known about it all along. He said nothing, however. Even though she was his prisoner, there was no need in showing his hand unnecessarily.

The sun finally came out and played hide and seek with scudding clouds. Katya lapsed deep in thought for a minute. Then her eyes switched toward the stream in the narrow valley. Immediately, her mood changed, as though she was about to grasp some opportunity.

"I am needing to take a bath. Is there being time?"

Brandon looked down among the trees to the pool through which the stream flowed.

"Leave your boots here," he directed. She couldn't go far or fast barefoot in these flintstone mountains.

The stipulation caught her by surprise. She hesitated. The look on her face provided clear evidence that her plans, whatever they were, may have been thwarted.

She braced against the boulder and ripped off her boots one at a time and chucked them at Brandon's feet. She turned in a huff and sashayed barefoot down through the trees.

"Enjoy," she flung back over her shoulder.

Mad Dog and Perverse rushed over to watch her walk.

"Chew look at that!" Perverse panted. "Is she going to take off her clothes?"

Mad Dog had an eye on the bump and sway of her hips. "You couldn't *never* wear that pussy out."

"This is no whorehouse, and it is no strip joint on Hays Street," Top Sculdiron interrupted. "I require a volunteer for first watch—Sergeant Sanchez. Sergeant Carson, you are next."

Brandon remained sitting on the boulder, but he turned his back to the stream to give Katya privacy. He soon heard splashing.

Gloomy Davis with Mr. Blunderbuss at his side hung around the cave entertaining Doc Red and Mad Dog with one of his stories. The day was mostly a down day, except for routine security and patrols. Brandon suspected the men were waiting for Katya to return from her bath, perhaps with expectations that she would do so wearing only a towel or a T-shirt or something. It annoyed Brandon the way her presence already disrupted the detachment's routine. Men with sex on their minds, no matter how professional they were otherwise, tended to be less vigilant and more prone to let their minds wander. Another very good reason why females did not belong in foxholes. Brandon had a hunch Katya was deliberately creating an atmosphere that suited some purpose of her own, purring around like a cat in heat.

"You are driving down the road on your Harley in a terrific rainstorm one night when you see three people stranded," Gloomy was saying. "One is an old lady who will die unless you save her. The other is an old friend who once saved your life. The third is the perfect girl you've been dreaming about your whole life. Which would you offer a ride to, knowing you can only take one?"

Doc Red thought about it. "I would give the motorcycle to my old friend so he could come back dreckly after he hauls granny to the hospital. I'd stay behind with the sweet li'l darling."

"And do what, Rhett Butler—play stink finger, cook up a mess of collard greens and black-eyed peas?" Mad Dog challenged.

"Them's all something a real Southern gal would appreciate."

They fell quiet, their mouths gaping in astonishment, when Katya came swinging back up the hill, fulfilling their wildest fantasies. Their expressions made Brandon jump to his feet and turn toward the girl. She did better than a towel or T-shirt. She traipsed out of the trees through the grass like a brown, bare woodland nymph, her wet skin glistening in the morning sun rays, her hair slicked around her face like a Roman helmet. She had washed her jeans and shirt in the creek and was carrying them, leaving her nothing to wear except a bikini panty. She held one arm across her bare breasts. She knew the impact her little show was having on the men. Perverse, high up on the pinnacle above the cave on watch, likely had his binoculars trained on her rather than on the surrounding potentially hostile terrain.

Mad Dog found his tongue. "Fu-uck," he exclaimed, awed. "I'd run over the old lady to put her out of her misery, give my motorcycle to my buddy and tell him to get lost and have some beers, and *then* . . ." He gestured toward Katya. ". . . I'd screw her until she went bowlegged."

Brandon angrily shoved Katya out of sight into some trees.

"Don't ever come around my men like that again," he scolded.

She dropped her arms away from her breasts. "Or you will be doing what? Shooting me?"

"Put your clothes back on."

CHAPTER 30

ASTRONAUTS OFFERED FOR RANSOM

Houston (CPI)—U.S. astronauts Roger Callison and Larry Williams and Russian cosmonaut Alexei Minsky are alive and possibly in the hands of al-Qaeda terrorists. NASA ground mission commander Alan Cunningham confirmed this morning that the Al-Jazeera TV news agency in Baghdad received a ransom note from an undisclosed source saying the space travelers are being held by unnamed individuals in an unspecified location. The note said they would be released in exchange for a $20 million ransom; it set a forty-eight-hour deadline after which the first of the trio would be beheaded.

The Soyuz space capsule containing the three spacemen returning from the International Space Station experienced a malfunction upon reentry last week, losing radio contact with NASA before reaching its targeted landing zone in Kazakhstan. Search teams spread out across the globe but found no sign of the spacecraft.

Today's message was the first indication that the spacemen may have survived.

Heretofore, space has been considered common ground for international cooperation and peace, off-limits and immune to warfare and strife on earth.

"We are not sure this is a terrorist situation," Cunningham said. "We assume it since the ransom note came through Baghdad. However, common criminals inspired by terrorist methods are beginning to use them to threaten and intimidate the world . . ."

CHAPTER 31

Partizanskaya River Valley

Horsemen at noon rode single file out of dark timber from the east, riding slowly but with purpose. Brandon counted an even dozen, all heavily armed and military-looking. The ponies were small and wiry, descendants of the steppe horses ridden by Mongols and Ghenghis Khan's hordes. The point rider in baggy kulaks, boots, and an open sheepskin coat dismounted and knelt to study the ground, an ancient Moison-Nagant sniper's rifle slung on his back. The others relaxed in their saddles, looking toward the rising escarpment of the southern Sikhote-Alin mountains.

They were at least five klicks away, about three miles, on the far side of the marshy opening the detachment had crossed two nights earlier in the darkness. On the high promontory above the cave, Brandon and Gloomy Davis sprawled on their bellies next to Doc Red, who was on watch, and glassed the scene, Brandon with binoculars, Gloomy with his high-powered rifle scope.

The riders were obviously tracking the detachment, but appeared to have lost the trail in the marsh and grasses of the valley. The Cossack-looking tracker on foot stood up. He looked at the rise of the mountains. He looked toward the river, a gleam of which could be glimpsed steeply downslope. Then he led his horse back to the others. A man wearing a black fur envelope hat seemed to be in charge. Cossack and Black Hat gesticulated and looked about in animated conversation.

Brandon had cautioned Ice Man and Diverse on point the night of insertion to select rocky terrain, creeks, and other hard-to-track routes as best they could in the darkness. Drizzling intermittent rain also helped cover tracks. Delta soldiers *knew* how to move in the woods without leaving much trace. Trackers down there knew their business to have followed the trail this far.

Or someone had secretly marked the trail for them. Although Brandon had kept an eye on Katya during the march, it would have been an easy matter in the dark for her to have dug markers in the soil with her heels or to have deliberately crushed grass and small growth to leave sign. The enigma that was Katya Sokolov kept growing in Brandon's mind. Questions surrounded her from the moment she appeared—the only answers so far being that she obviously wasn't the only one who knew of Cold Dawn's insertion.

"Those folks yonder are hunting *us*," Doc Red declared.

"You are one bright Southern redhead," Gloomy approved. "When you were in high school, did you ever read the short story 'The Most Dangerous Game'? Remember the quote, 'The ideal quarry must have courage, cunning, and above all, must be able to reason'?"

"Just because I'm from Georgia (he pronounced it *Jawgah)* don't mean I'm dumb. A Southerner knows the difference between a redneck, a good ol' boy, and po' white trash. I ain't po' white trash."

Brandon cut in. "Doc, go bring up the girl. Alert the others."

"Yes, sir."

He scooted away from the rocky brow of the pinnacle. Once he was out of sight of the distant riders, he scrambled to his feet and went leaping and running down the steep decline to the cave.

Distant thunder rumbled like the sound of a giant clearing its throat. The sun shone all morning and the land steamed from a good drying out, prompting everyone to hope the weather would give them a break. Now, Brandon hoped returning clouds would open up and begin raining horned toads and lizards, a real gully washer to eradicate all sign, whether deliberately left or not.

"Come on, rain," Gloomy murmured, voicing the desire for both of them.

Doc Red returned with Katya. Her jeans and shirt had dried from their morning washing. The clean scent tantalized Brandon's nostrils as she wriggled up beside him. Her curves touched him the full length of their bodies.

"Your friends," he said tersely, indicating the direction of the riders.

He trusted nothing about her. Most of the rest of the detachment just wanted to look at her without her clothes.

Katya took Brandon's binoculars, peered through them, and said, "I am having no such friends, *Americanski*."

"Who are they?"

She hesitated long enough that Brandon expected her to lie. Instead, she said, "Wearing the man in the black hat is Burian Topich."

"And he is . . . ?"

"He is being criminal. He and his men being with him are working for who is paying them best. I think they are working for Oleg Kopylov."

Brandon took the binoculars from her. "What do you suppose they are doing out here?" he asked, not trying to hide his suspicions.

She shrugged. "Perhaps Mikhail is being tortured and

is telling them about you before he is shot and is coming
to me."

Possibly. Brandon wasn't ready to buy it.

He watched the Cossack tracker mount. The entire cavalcade started downslope toward the river, breaking off
from the course that would have led to the cave. Brandon
followed them with his glasses. They traveled carefully,
apparently trying to pick up the trail they had lost, sweeping in a three-sixty. If they circled far enough out they
might come across a trace of the surveillance team on its
way to scope out the nuclear plant.

Brandon pressed the buzzer signal on his Motorola radio
to warn Ice and Diverse of unfriendlies on the move in the
area. The receiver on the other end should merely vibrate
without sound. Brandon received no response. He waited a
minute and pressed the signal again. Still no response.

In Brandon's mind, that indicated one of two possibilities: either both radios on the surveillance team had gone
on the blink, a highly unlikely probability; or Ice and Diverse were compromised. It wasn't enough for Cold
Dawn to face a virtually impregnable target forted inside
a mountain. Now, it had a bunch of armed cavalry on its
trail and more of its men missing.

CHAPTER 32

Brandon remained at the watch pinnacle above the cave after the cavalcade of riders merged into timber and terrain leading down toward the river. He and Gloomy Davis and the Russian girl Katya. Storm clouds continued to build over the mountains throughout the afternoon, boiling and blackening, stabbed frequently by bolts of distant lightning. The sun disappeared and the day turned as dark as Brandon's mood. Ice and Diverse on recon still had not reported in.

Top Sculdiron brought MRE packets for those on top and huddled a few minutes with his commander. "Sergeant Carson is on the Shadowfire radio. It has better reception, but so far he has nothing. His assessment is that the surveillance team is either inside another cave, deep in a canyon, or . . ."

He let the *or* stand on its own.

"Ice Man is too field-wise to get caught," Brandon said, wanting to believe it.

"Sergeant Carson is going to run a wire antenna from the radio to up here on top," Top said. "He doubts it will help, but he wants to try."

With that, he scuttled down the decline to assist Mad Dog with his antenna.

Katya opened a plastic MRE pouch and eyed the contents suspiciously. MREs took some getting used to by the uninitiated. Like the early bird eyeing the early worm and saying to his wingmate, "I don't know about you, but I think I'm gonna have to have some coffee first."

She scooted next to Brandon. "What is this being?" she asked, indicating the MRE.

Brandon looked. "Spaghetti."

"What is yours?"

"Chili con carne."

"They are both looking the same."

"They taste the same."

"It is being the American way?" she asked.

They had been jousting with each other ever since Katya decided Brandon and his detachment had been diverted to a second mission, each divulging nothing while trying to learn as much as possible about the other. So far, about all Brandon had got out of her was that she was a poor country girl born in a village near Nakodka. She had two sisters and a brother, all younger and still at home. She wasn't cut out for farming, she said, and therefore went to Partizansk a year ago to find a better job. She wanted to be a model or an actress. That was where she met Oleg Kopylov and Mikhail.

"What was Cage doing in Partizansk?" Brandon probed.

"He is saying he is import-export business. I am not knowing different for certain until . . . Well, we are both knowing now that his true business was other than that. What he is importing is *you*."

"I can see you're heartbroken about losing him."

"He say he is for helping me to get to Hollywood. He is lying."

"Yeah? Well. Men are like that."

"Kissing and leaving? Are you kissing and leaving too?" She moved closer.

"Leaving," Brandon told her. "Not kissing. Besides, I don't know anyone in Hollywood either."

A beautiful woman who used sex to get what she wanted was the most dangerous weapon on earth. Cage had found that out. Brandon wouldn't have touched this female with the proverbial ten-foot pole even if he didn't have Summer. Nonetheless, the promise of her nearness still made him uncomfortable.

Brandon gave up nothing in the little game they played, not even his name and the fact that the detachment was American, although Katya obviously assumed that by now. Brandon felt convinced she also knew his new mission. She had done nothing yet, however, to betray any ulterior motives. So far, nothing had come back on her photo Mad Dog relayed by SATCOM to Central Command.

She eased her lips next to his ear so that he felt her warm breath. "You are wanting me, I am feeling it," she whispered so Gloomy would not overhear.

She aroused him. Her beauty, her innate sexiness, her sheer availability. After all, he *was* human and a male. She let him know in subtle ways how she was his for the taking.

"Keep this up and I'll have you chained until we leave," he promised.

She moved away and pouted, picking at the contents of her MRE while Brandon lay back and studied the storm clouds. The best thing he could hope for was rain. It would wipe out tracks. If it rained hard enough and long enough it would also mask the detachment's approach to and withdrawal from the target.

Many things about the mission to this point troubled him: losing Cassidy; Cage's death; the girl's appearance; horsemen scouting the hills for them; having lost contact with the surveillance team . . . It all made him feel a lot like the narrator of an old Earl Emerson novel: "I was trapped in the house with a lawyer, a bare-breasted woman, and a dead man. The rattlesnake in the sack only complicated matters."

"Boss!"

Gloomy's tone announced trouble. Brandon shoved the girl to the ground and crawled over next to the sniper. Katya took Gloomy's other side.

"He's down by the creek," Gloomy hissed.

Together they scanned the little valley below and the creek pool where Katya tantalized the men that morning with her more-or-less public bath. A few minutes passed before Brandon detected anything alarming—a flash of movement against the cliff on the far side of the stream.

"See him, Boss?"

"I got him."

The Cossack tracker from earlier rode his little blood bay out of the timber and into view. He paused on the other side of the creek. He looked directly at the cave, but Brandon doubted he saw anything.

He was a short man who made his short horse look taller by contrast than it actually was. Sheepskin coat, baggy kulaks, Moison-Nagant sniper's rifle slung on his back. Through binoculars, the face appeared broad with Tartar eyes that reminded Brandon of Top Sculdiron's Slavic heritage. A young face, hawkish and watchful. A predator who, while not yet whiffing spoor, anticipated it at any moment. A dangerous man.

Brandon panned back through the timber and along the base of the far cliff. Gloomy did likewise. Forest and the twist of the canyon wall obstructed their view.

"See any of his pals?" Brandon asked.

"Not yet. I'd say he's scouting, waiting for the others to catch up."

Katya's breathing sounded harsh and raspy, excited and frightened at the same time.

The Cossack loosened the rein onto the horse's neck and fished around inside the lining of his coat. The bay dropped his head and picked at graze within his reach while its rider produced cigarette makings, built a cigarette, and lit it with a match. He drew smoke deep into his lungs, obviously relishing the break. Fresh breezes rustling through the canyon dissipated the smoke. Lightning flashed in backdrop above the cliff. A blast of thunder made the horse throw up its head.

"Boss?" Gloomy said. He had acquired the target in his scope. An easy shot.

"Not yet."

A firefight if the guy's buddies were hanging back out of sight was exactly what the detachment needed to really screw up the operation.

Brandon pressed the buzzer-vibrator on his Motorola for the second time to warn the others to stay down, danger near. He hoped they received the signal and that no one moved or made a sound.

The bay craned its head higher, its ears and eyes alerting in the direction of the cave. The Cossack stiffened. He flipped his cigarette into the flowing creek and in the same sudden movement unslung the old sniper's rifle and brought its sights swiftly to his eye.

"He's on to the Dog!" Gloomy said.

Mad Dog was stringing antenna wire up the face of the pinnacle. He must have left his Motorola below and hadn't received the warning signal. In another second the commo man was going to be dead meat.

"Take him!" Brandon ordered.

Gloomy was on his gun, ready. He had thought earlier, during mission briefing, of bringing along a noise suppressor, except a silencer reduced the range of a rifle and affected its accuracy. Better to chance the sound of a shot than to miss target and let the guy get away, report back to his cohorts, and reduce all doubt as to the presence of foreign intruders in the mountains.

The sharp crack of the .300 Winchester reverberated through the mountains, echoing and re-echoing. The jolt of the 173-grain bullet traveling at more than 2,500 feet per second slapped the rider out of his saddle. The spooked horse reared and trotted off a short distance before turning back to look.

The report of the rifle repeated itself in diminishing waves, followed by a startled silence.

"He's down," Gloomy said.

CHAPTER 33

Mr. Blunderbuss seemed to remain in recoil for long minutes after the shot that dropped the Cossack tracker off his horse. Brandon saw Gloomy's face harden into a mask. The little sniper was good at his business, had killed like this before, but Brandon feared that one day the protective crust around his heart would start to crack and disintegrate.

"He's not moving," Gloomy said, eye to the scope. "Winds are tricky at this range, coming out of a storm. But it looks like a clean kill."

Brandon was thinking defense, assuming the other Dirty Dozen riders were waiting just out of sight and would soon come charging up the hill. In Brandon's mind, there was no doubt but what Cold Dawn's six remaining operators could handle the scruffy indig cavalry. Top Sculdiron would already be setting up men and weapons to fight them off. In addition to carbines, the team had Ice Man's SAW, a light machine gun with a remarkable rate of fire, Perverse Sanchez's 60mm mortar, and Sculdiron's M203 grenade launcher mounted to his M4. ACOG scopes on the carbines let shooters reach out and touch someone at six hundred yards.

The complication lay in Cold Dawn's being pinned down in a firefight long enough for terrorists at the enrichment plant to escape with suitcase nukes they may have already manufactured, along with sensitive *Soyuz* materials likely in their possession.

Brandon waited, watchful, lying on the ground next to

Gloomy Davis and Katya, weapon ready. Lightning spider-webbed across the bruised sky. Wind came up and blew in darkness to replace the day. It riffled the loose bay's mane. The horse tossed its head and looked down past the cliff, whickering inquiringly. There was no answer except the crackling of thunder. A thunder boomer of heroic proportions was on the way. The bay shook its head, unsure of what to do with its new freedom, snorted in the direction of its fallen master, then began grazing.

"If there is being anyone hearing the shot, they will maybe thinking it is a hunter," Katya whispered, although there was no need to. "Russians are being good hunters."

"That guy could have been out on his own," Gloomy suggested hopefully when the victim's comrades still failed to appear.

Top Sculdiron's hard square figure came panting up the grade to the lookout point, carrying both the SAW and his M203. Other than his heavy breathing, he remained as neutral-faced and unflappable as a Berlin train conductor. Gloomy at his rifle and the loose horse below told him in a glance what had happened. He placed the machine gun on its bipod to cover the most likely avenues of enemy approach, sat down cross-legged beside it, and coolly threaded a belt into its feed tray. Katya looked at his M4/203 rifle propped on a rock nearby.

"You are giving me the weapon," she offered. "I will fighting them too."

Brandon looked at her. "I'd rather keep the rattlesnake in the sack."

Top's eyes remained glued on the horse, the creek running through the timber, and the edge of the cliff around which he expected a cavalry blitz. Tall grass concealed the dead man.

"Sergeant Carson needs five more minutes to set up the antenna and try it," Sculdiron said.

They waited some more while clouds scudded angrily above and the horse grazed peacefully below. Other horsemen still failed to materialize. There was only the wind beating at the trees. Brandon breathed easier.

A bolt of lightning struck nearby with a terrific crackle, illuminating the dreary landscape and bringing into relief the tense faces of the watchers on lookout. Hard, round, scattered drops of rain, vanguard of the approaching storm, stung when they struck bare skin.

Let it come! Let it come! It would wash out all tracks.

"Top, get the detachment ready to move," Brandon ordered. "Gloomy, stay where you are and cover me. We can't leave that horse loose to lead the rest up here."

He scrambled to his feet and started off the promontory. Katya sprang up with him.

"Where the hell do you think you're going?"

"I am being a farm girl, *Americanski*, are you remembering? You will being need help with the animal."

"What happens if I need help with you?"

"You are being man enough to handle it."

She trailed him off the precipice, slipping and sliding with him and kicking up loose gravel on the way down. A long bare wire, Mad Dog's directional antenna, lay draped over rock and boulders alongside their descent. Below at the mouth of the cave, Mad Dog hunched over his radio, speaking into a hand mike. He wore a floppy bush hat. His cammies were already starting to turn dark from the thickening rain, which he ignored. Doc Red and Perverse Sanchez kept watch, lying on their bellies nearby with weapons trained toward the creek.

"Good news, commander," the big commo man reported. "I've raised Ice and the Zulu."

That *was* news. Brandon took a knee next to him. "Sitrep?"

"Just as I thought. They were inside a mine shaft where the Motorola wouldn't work."

"A mine shaft?"

"They're out now and on their way back."

"Tell them to find a secure location and hold what they got. We're moving. We'll get back with them. Get your gear together, guys. Five minutes."

Brandon and Katya made their way farther downhill at a dog trot, passing the big boulder and on through the thick conifers already dripping from rain to the near bank of the creek where they forded at a shallows.

"Fu-uck," Mad Dog observed, watching them go. "How would you like to muff dive your red Georgia head into *that*, Doc? Parts of it are edible, you know. Ask our two gourmets when they get back."

The bay skittered about shaking its head and snorting at the appearance of strangers, its eyes white-rimmed and wild in the gathering rain dusk. Thunder rumbling and lightning flickering in webs across the half-globe of the sky contributed to its skittishness. Lightning shadows made the corpse appear to move as Brandon eased past it toward the horse, speaking soothingly to it, hand extended with the palm down. Katya stood back.

The Cossack lay face down in tall grass, the long rifle still in his hands. Rain was beginning to dilute a splotch of blood in the low center of his back where Gloomy's high-powered bullet exited.

Brandon reached slowly for the bay's rein as he approached. Just as he grasped it, the dead guy *did* move. The horse jerked back, yanking Brandon off-balance.

"Zafina!" the Cossack cried. *Zafina*, or a word that sounded like Zafina.

He swung the muzzle of his rifle toward Brandon. The spiteful *Pop* of a small-caliber handgun immediately followed. Brandon and the excited horse executed a pirouette together before he got the animal calmed enough to see what had happened.

Katya stood over the Cossack, who was really dead this time, having been killed twice. A small black .25 caliber auto pistol in her hand curled smoke out the barrel. Brandon cursed himself for having missed the concealed weapon when he body-searched Katya during their first encounter; he should have checked her crotch after all. A mistake like that could get a man killed.

On the other hand, it was a mistake that had apparently saved his life.

Lowering clouds split apart in a deluge of fierce rain.

CHAPTER 34

Russian Coast

Lina had to be a bit nutty, or so it seemed to Cassidy Kragle—the acceptance of which did nothing toward extricating him from her clutches. Margo had at times teasingly threatened to lock him in a room to keep him from running off with Delta Force to far corners of the world. Lina wasn't teasing. At least for the time being, he appeared to be her prisoner.

He might have been able to reason with her if they could communicate, or if she were more rational. Then again, someone more reasonable might have already turned his foreign invading ass over to the authorities and caused an international incident before they shot him.

After Lina knocked his crutch-chair out from under him in a fit of rage, she helped him back to bed, covered him, then went into the kitchen and returned with a big bowl of soup. Cassidy discovered he was famished in spite of everything. He could have fed himself—his *arms* weren't broken—but Lina insisted on doing it for him. Her mood had reverted to normal, if *normal* applied to her. She perched on the edge of the bed, looking at him adoringly with her sunken off-kilter eyes and smiling a little from her too-wide mouth while she spooned soup into his mouth.

Cassidy's mind raced while he ate, reviewing options of escape and dismissing them one by one as not only impractical but possibly even suicidal. He even thought of grabbing Lina and making her *his* prisoner. She was no match for his strength.

But then what would he do with her once he had her? All she had to do was kick his leg a couple of times to render him as impotent as Jell-O.

He obediently ate the soup, silently resentful of his dependence upon the Smurf but recognizing it as a fact of life for the present time.

Afterward, she took the empty bowl away and stood in the center of the room smoking a home-rolled cigarette and regarding him with gleeful possessiveness. Acrid smoke wafted about the room. Cassidy coughed and waved his hand. Lina looked at him, then looked thoughtfully at the cigarette before she snubbed it out in the ashtray by the kerosene lamp.

She removed both the straight-backed chair and the wheelbarrow to the other room to prevent another escape attempt. That accomplished, she turned at the door and showed Cassidy the skeleton key. She tittered, as though at a private joke, then locked the door behind her as she went out.

Cassidy heard her moving about in the other room. Dishes clinking, the scaly shuffling of her bare feet on the stone floor, giggling. She made up a husky little song, the lyrics of which were composed of a single word—*Mine*, mine, MINE, MINE . . . A chill clawed its way up Cassidy's spine, reminding him of how helpless he was that he could be held captive in her bed.

He sank back on his pillow with a mixture of frustration and smoldering anger as he stared toward the single window of his cage. Sunlight filtered by the chintzy curtains slowly muted and changed colors from light to straw color to stained-glass red. A splotch of light against the stone floor next to the bed resembled dried blood while shadows in corners of the moldy bedroom grew ominous. Occasional flashes and the muted rumble of distant thunder announced the approach of a storm.

It occurred to him that he still had no specific idea of where he was. He supposed he should be grateful to Lina for rescuing him. Otherwise, he might have found himself still crawling around on the seashore exposed to the elements rather than snug and warm in Lina's bed.

He slept fitfully the rest of the day. Sometimes when he opened his eyes, Lina was there in the room watching him. Once, rain pounding on the slate roof and against the window jarred him from troubled sleep. He lay awake for a long time watching the storm and thinking.

A sense of irrational betrayal and guilt swept over him—betrayal on his part for malfunctioning in the air and leaving the detachment with only half the demolitions it might require; guilt at knowing he should be with his people rather than in the feather bed of some Russian peasant woman.

Then again, he wryly conceded, Lina's bed might be the best place for him. With his broken leg and his broken head, he would have been more of a liability to the team than an asset.

Today was the first day of the three days allotted in-country for Operation Cold Dawn. What would happen to him if he failed to re-link with Det 3A for extraction and if he were unable to escape and evade? The U.S. Government disavowed all knowledge of such missions and their operators if they were captured or compromised.

Part of the Delta Force creed was that it never left a man

behind. Not even if that man was thought lost at sea, dragged down and drowned by his parachute and equipment?

Lina awoke him later when she came in to feed him dinner. She lit the kerosene lamp with a wooden match. Its flickering yellow glow cast highlights and hollows against her broad face. Wick flame from the lamp reflected deep in the hollows of her eyes.

"Lina?"

She looked at him and giggled coyly.

"I have to make you understand, Lina. I need my gear. The radio? Can you bring the radio? Understand? The radio? Telephone?"

She shook her head vigorously, refusing to even try to comprehend. She fed him another bowl of her soup-stew, then left the room, locking the door behind her.

Exhausted from his ordeal and injuries, Cassidy drifted back to sleep thinking of Margo. Maybe he *would* marry Margo when he returned to America, providing he made it back. He dreamed they were in bed together making love. It was all so real. She had him in one hand, stroking him teasingly the way she did while her dark hair fell over their faces and they kissed deeply and passionately.

It was *too* real.

He came awake to the overpowering odor of stale woman. It took him a moment or so to realize little Lina had crept underneath the covers with him. She had his sleep erection in both hands and was working it. Appalled, he wrenched away, enduring the sudden pain that shot up his leg and instantly softened his penis. He cried out in agony and disgust as he shoved the parasite away from him and out of bed. She thumped hitting the floor, but rebounded to stand nude and tearfully rejected in the faint glow of lamplight.

"What the hell do you think you're doing?"

That did it. She exploded in great boo-hooing tears, throwing her head back on her shoulders and slapping her arms against her sides like a flightless bird trying to take off. Baggy breasts thumped against her ribs.

Cassidy glared, repulsed at even the thought of making love to such a misshapen creature. Gradually, however, his outrage turned to begrudging pity. The poor, lonely bitch. Living out here without human contact, all by herself, wherever *out here* was. No wonder she was this way.

Lina was not nearly so forgiving. She stopped crying presently. Rejection and humiliation turned to indignation and anger. She glared at Cassidy with the flame of the lamp double-reflected in her cave-like eyes. After blistering him with a flood of Russian, she wheeled away as though intending to retrieve the thick walking stick she left by the door and render upon her prisoner the caning of his young life.

"Lina!"

She hesitated and turned back toward the bed. Cassidy softened his expression with an effort. Much as he abhorred the thought, he had to accept that he was at the mercy of this mean little Smurf. What might she do to him on a mere whim if he alienated her? He needed her if he ever hoped to rejoin his detachment and escape this shit-bag country.

Hadn't he done worse in the name of Mother Army, God, and country than be nice to some pathetic little hermit?

He flipped open the covers and patted the mattress to signal that he wanted her to come back to bed. After all, it *was* her bed. With a swift change of emotion, Lina giggled and rushed underneath the covers with him like a child allowed to get into bed with her parent in the middle of a scary night. She grabbed his penis.

He gently removed her hand. "We'll only sleep. Understand? Sleep."

He turned her away from him as though she were a child. He put his arm over her. Satisfied, she happily snuggled her bare back against his bare belly.

"Cass?" she said through tears of joy.

"Yes."

"Cass."

CHAPTER 35

Washington, D.C.

General Darren Kragle slumped over the little hotel desk in his room at the Washingtonian, poring over the paper in front of him. His craggy face looked more worn than ever, his short-cropped military hair silver in the lonely circle of light provided by the desk lamp. He was drafting his resignation as commander of the United States Special Operations Command and requesting retirement from the U.S. Army, effective once the Cold Dawn mission concluded. It was a difficult task, canceling out forty years of his life on a single sheet of paper. Forty years in the military and it was all about to end with his sitting alone in a hotel room. What had he to show for all those years?

He stared at the darkened window that overlooked Pennsylvania Avenue, hearing the faint cacophony of sound rising from still another antiwar, anti-Tyler midnight vigil. More naked fat women perhaps. Or enlightened celebrities hobnobbing with enlightened students who would all be better off guzzling beer and cheering local mud wrestlers. It was the Fall of Rome all over again. Spengler was right about the rise and fall of civilizations.

He sighed deeply and decided to dial his daughter-in-law Summer in Fayetteville, his way of postponing the inevitability of actually signing his resignation. When she answered, she sounded like she might go into labor immediately if he brought bad news.

"Relax. Brandon's okay," he admonished, trying to sound cheerful. "How's my future grandson doing?"

"Kicking me out of bed at night and starting to make me look like a balloon. Pops. Pops, we love you. Here. Gloria wants to talk."

"Brown Sugar—"

"Don't you go Brown Sugaring me none, Darren Kragle." He could almost see her wagging finger. "Is my boys doing all right? Don't you go fibbing to me now neither or the Good Lord will come down on you like . . . like I don't know what. You is always sending my boys off to them foreign countries where they is in danger."

He reassured her as best he could. No need to concern the womenfolk yet about Cassidy until he had more concrete information. Gloria detected a strain in his voice and mellowed suddenly. She could always tell, even over the telephone, when something ate at him.

"Darren, is you doing all right?"

"I'm fine, Gloria."

"You don't sound fine to me."

"I'm okay."

"Sure 'nuff?"

"Sure 'nuff, Gloria. Okay?"

She sounded like she didn't believe him. She pumped him for a few more minutes, trying to get him to open up. Then she said, "Darren, God bless you and them and all."

He hung up and gazed at the rough copy of his resignation. He stood and walked across the room and turned on the television. He turned it off again and resumed his place at the desk. He stared at the window and in his reflected image saw his own father's face being consumed by Alzheimer's. He pounded the desktop with the meaty side of his fist in sudden frustration.

"Damn it!" he exclaimed. "*Damn it!*"

The phone rang. He started to ignore it, then reconsidered. It might be CENTCOM calling about Cassidy.

"Kragle," he answered. "This is not a secure line."

"Darren Kragle?" A woman's voice. "This is Vanda Stratton."

"Vanda?"

"We met at Pleasant Valley . . ."

"I remember. I'm just surprised."

"I hope you don't mind. I called your office at Special Operations Command and persuaded them with a little sweet talk to tell me where you're staying."

Uncomfortable, the General didn't know what to say, so he hung fire. Vanda finally broke the awkward silence. "General Kragle, I have an embarrassing confession to make."

He still didn't know what to say. He remembered she had Rita's smile.

"Our encounter at Pleasant Valley wasn't exactly an accident," she said finally, in a diminished voice. "I know who you are. When I found out you were visiting your father, I arranged to be there as a volunteer-for-a-day to meet you. I hear you're one of the leading authorities in the nation on terrorism. I didn't know who else to turn to. It's about my daughter Jennifer. I told you I'd had some trouble with her . . . Well . . . Well, I think she's involved with terrorists . . ."

She stopped to catch her breath, everything having come out in a rush.

The General hedged. "Well . . . ?"

"Please? I need your help. Don't say no yet until you hear what I have to say. Will you have breakfast with me in the morning, early?"

CHAPTER 36

MUSLIM LEADERS APPROVE ATTACKS

Dubai (CPI)—According to a press account released through the Arab news agency Al-Jazeera, a "summit" of Muslim cleric leaders meeting in Dubai today approved al-Qaeda's launching preemptive strikes against the United States and its allies.

Reportedly, the clerics from Syria, Iran, Jordan, Egypt, Saudi Arabia, and elsewhere were hesitant about giving their blessing to attack civilians. However, after hearing arguments that the American people themselves, including children, were guilty by complicity in attacking Islam by participating in a democracy that elected leaders who did so, the summit voted to approve al-Qaeda's methods.

The summit issued a statement which included the exhortation: "Do not betray God and his prophet, and don't knowingly betray the trust. You must not wait for anyone and must begin resisting from now—and take experience and lessons from Iraq and Afghanistan and Chechnya. Strike at the heart of the Great Satan and kill in Allah's name . . ."

In a bid to disrupt and influence presidential elections, al-Qaeda may already be planning a new attack against the U.S., according to senior Tyler administration officials. Homeland Security Secretary MacArthur Thornbrew said, "We lack precise knowledge about time, place and method of attack. But the CIA, FBI and other agencies are actively working to gain that knowledge . . ."

CHAPTER 37

Washington, D.C.

Claude Thornton and his deputy director, Fred Whiteman, coordinated efforts to run down fugitive Patsy Koehler from their offices around the corner from the Capitol complex. The Capitol dome glimmered at them above the city in the afternoon sun as the two men stood at the wide window watching another antiwar protest in the street below. Placards denouncing both President Tyler and the War on Terror stabbed the air like drawn sabers. Distance and the building's walls and double-paned windows muted the demonstrators' chants and howls, turning the march into street theater in silent pantomime.

Whiteman regarded the distant Capitol dome. "If the Jihadia hit at the right time," he said, "they could wipe out our government in one stroke."

Claude paced the room. Waiting for something to happen was worse than being out in the streets trying to make something happen. The sheer scope and complexity of the Koehler case, however, had finally driven him back to his office. JTTF agents were scattered all up and down the eastern seaboard searching for Koehler through her various connections and associations in order to piece together the puzzle of what sleeper terrorists might be planning against the presidential elections. During the past two days since the Staten Island raid, Claude had learned more about Koehler than if he had been sleeping with her. Field agents fed a constant stream of information back to Claude's command post.

Agents promptly ran down Ronald McDonald, who had registered Americans Standing Up For People with the Manhattan bank, and who apparently had funding ties with Koehler. Whiteman took the call and passed it on to Claude.

"Sir, the guy's name really *is* Ronald McDonald, believe it or not. But that's not the most interesting point. Ronnie is only a surrogate. His buddy, the guy supplying the capital, is George Coalgate Geis."

"I thought he was in jail."

"He's a *multibillionaire*, Director." As though that explained everything.

Geis, who failed to see the incongruity of being both an avowed socialist and filthy rich, had previously funded an organization called the Committed from a collection of like-minded wealthy socialists, its purpose to install Senator Harris in the presidency, no matter what it took. General Kragle busted up the ring in a dramatic standoff during a Harris fundraiser at Geis's mansion in Arlington, killing two men in self-defense and suffering a wound himself. Harris avoided serious political contamination from it. Geis was already out of jail and apparently up to more crimes and dirty tricks.

"So far, Director, we can't find anything illegal about it."

"Keep digging," Claude urged.

Patsy Koehler was proving more elusive than Claude expected. She seemed to be moving from place to place, never staying anywhere for more than a few hours. News about the shootout at her residence, which she had not attended, spooked her completely. Agents kept the Director updated.

"I'm in the Bronx, Director. She was here. We're bringing in the maggot who harbored her."

"Do you have *her*?" Claude demanded.

"We're a few hours behind her."

"Go get her."

Another agent phoned in. "She was in Baltimore."

"*Was?*"

"We're still on her trail, sir."

Della Street, Claude's assistant, brought in takeout to feed the two men working late in the Domestic Preparedness Office. This time it was Chinese. She turned on the TV and the trio settled down to eat and watch the evening's keynote speaker at the Federalist Convention. Although security was heavier around Madison Square Garden than anywhere else in the world, every nerve in their bodies half expected the screen to erupt in a devastating explosion. The optimum time for an attack, however, would not be tonight but instead when President Tyler took the podium to deliver his nomination acceptance speech on the convention's last night.

Halfway through the televised speech, Agent Jonathan Barnes reported in from Charleston. "Claude, I got good news and I got bad news. Which do you want first?"

Claude was in no mood for games. "Get on with it, Barnes."

"The good news is—we've found Patsy Koehler."

Claude sprang to his feet. "Where?"

He could feel the other shoe about to fall.

"The bad news is—she's not going to tell us anything. She's been murdered."

CHAPTER 38

Partizanskaya River Valley

Katya remained standing over the dead man she had just shot, standing there blurred by the rain with the pistol hanging at the end of her arm, frozen in place by shock and disbelief. Brandon started back across the creek, tugging the bay horse by its reins. The fierce rain beat down upon him so hard it was like being pelted with stones, drenching him in seconds. Water poured off the brim of his bush hat. The elements had gone haywire.

"Come on!" he shouted at Katya above the crash and roll of thunder and lightning. "Bring the guy's rifle with you."

She gave a little start. "He was in aiming his rifle at you, *Americanski*," she shouted back.

"We'll talk about it later. Move!"

Rain drummed in the treetops, hissed on the surface of the little creek.

"I am not wanting to shooting him," she said, still looking at the body.

Brandon pulled the horse around to grab her shoulders and shake her back to her senses. She obediently picked up the Moison-Nagant and followed, trotting with Brandon and the horse back to the cave. Top Sculdiron ran out wearing a question on his hard face.

"She had to finish the guy," Brandon explained. "She saved my skin."

Katya still looked stunned, standing hunched in the

downpour, the rifle in one hand, the pistol in the other. Top took both weapons from her, slipping the handgun into one of his cargo pockets and slinging the sniper rifle on his shoulder. He didn't ask Brandon where the pistol came from.

"Saddle up!" Sculdiron sang out. "We are moving out. Doc, you and Sanchez go hide the dead man."

"Bury heem?" Perverse asked.

"I do not care if you stuff him up your butt, just so he is not found. But do it quick."

It was a move that had to be executed, compromised as the site was, but not a man failed to look back longingly in the deluge toward the dry and relatively warm cave, bat shit or no. It was rough going. Terrain alternated between stands of timber so thick the horse had trouble negotiating them to boulder-strewn hillsides. Brooks turned into creeks and creeks into brown roiling rivers that had to be forded. The drencher continued for hours, manufacturing mud and bogs in low places. Gloomy Davis, the Oklahoma cowboy, rode the bay across open stretches; it sank down nearly to its knees in the wet earth.

Twice the procession had to detour around dead-end canyons. Visibility was so reduced that Perverse at the rear of the march could barely discern the outlines of the commander and Top Sculdiron up front on point. Everyone was soaked, cold, and miserable, even though they wore poncho slickers.

Night settled with still no sign of the dead Cossack's cavalry buddies on the detachment's back trail. Nobody was going to do any tracking in that stuff. Top Sculdiron slipped down a ravine in the total darkness, tumbling and crashing through brush until he splashed into water at the bottom. Brandon shucked his pack and leaped blind into the abyss after him, pulling the team sergeant out of the raging torrent of water.

After that close call, Brandon soon called a halt for the night in timber on high ground. He figured they were within six klicks of the enrichment plant. He radioed his grid coordinates to Ice Man and Diverse Dade, who assured him they would rendezvous with the detachment within a few hours, around midnight at the latest.

"We're on high ground and making good time," Ice Man said.

The men stripped off their ponchos and used them to construct little hooch shelters low to the ground, under which they stashed their gear and huddled out of the weather. Efficient as always, Top Sculdiron positioned them in close defense. Barely four steps separated any one hooch from the next.

Doc Red and Perverse Sanchez erected their shelters on the back side of the perimeter. Mad Dog took the left flank. Gloomy Davis tethered the horse nearby and ducked underneath Mad Dog's hooch. Dog had already broken out an MRE and was burning a heat tab to boil water for coffee.

"We're dining in the parlor tonight, I see," Gloomy said as Dog made room for him. He ruffled through his pack and produced beans and frankfuckers. He seemed all right again after sniping the Cossack at the creek; neither man was going to talk about it.

"Fu-uck," Mad Dog bitched. "The Gods of War screw with us everywhere we go. I'm already missing the cave, bat doo-doo and all."

Nearby, Brandon and Top Sculdiron built their hooches. Brandon stretched his poncho between two saplings and placed Katya underneath its shelter. She was shivering.

"I think I'm in love," Dog said, looking in her direction

even though it was so dark he could barely make out the fluorescent digits on his watch. He could hear her talking though. Rain thrumming on the stretched canvas made conversation difficult.

"More like lust," Gloomy corrected him.

"There's a difference?"

"You're too ugly for love. Even Arachna thinks so."

"Looks ain't everything, not when you got a dong like mine. I wonder if Katya would like to sleep with me tonight instead of the major?"

"She'd probably rather sleep with the horse."

"You're a crude sonofabitch, know that, Gloom-an'-Doom?"

Brandon hunkered low underneath his shelter, bent forward, listening to rain pound on it. He was soaked to the bone and chilled even deeper than that. He opened his sleeping bag for Katya. It was relatively dry. They couldn't help rubbing against each other in the confined space and thereby becoming acutely aware of the circumstances.

"What is it you are doing if I am taking your bed again?" she asked.

He didn't answer. He sat back on his heels. She got very quiet for a moment.

"I . . . I am never shooting somebody before today," she said in a small voice. "It is being most awful on the inside where I am. I am wanting not to be alone. Not tonight. I am being most small. The sleeping bag is large enough being for two people, one of who is small like me."

In spite of himself, Brandon felt heat rising in his groin in anticipation of crawling into a bag with this beautiful and desirable stranger. He shook it off. She may have saved his life, but he couldn't help the little thread of suspicion that continued to worm around inside his mind.

"We will sleeping only," Katya promised, her voice thin and strained and almost pleading.

He thought about Summer pregnant with his child at home.

"When you shot him," Brandon said, nursing his doubts, "he yelled out something. What was it?"

He wished he could see her face.

"It sounded like *Zafina*," he clarified, pushing her.

"I am hearing only his pain. Please, *Americanski*. Let us not tonight be talking on it."

There were tears in her voice. Brandon felt guilty.

"I'll be back," he said, and left quickly in the rain.

He stumbled around in the dark from hooch to hooch, running a commander's check on the detachment. Doc Red and Sanchez were already sleeping. Mad Dog and Gloomy made room for him out of the weather.

"Want something to eat, Boss?" Gloomy offered.

"I'm having coffee with Top in a minute. We're waiting up for the recon team."

"Boss, I'm sorry for today."

"You made a good shot. It wasn't your fault."

"I should have finished him off when he was down. I could have got you killed."

"You couldn't have known."

"If it wasn't for Katya . . ." Gloomy sounded ready to forgive her of anything—if she was guilty of anything.

Mad Dog snorted. "That cunt doesn't do anything without a reason. Even in bed, she'd have a knife in her hand." He thought it over. "It might be worth getting stabbed over," he added.

Everyone knew she was sleeping in the commander's hooch, in the commander's bed roll. *With* the commander?

Top Sculdiron had coffee going in a canteen cup over a heat tab that burned a tiny blue flame.

"Is *Zafina* Russian?" Brandon asked him. Russian was the Polish immigrant's native tongue. "That's what that guy called out when she shot him. What does it mean?"

"Are you sure that is what he said?"

"That's what it sounded like."

The blue flame barely illuminated the bottom of Top's canteen cup.

"Zafina?" Top mulled it over. "There are words which might sound the same. It seems like a name, but is not Russian. Perhaps, Commander, she is Zafina and not Katya."

"I've thought of that."

The top sergeant was a born cynic distrustful and careful of everyone and everything. Katya's saving Brandon's life wasn't enough to win his trust.

They guzzled three canteen cups full of scalding black coffee before the returning reconnaissance team flashed a red-lensed entry signal shortly before midnight. A GPS was a remarkable instrument, allowing navigation from point to point with unerring accuracy under even the severest conditions. The entire detachment turned out to welcome Ice Man and Diverse back into the fold. Katya remained in Brandon's hooch; he wasn't sure if she was sleeping or not.

"Did you run into the horses?" Brandon debriefed the two Deltas, who, wearing ponchos, squatted in the rain at the end of Top's shelter. The rest of the team returned to their bags once they made sure Ice Man and Diverse had their correct quota of body parts.

"They're there all right," Ice replied in his usual tight-lipped manner.

"How's it look?"

"It can be done."

"We have sketches and photos," Diverse said. "Actually, the horses arrived at an opportune time."

Ice took up the story. "We ran across an old mine shaft to hide in."

He let Diverse take it from there. "The other end of the shaft opens into the cave that houses the plant, Major. It's not guarded at either end."

"It's not easy though," Ice put in.

"But it's do-able," Diverse said.

Both men were soaked and sounded exhausted. They had been humping those mountains since early the previous morning.

"You did good," the major approved. "Get in your bags and catch some sack time. We're all going to need it. Mission planning at first light."

He helped the two men stretch their hooches, then sat with Top a while longer drinking yet more coffee until everyone settled down. Top yawned, causing Brandon to admit to himself that he had delayed returning to his own roof this long only because of Katya. His throat went dry every time he thought of slipping into a warm bag and feeling the girl's slim figure curling up with his. Nothing would happen, he assured himself. These were extraordinary circumstances. Summer would understand.

Would he understand if the situation were reversed and Summer shared *her* bed?

Top correctly interpreted his commander's dilemma. "Sir, we can take turns in my bag."

"I can't take yours, Top. Thanks."

"Then you must sleep with her or freeze your bony butt for the rest of the night. The men are jealous, but they understand. It is your duty to share your bed, Commander. Nothing is too good for Mother Army and her soldiers."

Brandon detected the purring rumble of uncharacteristic humor in the sergeant's voice.

"Up yours, Top," Brandon said.

Sculdiron openly chuckled as Brandon crawled out and made his way to his own hooch next door in the darkness. Brandon's throat got dry all over again as he ducked onto his hands and knees and crawled in out of the rain. Katya was awake. He heard her open the sleeping bag for him.

"Getting in quick," she whispered. "You must being freezing."

"I'm soaked. I'll get the bag wet."

"You are taking off your clothes."

"Have you taken off yours?"

"Of course. Coming in, please. It is feeling wonderful. Our body heat is keeping us snugly."

He couldn't see her in the darkness, not even an outline, but he smelled her warm and soft the way a woman is in bed. He felt heat generated by the two of them about to come together. The air was so close he could hardly catch his breath. He sat cross-legged on the wet ground at the foot of the sleeping bag, hunched over underneath the stretched poncho, debating with himself.

This time tomorrow night he could be dead. What difference did it ultimately make if tonight he sought a few hours' pleasure with a woman who wanted him, whom he wanted? It wasn't like he hadn't been with his share of women before Summer.

"*Americanski! Americanski*, you are telling me your name?"

What harm could it do now? "Brandon."

"You are being the commander, Brandon?"

He let it pass.

"Brandon. I am liking your name. Coming in quickly and get warm with me."

God, how he wanted to.

What about afterward, if he wasn't killed in the operation? A man had to live with his *afterward*.

Then it occurred to him that seventy-two hours earlier she was sleeping with Cage or Mikhail, whatever his name was. Cage was dead now; she had saved Brandon's life and was offering to sleep with *him*.

All the heat evaporated from the shelter. He suddenly felt cold again.

He would never know whether he resisted temptation because of Summer and his own character or because he suddenly felt the frozen heart that must beat underneath Katya's inviting skin.

Gloomy made room for him in his sleeping bag. It was a tight fit, but they had managed before.

"Boss?"

"Don't ask."

"I'm proud of you, Boss."

He wasn't so proud of himself. It had been a struggle.

"Boss," Gloomy said sleepily, "do you remember the time the C-130 dropped us in the middle of the Won Ju River on the Korean DMZ and we all had to pile on top of one another underneath a barn full of cow shit to keep from freezing to death?"

"It's the thing memories are made of."

"Mother Norman was alive then."

So were Rock Taylor, Brownie, Thumbs Jones, and Gypsy Iryani . . .

CHAPTER 39

Russian Coast

The watery rise of the sun softened the chintzy curtains covering the single bedroom window and cast a yellow frame of it on the damp stone floor. It rained much of the night and, although there was an early sun, the skies threatened more rain. The room smelled moldier than ever. Lina snuggled close on Cassidy's arm, which had grown numb, but he left it where it was.

Time was wasting. That very night, late, Det 3A would complete its mission and exfiltrate by submarine. He could rot in this place for all anyone on the outside knew if he failed to join them. He also needed a doctor to correctly set his leg, else it grow back crooked and deformed. He needed *out of there.*

He had to admit Lina had done a credible job of splinting, using barrel staves and cloth bandages cut from a bedsheet. Doc Red would surely have approved. His leg felt better and his head no longer ached. Perhaps he might escape if he had a way of fashioning a crutch. He looked around the nearly empty room, thinking he might have overlooked something. There was the bed, the small table containing the ashtray and still-burning kerosene lamp. Nothing else. Lina had even left her walking stick in the other room.

He shifted his arm to relieve some of the pressure of Lina's lying on it. She snuggled near, not opening her eyes but rewarding him nonetheless with her vacant smile and a wet kiss on the lips. This whole damned thing repulsed him—sleeping with this pathetic girl to avoid being whipped with what he now thought of as Lina's "ugly stick."

He *needed* her. That admission also disgusted him with the implication that he depended upon her goodwill in a way he had never depended upon anyone or anything in his life. That meant manipulating her, *using* her emotions and her disturbed thoughts toward his own ends. It was something he had to do if he hoped ever to get out of this mess.

Brown Sugar Mama would never have approved of exploiting another's weaknesses, no matter the circumstances. Once when he was a kid he befriended a nerdy classmate because the boy's father owned a ski boat.

"Is you liking Kevin or is you liking his boat?" Gloria demanded, her scolding deadly finger at the ready.

She correctly translated his silence. The Kragle boys *never* lied to Brown Sugar and her finger.

"Dat's what I thunk, honey-chile. You just friends with him 'cause he be rich. What do dat make you? Dat make you a phony, and they's already enough phonies in the world to go around and then some. The Lawd done say if you bites and devours another, heed that you be not consumed you own self."

Maybe Brown Sugar would forgive him this one more time. He had to get Lina to take him outside the house as a first step so he could look around and try to formulate a plan of escape.

"Lina?"

She stirred. She had tossed back the covers in her sleep to expose bare breasts lying like thick flaps of skin on her muscular chest. She opened her sunken eyes, smiled drowsily, and flung her arm across his chest. The smile of adoration with which she regarded him made him feel guilty all over again.

"Cass. Mine," she murmured, lips fluttering against his neck.

He *had* to teach her more words.

He shook her gently. "Lina, look at me."

She rose to one elbow. Her breasts drooped against his chest. By way of explicit pantomime he conveyed to her the necessity of his using the bathroom. Understanding, giggling, she jumped out of bed, recovered the door key from where she apparently hid it the night before underneath a loose floor stone in the corner, unlocked the door, and closed it behind her as she hurried into the other room.

He could kill her with the rock and get away! Crush in her skull and attempt to make it to the river before Cold Dawn floated down it later that night.

The thought sickened him as soon as it arrived. He had killed before, but always in combat. Never had he contemplated *murder*, except for that one time after the anthrax slaying of his wife Kathryn. Besides, for all Lina's beastliness and her seeming willingness to employ the ugly stick, she had never been anything but kind to him. How far would he get anyhow on one leg if he neutralized her? The local police would catch him and lynch him, justifiably, from the nearest tree.

For better or worse, he conceded, they were married to each other until something better came along.

Still nude with one of her home-rolled cigarettes sticking from her lips, Lina rushed back in with the bucket he had employed before as a chamber pot. He shook his head and insisted on going to the toilet, explaining by gesture

that she could assist him. He doubted the house had in-
door plumbing. That meant an outhouse.

Lina looked uncertain. Fear and distrust worked the
muscles of her face: Perhaps this was a trick to allow him
to escape. Cassidy smiled. That worked wonders. Her
wariness vanished instantly into a smile that matched his.
She seemed to become more accommodating the longer
they were together, more under his influence.

She dashed out with the bucket and returned pushing
the wheelbarrow, having also got rid of the cigarette and
pulled on a colorless shift-like dress to cover her nakedness. In her case, at least, clothing made the woman.

"Cass?"

"Good girl."

Getting from the bed into the wheelbarrow under-
scored Cassidy's helplessness and his reliance on his
benefactor. The pain of moving around proved excruciating. He almost gave up the effort and asked for the return of the bucket. Finally, however, with Lina's help,
he gritted his teeth and, clad only in his underwear,
plopped into the wooden box with his legs up in the air
and lying on his back. It astonished him that his leg held
together.

Laughing, Lina wheeled him into the other room. She
seemed to live with the simplicity of a monk, in dimness
and dreariness. This room was larger than the bedroom
but just as sparsely furnished—a wooden bench-like sofa;
a crude table covered in debris, and two chairs pushed up
to it; a wood-burning cookstove; homemade cupboards
and diminutive kitchen counter; and two doors leading
outside, one in front and one at the back of the room. The
walls were bare, not even a photo or a framed cutout of
some flower or pastoral scene on them.

"Outside?" Cassidy asked, pointing at the front door.

"Outside?" she mimicked.

"Yes. Outside."

"Outside."

She burst spontaneously into infectious laughter, as though extraordinarily pleased with her accomplishment. Cassidy couldn't help laughing with her. She opened the door and wheeled him into the yard as effortlessly as if he were an infant and the wheelbarrow a baby carriage.

"Outside? Outside?"

"Now you know three words." He held up three fingers.

"Outside. Cass. Mine."

"You're a linguist. Lina the linguist."

Puddles of rainwater lay everywhere, the grass having been beaten down almost to bare mud through which Lina splashed with her bare feet. Cassidy eagerly took in his surroundings for future reference.

As he expected, the house was isolated in a clearing surrounded by forest. It was a typical two-room peasant structure built of native stone. Out of the forest on one side appeared a well-beaten footpath. He assumed this was the route by which Lina had wheelbarrowed him up from the sea. He listened but failed to detect the bashing of breaker waves against rock.

Some chickens pecking busily about in the mud rushed the wheelbarrow and followed noisily along behind. Four black-and-white milk goats inside a fence next to the forest bleated pleas to be fed. This appeared to be a place, as Brown Sugar would have noted, where sunshine had to be piped in and where you could holler and no one would hear you until next week.

Still giggling and laughing for no apparent reason other than the sheer joy of living and having her own man, Lina pushed him around the corner of the house toward a crude wooden privy and a larger building that seemed a combination henhouse and barn, both set at some considerable distance from her residence. Rugged mountains rose in the west beyond the outhouse and the timber, capped by black storm clouds snapping bolts of lightning. It was either raining or about to rain up there where Detachment 3A went about its clandestine business. Cassidy stared at the mountains and fought back a surge of despondency.

Here he was—almost naked in a wheelbarrow being trundled by a dim-witted Smurf across a chicken yard to an outhouse, chased by poultry, glared at by hungry goats. The picture *that* would present were anyone to observe it was enough to overcome his brief sense of despair. He began laughing as heartily as his tiny savior. They roared with uncontained mirth all the way to the one-holer.

"Can you say, Cass's ass is in a crack?" he asked her.

"Crack? Crack. Cass. Mine. Outside." She was an excellent mimic, whether or not she understood the words themselves.

"We're having a conversation!" Cassidy shouted.

It was no easy matter getting him into the toilet and out again. He leaned heavily on Lina as she patiently helped him maneuver back into the wheelbarrow for the ride home. As he twisted to sit down, he glimpsed through an opening in the trees a large, low structure on a distant ridgeline.

"Wait!" he said, pointing. "What is that?"

The laughter on Lina's face froze as though she were suddenly engulfed by a sudden arctic blast. Her eyes bulged with terror. Tears burst from them and rolled down her cheeks. She frantically shook her head and urged Cassidy into the wheelbarrow. In a panic, she pushed him running all the way back to the house, jabbering in tearful Russian, glancing fearfully back over her shoulder as though the Devil himself was after them with his red-hot pitchfork.

CHAPTER 40

Chased by her demons, Lina ushered Cassidy inside so hurriedly that she almost jostled him out of the wheelbarrow. She bolted the front and back doors, then locked Cassidy and herself together in the bedroom. She left him in the barrow in the middle of the room and darted to the window where she parted the curtains just enough to peep out, as though half-expecting pursuit. Shaking her head, mumbling in Russian, she looked scared to death, her face uncommonly pale and harried, her eyes sunken and flinty.

"Lina?"

It was frustrating not being able to communicate beyond the few signs needed to satisfy his basic needs. What was with the building and her anyhow?

Still shaking her head as though admonishing him not to even *think* of the building, she helped him back to bed, then returned to keep watch at the window. Gradually, she calmed when nothing or no one showed up to harm them. After an hour she was back to her old self, whatever that was. Cassidy decided she ran on a one-track mind incapable of entertaining more than one thought at a time.

She locked him in the bedroom while she made breakfast. Cassidy smelled eggs frying. She brought them to him presently, along with a chunk of hard bread and a stoneware cup of what he assumed to be goat's milk. She let him feed himself this time while she perched on the edge of the bed, occasionally reaching to touch him familiarly, possessively, on the chest or arm.

After breakfast, Lina sign-languaged that she was going outside to conduct morning chores—the chickens and goats. Cassidy indicated he wanted to go with her. That pleased her at first. But then her eyes seemed drawn against her will in the direction of the mysterious structure on the ridgeline. She scowled and muttered to herself.

"Lina?"

Saying her name was the best way to attract her attention. He gave her his most winning smile, even though it made him feel deceptive and dishonest. He was discovering that she might be willing to do almost anything to satisfy his whims as long as he couched them in the appropriate manner. She was like the mistress of a pampered poodle who catered to it as long as it didn't stray into the street or try to go next door to romp with the neighbor's schnauzer.

A prisoner incarcerated unjustly had the right, the obligation, to use everything at his disposal to free himself. Cassidy was going to be left behind otherwise, the detachment and CENTCOM undoubtedly concluding that his parachute had malfunctioned and dumped him into the sea to perish.

Lina relented finally and hurried out to bring back the wheelbarrow. Cassidy then asked for his clothing. It was chilly outside and threatening rain. He held himself and shivered to make her understand. Again she thought it over, the wheels in her mind almost visible as she considered how clothing might facilitate his escape attempts.

"Where can I go?" he asked, although he might as well have been talking to himself. "We're already as close to Siberia as we can get."

She padded out of the house on her thick bare feet to return shortly carrying his cammie uniform and one boot. That meant the rest of his equipment must also be nearby, though he figured he might have a tougher time convincing her to bring his weapons and the radio. She had found him, by God, and she was going to keep him.

He got dressed with some difficulty, wearing the one boot, and she wheeled him outside and parked him near the goat pen. She called the chickens and scattered grain out on the ground all around him so he would have company and be amused while she milked the goats. She balanced on a little three-legged stool behind each nanny and squirted rhythmic streams into a bucket with both hands. That amused him more than the chickens, for he had never seen goats milked.

Cassidy noticed that while she milked, indeed while she fed the chickens or gathered eggs or accomplished her other morning chores, she kept her back toward the distant ridgeline and the building nestled on it. She would not so much as cast a single fearful glance in its direction, as though to do so might subject her to some evil spell.

Her strange deportment, which Cassidy was beginning to consider another example of her paranoia about the outside world, intensified his curiosity. Where there was construction, there was civilization. Civilization meant other people, and other people meant hope. A plan slowly formed in Cassidy's mind. All he had to do was get away from Lina, somehow reach the ridgeline, steal a car, a donkey—anything except a goat, chicken, or wheelbarrow—and make his way to the river in time to link up with Brandon and the detachment upon exfil.

It wasn't going to be easy in his condition, but a long shot was better than no shot.

After Lina finished her chores, she wheeled him inside where he watched her strain the bucket of milk through a piece of cheesecloth. She poured half of it into a pitcher and the other half into a crock jar, the top of which she tied off with a clean cloth. Then she explained to him as best she could through sign that she had to run an errand. He couldn't understand how long she would be gone, only that she apparently intended to take the crock of goat's milk to sell to neighbors.

Cassidy was elated. He couldn't wait for her to depart. At first he thought she was going to leave him in the living room unattended. What luck! Instead, she ignored his protests and put him back to bed. He insisted on remaining clothed. That much she granted. Before she left, she clasped the palm of his hand hard against her lips and kissed it and kissed it until it was wet.

"Cass. Cass mine."

She locked the bedroom door as usual on her way out, and in a few minutes Cassidy heard her leave. He had to work fast.

Setting his mind against the anticipated pain, he rolled out of bed and landed on his good side. His injured leg banged. He almost passed out from the agony.

He recovered and, dragging his splints, pulled himself to the table that contained the Bible, ashtray, and kerosene lamp. He removed the lamp's wire damper handle and crawled to the door with it. Sweat rolled off his face. He dropped his head on his arms and rested a minute, letting the pain subside before he went to work on the door lock.

Like most Deltas, Cassidy had attended locksmith training under the best safecrackers in the business—inmates at the North Carolina State Penitentiary. The old-fashioned skeleton-key lock with its simple tumblers posed little challenge for his skills and the key he made from the lamp's damper handle. The door opened almost immediately.

Crawling on hands and one knee, dragging his injured leg, he made his way to the kitchen area where he located a broom to serve as a makeshift crutch. The ugly stick was nowhere about. The broom handle was too short for his considerable height, but he discovered he could still walk of a fashion by wedging the straw end of the broom in his armpit and leaning his weight forward over it. It was awkward, but still faster and less painful than crawling.

There was still one other problem. His bad leg dragged and bumped along behind him, shooting pain up his spine to pierce his brain core. He tore a dish towel into strips and braided the strips into a rope. He tied one end of the rope around his bandaged ankle and tractioned the lower half of his leg off the floor and secured it with the other end of the rope to the back of his belt. It was still painful to walk, but not as excruciating as before. He was now mobile, relatively speaking.

A quarter hour later, hobbling on the broom with his bad leg swinging out at a ninety-degree angle behind, anxious lest Lina return and catch him, he entered the forest beyond the goat pen and laboriously climbed through rain forest toward the building that had so frightened Lina.

The forest smelled of turpentine and decay and mold. Clouds moved over to blot out the morning sun and darken the way. Freshening winds carried the scent of coming rain as they moaned through the treetops. He looked back and saw how the broomstick punched holes in the humus, authoring a trail a blind man might follow. He would have to work fast if he hoped to hide out from the Smurf long enough to steal some kind of transportation that allowed him to reach the river in time for the detachment's extraction. He was also counting on Lina's intense fear to keep her from following.

Intermittent drops of rain fell by the time, exhausted, he reached the building. From habit and caution, he parted the foliage to look things over before he committed himself. From a distance the structure appeared to be an old abandoned schoolhouse, many of its windows shattered and boarded up and its yards overgrown with weeds. It hardly constituted anything that would so frighten Lina she refused to even look its way.

There was nothing else around that he could see. His expectations plummeted. He was about to write it off as a dry hole and postpone his escape plans when two men armed with Russian AK-47 assault rifles suddenly walked out a back door of the schoolhouse and stopped near a low crumbling rock wall to smoke cigarettes.

He was studying them, puzzled, when a terrifying screech of rage from behind jerked him around in surprise, dislodging the broom from his armpit. He dropped to the ground. A small screaming banshee with wild off-kilter eyes and hair frizzed out like electricity shocked through moldy hay charged him, her long ugly stick flailing the air.

"Mine! Mine! Mine!"

CHAPTER 41

Charleston, South Carolina

Patsy Koehler made one huge corpse. Her death was her final statement, but it had been made for her and not by her. Seagulls screeched across the gray morning sky, whipped about like dirty tattered rags. It would soon be hurricane season and the air smelled saltier and richer than usual, especially underneath the Exxon pier at the Charleston seaport where the body had been discovered. The incoming tide, oily and garbaged with the detritus common to ports, lapped in echo chamber resonance against the sand and around the huge barnacle-encrusted pillars that supported the wharf.

The heavy corpse lay belly-down on the wet sand. *Face down* would have been an inaccurate description, as her head had been severed and placed between her shoulder blades. Claude Thornton and FBI agent Jonathan Barnes looked the body over while plainclothed JTTF investigators, CSI experts, and Charleston homicide detectives, hardened pros at the grim business of violence, scoured the vicinity for clues and evidence.

Claude had changed into loose jeans and a sport shirt to cover his belted Glock 9mm after Barnes picked him up at the airport from one of the first flights in that morning. The perpetual frown worn into Barnes's features remained unchanged as the two Feebies looked back at the grisly head looking back at them. Her eyes were wide in perpetual surprise and shock, her mouth hung open as though still screaming in her last throes of agony.

Charleston detective Martin Wells, a powerful-looking man with a bushy mustache and a Deep South drawl, walked over. "Folks lose theah heads all the time ovah different things—lovers, horses, cards," he commented. "But this heah seems to be taking things to the extreme. Ya'all do understand, this is like them beheadings terrorists are doing in Iraq."

It definitely made a statement.

"When was the body discovered?" Claude asked.

"Just before I called you last night," Barnes said. "Some sailor lost his dog and came down here looking for him. He found her instead. He almost shit his jeans."

The Charleston detective, Wells, had taken off his coat and loosened his tie. He wore a .357 S&W on his belt. "We had a pickup order on her from ya'all. The feds, I mean," he said. "We identified her from mug shots and fingerprints. The flyer said notify the FBI if apprehended. Well, this ole gal has been apprehended big time."

"Director," Barnes said to Claude, "*you* tell me the motive. Why did the Jihads kill her if she was in cahoots with them?"

"She got too hot for them, Jonathan. Look at it this way: she knew too much about whatever the terrorists are planning. They knew we'd catch her sooner or later and that she'd probably squeal like a pig. Sound logical?"

Little about leftist radicals allying themselves with Islamic terrorists made much sense from a logical standpoint, but so-called intellectuals like Koehler functioned on an emotional, visceral level. By the looks of the crime scene, her killers functioned the same way, albeit more primitively. The body lay beyond the reach of high tide. Her executioners intended that she be found and not washed out to sea.

"So when, for some reason, she came down here to rendezvous with her terrorist buddies . . ." Barnes speculated in the abbreviated musing of lawmen probing a crime. "But why cut off her head?"

"She was a useful idiot—and then only an idiot when she was no longer useful. They're sending a message to other useful idiots to put up, shut up, and don't get caught. Beheadings these days are fashionable in terrorism. Maybe they're trying to show us they can do it inside our own country. Arrogance, Barnes. Besides, whoever said these guys are entirely rational?"

Charleston police and local feds had been working the scene most of the night.

"You guys pick up anything useful?" Claude asked Wells.

"Lots of blood. It appeahs she lost her head over somebody she came down heah to meet. Her rental car is parked in the lot at the head of the pier. We traced it to Avis. Theah was no blood inside the car. Outside either."

"Anything else inside the car?"

"Not even her purse. It looks like whoever did this made shore nothing was left behind. At first we thought it was some kind of sadistic mugging . . ."

He snapped his fingers.

"One other thing. Theah was a key to Room 212 at the Day's Inn that had slipped down between the seats. We went through the room. All we found was a pair of panties and a law book. Ya'all want to see the evidence? It's in my car."

Claude and Barnes accompanied him to the parking lot. Police vehicles, marked and not, were parked at odd angles and in all positions. The lot had otherwise been cordoned off. Uniformed cops guarded the perimeter to keep out unauthorized personnel. Groups of stevedores and dock workers watched from behind strung yellow tape.

The panties were in a paper sack; they would soon be on their way to the FBI lab to be checked for bodily secretions and DNA samples. The law book—*Federal Law, Codified*, edited by Patsy R. Koehler—was in a plastic bag. Wells said it had already been screened for prints. Claude took it out of the bag and opened it. The pages were stained by forensic spray.

The title page contained two notations in two distinct and separate handwritings. The first was a name in fine-pointed ink, legible and feminine: *Jennifer Stratton.*

"We're tracing the name now," Wells offered.

The author had signed the book to Jennifer, adding a memo: *We must do everything within our powers to help ensure that Tyler and his ultra-conservative administration are removed from the White House. If we are to survive, we must act now. Professor Pat Koehler.*

"Theah must have been another woman with her, this Jennifer," Detective Wells said. "Look at the panties. No way could that old woman in the sand have got her fat ass in them."

The panties were a black bikini from Victoria's Secret. Claude knew little of women's sizes, but even his ex-wife Edith, no big woman herself, could hardly have fit in them.

Barnes lifted a brow. "Jennifer Stratton?"

Claude looked at the panties. "Young, mod, and probably dead," he said.

CHAPTER 42

A meat wagon hauled away Patsy Koehler and her head in separate body bags.

"If you can keep your head when all about you are losing theah's . . ." Charleston homicide detective Martin Wells quoted cynically in his Deep South drawl. He watched the meat wagon leaving. "I guess she couldn't."

Claude Thornton assumed authority of the investigation and established a command post in a Charleston Police control van on the seaport parking lot from which he coordinated clues and directed the overall effort. Detective Wells oversaw the police end of the probe, Agent Jonathan Barnes the FBI side of the house. More than thirty lawmen and feds assembled to work the case. In Claude's world of facts, clues, and hard evidence, there was no room for coincidences. Patsy Koehler went to Charleston Seaport for a reason; she didn't end up there by coincidence.

"It makes no sense," Wells reasoned. "It was after dark when she got heah last night. She had no known official contact with anybody. What are ya'll looking for in specific? Theah are some twenty ships or more in port as of this morning, loading and unloading."

"Nothing is to be moved on or off any ship without my say-so," the director said. The Coast Guard had been summoned to make sure the ships complied. "Patsy meeting her Waterloo is connected to one of these ships. How? I'm not sure. It's like what Justice Potter Stewart once said about pornography: It's hard to define, but you know it when you see it. We need bills of lading on every ship in port, along with their nationalities and last ports of call. I also want crew manifests compared to lists of known terrorists."

He couldn't help feeling they were running out of time. President Tyler was always saying it: "We have to be right every time. Terrorists only have to be right one time."

Eighty percent of merchandise sold internationally each year moves by ship. Seventy-five percent of that passed through either the Panama Canal, the Suez Canal, the Strait of Gibraltar, or the Strait of Malacca. These commercial routes along with thousands of miles of deep-sea oil pipeline, hundreds of pumps, and the world's 2,800 ports made for tempting targets difficult if not impossible to fully protect. One of al-Qaeda's most ambitious strategies was to cripple the global economy by attacking ships and sea lanes crucial to world trade. A number of Jihadia had been apprehended attempting to illegally enter the U.S. via international shipping.

But, Claude had to concede, if terrorists were planning something involving shipping, why would they advertise it by leaving a beheaded corpse lying around?

"Dock of the Bay" played on his cell phone.

"Claude, this is Della," his assistant said when he answered. "Have you forgotten you're supposed to testify before the 9/11 commission this afternoon?"

"Oh, shit! Pardon the French."

"That wasn't French. I understood perfectly. I don't think they're going to be too happy if you put it off again."

"Tell them I'm just a dumb Mississippi nigger and I forgot."

"They *will* find you in contempt this time."

"Della, I can't leave here now. Do what you have to do to get me out of it until next week."

"You wouldn't happen to know jail visiting hours, would you, Claude?"

A uniformed policewoman and a police-records clerk stationed at a bank of telephones and computers in the control van sorted through incoming information and passed the more pertinent details on to Director Thornton. By noon, detectives had traced the name *Jennifer Stratton* to Harvard University, where she was a third-year social studies major active in the antiwar movement. BMV listed her driver's license address as an apartment off-campus in Cambridge. Claude recalled that Patsy Koehler had been, at various times, a visiting semester lecturer at Harvard.

"She doesn't live at the apartment anymore," an FBI agent reported from Massachusetts. "Somebody said she moved in with a boyfriend. You know how college kids are—musical beds and all that. Her home of record on her college application was sold three years ago after her father died in an auto crash. We're still trying to run down her mother."

"Keep at it," Claude encouraged.

"She might want her panties back," Barnes said.

Federal law prior to 2001 prohibited the exchange of intelligence among the FBI, CIA, NSA, and other federal agencies. Passage of the Patriot Act changed all that. Claude had kept a running contact with CIA deputy director of ops Thomas Hinds since the raid on Patsy Koehler's Staten Island residence, asking him to process names through his extensive network.

"Dock of the Bay" went off again. A gravelly smoker's voice interrupted by occasional coughing spoke up on the other end.

"Claude, this is Hinds. I might have something for you,

so follow me on this. According to the Brits, Iraq was one of five countries prior to 2003 that negotiated with Niger to purchase uranium yellowcake. In 1999, a senior Iraqi trade delegation headed by Dr. Huda Ammash went to Niger. Ammash is better known as Dr. Death, one of Saddam's scientists working on nuclear weapons research.

"Uranium accounts for nearly 80 percent of Niger's exports, the other 20 percent or so being cowpeas, onions, and goats. I'm doubting Saddam dispatched his Ba'athist big shots all the way to the dusty capital at Niamey because he had a sudden yen for goat and onion stew with a side of peas."

Hinds stopped to cough.

"Thomas, when are you going to quit smoking, again?"

"Keep up with me here, Thornton. In early 2003 before we invaded Iraq, guess who went to Baghdad via the United Arab Emirates and Dubai?"

"Patsy Koehler. We've known that."

"What wasn't known is who she stayed with while she was in Baghdad. Dr. Death herself, Huda Ammash!"

Claude let out a low whistle. "I'll be damned."

"So may we all be. It gets even more interesting. Dr. Death, along with a number of Saddam's other scientists, disappeared when the Iraqi War began. The last clue we had of Dr. Death's whereabouts was in Vladivostok, Russia. We think she's working on an enrichment project with al-Qaeda to build and export WMDs to the United States. One of our implanted agents in Partizansk, Russia, ended up murdered a couple days ago."

"So what are we doing to stop her?"

"We're doing," Hinds said, not elaborating. "It occurred to me that your Patsy Koehler may be—pardon me, might *have been*—the contact for smuggling WMDs into the U.S."

The same thought struck Claude. Russians had been caught slipping across the Arizona border from Mexico. They failed to make it via that route. So, maybe they were trying another. He hung up with Hinds and immediately dialed the harbormaster's office.

"Were any ships off-loaded during the night?" he asked.

"Not since you all found the dead woman. You guys are screwing up business and causing workers to lose pay."

"We're going to have to search every ship."

"Goddamn! What are you trying to do to this port? Shut it down? That'll take weeks. We're already starting to get protests from other countries about their freighters."

"Screw 'em," Claude said.

He scooted back in his chair, readjusted the Glock on his belt to a more comfortable position, and took a long thoughtful sip from coffee long gone cold. He ran a hand across his shaved head and was surprised to feel stubble. He had been constantly on the go for the past three days.

The harbormaster was right. It might literally take weeks, even months, to go through all that cargo. Bills of lading from various freighters and tankers were stacked three inches thick on the desk in front of Claude. They represented tons and tons of cargo—tea and coffee from South America, fruit from the Philippines, electronics from Russia and Japan, cheap knickknacks from China . . . A twenty- or thirty-pound nuke could be concealed almost anywhere and, like the proverbial needle in the haystack, be literally impossible to uncover without more specific information about its suspected location. The ships' nations of registry would be filing protests with the U.S. State Department even before the search began.

No wonder the terrorists who relieved Patsy Koehler of her head felt confident in leaving her body behind. They may even have counted on their merchandise already being off-loaded before she was found.

Claude took out a blank sheet of paper and began itemizing power points in the investigation. It was a habit he had developed years ago. Seeing things organized chronologically helped him understand the Big Picture. He had to find some link, some clue, to narrow the search to perhaps two or three ships, not twenty or thirty.

1. *1999. Dr. Death goes to Niger to obtain uranium for Saddam*
2. *2003. Patsy Koehler visits Dr. Death in Baghdad*
3. *2003. Dr. Death and other Iraqi scientists vanish. She last seen in Vladivostok, suspected of building WMDs for al-Qaeda . . .*

After listing more than a dozen power points, Claude studied them, tapping his front teeth with the end of his pen. So what could he conclude from all this? How about: Nukes were being manufactured in Russia for shipment to the U.S.A.; Patsy Koehler had been the contact to expedite their importing and to establish a safe operating site for potential attackers; protests in New York and Washington to "shut down" these cities were either subterfuge, diversion, or some unknown element of the plot to blow up *something*; billionaire George Coalgate Geis, previously embroiled in similar plots, was financing the whole deal in an effort to make sure Senator Lowell Rutherford Harris won the election; Harris's wealthy wife had already contributed some three millions dollars in the effort . . . ?

Damn! How much more complicated could things get?

So, Claude pondered, what was the common denominator? He went back over his list, jotting down *Vladivostok, Koehler, Dr. Death . . .*

Vladivostok! He shuffled through the bills of lading, having recalled one in particular. There it was. The freighter *Cristi*, a 1,250-ton cargo vessel registered in Saudi Arabia, had steamed out of the Russian port of Vladivostok three weeks ago.

Claude sprang to his feet. "Give Wells and Barnes a ring. They're around somewhere," he called back over his shoulder to his policewoman assistant. "Tell them to meet me at the *Cristi*—and get an EOD team on the way!"

Were nukes already in port?

CHAPTER 43

Russian Coast

Lina's tantrum was a terrifying thing to witness, all the more alarming if one happened to be its target. It was like the display of a wild gorilla who rampages about screeching and uprooting things to work himself into a frenzy before he actually attacks. Lina pounded the forest floor all around Cassidy with the ugly stick, thumping it hard and rapidly while she hopped up and down on her stubby legs and shrieked out her rage and fear.

Cassidy rolled around back and forth on the ground attempting to avoid the onslaught, shielding his head and face with his arms. She thumped him heartily several times on the back and arms before he managed to grab the end of the stick. He jerked it and pulled her down on top of him. He crushed her body to his and clamped a hand over her mouth to hush her damnable bellowing. She continued struggling for another minute, thrashing his legs soundly with staccato kicks that sent jolts of raw pain all the way up his spine. He had to bite his lip to keep from crying out.

Finally she started to run down. She went limp. In a moment Cassidy felt her body shuddering as she wept silently into his hand. He pushed her away a little so he could see her face; he kept his palm over her mouth. Her eyes bulged out of their caves. Tears streamed down her cheeks and over his hand. She looked as though she had lost him.

"Shhh! Shhh! Hush!" he warned, his own heart beating wildly. Surely the riflemen at the schoolhouse must have heard the commotion, even though they were some distance away.

In spite of the circumstances, Cassidy was touched by the effort it must have required for her to overcome her aversion to this place and follow him. From the looks of it, she might have good reason to shun the old schoolhouse after all. Ordinary farmers didn't run around the countryside armed with assault rifles. The two gunmen he saw smoking cigarettes posed far more potential threat than Lina and her ugly stick. Better to be the prisoner of a mad Smurf than corralled by hard cases with rifles.

He removed his hand tentatively from her mouth, ready to grab her again if her hysteria resumed. She cuddled close, moved even closer, as though for protection against some evil.

"Mine. Cass mine," she whimpered, raining sloppy smooches into his open hand.

"Right."

He grabbed her hand and pulled her after him as he crawled to a spot where he parted bushes and took another look at the schoolhouse and its sentries. He half-expected to find them charging him with their rifles, at which point his ass was grass and they were Big Boy lawn mowers. Lina shook her head in horror and refused to look. She trembled all over.

The two men had clearly heard the fuss in the woods but appeared unable to determine its source. One wearing baggy trousers and an even baggier shirt belted at the waist vaulted onto the stone wall and stood on tiptoes to scan the woods. He pointed the rifle and held an animated conversation with his partner. Maybe they thought they were hearing a wild animal—a tiger perhaps?

Who were they and why was Lina so afraid of them? Russian mafia? Criminals? Terrorists? They were standing guard over the abandoned schoolhouse for some reason. The Partizanskaya River couldn't be far from there. Downstream lay the sea, upstream the space capsule, target of Cold Dawn.

A third man joined the other two. He wore some kind of gaucho-looking hat, a short leather jacket, a holstered handgun, and was obviously in charge. He spread his arms in annoyance and gestured toward the forest. There was going to be a search.

"I don't know about you, ole girl," Cassidy whispered, "but I'd just as soon be somewhere watching *Friends* when they get here."

She couldn't have agreed more. She helped him up, his bad leg still tethered to the back of his belt, and inserted herself underneath his arm to take the place of the broom. She retrieved it along with her ugly stick as they hurriedly vacated the premises. A few large drops of rain pelted the trees, but it was not going to rain hard enough soon enough to wipe out their tracks. There wasn't enough time for Cassidy to cover them either. He had to hope these guys somehow overlooked their trail. Like they were stupid, perhaps, or blind.

They made good time downhill, Cassidy hanging on to the Smurf and hopping along on one leg, panting and sweating with exertion and fatigue. It had been a busy morning—and the day wasn't over yet.

Chickens in the clearing had their tail feathers splayed against the quickening breeze and the coming rain. Lina rushed him into the house, but he balked at being put back to bed and locked up. He pointed at one of the kitchen chairs and indicated he wanted it brought to the front window so he could sit and keep watch for any pursuit. He leaned against the wall with one hand and freed his bad leg, easing it to the floor, while she obediently brought the chair. He sat in it and looked out the window. Lina encircled him with her arms from behind and, still trembling, peered out anxiously over his head.

Cassidy thought their relationship may have reached and passed some kind of milestone within the past short while. The power structure was rapidly changing, she becoming submissive to some extent while he moved into dominance. That opened up new possibilities. He took her hand, pulled her around to face him, and demanded through sign language that she produce his Motorola and weapons.

Lina proved unready to go that far. She dug in stubbornly, shaking her head. She retained the upper hand, for all his new-found independence, and knew it.

"Damn it!" he exploded. "Don't you understand, Lina? I'm betting we're about to have company, and these guys don't have broken legs. What do you expect me to fight them with—the ugly stick?"

She teared up but held on nonetheless.

If he could only communicate with her, get some answers to his questions, explain to her what they confronted. This was worse than trying to talk to a very small child, what with the language barrier. In his desperation, he recalled reading once about KoKo the talking gorilla who learned to correspond using pictures and illustrations. His eyes scanned the room, settling on the pile of papers and other debris on the kitchen table.

"Pencil?" He indicated he wanted to write. She understood and obediently brought him a stub of lead pencil and what resembled the Russian version of a Big Chief school tablet. She watched curiously as he sketched a crude outline of the schoolhouse with the rock wall around it. He pointed out the window toward the ridgeline and raised his brows and hands in a question.

"Lina, what is going on up there?"

She caught her breath sharply and wouldn't look anymore. "Cass *mine*."

"Cass is going to be mush if we don't do something," he shot back. He squinted across the clearing, past the wind-excited chickens and the goats. The men couldn't be far behind.

"Lina? Look. Can you draw? Here. Take the pencil and paper."

The pencil turned over and over in her shaking hand while she stared at it.

"Lina, draw why you are afraid of the school."

Of course she didn't understand. Cassidy pointed at the pencil and paper. He took her hand with the pencil in it and forced it against the tablet, even starting to sketch with her.

Finally she caught on to what he intended. Bolstering her courage, she drew the schoolhouse, copying off Cassidy's example. Even that much daring brought tears to her eyes. She kept looking out the window as though expecting the world to end.

Exasperated, Cassidy urged her to continue. "More. More."

She drew in three stick figures with guns, then immediately drew in three more. Seemed like good enough reason to be afraid.

"Good girl, Lina." He smiled his approval, encouraging her. "Can you show me what they're doing there? More."

He wasn't sure what he expected from her, other than

more. Perhaps some clue, some revelation to explain the presence of armed guards and their purpose. If he was right, Lina and he were going to have visitors very soon. He had to get her to understand the danger and persuade her through their rudimentary art conversation that she had to return his rifle.

"Lina. More."

She put trees around the school. She drew in her farm and a stick figure with a dress and one in a wheelbarrow. She giggled and nodded. She filled in what he thought to be the ocean on the right and a river on the other side of the schoolhouse emptying into the sea. A crude map of sorts. He took the pencil and added a rifle to the figure in the wheelbarrow, pointing it in the direction of the six men she contributed earlier. She began to cry again.

"Lina. I have to have a weapon."

Her broad face hardened. Cassidy couldn't seem to make her understand that they were not safe merely because they ran home and slammed the door. The Big Bad Wolf was coming to huff and puff . . . And, boy, was he pissed off.

Lina had gotten into her art once she got started. She traced in the sky above the schoolhouse what appeared to be some kind of flying contraption attached to a parachute. It took Cassidy a moment to comprehend. It came to him with a jolt.

"Spacemen?" he asked, making flying maneuvers with his hands and creating a parachute with his palm over his descending fist.

She nodded eagerly. She took the pencil again and made three more figures, these with their hands conspicuously tied behind their backs and surrounded by the six with rifles.

My God! It was the missing space capsule, the *Soyuz*. It must have dropped to earth and its passengers taken prisoner by the men at the schoolhouse. No wonder Lina was afraid.

Lina glanced up through the window and her eyes flattened. Blood drained from her face. Time for further conversation had run out. Two riflemen stepped cautiously out of the forest on the other side of the clearing, weapons at the ready, sending the chickens and goats into a panic.

CHAPTER 44

Washington, D.C.

General Kragle pulled on a pair of tan Dockers, a long-sleeved shirt of a blue that Rita used to say brought out the gray in his eyes, and a pair of soft-soled hiking boots. Vanda had offered to pick him up in her car for their break-fast date, but he thought the walk would be good for him.

It was a clear, cool morning and leaves were just begin-ning to change on the Mall. Twice on his way he thought about standing her up and returning to the hotel. He had enough concerns of his own without taking on hers. All three sons in peril, one MIA in Russia; his father suffering from Alzheimer's; the pending presidential election, in which it seemed to him the entire nation was going down the tubes . . . But Vanda had sounded so desperate over the phone and had gone to such lengths to arrange a "chance" meeting with him. He *was* curious.

She was waiting for him at a small walk-in café two blocks from the Capitol and about a mile from the Wash-ingtonian Hotel. As the name implied, the Pig Out catered to a nearby working-class neighborhood and was jammed with big men in gray company uniforms or jeans and con-struction boots, along with busty women likewise in jeans and various service uniforms. Vanda already had a table for them at the front window. She accepted his proffered hand in both her small cool ones.

"I wasn't sure if you were coming until I saw you outside," she said.

He didn't tell her that he almost *hadn't* come.

She had done something different with her hair, pulled it back and curled it under in a French twist held in place by a ruby-studded comb. She wore comfortable slacks, a mauve form-fitting blouse with a wide collar, and, like him, sensible walking shoes. The General took in all this, along with the large brown eyes and the hesitant smile that reminded him again of Rita.

She explained her choice of restaurants, saying a little teasingly, "I took you for an eggs and steak and hominy grits sort of man."

"They have grits! In Washington?"

"You may have to substitute hash browns."

"It sounded too good to be true."

The waitress promptly approached. Bleached big hair, too much makeup, popping her gum and thrusting out one hip. Just the type for a place that would call itself Pig Out.

"What can I get you folks, honey?"

Darren and Vanda looked at each other and had a hard time suppressing laughter. Darren realized he hadn't laughed in weeks.

"Do you have grits?" he asked.

"Tell me what a grit is, sugar, and I'll see if I can rustle up one."

"I'll have hash browns, two eggs over, sausage, biscuits and gravy, black coffee." He found himself unexpectedly famished.

Vanda had toast and a poached egg. She made an effort to keep things upbeat, but her apprehensions kept sneaking out in little ways—the trembling of a hand, a sudden dulling of the eyes. She stopped him, however, when he broached the purpose of their meeting before breakfast was over.

"The least I can do is offer you a good meal first," she protested. "Men are so much more accommodating on a full stomach."

Finally, Darren pushed back his plate, took a second cup of coffee, and looked at her across the table. She averted her eyes, sobering, and gazed out the window toward the dome of the Capitol Building that stuck up over the city. She didn't hesitate in taking his hand. He gently removed it.

"Your daughter?" he prompted. "You said she was in trouble . . . With terrorists? Why did you call me instead of going to the police?"

"I *did* call the police."

Darren sipped coffee, holding the cup with both hands to prevent her reaching for them. Having his hand held evoked painful memories of Rita.

"What did the police say?"

She smiled pensively. "The desk sergeant told me there were one hundred thousand demonstrators in Washington, D.C., this week, most of them, he said, whacked-out students from left-wing colleges. He said, 'Lady, do you have any idea how many calls we're getting from concerned parents asking about kids coming here to protest the war?'"

"What makes you think I can help with your daughter . . . ?"

Her dark eyes penetrated his. "Jennifer was like our other daughter Patricia until she went away to Harvard," she explained. "She was never particularly . . . *political*. She began changing after she got into college. Darren, it frightened me to see my sweet little girl transforming into this . . . this strident, self-righteous stranger talking about how it is her personal responsibility to join in a revolution against the oppressive majority to change racist, capitalist America . . ."

"I get the picture," Darren interjected, not meaning to sound overly harsh.

Vanda tore a napkin in half and then began ripping the halves into shreds.

"Jennifer got caught up in every movement that came along—antiwar, animal rights, the environment, gay rights . . . Last year she went with World RSPONSE to pressure the INS to place water stations in the desert for illegal immigrants sneaking across the Rio Grande. I saw her on TV at a march that started cheering and celebrating this year when the PA system announced Ronald Reagan's death. Now, it's the election. To her, President Tyler is the embodiment of all that's evil in the world and all that's wrong with America."

She made a pyramid of the shredded napkin, concentrating, then looked up pleadingly into Darren's eyes. "This is what my daughter has become—but, Darren, she's still my daughter."

The General let her finish her pyramid. She crushed it flat with an open hand.

"Darren, I apologize with all my heart for deceiving you. Everything else I told you is true. My husband did die in a car crash, my mother really is a resident at Pleasant Valley. The police wouldn't help me. I read about you in the news when you busted up the Committed organization, and saw you on TV talking about terrorism. When I learned your father was also a resident at Pleasant Valley, I contrived to meet you that morning in the lounge. I . . . I didn't know anyone else to turn to . . . Darren, will you help me find Jennifer?"

"This is a big city. Do you have any idea where she is or why you think she's involved with terrorists?"

"I thought at first she was in New York with BUCKUS. She told me she was going to stay with a Harvard professor active in trying to shut down the Federalist Convention by causing huge disruptions to scare the delegates. Then she called me two days ago and said she was in D.C. She sounded . . . terrified. She said she found out something she wasn't supposed to know. Something about terrorism."

"Did she say what?"

"She whispered a telephone number. I heard somebody in the background. Then she hung up. That was the last I've heard from her. I've tried to call back, but whoever answers hangs up whenever I ask for Jennifer. The number is unlisted. Darren, I . . . I . . ."

Tears filled her brown eyes and rolled down her cheeks. The General sighed deeply and dropped his chin on his chest. One of the first things Rita said to him when they met nearly forty years ago was how the Kragles were knights in armor always prepared to mount a steed in defense of God, country, Mom, apple pie, and damsels in distress. He knew he shouldn't have had breakfast with Vanda. He should have bundled up his shit-blahs and hauled them back to Florida with him. But the way Vanda looked at him, her eyes both burdened and trusting . . .

He stood up from the table. "Do you still have the phone number? It's a place to start."

CHAPTER 45

Partizanskaya River Valley

An air of contained excitement infected the Cold Dawn camp in the wan light of a watery dawn. The overcast had squeezed out most of its precipitation overnight, leaving only a thin miserable drizzle. Detachment 3A would be moving out shortly for the assault on the terrorist nuclear plant.

With the coming of daylight, Brandon saw that the previous night's bivouac selected in the blind had been a good choice—within a conifer thicket so dense a snake would have detoured it. It was as secure a site as the detachment was likely to find in those mountains.

The detachment broke camp, answered calls of nature, checked individual weapons and equipment, stuffed rucks, and prepared for movement to the target. Mad Dog, tinkering with antennas and satellite probes, radioed in the morning SITREP and processed digital photographs Ice and Diverse snapped of the nuclear enrichment plant, which he then delivered to Major Kragle for his use in developing a plan for mission briefing. Gloomy Davis led the captured horse nearly fifty yards from camp before he located a small grassy clearing where he tethered the animal to feed. Doc Red prescribed Sudafed for a runny nose Perverse Sanchez contracted overnight in the rain, then commandeered some ponchos to build a large shelter for the team's briefing.

Katya was still snoozing in Brandon's sleeping bag. Brandon went to great pains to make sure everyone knew he had not spent the night with her.

"Fu-uck," was Mad Dog's assessment. "What a waste."

Things about Katya still bothered Brandon, never mind that she had saved his life. So far, she was unable to come up with a good explanation for why the Cossack shouted "*Zafina!*" with his last dying breath, other than to say, "Perhaps it is saying his wife's name." But whatever she was up to, *if* she was up to something, she couldn't do anything as long as the detachment kept tabs on her.

Brandon and Top Sculdiron gathered with Ice Man and Diverse Dade under Doc Red's big shelter to thoroughly debrief them on their patrol and begin a mission plan. Brandon tossed his full ruck on the pine needles underneath the stretched ponchos and sat on it. Ice Man dropped his on the ground and likewise took a seat, nursing a canteen cup full of Ranger coffee. He offered the cup to Brandon, who blew on the rising steam from its surface before sucking on it. Ice Man watched, his jaw stubbled with dark beard growth and the scars on the left side of his face standing out like gorged leeches.

"Good coffee," Brandon said.

"Ground it myself this morning." Which was probably true. Ice's gourmet tastes had never allowed him to get used to common army coffee.

Top Sculdiron riffled through the digital target photos; the recons had shot more than fifty to cover every aspect of the target. Diverse started to go check on his demolitions bag, which he had left in Gloomy's care while he was gone, but saw that the others were ready to begin and sat down on his ruck instead. Brandon passed the hot canteen cup to him. He looked at it with a critical eye, he being the detachment's other gourmet.

"It isn't army coffee," Brandon assured him.

The Zulu warrior looked at Ice. "Did you prepare it, Sergeant Thompson?"

"Exquisitely to your refined tastes, Sergeant Dade, my young African friend."

Diverse tasted it and nodded approval. "There's no reason civilization must be forsaken by civilized men," he said.

The debriefing began, from which the four men would hammer a plan to deliver to the rest of the detachment for discussion and modification. Although a detachment's leadership held dictatorial control in the field, a wise commander considered the advice and input of his subordinates, who were in many instances as experienced as he.

Gentle rain pattered on the stretched poncho canvas.

"We rendezvous with the submarine at 0500 hours, twenty-two hours from now," Brandon said. "That means we have to blow the target tonight if we hope to reach the coast to be exfil'd. Sergeant Dade, do we have the demo for it?"

"It's a big plant and deep underground," Diverse replied. "We could have used the rest of the demo—"

He broke off. His amber eyes met Brandon's. It was an unwritten rule that no one spoke of casualties suffered during an operation until after the mission was over.

"We don't have the rest of the demo, Sergeant."

"It can be done with what we have," Diverse concluded. Ice Man nodded agreement.

Utilizing photos, Diverse and Ice Man described the target, its surrounding terrain, and activities they had observed. Diverse did most of the talking while Ice Man, taciturn as usual, occasionally inserted a salient point. The four men drew their rucks into a tight circle, knees touching, and passed the photos around.

There were no roads leading to or away from the plant in the cave. Roads would have allowed satellite spies in the sky to detect new construction. About twenty people, among them Huda Ammash and her scientists, whom CENTCOM had identified as running the project, worked in the cave, commuting via the river using powerboats and small, flat-bottomed barges. The Sea of Okhotsk was some two hours downriver with the current.

Brandon, thinking of Murphy's Law, asked lots of questions. Where were the cavalry? Exterior sentry posts? What time did the scientists and workers arrive and leave? Buildings or construction in the area? Was there a way to cross the river other than by boat?

Obviously, the detachment's presence in the area was known; that called for extra caution. Brandon still thought Katya might be responsible for having alerted the terrorists.

A footbridge spanned a narrows in the river about fifty yards downriver of the cave entrance. Horseman, likely part of the mafia guard, were dispersed to either river bank at the bridge to guard all land approaches. There was an additional sentry post on the cliff above the cave and guards stationed inside the cave. The recons had seen no other construction in the area.

"It appears," said Diverse, "that the workers come up-river before dawn and don't leave again until after night-fall. They don't come all at once. We watched them leaving in ones or twos. To keep our spy planes from growing suspicious, I suppose."

The cave mouth, wide enough and tall enough to ac-commodate an eighteen-wheeler were it possible for a semi to float up to it, opened directly to the river itself and provided the only apparent entrance and egress. Over the eons the flow of the stream had cut out the bottom of the cliff to form a rock overhang where any number of boats could be tied off at the cave mouth in concealment against observation from above.

Brandon brought up the mine shaft. "Go through it step by step. Get us into the plant and out again."

"Cage may have had a better plan," Ice Man said.

Brandon nodded agreement. "But Cage is dead."

Ice glanced toward the hooch where Katya slept on. "I wonder how he died."

"We found the old mine shaft quite by accident," Diverse said. He displayed the series of photos showing the mouth of the mine overgrown with foliage and almost obliterated by rock slides. The river ran by in front of it, about thirty meters away. "It hasn't been used in a long time. It's some two hundred meters downriver from the cave. When the horses came, Ice and I ducked into the bushes to hide. We could just barely squeeze through what we thought was the opening to an animal den. There might have been a bear in there, but it was better than fighting all those Genghis Khan types. The mine shaft was on the other side. I doubt if anybody knows about it."

Exploring, using flashlights, the two Deltas crept deeper into the shaft as it elbowed in the direction of the cave. Soon, they heard water running and came to a dead end where an underground stream gushed from the roof of the shaft in a kind of waterfall and collected in a large black pool.

"We heard machinery on the other side of the dead end," Ice Man added.

Investigating, they stripped, eased into the pool and waded and swam toward the sound of machinery. The ceiling dropped into the pool, making it necessary to swim underwater in order to proceed. They took turns diving. After several attempts, during which they located rises in the ceiling that contained pockets of air, they surfaced again *inside* the main cave. The pool there lay in semishadow while the rest of the cavern was brightly lighted with electricity manufactured by river turbines.

They saw reactors and electrical generating equipment and all sorts of other machinery, near which a number of people in white or gray smocks toiled. Two armed sentries stood by the tethered boats at the cave's mouth.

"It reminded me of Osama bin Laden's cave in the Tora Bora when we ran the Iron Weed operation in Afghanistan," Ice Man said.

"I'll need ten minutes to set a charge to drop that mountain down inside the cave on top of the plant," Diverse calculated. "We should be out of there and halfway down to the sea when the explosives go off. They won't know what hit them."

Sounded good enough. They quickly formulated a mission ops order and contingencies using the KISS principle—Keep It Simple, Stupid. The detachment moving as a body would make its way to the mine shaft during the day and establish a mission ORP (Operational Rally Point). The assault team would enter the cave via the shaft to plant explosives while security teams positioned themselves to take out the cliff sentry post and keep the cavalry busy in the event Murphy stuck his nose in.

"We'll time the detonation to go off just before 1800 hours while the crews are still inside," Brandon directed. Central Command wanted Dr. Death and the other terrorist scientists destroyed with the underground plant. Otherwise, they moved somewhere else and started all over again. "By then it'll be dark enough that we can get the rubber rafts in the water and hang on for the ride to the coast. Our one concern is how long it'll take them to start a reaction force up the river when hell breaks loose."

"The fat lady will already have sung by then," Ice Man said.

His eyes narrowed. Brandon followed his gaze and saw Katya awake and sleepily wandering around the camp near where Gloomy and Brandon had slept.

"What about her?" he asked, the tone of his voice tight and disapproving.

"What do you suggest?"

"Tie her up and leave her."

"And if she isn't found?"

Ice Man shrugged indifferently.

Brandon ended the discussion. "We'll take her with us and turn her loose with the rubber boats when we board the sub."

Top Sculdiron corralled team members for mission briefing and last-minute adjustments to the ops plan. Mad Dog Carson trotted up with message traffic from CENT-COM, including a pair of grainy photos.

"Major, you'd better take a gander at these," he rumbled. "That bitch ain't who she says she is. Surprise, surprise."

The first photo was the one of Katya Brandon sent to CENTCOM for identification. The other showed Katya standing between an older woman in a burqa-like robe and an Arab man in his thirties. The background looked Arab. A succinct message accompanied the pictures: *Ref photo of female you request ID. ID her as Zafina Ammash. Ref photo from Baghdad. Other subjects her mother Huda "Dr. Death" Ammash, her brother Hakkim.*

Brandon looked up, his face grim. "Where is she?"

"Fu-uck!" Mad Dog exclaimed. "She was standing there when I downloaded the photos. Maybe she saw them."

"I saw the li'l darling going off in the woods," Doc Red volunteered.

"Go get her."

Perverse batted his eyes. "Chew think she might be peeing?"

"I do not care what she is doing," Top Sculdiron thundered. "Get her!"

Men rushed in the direction Doc Red pointed out. Barely had they cleared the shelter than the clatter of a horse's hooves on rocky ground caught their attention. An opening in the timber disclosed a section of hillside and a horse and rider scrambling up it in a series of lunging jumps. Katya and the bay were gone up and over the hill, heading in the direction of the cave, before Gloomy Davis had time to uncase Mr. Blunderbuss and zero in on her.

Barely had the ramifications of Katya's escape settled over the camp than Diverse Dade gave a howl. Always protective of his demolitions, he recalled seeing her last near the area of his demo bag. Running to check, he discovered his loss.

"She's stolen the detonators!"

All the explosives in the world were useless without a means of setting them off.

"That cunt wasn't peeing," Mad Dog scorned. "She was *pissing*—on all of us."

CHAPTER 46

Russian Coast

Lina panicked when the two goons emerged from the woods. Fear and childishness were not a good combination. Her off-kilter eyes bulged, her mouth hung open like a deflated balloon. She hopped around the room on coiled, uncontrollable springs, wringing her hands and whimpering pitifully. She couldn't seem to make up her mind what to do. Twice she darted to the back door and opened it. She ran back to Cassidy, her hands going like fans. She peeped out the window, screamed underneath her breath, and cut a fiery path out the back door, leaving it standing open.

Cassidy expected he had seen the last of her, that she had left him with his broken leg at the mercy of the intruders. He had no way to defend himself. He couldn't even stand on his own two feet. But he was not going to roll over and give up like a beaten-down cur. He lunged out of the chair and dragged himself on his belly toward the back door as fast as he could, his gut knotting against the pain.

He had almost reached it when, to his surprise, Lina returned, popping up in the door like a Jack out of its box. Under slower, more contemplative circumstances, her unwillingness to desert him in spite of her terror might have been touching. As it was, there was no time to think of anything except escaping.

"Mine! Cass mine!"

"Baby, just keep thinking that way."

Wind from the freshening storm gusted through the open back doorway, fluttering the pages of the Big Chief tablet discarded on the floor by the window. The invaders would know by the sketches in it that the harmless retard was not alone and that someone else may have discovered the secret of the missing spacemen. Cassidy thought of retrieving it, but Lina's blubbering and mewling, the way her terrified eyes fixated on the front door in anticipation of flame and brimstone erupting through it, told him her patience was limited, no matter how she might value him. She had come back for him. Wasn't that enough?

She helped him into the wheelbarrow parked outside the back door. He sprawled in the bucket, facing the rear and Lina at the handles. She sprinted across the backyard with him. Goats bleated in alarm. A startled hen flew past, sailing with the wind and cackling.

Good thing she possessed twice the strength of a normal person her size. Running on her short legs, gasping and bawling, she trundled him across the muddy clearing and into the shadows of the forest. Cassidy noticed his weight on the single wheel cut an easy-to-follow furrow in the soft ground. It shouldn't take their pursuers long to get the picture once they determined the house was empty.

Wet branches whipped and slashed at them in the wind. Light rain in the upper foliage went *tickety-tick* against leaves, not yet penetrating. Lightning skittered in terrible waves of electricity from one side of the heavens to the other, making awful shadows, the most hideous that of the gnomish little woman pushing the wheelbarrow with dog-like devotion. Thunder trembled the forest in some eerie replay of an old late-night horror movie. Cassidy felt a bit like the Frankenstein monster being chased by villagers bearing torches.

Strong as Lina was, as swiftly as she pushed the wheelbarrow, Cassidy soon realized she was no match for men unencumbered with a handicap like him. She was slowing now as she lost breath and strength. Cassidy figured they had five minutes at most to think of something. It would have been better for her if she had left him behind. He wasn't being fair in thinking only of his own skin.

"Lina!" He had to repeat her name before her wild eyes focused. He pantomimed his message. "Lina, you can get away if you leave me."

Finally she understood and vigorously shook her head negative. She refused to abandon him.

"You're a trooper, Lina. Crazy, but so what. You're going to die with me, unless—"

He threw his palm toward her face. "Lina! *Stop!*"

Startled, she dropped the wheelbarrow onto its stand and stared at him like *he* was the one who was crazy.

"My rifle. *Rifle!* Understand?" He pretended to aim and fire a weapon and slapped his chest to show ownership. "Bang! Bang! Lina, you have got to understand."

It had taken her only a few minutes that morning to leave the house and bring back his clothing. That meant the rest of his gear, hopefully, couldn't be far away. Her face clouded. Cassidy almost heard her thinking. She was afraid he might escape if she returned his equipment.

"Lina! It's our only chance."

She looked at him, she looked back toward the house as though also expecting villagers with torches. They were wasting time with this stupid argument.

"Lina! Hurry!"

She jumped when they heard voices calling out to each other at the edge of the woods behind them. That seemed to make up Lina's mind for her. Rejuvenated by her brief rest, urged on by pursuit, she grabbed the handlebars again and took off at a right angle to their previous route. Cassidy couldn't be certain if that meant she was acquiescing to his demands or not. She was so damned stubborn.

Voices gained on them, the men baying out to each other like hounds on a hot game trail. Rain still held off except for sprinkling against treetops. Lightning flashed frightening shadows through the forest. Lina sobbed with exertion and heartfelt terror. Cassidy could do little except lie in the wheelbarrow and chant encouragement.

Less than three days before, he was young and virile, easily the match for any man on earth in his combat training and physical prowess, reduced now to dependency upon a Smurf with a wheelbarrow. How quickly circumstances changed.

Lina paused and looked back. The hounds were coming. Fast. That seemed to be her final incentive to meet Cassidy's demands. She burst out of the forest where the sprinkling rain struck his face. He recognized the back of her ramshackle chicken house/barn where they had gathered eggs that morning. The stone house stood on the other side of the clearing, its back door ajar and no one in sight. They had gone in a big half circle through the woods. Cassidy hoped this meant what he thought it meant. Had his gear been in the barn all along?

She parked the wheelbarrow and scurried around the side of the barn to the door. He heard her inside. He heard brush breaking nearby, a shout.

Lina reappeared running, carrying his M4 carbine. A glance told him the magazine remained locked in the feed. Locked and loaded. He reached for it.

"Throw it to me, Lina! Quick!"

Gunmen charged out of the trees not twenty meters

away. They took in the scene at a glance—the big man in the wheelbarrow, his leg splinted, reaching toward the retarded girl running at him with a weapon in her hands. Lightning bared the wolfish expressions on their faces.

Lina hurled the carbine. It tumbled through the air, seemingly in slow motion while Cassidy desperately reached to catch it. Rifle fire ripped its own thunder against the approaching storm.

CHAPTER 47

Partizanskaya River Valley

Katya Sokolov, Russian. More correctly known as Zafina Ammash, Iraqi, daughter of Saddam Hussein's notorious Dr. Death. True believer. *Allahu Akbar* and all that. Willing, even eager, to unleash the energy of the universe upon innocent peoples. Everything about her had been an act, down to her saving Brandon's life. She shot the Cossack rider because he was about to expose her, no other reason. She likely participated in whatever happened to Cage.

One cold-hearted bitch. All that make-believe anguish over having killed the rider. The *Playboy* routine. A beautiful woman with a clever cover story dispatched to facilitate the *Soyuz* mission while her real purpose was to divert, delay, and sabotage any overture toward the nuclear plant. It occurred to Brandon that the plant may already be manufacturing nukes, that Zafina's job was to buy time for terrorists to complete their own goals and perhaps move whatever WMDs they may have already produced before they closed down the plant. In another seventy-two hours, Brandon was willing to bet, there would be nothing left of the plant.

Without explosives, or at least without the means to detonate them, Cold Dawn was dead in its tracks. Mission accomplished for the loyal daughter of Dr. Death. She was surely on the way now to warn her mother to get the lead out. There was no way to stop her. A man afoot, even a long-distance runner like the Zulu, was no match for someone on horseback.

Brandon expressed a rare moment of rage and self-recrimination. He let his guard down—and now, because of it, he had failed his second mission. He was getting soft. Notwithstanding Summer's pregnancy, maybe it *was* time for him to get out of the business. He had never failed before.

"Boss, there was nothing we could have done," Gloomy Davis offered, always ready to protect Brandon against threats from any source. "You can't live with 'em, and you can't shoot 'em."

Brandon couldn't have shot her, but he could have kept her tied to a tree.

"How bad is it, Diverse?" he asked.

The Zulu sorted through what was left in his demo satchel. He looked up, his fierce amber eyes startling against the deep blue-black of his lean face.

"The detonators, hell box, and time fuse are gone," he reported. "She left the roll of primadet. She probably didn't understand what it was."

Primadet was a fast fuse that burned at an explosive rate of *five miles per second*. That meant ignition at one end and detonation at the other end attached to demolitions occurred almost simultaneously, an extremely hazardous method of initiating a firing train.

"I might be able to ignite the primadet with a gunshot," Diverse offered.

"But chew will go up with it!" Perverse objected, horrified. "Chew do not have enough primadet."

Strained silence. The hiss of drizzle against conifers. All were thinking the same thing: Within the confines of the cave, especially if secondary explosions occurred, depending upon how far along Dr. Death had advanced in building nuclear WMDs, ignition might well kick off a mushroom cloud that would blow up the entire mountain and everything around it within a radius of several miles. Time-delay fuse would have allowed the detachment leeway to escape the blast area; primadet in limited supply did not. Sober faces in the rain revealed all too well how the detachment understood the risk.

"What are the chances that you can drop the mountain in on the cave without setting off nuclear materials inside?" Brandon asked Diverse.

Diverse thought about it out loud. "If I drilled and set the charges inside the cave walls, tamp the energy *into* the walls instead of toward the contents . . . Maybe . . . I'd say eighty-twenty . . ."

"Eighty being . . . ?"

"Eighty being the chance that we can do it. I've made a lot of successful four-to-one bets at the race track."

"How many times have you lost a bet?" Mad Dog wanted to know.

"I'm not a horse," Diverse pointed out. "I think you might go as high as eight-to-one on me."

Every CT mission carried with it certain odds that at least some members of a deployed detachment would not return alive. That was why survivor records were always kept up to date at Wally World.

Brandon lifted his eyes toward the treetops, considering options without having to look at the faces of the men his decision impacted. He had to think of the Big Picture, weigh the risk of a few lives against the many.

"We've got two things going for us, the way I see it," he said at last. "One is the mine shaft that they apparently don't know about. They'll be guarding the cave in force, never suspecting we can get in another way. The second thing is she'll think she's sabotaged the mission. They may not expect us to keep coming."

He paused.

"None of us may live through it," he continued. Delta operators could stand the truth. "I won't order you to go on what may be a suicide mission, but I want to remind you that millions of innocent lives back home may hang in the balance of what we decide now. If there are WMDs inside that cave—and we're told there are—they must be destroyed."

He scraped a line across the ground with his boot and stepped over it to the other side.

"Travis pulled this at the Alamo," Diverse said. "You'll need a demo."

He joined Brandon, followed without comment by Ice Man, Top Sculdiron, and Gloomy Davis, Mr. Blunderbuss in hand.

"Fu-uck," Mad Dog rumbled, looking at Diverse and joining the movement. "I'll go eight-to-one on the Black Stallion."

"Chew are all *loco en la cabeza*," Perverse exclaimed, then shrugged as he and Doc Red made the vote unanimous.

A surge of emotion swept over Brandon, although he was quick not to let it show in his expression. Where did America get such men? He had asked the question many times and it always left him dumbfounded. How could a society that seemed narcistic and self-serving produce such selfless acts of raw courage? The irony was that few Americans would ever know about it.

"Chew know Arachna Phoebe is going to miss you, Mad Dog," Perverse said.

Dog gave the Mexican-American a mellow look. "Chew know what, spic? Fuck her. I don't give a flying rat's ass."

CHAPTER 48

Russian Coast

For an instant as Cassidy launched himself out of the wheelbarrow, reaching, he thought he had missed the carbine Lina hurled through the air at him. It bounced off his forward hand, spinning through the air in seeming slow motion, his horrified eyes following it. He snatched at it with his other hand, using both legs to propel himself, ignoring the pain and grating of bone against bone.

The leg collapsed underneath him. As he went down in the mud, the fingers of his left hand wrapped around the rifle barrel. He combat-rolled on the ground to provide an elusive target. The other hand found the pistol grip, thumb automatically clicking the lever off SAFE. The carbine became an extension of his personality and his physical being, a result of the inordinate amount of time Delta soldiers spent on the firing range and in the House of Horrors at Fort Bragg's Delta Compound.

Lina unintentionally bought him precious seconds by capturing the assailants' attention. She had the weapon initially, so they fired at her just as she threw it, dismissing the cripple in the wheelbarrow as the lesser threat. Their rifles shattered the air simultaneously. From his peripheral vision, Cassidy saw Lina go down.

"Bastards!"

Cassidy was already returning as good as he took, *better* than he took, when the muzzle splashes turned on him and bullets chewed geysers in the earth around his head. Prone in the mud, point shooting by instinct, he tapped three quick rounds into the lead attacker. The guy shrieked in pain and disbelief, cut short by the last of the 5.56 slugs that ripped through center of mass and kicked him onto his back. His weapon went flying from his reach.

The second bruiser made the amateur's mistake of freezing in shock when he saw his comrade tumble. It was his last mistake in this lifetime. Cassidy's second *Bang-Bang-Bang* series dropped him in his tracks. There was no need for finish-off shots. A Delta trooper seldom missed the heart when he fired a target in CQB, close quarter battle.

One of the bodies kicked its foot spasmodically as its nerves died and its life force drained rapidly away. The other issued ghastly death rattles. Then both lay in the utter stillness of dead men. Rain fell a little harder and a magnificent display of lightning sanctioned Cassidy's victory.

Lina lay entirely motionless a few feet away at the corner of the chicken house, her face down and hidden from Cassidy's sight by her folded arm. Rain started to mold her faded old house dress against her thick body and stubby legs. One bare calloused foot rested across her other thigh. It was caked with mud and chicken manure.

"Lina?"

Panic surged at the thought of how much he depended upon her and her wheelbarrow. Others would come looking when the two men failed to return, even sooner if they

had heard the brief exchange of rifle shots above the clap
and roll of thunder. No way without Lina could he elude
them with his broken leg.

He crawled to her side, touched her wad of molded-hay
hair. There was no blood. Her eyes were open wide,
bulging from their sockets, staring at the dead men. She
blinked as rainwater ran into her eyes.

She was alive! Relieved and grateful, Cassidy lay next
to her and stroked her hair until her shock wore off. Finally, she lifted her face out of the mud and looked at him,
not comprehending at first that he was also really alive.
Tears mixed with rainwater began streaming down her
face. The wide, loose mouth trembled out a babble of
Russian. She wrapped both arms around his head and
yanked him to her bosom while she moaned and howled
with the happiness and devotion of a loyal dog over the
unexpected return of its master.

Embarrassed, Cassidy succeeded in extricating himself from her arms. She held on to one hand with a grip
like a drowning person clinging to a single floating
twig. He spoke soothingly into her ear as she went
back to staring at the corpses that seemed to be melting
into the earth. Thunder made her flinch. He feared she
might be having a breakdown, at which point she became more a liability to him than he to her with his
splinted leg.

He shook her gently. "Look at me, Lina, not at them.
We're going to join them unless we do something fast."

She seemed content to lie forever right where she was
and hold his hands. He shook her a little harder and tried
to make her understand by sign and gesture that more
bad men would be coming. He had no desire to make his
last stand lying in chicken shit defending a chicken

house in Russia. What kind of an epitaph was that for a Delta soldier?

"Is the rest of my gear in the barn?" But, of course, she failed to understand.

He pulled free and dragged himself painfully toward the chicken house door. He was sure Brandon and he could concoct a plan to get him out of this mess if he could get his radio and contact Cold Dawn.

Lina crawled on the ground with him, attempting to hold on while she sobbed and blubbered. He reached the open door. A single large stone acted as a sill stoop. It was dark inside. Rain beat on the tin roof. Chickens seeking shelter on inside roosts muttered irritably.

Cassidy rested a moment before attempting to pull himself over the sill. The exertion of the fight and its aftermath left him weak with fatigue. From the pain he thought he might have re-broken his leg.

He pulled himself over the sill. Inside reeked with manure, some of it fresh. Now was no time to be squeamish about crawling around in a few poultry droppings. He looked around, waiting for his eyes to adjust to the dimness.

"Cass?"

Lina lurched to her feet, as though at last either comprehending what he was seeking or resigning herself to letting him call the shots from now on. She motioned him to stay while she darted toward a covered feed bin beyond the roosting hens. She returned momentarily lugging the rucksack Cassidy had released and dropped into the sea.

"Where did you get it?" he gasped in astonishment. She beamed back, happy that she pleased him.

The ruck must have floated ashore after he hit the rocks and knocked himself unconscious. Since operations over water required that rucks be made floatable, Cassidy had deliberately left a small pocket of air in the rubber inflatable raft. He rummaged through the pack, finding it still contained the other half of the detachment's explosives, the rubber boat, extra ammunition, a change of underwear and socks, some MREs, his sleeping bag and poncho . . . Essential mission equipment.

He pointed into the henhouse. "Now the rest of it?"

She obediently brought out his load-bearing battle harness. The first thing he noticed was that it had been stripped of everything except the thirty-round magazine pouch and his SOG SK 2000 battle knife. The small butt pack containing compass, GPS, Motorola radio, SAT phone, survival gear, and other equipment was gone. He stared in disbelief, his hopes sinking into his remaining boot. He grabbed Lina by the shoulders.

"Where is it? What have you done with it?"

Lina hung her head, sensing his distress. No matter how hard he shook her, how fiercely he shouted, she simply knelt in front of him with her head down, tears running, attempting to clutch his hands. He fended her off, aghast at what she had done. For all he knew, she had viewed the radio and telephone as his link with the outside world and a potential aid to his escaping from her. She probably tossed them back into the sea. How could he possibly fathom the motives and thought patterns of a backward little farm girl, especially since he couldn't even speak her language.

Continuing to rant at her was futile. She wasn't going to beat him with the ugly stick again; that aspect of their relationship had changed. But he mustn't drive her off either. He needed her a lot more than she needed him.

He had to survive the rest of the day until later that

night if he hoped to rendezvous with Cold Dawn when the detachment came down the river. A man with a broken leg, a simple-minded Smurf, and a wheelbarrow could never outrun and hide from pursuers serious about the chase. The dead men made their pursuers more serious than ever.

Circumstances such as these required extraordinary countermeasures. A plan began formulating in Cassidy's mind. Although he had no idea yet how many enemy he faced, it didn't matter, for a good offense was always the best defense. If you couldn't outrun the hounds, the best thing to do was turn on them by surprise and kill them first. The last thing the bad guys expected was attack by a cripple and a little farm girl.

It was crazy, but crazy was all around him.

"All right, all right," he said to Lina as his anger dissipated. "This is not doing us any good. We've got to get out of here."

At his direction, Lina loaded the heavy ruck into the wheelbarrow. Cassidy buckled on his combat harness with the extra ammo mags and knife and Lina helped him and his rifle in on top of the ruck. It made the one-wheeled vehicle top-heavy, but the stout little Smurf quickly adjusted. She avoided looking at the dead men again as, obviously thinking the problem solved, she started pushing back toward her house.

Cassidy stopped her and managed to convince her that their problems were just beginning. She looked more frightened than ever and changed course to push him away from her home. They had another argument, all in gestures, sign language, and heated words before she submitted to his will.

She wheeled him uphill in a roundabout route through the rain-filled forest toward the schoolhouse, like a beast of burden spooked at shadows but nonetheless bowing to the discipline of its master. Cassidy pitied her suddenly. What would Brown Sugar Mama say if she saw how he was using this poor creature?

CHAPTER 49

Karbala, Iraq

Orders came down the pipe that army chaplains were not to accompany combat missions. Exasperated at having been restricted to 1st Infantry's tent city, Chaplain Cameron Kragle waited outside Charlie Company's TOC (tactical operations center) for his units to return from combat missions into terrorist-besieged Karbala. The sun rode high but was fading rapidly. Muezzins in the city called the faithful to five o'clock prayers.

Cameron had just learned his brother Cassidy was MIA. No details, other than that the youngest Kragle brother was missing on a mission. Cameron bowed his head and closed his eyes. He prayed for Cassidy's physical salvation, then for his spiritual redemption. Then he prayed that God would fill the hollow in his own heart left there by the news of his brother's missing. Casualties were a reality of war; the chaplain had seen his recent share of them during operations against Mullah al-Sadr and Abu Musaf al-Zarqawi and their gangs of masked bandits. From the beginning, Chaplain Kragle had sensed a streak of evil running through the city.

Dusk settled ominously over the terrorist haven that Karbala had become. A trio of Bradley fighting vehicles rumbled up to the assembly point and dropped their gates to receive troops. Armed soldiers, helmeted and flak-jacketed, filed into the armor for the exhausting and dangerous work that lay ahead that night.

The chaplain kept praying around the hollow in his breast. When he looked up he saw Captain "Ichabod" Crain walking toward the TOC for after-action debriefing. Charlie Company was returning from the day's combat. Captain Crain carried his Kevlar helmet and flak jacket. The look on his drawn face combined despondency and triumph, a reaction to the day's mixed results. Cameron walked to meet him.

"Maybe you'd better speak with Corporal Ellis," Crain greeted him.

Cameron grimaced. "Dusty Richards?" he asked.

"We found him today. It wasn't pretty."

Platoon Sergeant Dusty Richards had been seized by al-Sadr's men three days before during action at the Imam Hussein Mosque. Al-Sadr threatened to execute the soldier unless the U.S. capitulated to his demands, the same way he had beheaded a half-dozen other captured "infidels" during past weeks. United States policy forbade negotiating with terrorists. Dusty Richards and Corporal R.J. Ellis had been best friends.

Cameron accompanied the company commander the rest of the way to the TOC while Captain Crain gave him the lowdown on the day's events.

Since the morning, Charlie Company had raided six houses and recovered nearly a ton of munitions buried or hidden on various premises. Hopes rose each time that Sergeant Richards might be found alive in one of the safe houses.

Troops descended a steep staircase littered with glass shards and rubble to a dark basement displaying evidence of the horrors carried out there by terrorists of the Karbala insurgency. Electric lights revealed a steel cage and wall chains in one corner, with black banners on the wall as a backdrop for the video camera set up on a tripod. It was obvious from coagulated blood on the floor and the decaying stench of death what had gone on. Some of the beheadings had been filmed there for Al-Jazeera TV.

"They're not *human*!" a soldier gasped.

Tears streamed down R.J. Ellis's round cheeks. "Somebody tried to dig his way out of here," he said, indicating a bloody handprint on the wall inside the cage. Next to it were human fingernails left imbedded in the wall; someone had desperately attempted to tunnel out through concrete.

Sergeant Richards—or at least what was left of him— had been found nearby in a low mud building crammed against a narrow dirty back street. His head lay in one corner, his body in the opposite. Corporal Ellis led the squad that made the recovery.

"Where is Ellis now?" Cameron asked.

"He went back to the platoon area."

Cameron made his way through the dress-right-dress city that served as 1st Infantry's base. He came to the "street" that housed Charlie Company and 1st Platoon and stopped when he spotted Ellis on his knees in front of the GP tent medium that Ellis and Corporal Roddy Rutledge had shared with Sergeant Richards.

Several weeks before, Dusty had asked his wife to send him some grass seeds so he might once again feel grass instead of sand underneath his feet. Dusty's "lawn" was the only living green visible anywhere. It grew in a plot about five feet long and two wide next to the flaps of the tent. Dusty had irrigated it every day. He used to come in after a mission, take off his boots, and sit and wriggle his bare toes in the lavish growth.

Corporal Ellis was now trimming the lawn with a pair of scissors. He was bareheaded, his haircut white-walled. The look of despair and sadness on the big man's face almost wrenched Cameron's heart from his chest as he watched.

Suddenly, he would have liked nothing better in the world than to be back home at his little church on Smoke Bomb Hill at Fort Bragg preparing for Sunday's sermon. Perhaps Kelli would be there with him, Cassidy would not be MIA, and things would be "normal" again. Although he had concluded that the War on Terror, including the Iraqi War, fit St. Augustine's definition of a Just War, he could not help feeling that war under all circumstances was such a waste. He sometimes echoed Brown Sugar Mama's sentiments and wondered when, oh when, would Jesus come back to punish the wicked and install peace on earth, good will toward all men.

He sometimes wondered why he couldn't be more like his father and brothers with their practical, straight-forward mentalities and less like his softer, more-introspective mother. Brandon and Cassidy were seldom if ever plagued by questions and doubts when it came to the military and their job waging war against terrorists.

And now there was a good chance Cassidy was already killed in waging that war.

Corporal Ellis looked up and detected the silent chaplain watching from the other end of the street. Cameron shook his head to clear it of thoughts of home and the melancholia that threatened to set in. He walked the rest of the way down the street and got on his hands and knees next to Ellis.

"Dusty was like my brother," Corporal Ellis said. "Why would God let it happen?"

The chaplain placed an arm around the soldier's shoulders. "We must not lose heart. Even in the midst of pain and trial, God is at work in our world."

"Do you truly believe that, Rev?"

"There is no purpose in life, no reason for our existence, if the lives we lead on this earth come and go like a too-brief flame and there is nothing else. Mankind must have hope. God is our only hope. For every negative thing we say to ourselves, God has a positive answer."

"I am so tired, Chaplain."

"God says, 'I will give you rest.' "

"I don't know if I can do this anymore."

"God says, 'You can do all things.' "

"Rev, I'm afraid."

" 'I have not given you a spirit of fear.' "

Ellis continued to clip grass while tears wet his broad cheeks.

"Do you have another pair of scissors?" Cameron asked.

CHAPTER 50

Washington, D.C.

As soon as they were settled in Vanda's silver Saturn parked on a side street a short distance from the Pig Out café, General Kragle asked her for the telephone number her daughter Jennifer had supplied. He called it in to his FBI friend Director Claude Thornton, who had access to unlisted telephone directories, and requested he trace it. Claude asked no questions, simply saying he couldn't talk long; he was in Charleston on a matter.

"It'll take a little while to get the address," he said. "I'll have Della call you back on it. Yours was a short testimony before the 9/11 commission yesterday."

"I hear the commission has the D.C. police tracking you down, Claude, to bring you in."

"That's the problem with Washington—a bunch of clowns, but nobody has a sense of humor. General, you sound a lot better today than the last time I talked to you."

Darren glanced at Vanda. "I had a good breakfast," he said.

Vanda nurtured her innate effervescence in spite of the situation of her missing daughter. Her natural optimism buoyed the General while at the same time embarrassing him over his own inadequacies in coping with life's daily trials, temporary though they might be. Her hobby of photographing old barns, she said, hopefully would turn into a lucrative enterprise eventually. So they talked about barns while they waited.

"I'm collecting prints for one of those giant coffee table books that no one ever reads but everyone owns to keep out for company because it has a lovely cover that goes with the drapes," she said. She appeared nervous, alone with him, which surprised Darren. "Amazingly enough, there are quite a few old barns once you get away from Washington and out into the outskirts of Maryland. I search for them and just let my higher self guide me to the next, and the next and the next. It's exciting because I never know what's around the next bend in the country road, or over the next hill. I found a lovely, dilapidated little barn at a dead-end road. The windows were busted, the boards hanging hither and yon, but I snapped about six pictures of it just the same. I could only wonder that at one time, decades ago, this was a brand-new barn people were proud of. Now it stands in various stages of decomposure. I thought it the most perfect barn I have thus far found. I love it just as it is. It kind of reminds me of me—a little worn around the edges but still filled with life."

"Many of us get worn around the edges," the General said with a sigh. "Worn too much and then life begins to subside."

Vanda cast him a sharp glance.

"I have an old barn like the one you describe," he added quickly to shift the focus.

"Where?" she asked eagerly, going along.

"At the Farm we own in Tennessee. It's been in the Kragle family for generations, since around the time of the French and Indian Wars."

"That's wonderful. Permanence within families is rare these days. I'd love to see your barn—and your farm. To photograph, I mean."

The buzz of his cell phone saved him from making a ·

hasty commitment. It was Della. She gave him an address on Thirteenth Street.

"You seem more chipper than usual, General Kragle," she commented.

Vanda drove. Her fingers drummed impatiently on the steering wheel. As they neared the address, her brown eyes misted and she appeared simultaneously vulnerable and resolute. Darren gave her hand a reassuring pat. Maybe Claude and Della were right; he sounded better because concentrating on someone other than himself and his problems made him feel better. There seemed to be something about the atmosphere in Washington that spread into the hinterlands like a cancer in an election year and infected the whole nation with the shit-blahs.

"We shouldn't get our hopes up," Darren cautioned. A parent had to face reality at times. "She may not be there."

"I'm telling myself that. But, Darren, I *want* to be hopeful."

"I still don't understand how your daughter . . . how Jennifer got mixed up with a sorry outfit like BUCKUS," Darren said.

"Jennifer is an idealist—"

"So was Karl Marx."

"She believes in those old sixties notions about liberation and changing the world. Remember when we were on campus in the sixties?"

"I was in Vietnam," Darren said, then regretted saying it. He couldn't help the way he felt. His sons repeatedly went into harm's way, risking their lives for their own ideals of making America safe and keeping it free. And at home a bunch of spoiled, gutless brats like Jennifer and a bunch of retread sixties hippies swarmed the streets shrieking against better people than themselves and chattering about "making a difference."

Making a difference? Hell, *Stalin* made a difference. *Hitler* made a difference.

It was better that Vanda and he not talk about their children. There was too much of a gap between them when it came to that. They finished the drive in silence.

CHAPTER 51

The address on Thirteenth Street turned out to be a drab brownstone on a very unadorned street of drab brownstones. The lawn was left unshorn, the shrubbery unkempt, and there was a ratty, canary-yellow van with green spray-painted peace symbols on both sides parked out front and a used condom splatted on the door stoop. Vanda looked away and sighed, her lips compressed. She seemed to have passed into a state of shaky apprehension.

The man who answered the door was in his twenties, of medium height and rather thin. He wore a green army fatigue jacket with the collar turned up, ragged Levi's, an earring, a nose ring, a tongue ring, and, probably, General Kragle decided in disgust, a scrotum ring. His hair was dyed *pink*. Behind him in the room the General saw the edge of a brown sofa, a shaded window, and a cigarette smoking in an ashtray on the sofa's arm.

"What do you want?" the man asked.

"I want Jennifer," Vanda said promptly, and meant it.

"Just go away, both of you. We don't want you and we don't need you."

Vanda was not to be put off. She pushed her way past the New Generation Hippie and looked around the room. The General followed her.

"You're not invited in here," the man said.

"Then get some manners and invite us in," General Kragle snapped, staring him down.

The room was rugless and wretchedly furnished with

only the sofa, a small brown portable television playing soap operas, a telephone on the floor, and seven or eight mattresses scattered about where apparently any number of people normally crashed. There seemed to be no one else in the house.

Darren stepped into the kitchen and then into two bedrooms filled with mattresses on the floor and the heady odor of unwashed bodies. If cleanliness was next to Godliness, this bunch wouldn't get within sniffing distance of the Pearly Gates. He returned to the living room where Vanda still stood in the middle of the room, looking lost, and the hippie was standing across the room, looking sullen.

"What's your name, boy?" Darren asked.

The hippie type scowled. Darren took two steps forward. "Your name?"

"Smoke."

"Smoke what? Is it the fashion just to have one name these days?"

Smoke kept his place on the other side of the room. "Who the fuck are you to come in like this?" he demanded.

"I'm Vanda Stratton," Vanda said. "Jennifer's mother. Where is she?"

"How the fuck should I know?" He swept a hand across the mattresses. "They come and they go."

Smoke raised the window shade and stared resentfully into the backyard. Darren saw a rusty bicycle and an overflowing garbage can.

"Look, I don't want to disturb anything," Vanda said. "All I want is to talk to my daughter and make sure she's okay."

Smoke turned and looked at her with the same hostility he had worn from the beginning. "Listen," he said to the General, "tell this cunt to get out of here. She's with you, so tell her to go. I don't need a bad cunt in here criticizing us where we're at and how we live. She thinks she's too fucking good for us and I already heard that."

Vanda colored. Darren's temper surged. "You sleazy bastard," he said, unable to contain his temper. "Anyone *human* is too good for you. We're talking about this lady's daughter. Do you know where she is?"

"I don't care where her daughter is," Smoke said, looking back out the window. "I know what a bad cunt is."

Vanda suddenly looked sick. Her eyes went strange, as though clearly reacting to a great strain.

"Wait in the car for me, Vanda," Darren said.

That caught Smoke's attention. He looked unsure of himself. "What? What are you doing, old man?"

"Go on, Vanda," Darren said. "I won't be long."

He kept Smoke pinned with his eyes. The front door opened and closed.

This piece of crap, whatever the hell its name was, looked about the same age as Cassidy, but look at the difference in them. While Cassidy was out risking his life for folks, this scumbag was being disrespectful to the world.

Smoke attempted to dodge away as the tall man approached. He wore a look that said he thought he may have gone too far with the old guy. Darren latched onto Smoke's arm and jerked him back. With one hand he gripped Smoke's throat and slammed him against the wall. He pried the thumb and forefinger of his other hand into Smoke's mouth, caught the tongue ring, and levered the tongue out. Tears of pain and fear shot into Smoke's cloudy eyes.

"You and I are going to have a nice conversation," the General said in a low, measured tone. "Nod if you understand."

Smoke wasn't quite ready to give in. Darren yanked on his tongue. Smoke nodded and nodded and nodded.

"Good boy. Do you know Jennifer?"

Some more desperate nodding.

"See how easy this is when we understand each other? Do you know where she is?"

Smoke shook his head, mumbling and gurgling around his extracted tongue.

"We'll have a regular conversation, right, if I turn your tongue loose instead of wrapping it around your knees?"

Hopeful nodding.

Vanda was waiting in her Saturn when Darren came out. He got in and slammed the door.

"Jennifer was here," he said. "She left yesterday morning."

"Where was she going?"

"Smoke doesn't know. Have you ever met someone called Patsy? Maybe one of Jennifer's friends or a professor from Harvard?"

"There was a professor in New York she was supposed to stay with, but I don't know her name."

"Jennifer left with a fat older woman named Patsy and two guys Smoke said he had seen Patsy with before. They looked Middle Eastern. Smoke said Jennifer looked scared to death."

Vanda batted back tears. "Where do we go now?"

"This was in the house." He handed her a flyer advertising a Harris For President rally scheduled for that afternoon in Washington's Rock Creek Park. "Smoke thought she might go there."

CHAPTER 52

Charleston Harbor

"Am I being detained for a purpose?" Captain Boutros Igbal of the Saudi freighter *Cristi* objected.

Claude Thornton remained uncompromising. "You and your men will vacate the ship."

"It is piracy. This is my ship. I shall lodge a protest."

"It's in a U.S. harbor."

The rusty old tub rode a gentle tide moored to a pier opposite the Brazilian oil tanker *Maria*. Captain Igbal insisted his cargo hold contained legitimate exports from Russia and China. Three weeks ago, he said, he loaded at two ports of call—Vladivostok and Shanghai—and proceeded to Charleston via the Panama Canal. To Claude, it seemed a long route around when the freighter could have offloaded sooner and more economically at Los Angeles or San Diego.

"My ship and I sail where clients pay us to go," Captain Igbal challenged. "I am to offload in Charleston, then proceed to Cadiz."

A single large steel shipping container the size of a camping trailer had already been lifted to the dock, then left there when, backed by MacArthur Thornbrew and the President, Claude Thornton issued his order to close down the seaport. Crane arms extending above the cargo hold seemed to have frozen in midmotion. Captain Igbal and his crew, along with other merchantmen and dock work-

ers, watched sullenly from the heads of the piers until
Charleston police shooed them to safer grounds beyond
the yellow-taped parking lots. Not that anywhere in
Charleston was *that* secure should a WMD actually be
aboard the freighter and should it be rigged to detonate if
it were tampered with. Charleston would become a big
hole filled with seawater, contaminated and unlivable for
decades, perhaps centuries. The countryside around Chernobyl still glowed and no one dared enter the dead zone of
radiation following the blowup of that nuclear facility
nearly a quarter-century before.

EOD (Explosive Ordnance Disposal) teams arrived and
began the search, starting with the container on the dock.
It was tedious work, and time consuming. The door had to
be first checked for booby traps before seals were broken
and authorities personally led by Director Thornton in-
spected the contents.

"Ya'all sure about this," Detective Wells questioned
Claude and Agent Jonathan Barnes. "Ya'all might be
boogering over nothing. It still seems to me these terrorists would be crazy to leave that ole gal's carcass lying
around for us to find if they were trying to smuggle in
something. Seems to me, Mr. FBI, they wouldn't *want* to
draw attention to themselves."

Claude knew from experience that you couldn't always apply strict logic to terrorist behavior. It even occurred to him that terrorists intended to attract police to
Charleston, either to divert attention from elsewhere, to
attract the notice of the world to the WMD before it blew
up and thus demonstrate how they couldn't be stopped, or
simply as part of a continuing campaign to keep America
alarmed and on edge. Perhaps all three motives applied.
Whichever, it looked as though Patsy Koehler's political

lawyering had finally gone too far and turned to bite her in the ass.

It was slow work, considering the stakes, tedious and nerve-wracking. The EOD teams proceeded with extreme caution, taking one small step at a time, carefully planning each move, inspecting through procedure each obstacle they encountered. Terrorists might be mad, but they could also be ingenious and cunning. One mistake could lead to disaster.

It took hours to audit the single container. It held nothing more threatening than electric and electronic equipment, petroleum products, textiles, and other innocuous odds and ends targeted at the U.S. market.

The EOD moved into the ship's hold at midafternoon and approached a second container. Barnes and Detective Wells joined Claude to watch the bomb experts examine the sealed door. Auxiliary power from the ship's own energy source supplied unsteady weak light, thus requiring supplemental illumination from several high-voltage lamps powered by gas generators that lit up the hold like a movie set, sending shadows fleeing to corners. The EOD specialists used Geiger counters, X-ray, and infrared to examine the door inch by inch before they decided it could be safely opened.

"It's a little like King Tut's tomb in one of the old late-night horror movies," Barnes observed, adding, "just before evil is released into the world. Claude, do you ever get the feeling we're in the wrong line of work?"

The heavy steel door opened on its rusty hinges. Blinding light flooded into the container. Inside, among boxes and other materials, crouched two young Arabs wearing red Jihad headbands. They stared back at the Americans, squinting against the bright light. Astonished, Barnes and

Wells stepped in front of Claude, craning their necks to get a better look.

The cargo hold went up suddenly in a tremendous blast of flame and violence. Claude Thornton felt the searing flash all the way to his bones—and then he felt nothing else.

CHAPTER 53

Partizanskaya River Valley

It was raining, lightly, when the Cold Dawn detachment pulled up short of the Partizanskaya River and the mine shaft and went into a security perimeter in thick foliage. Leaving Top Sculdiron in charge, Brandon and Gloomy Davis left to conduct a leader's recon of the objective. They climbed high in order to come in and look down upon the target area where Ice Man and Diverse had run their earlier recon. At the last, they wriggled through short brush and tufts of withered grass to the edge of a dropoff where an old earthslide had spilled shale, soil, and rock two hundred yards down to the river, leaving a buildup of debris next to the footbridge.

Both men were breathing harder than normal from the steep climb. Sweat meant nothing since they were already soaked from rain. Neither wore a poncho; the slick material might give them away by its whispering and flapping in the wind.

Brandon caught his breath and took a swig from his canteen before breaking out a pair of binoculars. He soon detected five or six armed men patrolling back and forth across the narrow bridge, underneath which the water ran swift and brown from all the precipitation. Judging from their appearance, they were part of the Cossack cavalry the detachment observed earlier. Additional pairs of stationary sentries were posted at either end of the bridge and upstream a short distance near where the water darkened flowing out from underneath the cliff brow Ice and Diverse had described as concealing the cave's entrance. The boat dock below the overhang and the cave's mouth remained out of sight, as did the Cossack horses.

Gloomy cranked up the power on his variable Redfield scope and glassed the point of a pinnacle directly opposite the one he and Brandon were on and about eight hundred yards away across a deep saddle. Within this other peak, deep underground, lay the cave. Gloomy's pale handlebar mustaches twitched when he found what he was looking for.

"Boss?" he murmured into Brandon's ear. "One o'clock—see him?"

Brandon focused the high sentry into his lenses—a young bruiser of an Oriental with thickly folded eyes, a black rain jacket and cap, and a Moison-Nagant sniper's rifle of the sort first taken from the dead rider and then stolen by Katya when she escaped. From his high point, this sentry commanded an eagle's view of everything below. Nothing escaped his scrutiny.

"Can you reach out and touch him when we need to?" Brandon asked.

Gloomy concentrated on the guard and his sniper's rifle, calculating range and wind, humidity and temperature.

"Piece of cake, Boss. It's at about the same range as Carlos Hathcock once killed a VC sniper with a bullet directly through his scope and into his eye. They were aiming at each other, but Carlos got on the trigger first. He told me about it one time before he died. Good man, Carlos. The best sniper ever. I'm almost as good."

"They're expecting us," Brandon whispered.

"Big time," Gloomy agreed. "Katya must have got

here and warned them. That chink over there is carrying her rifle."

The cave and its surroundings appeared even more heavily guarded than Ice and Diverse described it from their recon, more evidence that Katya was already there. She undoubtedly had told her mommy and her mommy's buddies how she sabotaged the Americans, but no one was taking chances. The cave had been turned into a formidable redoubt requiring at least a company of soldiers, maybe a battalion, to overwhelm and destroy head-on. Brandon wouldn't have been surprised if more reinforcements were on their way upstream. Cold Dawn's only chance rested in the mine shaft. What Murphy took away, the Kragle Irish luck tried to replace.

An outboard river boat occupied by four figures floated out from the cave's overhang and caught Brandon's attention. The boat eddied with the current a few moments while the coxswain stood up and yanked three or four times on the outboard engine's starter rope. Brandon gave a little startle of recognition as he swept his binocs over the passengers. He nudged Gloomy, who swept his rifle scope toward the river.

"It's *her*!" Gloomy said, his voice grown taut and thin.

Katya—Zafina—rode in the bow wearing her jeans, heavy woolen coat, and a Cossack's fur cap from around the edges of which her dark hair stuck out. Brandon saw through his binoculars how her eyes, tension rife in them, scanned the overarching uplands, as though she half-expected to see the *Americanski* and his men, never mind that she had robbed them of their capability of blowing up anything. Although she appeared unarmed, an AK-47 was propped within the coxswain's reach and each of the other two men carried an assault rifle. One wore a white turban, the other a baseball cap. They also appeared tense and watchful.

A large oilcloth covered a mound of cargo amidships. Brandon immediately thought of WMDs, the evil spawn of this plant on its way out to annihilate Americans and their cities.

"I can do her if you say the word," Gloomy promised in a voice as dry and dead as old leaves.

Brandon had to make a choice. Either stop the boat and its *possible* shipment of nuclear suitcases or continue with the original mission. Even if the boat was hauling nukes and he destroyed them, the plant remained active and could produce replacements. Success in destroying the plant depended on stealth and not giving themselves away prematurely, not even to take out a rich target like the traitorous Katya and whatever she might be rushing out with her.

"Let her go," Brandon said, relieved that in spite of what she had done that he didn't have to decide her death. "She's not our assigned target. We'll radio out a report on her."

The outboard engine caught. Its angry buzz channeled up from the river between the heights. The coxswain sat down at the steering handle and turned the boat's prow downstream. The craft swept underneath the footbridge. Katya and the two guards remained vigilant. The sound of the engine throbbed back up the river a long time after the boat itself disappeared.

CHAPTER 54

Brandon and Gloomy eased back from the edge of the precipice to keep the Chinese on the opposite point from spotting them as they left. An hour later when it was already starting to get dark because of the cloud covering, the detachment with Ice Man leading the way worked its way cautiously to the mine entrance downstream of the nuclear cave. There, forested banks dropped steeply to the edge of the water where there was more cover of thick growth. Even though Ice Man had been there before, it still took him a quarter hour to find the shaft opening, it was that well concealed. Deltas slithered through the narrow slot on their bellies into a narrow subterranean chamber about eight feet wide and six tall. It was dry in the mine. Its walls shut out the patter of rain outside in the forest.

Brandon turned on a flashlight back from the opening to avoid spilling detectable light outside while he drew a map diagram of the target area in the floor's loose dirt. Using the diagram and reconnaissance photos, he made final assignments.

Top Sculdiron, second in command, would man the ORP and be responsible for the rubber boats and getting the team extracted should anything happen to Major Kragle. Gloomy with Mr. Blunderbuss and heavy weapons operator Perverse Sanchez would return to the high pinnacle above the footbridge where they could control the entire battlefield if something happened before charges could be set and detonated inside the cave. Mad Dog and his commo gear remained at the mine with Top. Ice Man and Doc Red would set up near the river with the SAW and Top's M203 grenade launcher as security to control access to and traffic on the river until the detachment reconsolidated and began its withdrawal.

That left Brandon and Diverse Dade unassigned.

"Sergeant Dade and I will set the charges," Brandon said.

Gloomy had already accepted it. That didn't mean he liked it. "Using the limited length of primadet," he said, "neither of you will make it out again."

"I'll go instead," Sculdiron offered.

"No." That was Brandon's final word. It was his fault the detonators were stolen in the first place.

He had thought about it—and if he could go alone and do the job he would do it. But he needed Diverse's expertise with explosives, as unfair as it might be to him. At least Diverse was not married. The situation reaffirmed his conviction that family men should never be accepted into Delta, and that he had done the right thing in culling Doc TB from the detachment.

Ultimately, it might make no difference *who* actually went into the cave to set the explosives, not if the nukes went off.

It hurt, the possibility that he might never see Summer again, that his child might never know him other than through a few snapshots that gradually faded over the years. Brandon accepted the risks when he came into Delta, accepted that such a day as that might come; he would do it all over again given the choices.

Mad Dog went from man to man shaking hands. "Fu-uck," he said. "Nobody promised we'd live forever anyhow. I suppose I'll see you all on the other side. If there is an other side."

CHAPTER 55

Russian Coast

Cassidy urged Lina on, feeling like a scoundrel but rationalizing that it was as much for her good as his that they put distance between themselves and her little farm. It wouldn't be long before the dead men's comrades discovered the bodies and came howling after their slayer. He called frequent listening halts, but heard no sounds of pursuit above rain in the trees, the crash and rumble of thunder, and Lina's raspy breathing as she bent over the wheelbarrow handles to catch her breath.

A shaft of weak yellow sunshine pierced a low western hole in the cloud cover as the odd couple with the wheelbarrow broke out of thicker timber onto the ridgeline west of the schoolhouse. Lina collapsed from exhaustion, trembling with terror, and refused to look at the panoramic view of the schoolhouse and surrounding terrain. She whimpered, anxious to be gone.

"Shhh!" Cassidy said.

The schoolhouse looked more rundown than he had gathered from his limited view of it earlier. It was actually little more than a low crumbling ruin being carved into consumable bites by ivy and other creepers. A sentry out front stood guard on the rock wall that enclosed the school, rifle slung over his shoulder while he scanned the sky to the north. A second man came out with a parka drawn over his head against the rain and also looked at the sky before going back inside.

Terrific webs of lightning reflected against the surface of the Partizanskaya River where it wound through the bottomlands toward the gray slate of the sea Cassidy saw in the distance, very much like the map Lina drew. While there was good timber cover along the ridgeline to within a few yards of the school, the terrain opened up onto a meadow in front. It spread out across a plateau about two hundred meters wide before it dropped abruptly to the river bank. The clearing was at least five hundred meters long, maybe longer; the westward end of it disappeared around the curve of the ridge. A flutter of wind inflated a wind sock on a pole at the other end of the clearing. An *airfield*?

Why would an abandoned country school have a runway?

The clearing complicated matters further. In order to reach the river and link up with Brandon and 3A by that night, Lina would have to push Cassidy across the clearing, out in the open. Even if they waited until after dark and weren't seen, the wheelbarrow's single deep furrow in the rain-sodden ground would lead pursuers directly to them. The best defense was still a good offense.

They didn't have much time left either. Two armed men came out the back door of the school and set off in the direction of Lina's farm, obviously on a mission to find the first ones now lying dead outside Lina's chicken house. It wouldn't take them long to read in the mud what happened—tracks, spent cartridge casings—and take up the wheelbarrow's trail.

Cassidy glanced anxiously at the skies. Purple evening haze was starting to creep across the drenched landscape, darkening the skeins of straight-falling rain, but even nightfall would not delay the trackers by much. Cassidy figured they had about two hours to work out a plan, three at the most.

Lina picked at his sleeve, begging him to go.

"We have nowhere to go, Lina. Don't you understand that?"

Of course, she didn't. She stood and hooked herself to the handlebars. Cassidy shook his head. She dropped the wheelbarrow back onto its stand and hunkered next to it, as though to hide, her back to the school. Rain and wet grass had washed her bare feet almost clean.

Any plan that a cripple in a wheelbarrow and a Smurf might execute required every advantage of weather and timing. Cassidy thought he had enough C-4 and RDX to blow the school all the way to China if Lina pushed him up to it unseen under cover of darkness. After, naturally, they heroically rescued the space travelers.

Proof that the astronauts were actually being held there came sooner than he expected. Light from the unseen sunset illuminated a flurry of activity in front of the school. Two riflemen came out leading three men whose hands were bound in front. They were linked together by rope tied around their necks. Even at a distance and without binoculars, Cassidy recognized the blue jumpsuits worn by NASA astronauts. The third man wore a tan jumpsuit; he must be the Russian.

Lina was right after all. The *Soyuz* crew had been taken captive. Cassidy shook Lina's shoulder and tried to get her to look. She ducked her head stubbornly and hunched lower into herself. He couldn't tell if she was shivering from being cold and wet or trembling out of fear. Probably both.

Guards had obviously brought the *Soyuz* crew outside to relieve themselves before night set in. The three men were resolutely attending to this function, standing side by

side, when additional activity brought more men running
out of the school. At first, Cassidy failed to comprehend
what was going on. Then he heard a high-pitched drone
and understood why the sentry kept watching the sky.

Even though the thunderstorm had moved toward the
west, taking with it the harder rain and most of the wind,
only a pilot with a suicide wish or a vital mission dared fly
in that weather. The high-pitched whine of the approaching aircraft intensified, echoing off the ground since it had
to fly low underneath a ceiling. Presently, it materialized
out of a thin fog bank, silhouetting itself against a backdrop wall of lightning. Its dual wings wobbled erratically
in aloft wind gusts. Cassidy recognized it as either a
Russian-made Colt An-3 single-engine light transport biplane or the Chinese equivalent of the same model, the
Fung Chow 2. Either version was equipped with a turboprop engine that gave it a range of about six hundred miles
with a light payload.

Wings still wagging, it executed a straight-in approach
against the wind sock, touched down and rolled out, stopping in the middle of the field closer to the river than to
the school. Cassidy thought it curious why it didn't taxi on
up to the building. The pilot and copilot climbed out,
stretched, and began tying the plane down for the night. If
it had come for the prisoners, it apparently wouldn't be
transporting them out until the next day when the weather
cleared.

The spacemen finished their business and were escorted back inside. One of their guards broke off and
walked down to the airplane. The pilots finished securing
the aircraft. Cassidy found it even more curious that all
three remained with the airplane, crouching underneath
the lower wing out of the weather rather than seeking

shelter in the school. It was almost as if they were waiting for someone else.

Visibility grew difficult, but enough daylight remained for Cassidy to make out an outboard power boat as it glided swiftly to bank on the near side of the river. Four figures jumped out and paintered it to a sapling. Three of the figures were armed with rifles. One wore a white turban. The fourth was smaller than the others and wore a heavy woolen coat, jeans, and a Cossack fur cap.

It looked like old home week at the school.

Turban got back in the boat and relayed two heavy-looking canvas bags to those ashore. Two of the forms hoisted these onto their backs by carrying straps and all four started up through the fringe of river growth toward the airplane. Cassidy lost sight of them until they emerged onto the plateau and strode across the runway, the two with the packs bent forward underneath their burdens. The pilot opened a large door on the left side of his biplane and hoisted himself inside to receive bags the newcomers handed up to him. It took him a few minutes to lash down the cargo.

He jumped back to the ground. He, his copilot, and the four boat people trudged toward the schoolhouse, leaving the sentry squatting underneath a wing, AK-47 resting across his thighs. Cassidy identified one of the group as a young woman, but he failed to make out her features.

Things, as Brown Sugar Mama would have put it, kept getting curiouser and curiouser. What did the canvas bags contain that required an armed guard? Cassidy recalled how, during the OpOrder for Cold Dawn, the CIA had briefed the detachment on how rogue scientists might be operating in Primorye Province to build WMD devices. Was it possible the canvas bags contained nuclear explosives? The situation seemed suspicious enough that he knew he had to take a look. He silently cursed the luck that confined him to a wheelbarrow, a *wheelbarrow*, for God's sake, and to the care of a simple-minded peasant woman with whom he could barely communicate.

He had a long night's work cut out for him. For him and for Lina.

CHAPTER 56

Partizanskaya River Valley

Sergeant Diverse Dade took lead in the mine shaft since he had traveled the route before, his lean face so black it blended with the near-total darkness of the tunnel, the backwash of his flashlight making his eyes glow like eerie disembodied orbs. Brandon had dumped his ruck before setting out, carrying only his carbine, the Ka-Bar his grandfather gave him, a Colt semiautomatic pistol, and his combat harness laden with extra ammo. Diverse insisted on bearing the entire load of C-4 and RDX, about forty pounds, rather than split it and chance not having the explosives within his personal reach when he needed them. Neither man spoke. There was no longer a need for words.

Brandon assured himself that, although they might die doing it, this was *not* a suicide mission. They were going in there to do a job and get out again, if possible, not to sacrifice their lives to Allah and go to heaven to receive seventy-two virgins or white raisins, whichever, as a reward. Leave that to the Islamic nut jobs.

Summer's face crept unbidden into his thoughts. Her bright emerald eyes and sunburnt ash-blond hair. She was one of those women who blossomed with pregnancy, became more warm and loving as she "waddled about like a mama duck." Her description of it.

He thought also of his father, his brothers Cassidy and

Cameron, and of Gloria, dear sweet Brown Sugar Mama, who had been his mother for almost as long as he could remember. The General was going to catch hell when she unleashed that terrible finger of hers for a good scolding if Brandon and Cassidy went and got themselves killed.

He wondered if you remained aware when you died, if you missed those people you loved when you were alive. He would have to ask Cameron about it if he survived the night.

Then his warrior's celebrated direct-action mentality kicked into gear to allow him to concentrate only on the task at hand. He shook off all extraneous thought.

Soon, he heard the musical tinkle of the waterfall. Diverse's flashlight played over it, refracting prisms of light in happy dancing colors on the walls, floors, and overhead. Its beam glared back at them from the black pool that spread in beneath the forward wall of the underground chamber. Diverse sat on the rock slag next to it, lay the flashlight on the ground as a lantern, and began removing his boots. Brandon did likewise after taking off his combat harness and jacket. He slipped an extra thirty-round magazine into the cargo pocket of his trousers and buttoned it in.

Diverse switched off his flashlight after they prepared for swimming. They sat in darkness as complete as anything Brandon had experienced before, waiting for the other teams to get into place before H-hour. He wondered if Death was that dark.

"Do you hear it?" Diverse asked. Even a whisper echoed before the darkness swallowed it.

Muted whirs and grinding of machinery filtered from out of the pool and through the wall.

"I hear."

"It isn't far to the other side. Perhaps fifty feet. There's one place at the end where we have to swim underwater to come up in the pool on the other side. We can't use a light from here on. It might be seen in the cave. I'll have to leave my weapon behind since I have the ruck."

"I have mine."

The illuminated hands on their dive watches said it was time. Diverse touched Brandon's arm, offered a hand. They gripped.

"Major, it's been an honor serving with you, sir. No matter what happens, I have no regrets."

"Likewise, Sergeant Dade."

"What if we find the astronauts inside?" Diverse asked.

"We'll have to work that out once we're inside." He took a deep breath. "Sergeant Dade, let's do it."

They slipped soundlessly into the water after Diverse secured one end of his short roll of primadet to an old mine piling half-rotted on the floor. He floated the ruck full of explosives with one hand, leading the way as he paid out the detonating cord. Brandon held on to the tail of Diverse's T-shirt in order to prevent their getting separated in the darkness.

Water rose to their waists. It soon deepened and the ceiling lowered until their heads banged against it and only their eyes and noses remained above water. Sounds from the cave beyond grew louder, sharper, vibrating through the water like a giant third heart, reminding Brandon of drumbeats in old African movies just before natives surrounded the hero and attacked.

Terrorists were like rats who burrowed into remote places; you had to go in and dig them out.

The space between water surface and ceiling decreased until Brandon had to turn his head sideways to gulp air. Diverse tapped him to let him know they must swim underwater from there. Water swirled as Diverse sank into a one-armed sidestroke, dragging the demolitions bag with his other hand while det cord continued to uncoil out of it. Brandon followed, guiding on the throb of machinery, relying totally upon his sense of hearing.

Soon he saw a glow ahead and above. He had plenty of breath left. He surfaced next to Diverse, who remained sheltered underneath the rim of the shaft opening. The pool was shallow enough to allow them to stand with only their heads and shoulders exposed. It lay in shadow, but light blazed deeper inside the cave's enormous main chamber.

Brandon took in everything. The room was about the size of a football field from the thirty-yard line to goal. Turbines, generators, vats, and other equipment and machinery dominated the center of the cave while "labs" and "offices" lined the walls, each partitioned off with plywood. Men and women, a dozen or so, some wearing white or tan smocks, others light cotton coveralls, went about their nefarious business in what seemed to Brandon an accelerated production mode, as though working overtime and in a hurry to finish the job. Men wore turbans and women covered their heads in black scarves in recognition of their Muslim heritage, the exception being the two armed guards near where the cave opened onto the river. They looked Russian and were undoubtedly part of the mafia hired as security.

It was in this place, deep inside a mountain in Russia near its border with China and North Korea, that radical Islamics labored to construct devices for the random wholesale bloodletting of distant men, women, children, and babies. *Allahu Akbar!* Little did they realize that Delta Force had arrived among them and that a cold dawn was going to rise over the ruins.

Diverse whispered directly into Brandon's ear. "The

walls of the cave look weakest near the entrance. If I drop them, we might be able to demolish this sucker without kicking off secondary nuclear explosions."

He pointed.

"I'm going to try to reach that point, if I have enough det cord. Maybe they won't see me if I stay in the shadows next to the wall."

"How much time do you need?"

"Five minutes to drill and tamp, maybe another minute or so."

"I'll give you whatever you need. We're going to have to look inside those closed rooms afterward for the *Soyuz* crew."

Brandon cleared his carbine of water while Diverse unpacked demo and his tool kit and made last-minute preparations. Workers continued their frantic duties without so much as a glance toward the pool, the one dark place in the entire cave.

Both men froze, sinking lower in the water, when a middle-aged woman in a tan smock and a tall man wearing a great green turban came out of the nearest plywood office. They stopped to make adjustments to a reactor, barely interrupting their animated conversation. The woman looked Middle Eastern, but wore no head covering like the other females. Brandon recognized her from the photos Mad Dog SAT-downloaded from CENTCOM. Katya's mama. Huda Ammash. Dr. Death herself. The Queen of Hearts on the deck of America's Most Wanted war criminals.

"She's toast," Diverse commented, also recognizing her.

Brandon consulted his watch. "H-hour," he said.

Diverse took a deep, steadying breath, waded to the end of the pool and climbed out onto dry land. He looked back at Brandon, his long face expressionless, water running off it. Things from here on got ticklish. His chances of being detected doubled and then doubled again the nearer he came to reaching where he needed to place explosives in order to demolish the plant without also destroying himself and Brandon and perhaps the entire Cold Dawn detachment.

Barely had he undertaken his short perilous journey, however, than gunfire erupted from somewhere outside, distant-sounding and muffled inside the cave, at the same time carrying a chilling forewarning of just how hairy things could get.

Brandon flinched. The excrement, as Mad Dog would put it, had struck the oscillator, prematurely.

CHAPTER 57

Russian Coast

Night settled purple, thick and wet-cloying. Cassidy waited impatiently in his wheelbarrow, anxious to get the action started. He dared not wait much longer. By now the mafiosi sent to Lina's farm must have certainly discovered their dead pals and were on their killer's trail. Surely in the annals of history there could be found another occasion in which a warrior rode into battle in a wheelbarrow.

His considering the odds was a bit disconcerting. Counting the recent arrivals from the airplane and the boat, he estimated at least a dozen arrayed against Lina and him, six to one against a cripple and a Smurf. Not too bad. The General always said cunning, deceit, and boldness of action trumped raw force every time. The key to victory, he decided, rested in freeing the astronauts and the cosmonaut and arming them to even up the odds a bit. Might as well plan big.

While Cassidy waited for full darkness, he fished malleable C-4 from his ruck and fashioned a half-dozen balls out of the putty-like explosive, into which he pressed gravel he set Lina to gathering. He then stuffed into each a blasting cap crimped to a five-second length of time fuse and an M-60 igniter. Grenades.

He spoke softly to Lina as he worked. She understood nothing he said, but the sound of his voice seemed to calm

her. He needed a serene Lina for the job ahead, not the
Lina apt to explode at the first provocation.

"The airplane has to go first," he explained. "We can't
chance the tangos escaping in it with the space guys. Plus,
it will serve as a diversion." He gazed off in the direction
of the airplane, now obliterated from sight by darkness
and rain drizzle. "I wonder what the boat brought?"

"Cass mine?" Lina murmured, rubbing her cheek
against his hand.

"I have *got* to teach you new words if this relationship
is going to grow."

He inserted a fresh thirty-round magazine into his carbine, arranged the "grenades" in the wheelbarrow for
quick access and looked around to test the quality of the
darkness. Rain fell in a steady but light mist and infrequent sheet lightning flash-glowed in the lower cloud
cover. Conditions were not apt to get any better. Trackers
couldn't be far off.

"It's time to start the party, old girl," he said.

It was going to take some persuading to get Lina hitched
to the wheelbarrow again and headed in the right direction
without her whimpering with every step. He raised the
poor wet miserable creature by her shoulders from the
ground and wrapped her in his BDU jacket; he still wore
his T-shirt and combat harness. Grateful for the smallest
kindness, Lina snuggled up to him in the wheelbarrow.

Cassidy drew her into his arms and held her tight,
warming her, feeling rotten for using her emotions
against her like this. Such a simple thing. A puppy would
have been wagging its tail all over. Once devoted to its
master, a dog will do anything for a pat on the head and a
crumb from the table. This was not, Cassidy confessed,
his finest hour.

They started out on what Cameron, being more reflective, might have called a quixotic quest. Cassidy faced forward in the wheelbarrow this time. Lina insisted on stopping every few yards to touch Cassidy for reassurance, but otherwise she proceeded across the open toward the airplane in silence, the only sound of their approach the whisper of the conveyance's single wheel in wet grass.

Rain and low ceiling made it one of the darkest nights on record, broken only by intermittent blips of lightning. Its revealing them to observers in the schoolhouse was something they had to risk. Cassidy counted on the aircraft sentry being one pitiful human being by this time, on his knees seeking shelter underneath the wings, crouching down inside himself and becoming unaware of his surroundings as men will when they are extremely uncomfortable.

They were almost within touching distance of the Colt before Cassidy made out its outline slightly darker against the skyline. Rain hissed against wings. Cassidy grabbed Lina's hand to halt her. She had also spotted it and sounded about to hyperventilate.

"Khto?" a voice challenged.

Cassidy waited, one hand on Lina, the other drawing his combat knife. The younger Kragle brother was known in Delta as its best knife thrower, a skillful technician who could hurl a knife fifty feet or more with deadly accuracy and who often demonstrated it for Delta recruits.

"Astanofka! Khto?"

Lina panted with near hysteria. Cassidy feared the sentry would hear her. Only the drum of rain on the aircraft's metal skin drowned her out and saved them. He patted Lina's hand. *Please, Lina!*

The sentry appeared as a darker piece of the moving night. Lina cried out, unable to further contain herself. Cassidy launched his knife at the same instant and heard the solid, satisfying *Thunk* of a score. The man fell with a heavy sound and Cassidy heard him gurgling and thrashing about in the grass. Why couldn't they die clean and instantly like they did in the movies?

Lina bolted and would have fled all the way to China if Cassidy hadn't grabbed her hand. She was like holding onto a wild mustang. The wheelbarrow capsized and spilled out Cassidy and his gear. She dragged him through the wet grass until she collapsed from the dead weight, huffing and mewling in terror. Cassidy embraced her to settle her down.

"It's okay, sweetheart. It's over now. I have to finish the job. Understand?"

Of course she didn't, but Cassidy was getting in the habit of talking to her anyhow. In the background the wounded sentry thrashed about in the grass. He kept trying to scream but only managed to gurgle on his own blood.

After a moment, Lina calmed and signified she was okay. Cassidy released her and dragged himself and his bad leg through the wet grass toward the downed guard. Lina followed, also crawling.

A hand reached out of the blackness, seized Cassidy's arm with a death's grip, and jerked him into the dying man's clutches. Warm blood spilled into Cassidy's face. He whiffed fetid breath in his nostrils and the coppery stench of fresh blood. They rolled in the grass. Searing pain shot through Cassidy's leg. The damned thing would never heal if he kept re-breaking it.

Grappling, Cassidy found the haft of his knife with the blade lodged up to its hilt in the guy's upper ribs. He leaned into the handle and twisted the blade, ripping viscera and arteries and vitals in the enemy's chest cavity. Lightning flashed the hideous scene into relief. Trailing thunder covered the dying man's final shriek before he went still and silent.

Cassidy wrenched his combat knife free of flesh and rolled away from the corpse, retching violently with his face against the ground as he sought fresh breath. His stomach roiled with disgust. Killing was nasty business, and killing close up where you smelled and touched your adversary was the nastiest of all.

He looked up finally and, not hearing Lina, figured she must have bugged out on him. Now it was his turn to feel something akin to terror. Without Lina, he might as well be a slug crawling helplessly about in the mud.

"Cass mine?" Plaintively.

Relief flooded over her. "You betch 'um, Red Ryder. Bring the wheelbarrow. We have work to do."

Lina finally understood what he wanted. She retrieved the wheelbarrow, gathered up his ruck, grenades, and rifle, and helped him into the bucket. Cassidy doubted those at the schoolhouse heard the struggle; they would have had to be looking out a window at the precise instant of a lightning flash to have seen anything.

He directed Lina to wheel him around to the other side of the airplane. Using her as a prop to lean on, he struggled to his one good knee in the bucket, found the handle, and slid the cargo door open. It was darker inside than outside, if that were possible.

He lifted himself into the bay, using only his arms. His legs were afire with pain from the thigh down. Lina sprang into the airplane after him, reluctant to let him get out of her reach. The plane seemed empty—or at least almost so. Cassidy slithered about, feeling with his hands until he found the twin canvas sacks brought up by the boat crew. Each weighed forty pounds or so. He opened the flaps on one and felt inside. It contained a single, large metal box.

Realization sank in immediately. He had had experience with methods terrorists were most apt to use in transporting nuclear materials, most recently in the Philippines on Operation Deep Steel. What he encountered now was a lead-lined container inside which, he suspected, was a WMD commonly called a suitcase nuke. The other pack undoubtedly held its counterpart.

Mightn't other bombs have already been flown out? Destination the United States of America?

CHAPTER 58

Washington, D.C.

The General was unconvinced that Smoke the New Age
hippie had spilled everything he knew, for all that Darren
had had him by the ring in his tongue. The only clues
Smoke divulged as to Jennifer's whereabouts were am-
biguous ones concerning a Harvard acquaintance named
"Patsy," who was possibly a professor, two Arab-looking
men who were with Patsy when Jennifer left with them,
and the Harris For President Rally in Washington's Rock
Creek Park that Jennifer and Patsy *might* attend. The rally
appeared the place to start, and it, in Darren's mind, a
long shot.

   Both Darren and Vanda felt out of place in the throngs
of loud, slouchy-trousered, caps-on-backward youth and
the even-louder boomer generation hippies with their pony-
tails, flower-child dresses, double chins, and paunches.
They worked their way through the crowds, searching
faces for Jennifer's. The sick-sweet odor of commingled
beer and marijuana lingered in the air, along with the
smells of hot dogs, onion rings, and body odor. Vanda's
slacks and French twist made her look slim and way
younger than the gray in her hair indicated. Darren
thought she had a quality almost everyone else at the
rally lacked—class. His own Dockers and blue shirt accented his height, military walk, and military buzz cut.

•

Rally goers stepped aside to stare after them. Darren heard someone sneer *"Bourgeoisie"* in a tone that suggested he had come up with the Marxist term on his own and was so proud of it.

A stage had been erected near the creek, around which the crowds milled, and from which speakers bawled and howled over the PA system. Every few minutes, devoted Harris followers cheered mightily, as though on cue; a sea of the usual antiwar placards jabbed and poked at the sky, among which appeared a large number of additional ones raging against a "corrupt" president and his administration. One young thing in low-rider jeans, a high-rider top, and a sign that read TYLER TORTURES POWS gushed, "This campaign is all about allowing people to come together and tell their life stories."

The General shook his head in dismay. Perhaps universal suffrage was not a good thing after all.

The bullet wound in Darren's arm burned suddenly and his hackles rose at sight of avowed socialist George Coalgate Geis on the stage with Senate minority leader Tom Talmadge and POP national committee chairman Russell Pope. The bushy-haired old man sat glowering out from the stage like a resurrected Stalin while Senator Talmadge at the lectern explained that while candidate Lowell Rutherford Harris could not be here in person, he was definitely here in spirit. How was it that Geis kept showing up whenever things were going wrong? The General stared directly at Geis. The billionaire either failed to see him or refused to acknowledge him.

"Who is he?" Vanda asked. "I've seen his picture somewhere, but I don't recognize him."

"George Coalgate Geis." The name tasted bitter on his tongue.

"The man who shot you?"

"He didn't shoot me personally. One of his goons did."

"There were a bunch of newspaper clippings about how Geis was working for Senator Harris to make sure he became the next president. Wasn't there also some kind of murder involved when you broke up the Committed?"

"Geis isn't working *for* Harris," Darren corrected, "but he *is* one of Harris's main benefactors. He sees himself as a kingmaker in the vanguard of socialism."

As far as Darren was concerned, still smarting from his experience with the California Assembly in Sacramento and his even more recent encounter with the Second 9/11 Commission, Geis was not much worse than most Washington pols. All, or at least most, of them, it seemed, went around stabbing each other in the back, concocting dirty tricks, and bending the law in their quest for the Holy Grail of power. Diogenes would have had to look a long time in D.C. to find an honest man. Honest men like Woodrow Tyler rarely made it in big-time politics when the common guiding credo seemed to be: *These are my principles. If you don't like them, I have others.*

"If you want the easiest way to define the Tyler Doctrine," Talmadge was saying through his megaphone, "it's what I call a Testosterone Presidency. They've worked hard making him look like Gary Cooper in *High Noon*. Mr. Tyler acts like he was anointed by God after 9/11 and is leading the world through a vicious cycle of escalating violence. His views are the views of extremists, not adherents to a peaceful world where we can all get along together . . ."

"If a politician found he had cannibals among his constituents," the General commented, "he would promise them missionaries for dinner."

All of a sudden Vanda went up on her tiptoes and started jumping up and down in her attempt to see over the heads of the crowd. "Oh! Oh! I think I see her!"

"Where?"

"See the long dark hair?"

Darren ran interference for her. The girl with the long, dark hair turned in astonishment as they rushed at her. Vanda physically deflated with disappointment. Tears welled. Impulsively, Darren drew her into his arms. She melted against his chest. After she began to collect herself, Darren felt awkward and presumptuous. He didn't want to let her go. At the same time, he didn't want to hold her either. The Ambassador always said there was no damned fool like an old damned fool.

"We'll keep looking," Darren promised. "We'll find her."

A few minutes later, while they continued to work the crowds, Darren caught sight of Smoke, who was also apparently looking for Jennifer. He took Vanda's hand and drew her quickly behind a Coney cart to avoid being seen. The General's height provided him a commanding vantage point.

While they watched, a Middle Eastern type in his early twenties shouted at Smoke from out of the crowd. The guy reminded Darren of photographs he had seen of the 9/11 airline hijackers—the same predatory look, the furtiveness of a fox among hens . . . So he was racial profiling. Irish Catholic altar boys weren't the ones committing terrorism worldwide.

From the looks of the encounter, Smoke and the Middle Easterner were not meeting by chance. The meet seemed planned. The two argued briefly, gesticulating and pointing. The Arab type seemed to finally give in. He motioned to Smoke and the two of them filtered out of the park, heading toward Sixteenth Street.

"Maybe they'll lead us to your daughter," Darren said.

CHAPTER 59

Walter Reed Medical Center

Doctors warned the big black man in ICU 414 that he was in no condition to work, but the first thing Domestic Preparedness Director Claude Thornton of the FBI asked for when he regained consciousness was a secure telephone system. Both legs and one arm were in casts and traction, a helmet-like dressing encased his shaved bowling-ball head, and his face had been scorched, giving him a peeled-skin appearance. Detective Wells was dead and Agent Jonathan Barnes was in critical condition; they took the brunt of the explosion when they stepped in front of Claude just before the bomb went off, thus saving Claude from more serious injuries or even death.

The last thing Claude remembered before, hurting like hell, he woke up in a Homeland Security jet bound for Walter Reed were the two Arabs in red headbands crouching in the shipping container, staring unblinkingly out into the bright lights when the steel door swung open. "*Allahu Akbar!*" they shouted in unison.

Still somewhat dazed on the airplane, he had mumbled, "What was it? A nuke?"

Whoever was there said, "You'd be on a cloud by now if it was nuclear, Director. With lots of other folks."

Three hours later, injuries treated, groggy from sedatives, he worked the phone with his remaining good hand

and arm. He had Deputy Director Fred Whiteman on the hook.

"You are one hard-headed African American intent on killing yourself sooner or later," Whiteman scolded.

"Would you miss me, sweetheart?"

"Not much. You know how we honkies are. You really opened a box this time, Claude."

"Literally. Tell me about it. I don't remember much."

"It appears the two assholes had rigged themselves with C-4 in case they were discovered. Martyrdom and all that, you know. It turned out successfully for them. Even all their little pieces are dead meat. It was a bloody mess in there, but from what we can determine so far it was a command-and-control center full of operable computers, phones, and satellite equipment. One of the scumbags was an Egyptian carrying airport security passes for New York's Kennedy Airport, Washington's Ronald Reagan, and Newark International. There was also the usual stuff like you found on Staten Island in Patsy Koehler's house— schematics and photos of the Capitol Building, plus some stuff on BUCKUS and Geis's Americans Standing Up For People."

Claude pondered it. His head continued to ring from the explosion and he wasn't thinking clearly. "C&C Center? There *is* something big going down. Who was the container being shipped to?"

"I have the address here. B&S Enterprises in Bethesda, Maryland. The address seems to be good. Guess what? We may find our CEO there is the clown with the red nose, green hair, and big shoes."

"Ronald McDonald!"

"The one and only— Well, not the *only*. It's a front company."

"Have you talked to Ronnie McDonald again?"

"He seems to be out of pocket. I know what he's going to say, Claude, even if Geis is behind it. We're not going to be able to prove he ordered that container shipped to B&S. I assume that's why Patsy Koehler was in Charleston, so she could receive it, arrange for it to be transported to B&S, and then disappear with no link. The container would have vanished the same way after it arrived in Bethesda. No one would ever have been the wiser if the tangos hadn't gone crazy, cut off Patsy's head, and left the parts lying around. Sloppy. That was dumb."

"Arrogant," Claude corrected him. "They never thought we'd make the connection in time. So do we have any idea who was going to receive the shipment in lieu of Koehler once she was dead?"

"Jennifer Stratton?"

"I don't know. The way these cells work, one bunch has no connection with another. The one that beheaded fat mama Koehler may not even have known about the shipment. That's how disconnected they are. I'm also betting the cell working out of B&S knows nothing except the container is on its way. That could work to our advantage. Fred, we got to work fast before news of this gets out. Here's what I have in mind: I want JTTF to deliver ASAP a container to B&S . . ."

He hung up the phone when he was done and immediately dialed Homeland Security. There might not be much time left; Claude had a feeling all along that they were working under a deadline. He had to consider the possibility that a WMD was already inside the United States just waiting for an attack to be coordinated.

"Mac, we've been concentrating on the Federalist National Convention in Manhattan," he said when he got through to MacArthur Thornbrew. "That's not the target. All their claptrap about shutting down New York is nothing but a diversion to draw our attention away from the actual target. Mac, they're going to nuke the Capitol Building in Washington."

He explained about the C&C container, Patsy Koehler, B&S Enterprises, the whole thing . . .

"Do you know about Operation Cold Dawn?" Thornbrew asked when Claude finished.

"I must have been out to recess when that happened."

"Get in touch with General Kragle at USSOCOM or General Etheridge at CENTCOM. Nukes *were* coming in, but Delta Force, I hope, has stopped them."

"We have to be certain, sir."

"You can never be certain about anything in this business. Claude, I think we've covered our end. Do what you need to do on yours, but get some rest too."

"After this is all over. Some days make me think I should go back to Mississippi and farm for a living."

"I've always wanted to teach," Thornbrew said.

Claude then rang General Kragle's secure cell phone. The General sounded rushed. Apparently, he hadn't heard about Charleston.

"Claude, let me call you back in a bit."

"It's important. What are you doing—jogging in a crowd?"

"Something like that. I'm chasing a female."

"At your age."

"Gotta go."

Claude's day was a long way from over. He telephoned Justice to bat around the facts with the attorney general. As usual, he laid them out discussion point by discussion point: the six Jihadia he apprehended on Flight 427; how that led him to lawyer Patsy Koehler in New York; the raid on her home resulting in a killed FBI and a dead terrorist and the seizure of plans for using WMDs; Koehler's asso-

ciation with radical Muslims and with BUCKUS and
Americans Standing Up For People, whose expressed
purpose was to shut down New York and radicalize public
opinion against the war and President Tyler, but whose
real purpose might be to cover up and assist in a much
more diabolical criminal operation; how George Coalgate
Geis funded those groups with the help of donors like
Senator Lowell Rutherford Harris's wealthy wife; Patsy
Koehler's murder in Charleston Harbor while attempting
to receive the covert terrorist command-and-control center; the blowing up of the shipping container and its two
residents, which also killed a cop and injured another two
FBI agents; B&S Enterprises; Ronald McDonald . . .

It was all there as far as Claude was concerned. Murder,
conspiracy to import WMDs, illegal alien smuggling,
conspiracy to commit sedition . . . All violations of either
the RICO statutes or the Patriot Act.

"Geis is already facing charges," the attorney general
noted.

"Yes, sir. It's involving another one of the organizations
he funded—the Committed. That goes toward showing
common scheme with all Geis's other crimes."

"We have to be careful that this isn't seen as piling on
in an election year."

Like the General, Claude Thornton was not a political
animal. Lawmen saw things in black and white, right and
wrong, legal and illegal.

"What are you saying, sir?"

"Work up your reports and a prosecution and I'll take a
look. We have to be circumspect and make sure we have
all the evidence. Otherwise, with the election approaching, this will be looked upon as a witch hunt against Party
of the People and Harris."

"So what you're saying is we take a chance on their

shutting down New York and bombing Congress—but if we act to stop them we're witch hunting? That's fucking incredible."

"That's politics, Claude. It's a dirty business."

CHAPTER 60

GEIS PUNCHES FOR HARRIS

Washington, D.C. (CPI)—One of the wealthiest men in America, George Coalgate Geis, whose fortune is estimated at $8 billion, is using his money to fund drug legalization, euthanasia, abortion, freeing of all prisoners . . . and that's just the beginning. The avowed socialist's stated goal, his mission in life, is to defeat President Woodrow Tyler and replace Tyler with a president more accepting of his position—Senator Lowell Rutherford Harris.

Geis has begun a twenty-city tour to bolster Harris's campaign. He's also published a pamphlet—"Why We Must Not Re-Elect President Tyler"—that's being mailed to 3 millions voters. He regularly plays Saudi banker to left-wing groups such as Americans Standing Up For People, World BUCKUS, International ANSWR and Americans Coming Together. BUCKUS alone has received more than $10 million from the currency speculator. Geis is now out on a $20 million bond pending trial after being charged with a myriad of crimes involving activities of one organization he funded, the Committed.

"We admire Mr. Geis's dedication to the ideals of a fair and open society and to his support of public policy that promotes economic growth and social equality both here and in the world," said POP National Committee Chairman Russell Pope . . .

CHAPTER 61

Partizanskaya River Valley

Staff Sergeant Steve "Doc Red" Mancino was nervous. His mouth felt so dry it was like he had cotton stuck in his throat. He and Ice Man Thompson made their way through rain-dripping timber so dark that, even wearing NVGs, he had to depend upon the glow strip sewed to the back of Ice Man's Ranger cap to keep from getting lost.

The redheaded little medic had left Georgia two years earlier after enlisting in the army under a contract specifying he be provided the opportunity to qualify for Special Forces. His Uncle James had worn the Green Beret in Vietnam and was killed during the siege of the Special Forces camp at Long Vei in 1968. Steven Mancino grew up on stories of how U.S. Army Special Forces Team A-101 and several hundred indigenous soldiers held off a numerically superior force of North Vietnamese tanks and infantry in one of the most exciting examples of collective bravery, endurance, and will that any war had ever produced. A book had even been written about it. It was only natural that the nephew might grow up yearning to emulate the hero uncle—in everything, that is, except the *posthumous* awarding of the Silver Star.

Doc Red made it through parachute training, the SF "Q" Course and graduated with honors from the SF Medic School. He applied for Delta Force and was accepted because of his school grades, his dogged determination to succeed, and a letter of recommendation from the Medical Branch at Fort Bragg. Assigned as a backup medic to Major Brandon Kragle's Troop One, Doc Red received his first combat mission assignment only because Major Kragle cut Doc TB Blackburn from the detachment because Blackburn's wife gave birth. Blackburn had given the new medic his orientation to Troop One; he sounded disappointed but not resentful.

"Major Kragle is Delta's best Troop commander," he told Doc Red. "We've been in some shit together, in places like Afghanistan, the Philippines, and Algeria. The man knows his business. Stick with him and listen to what he has to say. He'll get you out again if anybody can."

"He dumped you because you have a wife and baby!" Mancino found that hard to believe.

"He doesn't ask anything of others that he doesn't live up to himself. He's resigning from Delta after this mission for the same reason he cut me—his wife's having a baby. You're lucky in going on a real man's last mission."

Doc TB had no intent in sounding prophetic about the mission literally being Major Kragle's last—as it might very well be from the looks of things. Major Kragle, Doc Red was discovering, was all his men said of him and then some. Mancino was determined that, on this his first combat counterterrorist mission, he would make the detachment commander proud of him, whether Major Kragle ever knew about it or not.

He and Ice Man worked downslope from the mine entrance to the river's edge, cautiously picking their way and depending upon darkness and rain drizzle to mask their movements. Ice Man knelt next to the water to listen, his SAW braced barrel down across one shoulder. The river rushed past with a deep-throated gurgling, a lapping against the mud rind of the bank, and the delicate hiss of fine rain on the surface. Ice sniffed the wind; Delta folk-lore said the taciturn weapons man had developed the senses of a killer wolf during his long sojourn with Delta Force.

They eased on upriver toward the footbridge, their assignment to get in position to block forces from interfering with movement when it came time for Cold Dawn to clear out. Soon, through NVGs, Doc saw the footbridge inscribe a darker Rorschach blot against the lighter hue of the river. Ice froze when they heard a man speak to another somewhere in the blackness of the forest not far away.

Ice backed slowly, placing his feet in the tracks he had previously made, intending that they should withdraw a few yards and find a location to set up and block while they waited for the mountain to erupt like a long-dormant volcano. Doc Red, also backing into his own footsteps, made a fundamental error of judgment that a more experienced operator might have avoided. Whereas Ice Man habitually felt all around with his toe before placing weight on his foot under blind conditions, the medic hurried his procedure.

His footing on the edge of an unseen shallow washout gave way. He plunged into it with a crashing of brush loud enough to rouse an entire cemetery of dead. The night around the end of the bridge immediately lit up like the flickering lights on a Christmas tree as the jittery mafia guard, already on alert, lay down on their triggers in a mad minute.

Gloomy Davis and Perverse Sanchez high above the river on their pinnacle lookout were startled by what sounded like a premature hell-for-leather firefight breaking out in the woods near the footbridge. Muzzle flashes winked and the hard spate of firing filled the river valley, echoing and re-echoing in diminishing waves both upriver and down. It was too late for sneaking-and-peeking, snooping-and-pooping when the shooting started. Gloomy got on his Motorola and raised top at the ORP.

Top Sculdiron's accented voice sounded all business: *"Sergeant Thompson must have encountered opposition. Sergeant Davis, you and Sergeant Sanchez let nothing move. The commander and Sergeant Dade must have time to work."*

"Roger that, Top."

For night work, Gloomy Davis had changed out his Redfield scope for an experimental AN/PVS third-generation Starlight telescopic rifle sight with FLIR (forward-looking infrared) heat-detection capability and computerized range finding. This state-of-the art piece of equipment required little ambient light to be effective, certainly not as much as NVGs needed, and the view it provided was almost as clear as daylight vision through the Redfield. With it he had been keeping tabs on the Oriental with the Moison-Nagant on the opposite peak from him.

The enemy sniper jumped to his feet in alarm when sudden shooting rattled out from below. *What a fucking amateur!* Gloomy watched him through the Starlight. The Chinese stood there, obviously feeling secure in his lofty perch, and aimed his long rifle toward the footbridge. He wore NVGs, which could be awkward in effective shooting, but he appeared to have found a target. A stab of flame speared from the muzzle of the Moison-Nagant.

Ice Man and Doc Red were down there and perhaps vulnerable.

Gloomy already had range and wind cranked into his sights. In his prone position, he settled crosshairs on the Oriental and watched him work to bolt in a second round. A shot he never got off. Gloomy gently stroked his trigger and came down out of recoil in time to see the target jerk when the bullet struck him. The impact knocked him off the edge of his hide. The body rolled and tumbled downhill until a twisted and gnarled cedar caught it.

"Velly, velly solly, asshole," Gloomy mocked, then wondered when he had become so cavalier about killing a fellow human being.

He would deal with that later. Right now it looked as though Ice Man and Doc had shoved a stick up the ass of a bunch of hornets.

He swung Mr. Blunderbuss to cover the footbridge, the Starlight brightening the view. Several perps at the bridge's near end continued to pop rounds downrange, but as far as Gloomy could tell there was no return fire. Four or five men were running across the bridge from the other side to join the melee.

"Do you see 'em, Sanchez?"

Perverse's regular NVGs were inferior, but he made out the targets anyhow, vaguely.

"Chew know I do, Gloomy."

"Can you hit the bridge?"

"Do a bear shit chili peppers in the woods?"

Perverse already had his 60mm mortar set up and ranged in. The little mortar emitted a tubed pneumatic sound as it lobbed an HE shell on a low arc toward the bridge. Gloomy watched through his scope, ready to adjust. The running men were halfway across when the shell exploded in the water alongside, geysering the poor bastards and making them mill in momentary confusion.

Gloomy seized the moment for a second shot. A man went down hard and slid off the edge of the bridge. He caught himself on a railing bar and hung on. He seemed to be yelling for help. *Fuck you, Jack.* The others panicked and abandoned him to his own means, retracing their steps to the far side even faster than they came. The wounded man succeeded in pulling himself back onto the walkway where he writhed pitifully in a futile attempt to get to his feet and follow his buddies.

"Let 'em go," Gloomy said. "Get this end of the bridge."

Perverse dropped fifty meters and lobbed several more rounds. Bright eruptions blinked in the timber, puffing up luminous white smoke. The shooting stopped. Perverse also ceased fire to save his remaining rounds for another crisis. He watched the wounded man on the bridge through his NVGs.

"*Cabróne pobre,*" he muttered. "Gloomy, finish the mother off, will you, and do heem a favor?"

"I don't do favors," Gloomy said. He also declined to kill without a purpose, and this guy was clearly out of the action.

Now they waited for the mountain to go up.

Top Sculdiron couldn't be certain if Major Kragle and Sergeant Dade in the mine shaft heard the racket outside. He vibrated their Motorola to warn them, the agreed-upon signal, but wasn't sure if they received it. Reception proved tricky in places like that.

Mad Dog and he huddled in the dark rain outside the entrance to the mine, Mad Dog sitting on the three rubber boats rolled up and ready to be lugged down to the river and inflated with CO_2·when the elements returned and it came time to bug out.

"Fu-uck a toad!" he exclaimed as mortar rounds thumped at the bridge and the ringing bark of Mr. Blunderbuss accented the fray from high above the river.

Then there came that awful uncertain silence that always followed action. Rain whispered in the trees. Top attempted to raise Ice Man on the Motorola. "Dawn Romeo, this is Delta Dawn . . ."

Finally, Ice came up in a hushed voice. *"Top, all the rotten luck. Mancino is down."*

"How bad is it?"

"Bad. He somehow caught a stray round in the leg."

"Do you require assistance, Dawn Romeo?"

"Negative. I'll bring him out when it's over."

"It should not be long now," Top said, adding, "Do not let the kid die, Dawn Romeo."

CHAPTER 62

Although the cave was warmer than most caves because of all the machinery and electricity, things were about to get a whole lot warmer. Some giant chimp might have stuck his twig into the ants' nest for all the commotion the outside bursts of rifle fire and mortar explosions generated inside. Workers shouted and screamed at each other as they scurried into hiding. Huda Ammash, Dr. Death, and her associate, the Arab in the green turban, ducked among the vats and generators and Brandon lost sight of them.

He let them go. The two guards at the cave entrance posed the most immediate threat. They looked confused for the moment, running back and forth, heads twisting and rifles sweeping, concentrating on the cave entrance rather than on the interior since they *knew* no one had gotten past them. Still up to his waist in the pool, Brandon leaned out into the cave with his carbine elbowed up for support and the safety *off*. He held his fire, giving Diverse as much time as possible before the guards discovered him.

Diverse forsook stealth altogether. The tall black man, barefooted and wearing only his drenched BDU trousers and brown T-shirt, the ruck full of explosives thrown over one shoulder, broke free of the shadows near the wall and hurried toward the cave entrance, still laying out prim-adet, paying no attention to anything other than the task ahead, depending upon Brandon to watch over him.

Someone inside the cave out of Brandon's field of view shouted a warning. The guard wearing the sheepherder's shirt whirled around. Brandon was ready. He tapped him to the floor with two quick rounds, the reports magnified inside the confined area.

He took out the second sentry with equal efficiency.

Diverse had dropped to his knees to study the situation. He looked back. "Major, I'll have to spike walls on both sides of the mouth."

"Do what you gotta do."

Brandon scrambled out of the pool and stood dripping at its edge, crouched down on the balls of his bare feet and ready for action as he scanned for the next threat. Machinery whirred and snarled and coughed, filling the chamber like continuous growling in the throat of some fantastic predatory beast. Brandon sprinted forward into the cave and dropped a knee behind a pile of slag metal where he could keep an eye both on the entrance and the interior. He wondered if there might not be an escape route; Dr. Death and her workers seemed to have vanished.

Diverse worked rapidly. His battery-powered drill issued a high-pitched whine swallowed almost completely by the cave's heavier and louder appliances. He finished one set of holes, stuffed them with RDX and a plug of C-4 on the outside, then packed another twenty pounds of explosives into a deep-cut ledge above the holes. He looped primadet into both places, made sure it was secure, then rose to his feet with the rest of the explosives and roll of detonating cord to scurry past the entrance to the opposite wall.

The bang of a pistol shot filled the cave. The bullet splatted rock and dust from a stalactite next to Diverse's head. A second shot in instant followup made him grunt in pain and drop out of sight behind the cave formation.

"Dade!"

"I'm winged, Major, but I'm okay. Can you see him?"

It was hard to tell origin of sound because of the cave's acoustics. Brandon figured the shots must have come from near the other wall, beyond the machinery in the middle.

"He's got me pinned down, Major."

"Hold what you got. I'm working on it."

A giant conduit ran in from the river through the cave mouth to a huge holding tank that occupied much of the floor all the way to the ceiling. Brandon ran to it, bent over with his weapon at port arms. He flattened his back against it and glanced toward Diverse. Diverse remained out of sight.

His ears still rang and the cave seemed to vibrate from the gunshots. He eased around the curve of the tank. A half-dozen workers cowered behind it. They looked up at the armed intruder, fear writ huge in their paled expressions. None appeared armed.

"Shit!" Brandon exclaimed, feeling like the Monster from the Black Lagoon. He couldn't leave them behind and he couldn't take them with him.

Another shot from the pistol rang in his ears. "Okay!" Diverse shouted to let Brandon know the shooter failed to score. It wouldn't be long before the gunman realized Diverse was unarmed and became more aggressive.

The workers went into fear overload. They threw up their hands and, kneeling, began either praying to Allah or begging Brandon not to kill them, sometimes both simultaneously. At least this bunch was in no hurry to commit martyrdom and collect their virgins.

Brandon noticed a closed door to a room apparently cut into the cave's stone wall. He jabbed the workers with his carbine and urged them toward it, keeping behind them to avoid exposing himself to the unseen shooter any more than necessary. He ordered them inside. They seemed all too happy to obey. Other workers were already huddled together in what appeared to be a small grotto office. Huda Ammash was not among them. Neither were the spacemen. Brandon shoved in his last captive and closed the door on them. It was made of steel with a heavy hasp and an open padlock. He slipped the ring of the padlock through the hasp but left the lock open in case he ran across other people who needed confinement. Like, for example, Dr. Death.

Now for more pressing business. He padded around the outer edges of the industry buildup that took up most of the center of the cave. Intense overhead lights glared down, almost totally eliminating shadows. Steam hissed. Something clanged and rattled like a malfunctioning diesel engine. His bare feet left wet prints on the stone floor; his clothing dripped puddles.

He dropped on hands and knees and scouted to the end of a low vat of some sort. He peeked around the end toward the opposite wall from which the gunshots seemed to originate. He saw that the cave overhead slanted downward in that direction to form a kind of low-ceilinged alcove that shut out much of the light from the main area.

As he watched, the character in the green turban slipped out from the shadows and stood tall, craning his neck as though trying to pinpoint his hapless target and get off another shot. He suddenly looked excited and threw up his pistol to fire.

"Hey, raghead!" Brandon shouted in diversion.

The terrorist pivoted toward his voice. Brandon squeezed a double into his chest. The impact of the bullets sounded like a butcher's mallet pounding on a beef carcass. The guy dropped without making a sound.

Immediately, a shriek of rage from the shadows. Huda Ammash, the Queen of Hearts herself, Dr. Death, leapt for the dropped pistol. Brandon could have shot her, but he preferred not to. He beat her to the weapon as she threw herself on the floor and grabbed for it. He stomped on her outstretched hand and jabbed the muzzle of his carbine against her forehead.

She looked up at him like a cornered cobra. Brandon immediately recognized the resemblance between her and her daughter. He thought Dr. Death must have been a beautiful woman in her youth, but hate had leached the softness from her features and left them hard and ravished. One day Katya would look like this, if she lived long enough.

Huda Ammash spat out in English, "Shoot me—if you have the balls."

"Are women also rewarded with virgins in heaven?" Brandon shot back.

If looks could kill.

Brandon used his bare toes to pull the dropped pistol toward him and out of her reach. He picked it up while still covering the woman with his rifle. He slipped it into a trouser cargo pocket and scanned the area for other holdouts. There seemed to be no one else—just the two dead guards, the equally dead man in the turban, the workers locked in the office, and the Queen of Hearts.

"Get up," he commanded.

"Or—?" she taunted.

"I'll shoot you where you lie."

She believed him. She got to her feet, a dumpy little Iraqi woman in a soiled smock. Her glower revealed the torture she would enjoy inflicting on him if she had the chance.

"Sergeant Dade?" Brandon called out, keeping his eye on Dr. Death.

"Yo!" Diverse responded.

"All clear. Can you do it?"

"A few more minutes."

Brandon prodded Dr. Death with his rifle. "Let's go."

"You are . . . Brandon," she guessed.

"Is that what Katya told you?"

"Katya?"

"Your daughter Zafina."

Huda Ammash looked him over. "I can see why my daughter may have been taken with you," she admitted. "She talked about you with regret. She said you would come anyhow, but I did not believe her after she stole your detonators. I see now why my Zafina may have admired you, infidel that you be."

"I'd like to continue this stimulating conversation, Doctor, but you know how it is. Move."

She stood rooted and laughed directly into his face. "American, you must realize you will never leave this cave alive. Neither will any of your men within a mile of here. Even a small explosion inside this chamber will set off a chain reaction the likes of Hiroshima. Won't it be thrilling to ride a mushroom cloud seen all the way to Japan? I have prepared a fail-safe program that cannot be undone."

Mocking laughter failed to touch her eyes. They hardened into agates, telling Brandon that this mean-assed bitch would die before telling him anything. The only question was—was she bluffing?

Bluff or not, Brandon had a mission to accomplish. In Delta Force, mission always came first, above all else, including human life down to his own.

Enough talk. He shoved her across the cave toward the office. He opened the door and pushed her inside with the workers. She turned and faced him defiantly.

"Goodbye, Brandon," she said. "It is not over—and we

will win in the end. You must realize that. Soon there will be mushroom clouds in America, and we will win."

Her bitter cackling penetrated the steel door. Brandon hesitated over the lock. Then he clasped it shut, locking the terrorist scientist and her minions inside. He would consider the ethics of it later. If there was a later. After all, should the Queen of Hearts not be bluffing, the entire mountain would soon go up anyhow, turning miles of southeastern Russia into another barren Chernobyl.

He turned his back on the locked door and trotted toward the mouth of the cave where Diverse worked, checking other offices for the spacemen on the way until satisfied that they were not here. He set his mind not to think of outcomes and the future, only of the immediate now and what had to be done.

Mortar rounds exploded outside as Gloomy and Perverse kept everyone back from the cave entrance. Good men, all. Never would there be their likes again after this generation of Americans passed.

Diverse was about finished with his second charges. Primadet ran across the floor from the first set to the second. Diverse finished tamping RDX into large cavities he breached into ledges in the wall. He quickly packed the rest of his explosives around it and stuffed the cut end of the primadet deep into C-4.

"Where were you hit?" Brandon asked as he kept watch.

"In the *dierreriere*!" Diverse replied in disgust. His wet trousers kept blood from showing. "In the ass! It's a minor flesh wound, but I'll never live it down."

Brandon didn't bother to pass along Dr. Death's threat. What good would it do?

Diverse tossed aside his empty ruck. They met each other's eyes. There was nothing else to say.

They hurried back to the pool and dived in, surfacing a minute later inside the mine shaft. Brandon felt for his flashlight where he had left it. Its beam cast back the darkness enough to allow Diverse to untie his end of the primadet from the rotted timber where it was secured. Working silently, he stretched it down the tunnel and lay on his belly as far away from its end as he could and still reach it with the muzzle of his rifle.

"Major, no sense in both of us taking the shock," he offered. Primadet burned so rapidly that it was a minor explosion in itself. "I'll give you two minutes."

"Sergeant Mozee Dade, we're either leaving together or not at all."

The black man turned his head and gave a searching look into the darkness toward his commander's face. Brandon sprawled next to him on his belly. They shook hands before Brandon directed the flashlight beam to illuminate the end of the detonating cord. Diverse extended the carbine one-handed until the end of the cord was almost inside the muzzle. Both turned their faces away and buried them underneath their free arms for protection.

"Do it!" Major Kragle said.

CHAPTER 63

Russian Coast

So many variables were involved in the transportation and use of nuclear weapons that Cassidy couldn't be sure if the nukes would detonate or not when he touched off the airplane. Rather than take a chance on making another Grand Crater in Russia, he worked Lina to exhaustion wheelbarrowing the canvas sacks back to the river and transferring them into the skiff in which the boatmen arrived; he would simply take the nukes out with him. His rubber inflatable was built to accommodate two passengers. If all went as planned, he and the *Soyuz* crew made four persons, not counting Lina, requiring a ride downriver to its mouth and out to sea to link up for extraction. They would have to use the skiff.

Not counting Lina. The thought gave Cassidy pause. Seated in the wheelbarrow, he watched Lina struggle with pulling the canvas bags through bankside growth and hoisting them into the terrorist boat. Backlighted by lightning from the distant storm, she resembled some gnome stealing corpses from a midnight graveyard. In a matter of only two days—had that been all?—she no longer seemed so disagreeable and grotesque to him. Loyalty and devotion such as hers required decades to develop in normal people.

And how would he repay her? He couldn't take her with him, not a foreign national from a country where officially

America had never been, not after the dead men Cold Dawn was leaving behind. After that night, after the mafia or terrorists or whoever the hell these people were discovered the corpses left at her farm, he wouldn't give a proverbial plugged nickel for her chances of survival if she stayed behind.

Collateral damage. Little people in the world became collateral damage in war. That didn't make it right, but that was the way it was. Some lives had to be sacrificed for the greater good. Including, Cassidy acknowledged, his own if it became necessary.

From the earliest days Cassidy could remember, the General had drilled into his sons a sense of obligation and duty. Of mission. The General placed mission ahead of everything else. So did his sons.

Lina staggered back to the wheelbarrow and collapsed into Cassidy's arms. He patted her and whispered comfort while she rested.

"Cass mine?" A question.

He placed her hand on his cheek. The palm felt wet and labor-rough. He wanted her to feel him nod.

"Cass mine!" she exclaimed in delight. His heart went out to her.

After a few minutes he urged her to push him back up the hill to the airplane. She rested and kept watch for trackers while Cassidy, working out of the wheelbarrow, molded C-4 to struts underneath the wing tanks. It wouldn't take much of an explosion to incapacitate the Colt, but he used four times the plastic necessary. He wanted one damned big boom and a gasoline blaze to draw the enemy out of the school the front way while Lina and he busted in the back way like the U.S. cavalry.

He attached electrical blasting caps and miniature receivers to the charges, which allowed them to be detonated from a distance using a tiny radio-like "hell box" that transmitted an electrical impulse. That accomplished, he repacked the remaining explosives and figured he had two hours, maybe three, remaining before his detachment members passed the school in their rubber boats heading for a rendezvous with the submarine.

He had to work fast. They had been lucky so far in that their trackers seemed to be having difficulty following a trail through the forest in the dark, plainly inscribed though it might be in the soft soil.

Lina had apparently adjusted to her role as beast of burden. Her childlike faith in Cassidy's ability to protect them grew with each passing hour, even though he was handicapped and she had to do most of the work. She had gone from refusing to even look in the direction of the schoolhouse to wheeling him freely about its grounds.

"Good girl, Lina," he approved, feeling rotten all over again.

Dim lights shone through the front windows of the schoolhouse. Likely kerosene lamps. Cassidy envied the terrorists their shelter. They remained out of the elements while Lina and he suffered tremendously from exposure. Both were chilled and shivering in the light mist of rain. Neither had had anything to fuel their bodies since breakfast.

At his direction, Lina propelled him wide of the school to approach through the cover of forest on the ridgeline where there was less chance of their being seen during intermittent lightning flashes. He had no way of knowing how near the two sent out to look for them might be. Lina and he merely played hide-and-seek with them in hopes of delaying the inevitable.

Traveling through the woods was tough on Lina. Pushing him, she was panting heavily by the time the black outline of the decaying building came into sight only a few yards ahead. There were no windows at the near end, and therefore no light.

It took some doing to transfer Cassidy, his explosives, weapons, and the wheelbarrow across the crumbling stone fence without making noise to alert those inside the schoolhouse. Afterward, Lina hugged the side of the building with Cassidy in the wheelbarrow and listened for a sign that their intrusion may have been detected. Lightning fire-glowed in the forest behind them, forming shadows flitting and dodging furtively about. Lina's eyes bugged out of their recessed caves.

After a few minutes' listening halt, Cassidy signaled Lina to proceed. The wheelbarrow's tire whispered in the grass and the un-oiled wheel issued a tiny squeaking that Cassidy had not noticed previously. Alert for danger, he rode the wheelbarrow with weapon locked and loaded in the manner of a stagecoach shotgun rider of the Old West passing through Apache country.

They blundered into a pile of trash in the darkness. Old tin cans and other junk rattled horrendously in the night. They froze for a full two minutes. When nothing happened, Lina carefully extricated them from the hazard. Cassidy decided the occupants of the schoolhouse must be congregated in the front area where the lights were, else they would have heard the racket.

Good. That made the job easier.

He tried the knob on the back door. It was unlocked, as he expected. There probably weren't even keys to it anymore, even if the lock was operable. Leaning forward in the wheelbarrow, he inched the door open until he saw a hallway illuminated by a dim glow at the other end. These guys must feel awfully secure not to have sentries stationed at every possible avenue of approach. It meant the two men sent to Lina's farm had not yet returned with bad news; they were still out there somewhere, tracking. Wait until they discovered the dead sentry Cassidy knifed at the airplane.

Lina was about to hyperventilate again. Cassidy squeezed her hand until she breathed normally. Then by a series of signs and gestures he informed her that on his command she was to propel him inside and down the hallway toward the front lights. He thought she understood. He only hoped she proved capable of following directions when things got hot. He might as well be a turtle tossed onto its back if she went all to pieces on him.

A comforting thought.

He switched the miniature hell box into the firing-sequence mode. He looked up at Lina, whose face the darkness concealed. Her breathing sounded regular. A good sign.

He pressed the button. Instantly, a tremendous explosion seared across the lowering skies and rattled dust from the old school building as the airplane vanished in a fireball. Cassidy flung the door wide.

"Go, Lina! Go!"

CHAPTER 64

Bethesda, Maryland

The General and Vanda trailed Smoke and the Arab as they left the Harris For President rally at Rock Creek Park. It appeared the Arab had been sent to meet Smoke and was now taking him somewhere else.

"Run and get your car and pick me up on Sixteenth Street," Darren said. "I'll stay on them."

She hurried off. Darren stalked his quarry north through wads of students and professor college-types congregating at the park for another of their interminable protest marches that afternoon after the rally. The shifting crowds provided Darren reasonable cover and concealment as they casually blocked traffic in the street and openly defied police officers who tried to keep things moving.

The two men were getting into the same ratty canary-yellow peace van parked earlier at Smoke's house. Darren was afraid he was going to lose them when Vanda broke her Saturn through the mobs to pick him up just in time. He jumped into the passenger's side, slammed the door, and pointed as the van pulled away from the curb.

"Follow that car!"

Vanda tossed him an amused look.

"I always wanted to say that," he added.

"Being a detective might be exciting if I knew Jennifer was going to be all right," she said.

Darren knew all too well from his years in combat, and from deploying SpecOps, that things didn't always turn out well.

The peace van, coughing out greasy clouds of smoke that all but consumed it, obeyed all traffic laws, and seemed in no particular hurry as it proceeded north on U.S. 29, then turned west on East West Highway toward Bethesda. Vanda drove skillfully, weaving in and out of traffic to keep from losing the van that now took on some speed as it hauled toward Maryland. Its color and size made it easy to trail.

"Do you suppose they've seen us?" Vanda worried.

"I think our friend Smoke is just a bad driver."

"That foul-tongued creature is no friend of mine." She was still peeved from their previous encounter with him.

Darren returned Claude Thornton's earlier phone call while Vanda drove. He couldn't get an answer on Claude's cell phone. Odd. The General dialed the Domestic Preparedness Office.

"Where's Perry Mason?" he asked Della Street.

"Walter Reed."

"As in hospital? What's he doing there?"

She filled him in on Charleston without going into details. "He's lucky, but he's going to be laid up for a few weeks. He didn't get off as easy this time as he did in Tulsa. I can give you a number at Walter Reed, but it's hard to get through to him. I've been trying for a half hour myself. His cell phone's out of order from the blast."

"Do you know why he was calling me, Della?"

"He said something about . . . cold dawn? That ring a bell?"

"It does."

"Do you want to leave a message, General? I'd let you talk to Fred Whiteman, but Fred's on his way to Bethesda."

"Bethesda?" That was curious. "What he doing in Bethesda?"

"Search me. He spoke to Claude on the phone, then jumped up muttering something, and ran out of the office. I'll tell them both you called when I see them—which I expect may be around election day the way things are going now."

"Vote right," the General said.

"I always do."

There wasn't time for the General to make followup calls. The yellow van swerved off the first exit to Bethesda and executed a number of turns before it pulled up in front of two large sheet-metal warehouses surrounded by a vacant parking lot and a high chain-link fence. It stopped before a locked gate.

Darren instructed Vanda to whip into an alley a block away. She turned the Saturn around in a loading area and nosed it out toward the street ready for action. By that time, two men were walking out of the larger of the two warehouses to open the gate for the van. The van drove through. The gate was re-padlocked. A double cargo door slid open and swallowed van and gatekeepers before it closed again. The westering sun shone on the bare concrete parking lot, and a flock of starlings undulated by and landed in a swarm on the warehouse roof.

Darren got out. "I'm going to take a look inside. Wait here."

"Don't you dare order me, Darren Kragle. My daughter may be in there . . ."

Rita also had had a mind of her own. Vanda got out. They left the Saturn in the alley to make their way on foot down a series of other alleys until they came to the fence at the back of the warehouses. There were windows on the side of the main building, but a huge Dipsy Dumpster blocked the view of anyone looking out them.

Vanda's face appeared flushed, but she eyed the building with determination. "Judging from today," she said, "I suppose I should always wear slacks when I'm with you."

"You look good in slacks."

Her face flushed brighter.

Darren looked around and found a discarded metal post, with which he pried up the bottom of the fence. They crawled through and reached the Dipsy Dumpster in a low rush without being seen. When they paused to catch their breath, Vanda had a smudge of dirt on her nose and perspiration matted loose strands of hair to her forehead. Darren wondered if Rita would have liked her, then concluded she probably would have.

Vanda looked around. "Don't the police call this breaking and entering?"

"The army calls it expediency."

"I'll side with expediency."

Everything looked abandoned and quiet except for the starlings crackling on the roof. Darren espied a pile of cardboard boxes and shipping pallets lying on the ground next to the wall by the nearest window. He took Vanda's hand and showed her.

"I feel like a grandmother pretending to be Nancy Drew."

"That must make me a soon-to-be Grandpa Bobbsey Twin."

"We're dating ourselves. But we can be the Cisco Kid and Pancho as long as it returns my daughter."

Darren hesitated. "Vanda, don't get your expectations up. She may not be here."

"Then we'll keep looking."

"Yes," Darren said after a pause. "We'll keep looking."

A car passed by on the street out front. As soon as it was out of sight, Darren tugged on Vanda's hand and they dashed to the pile of boxes. Vanda breathed hard from exertion and excitement. Darren eased underneath the low window and peeped through a corner while Vanda impatiently picked at his sleeve.

"Is she in there?"

"Shhh."

The van with the green peace symbols painted on its sides and a late-model blue Chevrolet Cherokee were parked together in the middle of the otherwise empty warehouse. Banks of overhead lights blazed even in the daytime. Several closed doors on the far side indicated offices or storage rooms. No one was about, not even Smoke and his friend.

"Is she?" Vanda persisted, whispering.

"I don't see anyone. Hold a . . ."

Two Middle Easterners in jeans and T-shirts came out of one of the offices and walked briskly to the front where they looked out a window toward the street as though expecting other arrivals. Vanda edged closer to Darren. He made room for her. She knelt between his knees, her back snugged into his front. The window was dirty and fly-specked and hampered views from both sides. Darren showed her the two men. She sighed.

"Where's that . . . *that creature*?" she asked.

Darren shrugged. They kept vigil for several more minutes until another office door burst open in response to a buildup of loud voices speaking Arabic. Two more men surged out into the warehouse in heated argument, shouting at each other and flinging their arms. One of them was the predatory-looking character who had fetched Smoke there from the park.

Smoke followed them out. Overhead lights glinted off

his nose ring, lip ring, and earrings. His pink hair resembled some outlandish wig a skinny circus clown might wear. Following came a third Jihad type wearing a Polo shirt, trailed by a young woman in low-rider jeans and a green sweater. Darren knew right away from the large brown eyes, dark hair, and her full lips that this was Vanda's daughter Jennifer. There the resemblance ended. The girl's hair was long, tangled, and oily-looking. She was barefooted and looked either sleepy or drugged. Vanda emitted a pained gasp of both astonishment and joy.

"Oh, my God! What have they done to her?" Vanda moaned.

Contrary to the impression Smoke tried to convey earlier that Jennifer meant nothing to him, the couple was obviously elated at their reunion. Smoke tousled her hair while she casually stroked his butt. Vanda almost choked, watching this.

Darren had a hard time deciding whether or not Jennifer was being held against her will. She seemed to know the other men and, although she had told her mother on the phone that she was afraid, she appeared quite at ease. Everyone stood by and waited for the quarrelers to finish. They kept glancing toward Jennifer and Smoke, as though they were the subject of the debate, but the couple, more engrossed in each other than in a catfight, didn't seem to notice. Besides, they didn't understand Arabic.

"What's happening?" Vanda sounded distressed. The scene reminded Darren of two foxes snarling at each other over a pair of geese.

The fight between the Arabs ceased all at once with a final loud decision. They turned and stared at Jennifer and Smoke. Jennifer stopped stroking Smoke's butt. The silly smile froze on her face.

"What the fuck—?" Smoke began.

The pair from the front window stalked over to join the gathering. Saying nothing more, the five Middle Easterners surrounded their intended victims and pounced on them like a pack of dogs attacking young house cats. The pack had the couple pinned to the floor and bound hand and foot within the time it took Darren to restrain Vanda from rushing to her daughter's rescue and thus giving away their presence.

The guy who brought Smoke from the park hurried into an office and returned carrying a long scimitar-like knife and slipping an automatic pistol into his waistband underneath his shirt. Smoke and Jennifer were dragged to the yellow van and tossed into it like bags of grain.

CHAPTER 65

Partizanskaya River Valley

Gloomy Davis grabbed the earth with both outstretched arms when the explosion detonated with a muffled but mighty bark inside the mountain and the ground began to shake underneath him like an earthquake somewhere off Richter's scale. At that moment, filled with sudden dread and resignation, he knew he was about to die when the nukes in the cave went off and he and his little piece of real estate were blown into kingdom come. Oklahoma was going to feel this one!

"*¡Hijo de Dios!*" breathed Perverse Sanchez, awed.

The pinnacle opposite them where the Chinese sniper lay dead went first. It convulsed much more violently, like a giant wet dog shaking itself. It began to collapse into the cave, slowly sinking into the upheaval below, coughing enormous clouds of dust that, like osmosis, merged into clouds and rain to form a mixture that was neither earth nor atmosphere but a combination. Dust filled Gloomy's mouth. It blinded Perverse so that he cried tears of mud. Mud crusted their bodies.

Holding on, they waited for the big one to follow, the secondary explosion that would end them before it really began. Gloomy squeezed his eyes closed and held his breath. He had heard that a nuke going off seared out the eyes of anyone who viewed it other than through very dark glasses. He didn't want to die blinded.

They waited, and they waited some more, and at long last when the ground began to settle down a bit, Gloomy opened one eye tentatively and discovered that Sanchez gripped his arm in a vise and that both were still on earth as they knew it. It took him another minute or more before he caught his breath normally. His mouth and nose caking full of the taste and smell of dust turning to mud was the most extraordinary thrill of his life. It assured him that he was still alive.

The nukes had not gone off!

He felt like jumping and shouting with relief and glee. Perverse's Latin nature was less restrained. He rolled over toward Gloomy and folded the sniper into a giant *abrazo*, hugging him so soundly while he laughed with relief and poured out volumes of Spanish that Gloomy thought he was going to have his breath squeezed out. He finally extricated himself.

"Easy, Perverse. This is a bit more diversity than I'm prepared for."

"Chew know, Gloomy, we are *alive*!"

"Either that, or heaven ain't what I thought it'd be."

The cave's mountain opposite them continued to burp smoke and dust. Gloomy tried to use his rifle scope to glass the area below, but found the air so clogged he saw nothing except a black abyss. There was nothing else they could accomplish there.

"Bug-out time," he said.

It crossed his mind how much worse the explosion and earthquake must have been inside the mine shaft compared to up there on top of a separate peak. As he scrambled to his feet and started feeling his way down the pinnacle to rendezvous at the ORP, the dread he felt when he thought the nukes might go off paled against the thought of never seeing his commander and friend alive again.

* * *

Down by the river, Ice Man and Doc Red experienced the explosion as an initial teeth-rattling concussion that blew through the forest like a miniature cyclone, rattling and shaking trees, stirring up minitornadoes of leaves and forest debris and whipping rain sharp as needles through the air. Ice Man threw his own body across Doc Red's wounded one in a protective but otherwise useless gesture. If the detonation went nuclear, nothing they did would deter it from vaporizing them into their individual molecules and cells.

As with Gloomy and Perverse, Ice Man knew they had made it only when the belly howls of the mountain dropping into the cave produced a blinding groundswell of dust and airborne mud. Grit blasting and sifting through the air gabbled in the trees. Ice placed a hand on the Doc's chest. He was still breathing. He coughed weakly.

"It's over?" he asked hoarsely.

"Yeah."

"I reckon I'm in a bad way," the medic said. The bullet had punctured his outer thigh and exited near the groin.

The cave was still deflating. Ice Man heard tons of rock and soil avalanching into the river not far away. He got on his knees and checked the web belt tourniquet he had tightened around Doc's upper thigh at the groin to check femoral bleeding. The entire upper leg was mushy and bloated to twice its normal size, proof that the tourniquet was failing because of the location of the wound. Of all the rotten luck. A man could bleed to death inside his own leg while hardly losing a drop of blood on the outside. Ice Man cinched up the belt. Doc cried out in pain.

"Ice, you go on down the road," Doc Red said. "I'll be along dreckly. Do you hear me, Ice?"

"I hear you."

"Ice, you can't carry me through this, dark and dusty as it is."

Ice Man coughed up mud and spat. "Doc, have you ever had tender roast lamb with mint sauce the Scottish way?"

"What?"

"I know it's not a mess of collard greens and hog jowl and black-eyed peas like you Southern boys generally like, but Diverse and I have talked it over. When we get back to Bragg, he and I are going to prepare the best dinner Troop One has ever passed between their teeth. You're going to be there, Doc. So, damn you, hold on."

That amounted to an entire speech in Ice Man terms.

Top Sculdiron came up on the Motorola. *Dawn Romeo, this is Delta Dawn . . . Cold Dawn. I repeat, Cold Dawn.*

That was the signal for the elements to disengage and reconsolidate for exfiltration downriver.

"Top, how about Earth Dawn?" Ice asked. *Earth Dawn* was the commander's call sign.

There was a pause in the ear before, "*Nothing yet.*"

Ice man scratched the bullet scar on his cheek. Then he rose to his feet, slung the SAW and Doc's carbine over his back by their carrying straps, and bent over to hoist Mancino into his arms.

"Sorry, Doc. This may hurt—but we're getting out of here."

Team sergeant Sculdiron and Mad Dog Carson had set up outside the mine shaft and to one side of the opening. They expected the explosion to blast through the shaft like through the barrel of a gun. Since neither Top nor the Dog were much at casual conversation, they waited in silence through the separate episodes of gunfire for the expected explosion, nuclear or not.

They heard the powerful, deep-throated *crump* and felt

the detonation moments later through the crust of the earth. Wearing earphones connected to his Shadowfire radio, Mad Dog looked up to catch a glimpse of the mushroom cloud he half-expected to follow. He saw only a brief flash of light through the trees as the detonation shot fire out the mouth of the cave before the mountain folded in on itself, disintegrating faster and faster as it absorbed energy, vomiting debris and waste into the atmosphere. Smut spewed out the narrow mine shaft in a giant's hiccup of released wind, then continued to hiss out smoke and dust.

"Fu-uck!" Mad Dog muttered after it became clear there was going to be no followup nuclear explosion. "I was kinda looking forward to seeing the other side."

"You are a strange man, Sergeant Carson. You can send the message now. Mission accomplished."

Dog murmured through his mike. After a minute, he began breaking down his equipment for movement.

"Message receipt confirmed," he reported. "Central Command is tickled plumb shitless. If them nukes had'a gone off, they'd have felt it in Florida when our rosy red airborne asses fried."

Top issued the "Cold Dawn" signal to each of the outlying elements through his Motorola. Major Brandon and Sergeant Dade failed to respond. Top tried them again, waited a few minutes, then attempted a third time. He and Mad Dog crouched next to the mine opening. Dust continued to percolate out of the shaft. Rain hissed on the river below.

"Take the rafts down to the water and inflate them," Top finally ordered.

Mad Dog made three trips to the river to transport the three rubber boats and his commo gear. On his second run, he heard brush breaking. He knelt, weapon ready, although he personally doubted the surviving terrorists and guards had the balls left for encounters of the second and third kind. Most likely they were fleeing to the hills and congratulating themselves on their good fortune at still being alive.

Ice Man struggled out of the forest with Doc Red unconscious in his arms.

"How is he, Ice?" Dog asked.

"Not good. What do we hear from the major?"

"Fu-uck." A tone that told Ice everything.

Dog had already inflated the first two rubber boats. They bobbed against their painters on the swift-running river, unseen in the night. Rain made them sound like balloons sprayed with a water sprinkler. Dog pulled a boat close to shore and helped Ice settle Doc Red into it. He had to feel around in the darkness to make sure the medic's arms and legs were all in. Ice stifled a cough against the thick air.

"We're not bugging out on the major and Diverse?" Ice Man said as Dog started back up the hill.

"No," Mad Dog said.

Gloomy and Perverse were back when Dog reached the ORP to carry the last raft to the river. Gloomy lay belly down with his head stuck inside the shaft opening, probing the tunnel with a flashlight beam while dust hissed out around him. Mad Dog said nothing. Perverse helped him take the last raft and commo gear to the river. When they got back, both Top and Gloomy were on their knees at the shaft entrance shining lights inside.

"Do not forget that mission is what is important," Top was saying in his accented English. His patience sounded sorely tried.

"Mission *is* accomplished," Gloomy shot back. "We leave no one behind. Remember that?"

"When I command, I think of what Major Kragle will

do," Top argued, his voice thin. "He would never trade other lives for lives already lost. The mine shaft is perhaps weakened and could cave in at any time."

Gloomy dug in. "The boss is not dead. We need to go in after him."

"We will wait another quarter hour," Top compromised.

Gloomy gazed as deeply into the shaft as his flashlight beam and the dust allowed. Although he knew the top sergeant was right, even acknowledging that Major Brandon would have made the same decision under similar circumstances, he felt responsible for Brandon and had for years acted as the officer's personal security whether Brandon needed it or not. But sometimes there had to be compromises when equal duties and principles conflicted. As, for example, when Sergeant Cassidy Kragle turned up missing upon insertion. No way must a detachment risk its mission and the lives of men searching for a member who was undoubtedly dead.

That same principle applied now. But, damn it! Gloomy couldn't go off and leave his friend without at least giving a shot at bringing him back.

Top was one hardcore sonofabitch. "Sergeant Carson, you and Sanchez go down to the river and set up a security perimeter for the launch site in case these assholes have not had enough yet. Don't pull out too far in the woods."

"I'll go with you inside the cave, Gloomy," Mad Dog offered softly over his shoulder.

"A quarter hour," Top Sculdiron repeated.

CHAPTER 66

Russian Coast

Cassidy Kragle expected touching off the airplane would draw the schoolhouse occupants rushing outside—and he wasn't disappointed. He heard the front door fly open as soon as the plane went up. Lina charged him in the wheelbarrow down the hallway toward the lights, galloping as fast as she could on her stubby legs, chuffing and wheezing from excitement. As they stampeded out into the dusty rotunda, two kidnappers who stayed behind as guards turned toward them in astonishment. Firelight outside from the blazing airplane flickered wildly through an open window and the doorway and across faces stunned at being attacked by a man riding a wheelbarrow.

Hesitation cost them their lives. Cassidy tapped both of them with his carbine. It was easier than CQB drill in the House of Horror back at Fort Bragg. They dropped side by side. Kerosene lantern light washed yellow and dull across their twitching bodies and illuminated corners where old boxes, desks, chairs, tables, and other discarded junk were piled at random among cobwebs and dust. Cassidy saw no sign of the spacemen.

Lina was in a dither and couldn't seem to stop moving. She pushed him in fast circles, her bare feet slapping on the floor.

"Lina! *Lina!*"

He needed her listening to him, paying attention, not fugue-ing out.

"Cass! *Cass!*"

"You're doing great, old girl! Get me to the door. Hurry!"

He pointed and waved her forward. She understood. The group that had stampeded outside milled about in utter confusion, torn between gunshots from inside the school and the flaming runway. Fire backlighted them into wonderful shadow targets. Cassidy squeezed off bursts from the open door, sweeping his flickering muzzle back and forth. Delta troopers, the best riflemen in the world, trained their skills and instincts for such occasions. Cassidy knew he was scoring from the *Thuck-Thuck* of bullets striking flesh, screams of pain and fear, and the way several figures jerked and crumpled in the savage firelight.

Survivors bolted for the concealment of the darkness and the cover of the stone wall. One or two dragged body parts and wailed in anguish. Cassidy recognized the girl in the wool coat and Cossack hat as she vaulted over the fence with the others and disappeared from sight.

He knew he had cut down the odds considerably, what with the casualty at the airplane, the two fresh corpses inside, and however many others he may have fatally drilled or winged out front. Those left wouldn't be in that big of a hurry for a return engagement. He had bought precious time.

He dropped the empty mag from his carbine and replaced it with a full one. Lina crouched fearfully behind him and the wheelbarrow. Gesturing, he instructed her to pull the wheelbarrow out of the doorway. He looked around while she slammed the door shut.

"Americans?" he shouted. "Where are you? We're here to take you home."

After a moment, a cautious voice piped up from behind

a closed office door, sounding as though its owner found this too hard to believe. "Who are you?"

Cassidy glanced at Lina. "You wouldn't believe it," he said.

Lina was hyperventilating again. Cassidy mimed taking deep breaths. She followed his example and in a moment, somewhat recovered, wheeled him to the closed door. It was locked. Under normal circumstances, he would have kicked it in.

"Stand back in there," he called out. "Get as far away from it as you can."

He heard movement beyond. He waited a second, then fired. A single bullet smashed the door lock and shook plaster dust from the ceiling. Lina pushed the door open for him with a broom leaning against the wall, then jumped back with the broom ready for ugly stick action.

The room was dark except where yellow lantern light flooded a square through the doorway. An astronaut in blue NASA coveralls shuffled hesitantly into view, blinking against the light. His hands were tied in front and his ankles hobbled, but he could still scuff along. Two other spacemen, one American, the other Russian, slowly joined him in the light, all three looking gaunt, worn, filthy, and totally incredulous as they stared at the man in the wheelbarrow and the diminutive, wild-looking girl wielding her broom.

"My God!" the first astronaut exclaimed, he the taller of the three, space station commander Roger Callison.

"I told you you wouldn't believe it," Cassidy said.

"Where . . . where are the others?" astronaut Larry Williams asked.

"I'll explain later when there's time," Cassidy said. "Stick out your hands."

He whipped out his knife and sliced through the ropes that bound the astronauts' wrists.

"You had secret Star Wars technology aboard the capsule . . . ?" Cassidy said aside to Callison. "Where is it?"

"They brought it with us. The leaders were using another room. It might be there."

"Get it. Quickly."

Callison hurried off down the darkened hallway.

"Do exactly as I tell you if you want out of here alive," Cassidy instructed the other astronaut, Williams. He gestured toward the dead guards sprawled in widening pools of their own thickening blood. "Take one of their AK's and watch the front. Shoot anything that moves. Understand? Come on, man. Move it!"

The astronaut asked no questions. He hurried to comply. The cosmonaut extended his hands. Cassidy sliced through his bindings. "Do you speak English?"

"But of course," Alexei Minsky said.

"Good. Lina doesn't. I need you to help me. You and I are going to rig this room with explosives. When we're through, we're going to get out of here and let that bunch outside have it back."

If all went well, the rest of the kidnappers outside would be lured back into the schoolhouse in time to be caught in the resulting explosion, allowing Cassidy and his little band the chance to escape without pursuit. It was iffy, but it was the best plan time had to offer.

"I understand," Minsky said. He eyed Lina curiously. "She is Russian?"

"A brave Russian woman. I couldn't have done this without her."

Minsky spoke to Lina in her native tongue. She beamed and responded in Russian.

"She is not quite right in the head," the cosmonaut explained, dismayed.

"She is more right than anyone I've ever known. Now, let's get busy."

Commander Callison returned carrying a ragged daypack stuffed with materials. "Everything seems to be here," he said.

"Good. You hang on to that, no matter what."

He gave each of the astronauts two of his homemade C-4 grenades and showed him how to use them. "Save one of the grenades for the backpack," he advised Callison. "Blow it up if everything turns to shit and it looks like we're going to be overrun. We don't want that stuff back in their hands."

He then wrestled his ruck into position in the wheelbarrow so he could get to his remaining demolitions.

"You blew up the airplane," Minsky said.

"Guilty. We're going to make a bigger bang now."

He began work, constructing several charges of RDX by quickly wrapping bags in demo wire, cutting them off and adding a booster of C-4 to each. Into the C-4 he planted electrical blasting caps attached to tiny radio receivers that allowed him to set off the charges from a safe distance with his hell box. He showed Minsky where to place each charge for optimum effect. He wanted the entire schoolhouse to go up like a nest of five-thousand-pound bombs when they allowed the enemy to drive them out of it.

It was slower work than he anticipated. Luckily, he had a pair of legs at his command in the cosmonaut. Bossing around Russians from his wheelbarrow, first Lina and now Minsky, seemed to be the only thing he had done all day.

Williams at the front window threw one of his grenades and fired a short burst from his purloined AK-47. "The natives out there are getting restless," he reported.

"We're on the last charge now," Cassidy said.

He was imbedding the blasting cap into the charge when Lina cried out in alarm. Cassidy snapped to attention in time to spot two bruisers thundering out of the back hallway into the rotunda, leading with their assault rifles. Damn! In his concentration over the demo, he had forgotten all about the two men sent out earlier to check on their comrades now dead behind Lina's chicken house. They were better and faster trackers than he thought. Carelessness like this could get him killed.

He had propped his carbine against the edge of the wheelbarrow while he worked. He reached for it, knowing already he was too late. The sudden movement upset the wheelbarrow, spilling him out onto the floor in a scrambling heap. He combat-rolled away as the intruders' weapons bark-barked in unison, deafening in the enclosed room, splashing fire and smoke. Bullets splintered wood where he had been, chased him as he continued to roll across the floor.

Minsky ducked through the door into his former prison, a diversion that likely saved Cassidy. Both shooters caught the movement and interpreted it as assault from a different source. They wheeled to confront the new threat—and in that instant Lina erupted into one of those rages Cassidy knew her capable of from personal experience.

Armed only with the broom, she hurled herself at the intruders, swinging savagely with all her considerable strength. Dervish-like, she was all over them, whipping hell out of them with the broom in a fight driven by passion and protectiveness for the man she fished out of the sea. A short, stout troll, soaking wet, with bushy hair, shrieking war cries that seemed to boil out from the depths of her soul.

It was a fight she could not win; it ended quickly. One of the invaders took a little hop back from the broom's reach and sawed her almost in half with a point-blank burst from his assault rifle. Her little body in the nondescript old house dress jerked spastically with the multiple impacts, like a puppet out of control. Blood sprayed all the way across the rotunda. The beginning of an unearthly scream shorted out almost before it left her lungs.

"No! No!" Cassidy bellowed. He felt every bullet that pierced her flesh.

Combat-rolling slammed Cassidy against a wall. Sprawled on his belly, consumed now with Lina's own rage, he pounded lead into her killer, kept pounding it in on full auto, filling him with it before the dead man knew he was dead and before he could fall.

Astronaut Callison, from the front window, shot the second bandit. Cassidy turned his carbine on this dying terrorist and emptied the rest of his ammunition into him before the body struck the floor. He held such a death's grip on his weapon that he couldn't let go the trigger even after he expended his ammo and the bolt locked open. He heard somebody roaring with pain and fury and realized only after the shooting stopped that it was himself.

Glaring at his downed enemies, he tossed the empty carbine away and rolled to one side to draw his knife to finish them off if they so much as gasped a final breath. Splattered with blood and gore, some of it Lina's, he dragged himself across the floor toward her killers, knife in hand.

They remained motionless. It seemed that even while dying they dared not so much as gurgle lest they be carved into pieces.

Gradually, Cassidy's wrath drained away and left him feeling numb. He crawled to Lina's side. She was breathing Cheney-Stokes, gulping for air, her chest heaving. From her loose breasts to her pubic was a mass of raw flesh chewed and shattered into hamburger. The fresh stench of it almost made Cassidy sick. Her dress had been blown up around her waist. She wore no underwear. Cassidy tugged her skirt down to cover her nakedness.

"Lina?"

Her eyes looked unfocused and dulling, sunken into her skull deeper than ever. A trickle of blood and drool escaped her trembling lips as she attempted to speak. "Cass . . . ?"

Her head lolled to one side, toward Cassidy. She stopped breathing. Her eyes glazed and the pupils fixed. Cassidy sat up against the wall with the leg she had splinted for him sticking out straight in front. He pulled Lina's body into his lap, painful though it was, holding her close and burying his face into her neck, stroking the dead girl's frizzy hair, smelling her and her blood as it soaked into him. He wanted to always remember that peculiar scent of earthiness that belonged exclusively to her.

Collateral damage.

CHAPTER 67

Bethesda, Maryland

The predatory-looking Arab who brought Smoke from Washington tossed his long-bladed knife into the yellow van through its open window, adjusted the semiauto pistol carried underneath his shirt and climbed into the driver's seat. One of his cohorts got into the passenger's side and looked over the back of the seat into the cargo space to make sure Jennifer and Smoke remained securely tied. He laughed and brandished his knife. The driver rolled up his window and kicked over the engine, boiling smoke out into the warehouse.

"They're taking my baby!" Vanda cried. "I'll never see her again!"

Jihadia types had a bloody penchant for cutting off their victims' heads, as events in Iraq were making all too clear to Americans.

The General had little time to puzzle over what in hell this was all about, what these foreign-looking men were up to, why Jennifer was with them in the first place, and why they had turned against her like this. For some reason, evil men where shanghaiing Vanda's daughter and her worthless pink-haired boyfriend and were obviously going to murder them, for whatever motive. The General could care less if Smoke had his throat slit, but Vanda didn't deserve losing her daughter. It would break her heart, and that, the General suddenly realized, mattered to him. He had to stop the van.

He looked around for something to use as a weapon, finding only a short length of steel tubing, an old-style water pipe common before PVC plastic came into use. He hefted the pipe and decided it would have to do.

The warehouse's overhead doors screaked open and the van eased forward. Darren had no time for planning, only for reaction. He broke for the front of the warehouse, running close to the building, Vanda trailing him but losing ground. He felt winded by the time he reached the front corner. Damn! There ought to be a law against getting old; there was a law against everything else.

The van nosed out onto the parking lot, the setting sun red-washing the yellow sides and the green peace symbols painted on them. The driver looked directly at the larger, older man blitzing toward him with grim determination, behind which charged a graying-haired woman wearing her hair up in a French twist. The length of pipe in the old man's hand was already ripping through the air.

Darren shattered the driver's side window with his pipe, exploding shards of glass. The driver stomped on the gas to get away. Not quickly enough. Darren grabbed the window frame, feeling remnants of the window slashing into his palm. He held on anyhow, running alongside and jabbing the end of the pipe viciously into the driver's face again and again, wanting to hurt the bastard and hurt him badly.

Blood sprayed. The driver screamed and grabbed his face, releasing the steering wheel and reflexively jamming the gas feed against the floor. The van caromed in a tight circle on smoking tires, whipping the General about so violently that he almost lost his grip.

He couldn't let it get away. Concrete split the knees of

his Dockers. A shoe went sailing. He discarded the pipe to free his hand to reach through the window and grab the driver's clothing.

The guy pounded back with his fists, raining blows into Darren's face, but his foot slipped off the accelerator and the van lost momentum. Darren wrenched the door open and threw the terrorist out onto the tarmac. He scrambled into the driver's seat in the same movement and lunged across the center console to get to the Jihadia with the knife. The guy yelled and slashed at him as the van coasted toward the fence.

On the tarmac, Vanda propelled herself at the discarded driver, who rolled across the pavement with the momentum of having been ejected from the moving vehicle. He struggled to his knees and was drawing his pistol when Vanda threw every ounce of her petite five-one frame into a brawling tackle that would have done any NFL player proud. She and the terrorist tumbled on the parking lot, locked in deadly combat.

She was on her own. Darren had his hands full inside the van. Somehow he had ended up jammed head and shoulders down against the passenger's floorboard with his foe on top. Unable to gain leverage, his legs flailing the air, he grasped the wrist of the hand that forced the sharp point of the knife toward his exposed throat. It was only inches away. As the guy bore down against Darren's resistance with his entire weight, he chanted maniacally, *"Allahu Akbar! Allahu Akbar!"*

Occupied as they were with life-and-death struggles, neither the General nor Vanda was aware of events unexpectedly unfolding around them. The unengaged Jihadia were not so tunnel-visioned. As they surged from the warehouse to join in the one-sided fray, a flatbed truck carrying a huge steel shipping container drove up the street, followed by a plain blue sedan filled with burly men. Instead of stopping at the locked gate, the truck revved its engine and rammed through the chainlink like a Caterpillar tractor.

The door on the shipping container, a Trojan horse, swung open. Teams of SWAT officers poured out, vaulting onto the parking lot and giving chase as terrorist suspects, jumping around in consternation and surprise, attempted to flee.

"Halt! Halt! FBI!"

A shot or two rang out. One SWAT officer executed a beautiful kick into the face of the man who had Vanda pinned to the tarmac. The guy flipped over backward. Other agents swarmed over, wrenched the gun from his hand and handcuffed him none too gently.

Vanda sprang to her feet. "My daughter!" And she was off to where the van had rolled to a stop against the fence.

Darren was bigger and stronger than his opponent, but being wedged on his back between the seat and the dash robbed him of any edge. He gripped the knife hand posed over him, straining and quivering with his every muscle and sinew as the terrorist threw his weight again and again into a desperate effort to end the struggle. Veins in his forehead and neck stood out like cicatrix scars. Sweat made the guy's wrist as slippery as holding onto a wet eel. Darren felt the knife point pricking his throat, drawing blood. He was losing his grip.

It occurred to him that this was a hell of a way to die after all the foreign wars in which he had fought for the past forty years—at the hands of an Islamo-fascist in the seat of a rusty van inside his own country.

The van door sprang open. Someone yanked the knife-man out and off him. Darren gasped for breath.

After a moment, befuddled about what had happened

but thankful it had, he slowly sat up and looked around. JTTF agents were running all over the warehouses and parking lot, rounding up suspects. Darren's assailant now lay on the tarmac sullenly handcuffed and guarded by two SWAT officers. Other agents helped Jennifer and Smoke out of the van and untied them. Vanda and Jennifer collapsed into each other's arms, sobbing with relief.

General Kragle climbed wearily out of the front seat, still winded, blinking against the dying rays of sunshine, wondering. Cavalry seemed to have arrived in the nick of time, just like in the movies. Only instead of charging in on horses they came on a flatbed truck inside a shipping container.

Darren realized Claude Thornton had something to do with this when Claude's burly and balding deputy director, Fred Whiteman, walked up with a puzzled grin and shook his head in amazement.

"General Kragle," he said. "What in the world are you and that pretty lady over there doing brawling on a parking lot in broad daylight?"

CHAPTER 68

Partizanskaya River Valley

Sergeant Gloomy Davis played his flashlight beam as deeply as it would penetrate the dust and smoke inside the mine shaft. He felt conflicted. Top Sculdiron was right. The longer the detachment remained at the crime scene, so to speak, the greater its chances of being detected. Every man accepted the risk when he signed on with Delta Force that one day on some far-flung mission no one in the civilized world would ever hear about he could end up owning for eternity his own little plot of dirt. Therefore, a Delta trooper had to be hard, calloused, cavalier about death and dying, whether his or his teammate's.

"When I buy the farm," Mad Dog Carson had asserted, "I want to be buried in the East with my bare cheeks up so any time a raghead tango bows toward Mecca he can kiss my ass."

Gloomy pushed up his NVGs and rubbed moisture from his eyes. He told himself it was mud from rain and shaft dust blurring his vision. Interminable minutes passed. Top had waited for the boss about as long as he dared. Gloomy would have to go against the top sergeant's orders if he entered the mine to search for Major Brandon and Sergeant Dade, at which point Top had every obligation to leave him behind as well.

"Sergeant Davis!" First Sergeant Sculdiron barked unexpectedly.

Gloomy bowed up to protest. "Top—"

"Get in that mine, Sergeant Davis. Find them—but be back here in five minutes. Understand?"

"Roger that, Top. Five minutes."

Mad Dog had offered to accompany him, but there was no time to delay. Besides, Top would never go for risking another man. Gloomy scrambled through the tight opening into the shaft like a lizard. It was so dark and dusty inside that Gloomy's NVGs, even though he used a flashlight, proved of little value other than to keep the dust out of his eyes. He hadn't gone far before the shaft turned muddy. Water dripped from the walls and ceiling. Either the mine leaked or explosions inside the cave discovered the pathway of least resistance and blasted dry the pool of water at the other end of the shaft.

Gloomy broke into a trot to cover as much ground as he could in the time allotted, although sand and dust in the air refracted his flashlight beam and reduced illumination to only a step or two in advance. The mine narrowed and twisted sharply. Almost blind, he collided with a wall of rubble, from which thin webs of rock dust still issued. The wall was dry, which meant the shaft had caved in *after* the detonation.

The Boss and Diverse were trapped on the other side. Gasping with desperation and lungs full of dust, Gloomy tore at the rock with bare hands, starting near the ceiling where the thickness would be less. Soon, he opened a small mouse hole through which he shined his flashlight.

"Boss?" he shouted. *"Boss?"*

No response.

He clawed out more debris, enlarging the opening. He slithered through to the other side. It was wet again. He shone a light on his watch as he continued. Two minutes to go. Still no sign of Brandon and Diverse. He was almost running now, splashing in the mud and slop, calling out again and again.

Knowing that the concussion might have taken out Brandon and Diverse. If not that, then the main shaft collapsing, blown rock, shock . . .

He stopped. He heard a sound. An echo of his footsteps . . . ?

Someone in the blackness ahead coughed. Was it his imagination?

There it was again. "Boss? Is that you?"

He knelt and extended the flashlight high above his head to cast less glare and refraction and provide a better view. Scuffling sounds, more coughing. Two preposterous forms materialized into the strange, glowing light, as though creating themselves out of nothing before Gloomy's astonished eyes. Bog monsters caked with mud from head to bare feet so that only the whites of their eyes shone. They were hatless, shirtless, Brandon assisting Diverse, half dragging him while the Zulu held on with an arm around the major's neck. Brandon still had his carbine, but Diverse's head lolled forward and even his combat harness was gone. Gloomy's heart raced with relief. He leaped forward and got underneath Diverse's other arm.

"I'm so glad to see you, Boss, I could pee my pants," he effused.

"Save the peeing. The detonation addled Diverse and he caught a bullet. I think he'll be all right when he gets some air. What's the situation outside?"

Gloomy told him about Doc Red's wound. Brandon took all casualties hard, although he went to great pains to maintain his professional impenetrable crust.

"Otherwise, Boss, it's all quiet. I don't think anyone will be chasing us soon."

They made better time now with both men helping Di-

verse. Gloomy crawled back through the cave-in first and
with him pulling and Brandon pushing managed to
squeeze the injured demo man through the narrow hole.
Soon, all three coughing, they emerged from the mine
into the drizzling rain. Although they were two minutes
late, Top Sculdiron still waited. He greeted them in his re-
served, matter-of-fact manner, as though he expected
nothing else but that they should return. Brandon handed
off Diverse to Top and Gloomy.

"The boats are ready, Commander," Top reported.

"Good. Let's haul ass."

Major Kragle was back and in charge. The others on the
riverbank slapped him and Diverse on their shoulders in
passing but otherwise saved their greetings and congratu-
lations until later when the job was finished. The eight
men clambered into the three two-man inflatables. One
raft short reminded them that the detachment was also
missing one man in Cassidy Kragle.

Ice Man took Doc Red and Perverse Sanchez in one
boat. Perverse cradled the unconscious medic in his lap
while Ice unfolded metal paddles. Doc's feet dragged in
the water over the gunnel while Perverse sat between Ice
Man's feet and extended his own legs across Ice's.

Not to be separated from the boss, Gloomy climbed
into Brandon's raft. Top Sculdiron, Mad Dog and Diverse,
who was starting to recover, occupied the remaining boat,
crammed together, as Dog observed, like "rub-a-dub-dub,
three men in a tub . . ."

Wading, Brandon pushed his rubber inflatable away
from the bank and piled in on top of Gloomy as the current caught it. He rode the prow, navigating and keeping
watch while Gloomy paddled. The others guided on them.
NVGs worked more efficiently in the open out of the
forests and tunnels.

Current fed by flooding rainfall caught the three tiny craft and swept them downstream at an amazing speed. They should reach the river mouth at the sea within less than two hours. Behind them, the mountain was starting to settle down after its eruption. A single boulder of some immense size rolled down and splashed heavily into the water. Otherwise, there was blessed silence.

CHAPTER 69

Russian Coast

The main part of the storm moved east and out toward the sea where lightning still boiled and popped, leaving the more-western stretch of river relatively undisturbed and mostly in black darkness. In the lead inflatable, Brandon kept close to the bank where they might dart into marsh grasses or beneath overhanging trees should they encounter boats pushing upstream to investigate. Paddlers worked quickly but silently. Splashing or indeed any sound could be heard at incredible distances over water at night.

Reason told Brandon that his brother was undoubtedly lost since his parachute malfunctioned over the sea, but he steadfastly refused to accept it. Escape and evasion plans called for a Delta operator who became separated from his detachment to attempt to link up with it during the exfiltration phase. Cassidy had one of the rafts when he went down, along with his weapons and half the detachment's explosives. If he *were* alive, and able, Cassidy would make it to the mouth of the river and be waiting.

Brandon dreaded breaking the news otherwise to the General and especially to Brown Sugar Mama. Gloria would literally die of heartbreak should anything happen to one of her "sons."

Sounds of boat engines laboring upstream sent the tiny flotilla skimming into tall grass beds in a shallows where conventional boats could not follow. The detachment huddled breathlessly in the grass like geese hiding from predators. Brandon gripped his carbine and bent low with the others to cut down on what profiles they might make on such a dark night. Rain still hissed on the river surface. Downstream toward the sea, lightning played from one horizon to the other, backlighting a pair of skiffs loaded with men chugging their way against the strong current, engines grinding on full throttle.

Doc Red cried out something in his delirium. Perverse, on whose lap the Doc rode, clamped a hand over the medic's mouth to prevent further outcry. Brandon kept his NVG eyes on the approaching skiff. None of the boatmen appeared to have heard. They seemed more anxious to reach the cave to find out what had happened than they did in looking for transgressors.

It took the skiffs an eternity to disappear around a bend in the river.

"How's Doc doing?" Brandon whispered. The three rubber boats bumped against each other in a tight cluster.

"He's still unconscious," Perverse replied, clearly worried. "He cannot hardly breathe."

Ice Man checked Doc Red's tourniquet and reported it holding as best he could expect, considering the location of the wound. The leg continued to swell as it filled with more blood.

"Can he last?" Brandon asked. A regular Special Forces team of twelve operators had two medics assigned to it in case one became incapacitated, like now, and required medical treatment himself. A detachment rarely had such luxury.

"He has to last," Ice Man said.

A half hour farther downstream, Brandon detected lights from a village along one bank. It had rolled up the streets after nightfall, like most such small towns anywhere in the world. Rain and the storm kept even the more active and adventurous indoors. For a moment Brandon considered dropping off Doc Red in the town where a doctor could be summoned. Let diplomacy work out the details of his recovery.

He changed his mind. It would cause an international incident should Americans be implicated in blowing up an "electrical plant" inside Russia and killing Russian citizens. The mission was a "sheep dip," meaning the U.S. government would disavow all knowledge of the detachment should it be compromised. Better to take a chance on Doc's living to reach the submarine than consign him to endure months, even years, of confinement, trials, and eventual execution.

Boats tied up to three or four short unlighted piers along the waterfront lapped gently in the current. The inflatables were gliding past when a tremendous flash from downriver flared away a portion of the distant night. Moments later, the muted boom of the explosion reached Brandon's ears. Astonished, he held up the detachment. Who else except a Delta trooper in this part of Russia was capable of firing off a blast like that?

This newest detonation changed the situation. People might want to investigate it as well, if someone happened to distinguish it from lightning and thunder.

"Top, transfer Diverse to my raft. You and Dog set all those boats adrift. No use making it easy for them to follow us."

"I'm all right now, Major," Diverse spoke up. "I'll help them."

"I hear you got shot in the ass," Mad Dog noted. "For the record."

"Dog, that's none of your business."

"So it is true."

Soon skiffs, rowboats, and small outboards were drift-bobbing like corks on their freedom run to the sea. Top Sculdiron rejoined Brandon just as a second, more-violent explosion jarred the water and flashed like the most remarkable lightning strike. If the boom that followed failed to awake the dead, the dead were incapable of being awakened. Gloria would have thought Jesus was coming back.

"It's Cassidy!" Gloomy stared downriver in amazement. "What on God's earth is he doing?"

He was apparently alive and kicking butt.

As the detachment neared the site of the detonation, Brandon passed the word to be on the lookout for Sergeant Kragle, an unnecessary instruction as Deltas were already craning their necks for him. Fires blazed on a ridgeline that lay a quarter mile back from the river—a smaller flame burning like a bonfire on an open meadow and a fiercer conflagration consuming some form of large structure.

The rubber boats drifted past, staying in the darkness out of the reach of firelight. No one seemed to be about. Ice Man broke the concentrated silence.

"Major, the Doc didn't make it. He's dead, sir."

The epitaph, coming as it did out of darkness and silence in Ice Man's terse vernacular, cast a pall over Det 3A. Mad Dog responded for everyone, with feeling, "Fu-uck."

Perverse Sanchez continued to hold the redheaded medic in his arms as the little flotilla of Deltas passed by the fire, seeing no activity ashore and nothing on the water. It was smooth sailing from there on; the mouth of the river began to widen there before it emptied into the deep sea. Cold Dawn, what was left of it, was on its way home.

"Boss?" Gloomy said, alerting.

Brandon spotted the motor skiff ahead of them in the middle of the river, its engine idling to maintain its position against the flow. He discerned four figures in it through his NVGs.

Tense minutes passed as Brandon maneuvered his rafts toward the boat. It appeared to be waiting. Delta trained a variety of weapons on it, approaching cautiously, until Brandon recognized the man in the bow. Cassidy, his own NVGs having been lost, failed to notice the rubber boats until Brandon called out.

"Cassidy!"

Rafts surrounded the skiff. Each man greeted 3A's lost member with quiet effusiveness. Brandon reached from one boat to the other to shake hands with his brother, both men controlling their emotions. Tears were for *Oprah* and not for some river behind enemy lines.

"I heard detonations upstream," Cassidy said. "You?"

"A nuclear plant," Brandon explained. "What's this all about?" He nodded toward the fires.

"I've been busy."

"I can see you have."

They exchanged casualty reports—Cassidy's broken leg, Diverse Dade's flesh wound in the butt, Doc Red KIA, a bit of news that sobered what would otherwise have been an upbeat reunion. Cassidy introduced his three companions, two of whom wore NASA jumpsuits while the third was the cosmonaut Alexei Minsky.

"The crew from *Soyuz*?" Brandon asked in astonishment. "How about the documents?"

"We have it all, brother."

"You *have* been a busy little beaver," Mad Dog muttered, impressed.

"You don't know the half of it, Dog."

"There's time enough for war stories later," Brandon

said. "Cass, can you make it the rest of the way with your bad leg?"

"I've made it this far. Thanks to Lina . . ."

"Who's she?"

Cassidy glanced at the fires blazing on land, then toward a dead girl in the boat that no one had noticed in the darkness until now. NVGs allowed Cassidy's teammates to see the pain in his face.

"Lina. She . . . she saved my life and gave hers in doing it." He fought to keep from choking up. "She may also have saved thousands of other lives, including the *Soyuz* crew. I couldn't have done anything without her. See those bags in the bottom of the boat? Suitcase nukes. They brought them downriver and were trying to smuggle them out by airplane. I assume we all know where they were going."

And where they came from. Brandon thought of Katya. "Was there a woman . . . ?"

His head twisted toward the fires.

"A pretty woman and three men," Cassidy acknowledged. "Dark hair. Wearing a woolen coat and a Cossack-type cap? You know her?"

The boats bobbed in a dark pod on the swiftly running river, the rafts tied off to the skiff as it floated with the current. Brandon nodded as the fires receded. "We knew her," he said.

"Everybody went up with the school when I blew it," Cassidy explained. "I think she's probably dead too. There's been no activity since."

Brandon nodded again. He sighed, feeling a sadness seep into his soul. Katya was tricky, deceitful, a killer, but . . . But what? Beautiful? She had a way about her. In some respects she reminded Brandon of Summer when Summer worked clandestine for the CIA. Except Summer would never have conspired to murder innocent people, thousands of them, hundreds of thousands . . . That was the big difference, the major difference . . .

It was better that Katya died now, young, along with her mother Dr. Death.

"I'm taking Lina with us," Cassidy avowed in a tone that brooked no discussion. "I can't leave her here. She has nobody except me. I want her buried at the Farm in the Kragle plot. No one will ever realize how much she deserves it."

Brandon cast a last look at the fires.

"Let's move out, Cold Dawn," he said. "Welcome back, space travelers. We have a ride waiting to take us home to America."

CHAPTER 70

Karbala, Iraq

The ceasefire with Mullah al-Sadr, such as it was, broke down for the fifth or sixth time after he and Abu Musaf al-Zarqawi beheaded Sergeant Dusty Richards. Filled with rage and vowing revenge, 1st Infantry moved into action shortly after nightfall, its Bradleys, Abramses, and Strykers spitting flame and destruction as they rumbled into the city like monstrous armed carapaces. Strobe-like explosions flashed in alleys and streets. Small arms and machine guns rattled and chattered viciously. This time there would be no further ceasefires.

Fire glow reflected grimly against Chaplain Cameron Kragle's desert-burnt face as he stood on the outskirts of the tent city and watched the assaults on insurgent strongholds. He prayed silently, lips moving but his eyes wide open against the warring city. Vengeance belonged to the Lord, not man, but Cameron fought his own war inside himself, struggling not to succumb to his darker emotions. He felt his heart knotted and un-Christ-like in his chest. Surely the god who told al-Zarqawi to saw off the heads of his helpless victims could not be the same God Cameron served.

But if ye forgive not men their trespasses, neither will your Father forgive your trespasses.

Cameron had held a memorial for Dusty at Dusty's little lawn in front of his tent before the offensive began.

Men from 1st Platoon built a monument on the green patch of grass, consisting of a spare pair of Dusty's combat boots, a helmet and an M16-A4 rifle. Most in the battalion attended, filling the walkway between the row of tents with helmeted, armed soldiers heavy with the tools and accouterments of battle. Clutching his Bible and Shield of Strength dog tags, Cameron knelt and the battalion knelt with him. He led the young soldiers in prayer and then he spoke a few words of encouragement, assuring them that their mission was just, a Just War, in bringing freedom and hope to twenty-five million Iraqis who had never known it.

But did such platitudes mean anything to those families who received folded flags at graveside?

The soldiers seemed to take solace from the Word. They replaced their helmets on their heads, buckled them, and marched off to generate more widows and orphans. Wars and rumors of wars, forever and ever, amen. Watching them depart, Cameron felt hollow inside. God was his anchor. The way, the truth, and the life. But the Lord had not comforted him this time, bringing him to the question: Was God enough? *Was God enough?*

There were evil men in the world—Saddam Hussein who tortured, enslaved, raped, and murdered hundreds of thousands of his own people; Osama bin Laden; al-Zarqawi; assorted Jihadists; anticivilization radicals and zealots and crazies, all of whom worshipped chaos and devoted themselves to replacing order with an anarchy where every man turned his hand against his neighbor. The two forces in the world—good and evil—constantly warred with one another.

All that was required for evil to prevail was for good men to do nothing. Men of God, *especially* men of God, must never stand on the sidelines and overlook evil, from whatever its source. God expected his servants to fight the good fight on the front lines, to be warriors in the ongoing struggle against the forces of darkness. Still . . .

Was God enough?

Karbala began exploding in fire and destruction and Cameron, watching from the gathered darkness, ached from the emptiness inside, from the sense of frustration that settled over him darker than the night itself.

Lord, forgive my doubts . . . I am your servant . . .

CHAPTER 71

Walter Reed Medical Center

General Kragle rushed directly to Walter Reed Hospital
from the B&S warehouses in Bethesda where Agent Fred
Whiteman and his JTTF were still trying to sort out
things. Vanda drove to the Justice Department where Jennifer and a sullen but shaken pink-haired Smoke were under interrogation, along with a half-dozen suspected
terrorist sleepers rounded up at the warehouses. Jennifer
might be charged with crimes herself, as she most certainly conspired to some extent with those who ultimately
turned against her. Agents informed her mother that she
might expect leniency if she cooperated.

Confined to his hospital bed in ICU 414, even for only
those few hours, seemed to have turned Claude Thornton
philosophic.

"The War on Terror is a messy business," he was saying to the General. "It's a confusing mess where nothing
is neatly packaged and where there are always lots of
loose strings even when we win a round. But we have no
choice but to keep fighting while we try to withhold as
much from the media as we can. Imagine the panic if
people knew we bust up a terrorist cell right here in the
U.S. at least once a week, or that hundreds of potential
terrorists are coming across our borders every week—
Russians, Iraqis, Saudis, Iranians, al-Qaeda . . . We cer-

tainly can't expect the public to react any better than official Washington."

Congress had demonstrated solid statesmanship when someone sprinkled a few grains of anthrax in the Capitol cloakroom. Politicians knocking each other out of the way, scrambling down the Capitol steps and hurrying to be first in line at the airports told it all.

"It would be an even uglier sight if our esteemed leaders should find out terrorists were planning to nuke them," Claude said. "It could shut down the federal government."

"Which might not be a bad thing," General Kragle wryly suggested. "Claude, how did you know to send agents to the warehouses? They arrived just in time, I might add."

"It's a long story. You got the time?"

"I'm picking up Vanda from the Justice Department later. She may be there for a few hours."

Claude lifted a brow. "Vanda?"

"I'll tell you later."

Something appeared to have renewed the General's outlook on life since Claude and he had lunched together a few days earlier. Claude wondered if "Vanda" had something to do with it.

Claude took a telephone call. When he hung up, he said, "That was Fred. He's at Justice now. Your Jennifer Stratton and the scumbag called Smoke are confirming what we suspected. Terrorists at the B&S warehouses were expecting the Command and Control Center to be delivered from Charleston so it could be used in setting up operations targeting U.S. sites. Professor Patsy Koehler was coordinating the whole thing—or at least she was until she became high profile. She would have received tactical nukes either tomorrow or Friday if her terrorist buddies hadn't got hinky of her new fame with the FBI and cut off her head."

"I think we've intercepted the nukes—at least this time," the General said, filling Claude in on Operation Cold Dawn and how Major Brandon Kragle's detachment had destroyed a nuclear plant in Russia. Detachment 3A was even then in the process of being recovered in the Sea of Okhotsk, along with the missing *Soyuz* crew and suitcase nukes that had almost been smuggled out of Russia on their way, presumably, to the United States.

"Do you know the intended target, Claude?" General Kragle asked.

"We were concentrating on New York because of all the antiwar activity to shut down the Federalist National Convention," Claude said, trying to shift his weight in bed against traction that held him captive. "That's where we expected the attack. Gradually, it occurred to us that all the terrorist chatter about the convention was nothing but a diversion to keep us from looking at the actual target— Congress. Your Cold Dawn might have answered the question of *where* the nukes were coming from, Darren, but we still don't know how WMDs were to be smuggled in, nor how the plot to nuke the Capitol was supposed to go down. There are a couple of possibilities for infiltrating them. One is by the shipping lanes; the other is across the Mexican border, where we caught some Russian Muslims earlier this week. All we know so far about the plot to bomb Congress is that there would have been a nuclear mushroom over Washington, D.C., on the last day of the Federalist Convention this week, and that it would have been carried out using planned antiwar demonstrations as a diversion."

He took a deep breath. "Okay, General. Your turn. How did you end up in the middle of all this?"

The General explained about Vanda and her missing daughter Jennifer. Jennifer had unintentionally discovered elements of the plot to bomb the Capitol, but only enough details to frighten her and make Patsy Koehler's terrorist buddies suspicious. Patsy turned Jennifer over to the Jihadia who kept her drugged and in captivity at the B&S warehouses. Terrorists eventually lured Jennifer's boyfriend Smoke there when he started getting nosy.

"Tangos were about to do away with both of them," the General concluded. "They clearly couldn't trust Jennifer after what she had found out—and I wouldn't trust Smoke myself to carry out my garbage. Then your FBI guys showed up concealed on the back of a truck in a shipping container."

Claude grinned. "That was a nice touch, don't you think? The warehouse was expecting the delivery of the shipping container from Charleston. Since terrorist cells are insulated from each other, we thought delivering the container was the best way to get inside the warehouses and prevent the detonating of a WMD if the terrorists already had one. Sort of like a Trojan horse to get past the walls. But when we got there, there you were, Darren."

"It's a messy business, Claude. We can't be everywhere and know everything."

"We may never know the full story," the FBI agent conceded. "It's even unlikely this terrorist cell knew the entire plan. Sleepers are merely foot soldiers ready to carry out last-minute orders from their leaders, radical mullahs, and Allah. There were no WMDs present this time, yet. We might have stopped this one, but it won't be the last. They'll keep coming, and they'll keep coming. Every morning I read the intelligence summaries and I think we're all going to die. The next morning I wake up and do it all over again. That's the way this war is fought—and we're going to lose it when we lose the courage to keep fighting."

CHAPTER 72

TYLER ACCEPTS PARTY'S NOMINATION

New York (CPI)—In a rousing nomination acceptance speech on the last night of his party's convention, President Woodrow Tyler vowed that, if he is reelected, America will continue to fight on until terrorism throughout the world has been eradicated. He said if the world would live in peace, it has no choice but to fight for it.

In a thirty-minute speech sometimes laced with the malapropisms that so annoy his opponents and provoke the most acerbic to question his intelligence, President Tyler began by saying, "Three years ago, the world was very different. Terrorists planned attacks with little fear of discovery or reckoning. Outlaw regimes supported terrorists and defied the civilized world without shame and with few consequences. But no more. The world changed on September the 11th, and since that day we have changed the world. We have not forgotten September the 11th, and we will not allow our enemies to forget it either . . ."

Outside Madison Square Garden, while President Tyler delivered his speech inside, several thousand antiwar, anti-Tyler demonstrators marched by with placards describing Tyler as a "Nazi" and "warmonger." Protestors had threatened to "shut down" the Republican Convention and New York City, but failed to attain that goal.

"On September the 11th," President Tyler said, "we saw the cruelty of the terrorists, and we glimpsed the future they intend for us. They intend to strike the United States to the limits of their power.

"To overcome the dangers of our time, America is also taking a new approach in the world. We're determined to challenge new threats, not ignore them, or simply wait for further tragedy. We are defending the peace by taking the fight to the enemy. We will confront them overseas so we do not have to confront them here at home. We are destroying the leadership of terrorist networks in sudden raids, disrupting their planning and financing, and keeping them on the run. Month by month, we are shrinking the space in which they can freely operate by denying them territory and the support of governments.

"Senator Harris says if we only avoid any direct confrontation with the enemy, he will forget his evil ways and learn to love us. Well, as Ronald Reagan said of the Cold War, the choice is not between peace and war, only between fight and surrender. There is only one guaranteed way you can have peace, and you can have it in the next second—and that is to surrender . . .

"If America shows uncertainty and weakness in this decade, the world will drift toward tragedy. That will not happen on my watch. We are winning and we will win. We will win by staying on the offensive. This is how I see it: we will win, they will lose . . ."

CHAPTER 73

Washington, D.C.

General Darren E. Kragle sat pondering at the little desk in his hotel room at the Washingtonian, before him his resignation from USSOCOM and request for retirement from the U.S. Army. White noise in the background from CNN on the television barely registered in his concentration. Talking heads still babbled lead stories—the recovery of the two missing American astronauts and the Russian cosmonaut; the beheading of the 1st Infantry sergeant in Karbala. There had been nothing at all on the destruction of the nuclear plant in Russia, nor was there likely to be.

Officially, American warriors from Operation Cold Dawn were never in Russia. Officially, the al-Qaeda nuclear plant had not been blown up. Except for high-profile instances like Afghanistan and Iraq, and in the political arena where it was nastiest and most vicious, America's War on Terror was waged mostly in the shadows by Shadow Warriors whose valor could never be officially and publicly recognized.

The General stood up and pulled back the window curtains above the desk to let in the morning sun when it finally rose. It was Sunday and too early for protestors to take to the streets. Most of them had gone home anyhow after the Federalist Convention ended in Manhattan. Pennsylvania Avenue that ran past the hotel and on across the bow of the White House lay quiet outside the window. President Tyler reopened the famous avenue to traffic the day before for the first time since 9/11. Almost immediately, some wacko set himself afire in front of the White House while shouting *"Allahu Akbar!"* until flames scorched out his tongue.

Darren glanced at his watch. Vanda was meeting him in the hotel lobby in an hour to pick up her mother and his father at Pleasant Valley and drive south for what the General liked to call the Gathering of the Clans at the Farm in Collierville, Tennessee. Although Vanda expressed a desire to photograph the old barn at the Farm, the General had been reluctant to invite her at first. Too many memories of Rita and him together inhabited the Farm for him to let another woman intrude. There had been a moment at Pleasant Valley on the previous day that changed his mind.

Vanda met him there and walked with him to meet the Ambassador.

"How's the old gentleman doing today?" Darren asked Dolores, his father's nurse.

"He's on the patio. It's a mite cool, but he has a blanket."

The Ambassador sat wrapped in his blanket gazing solemnly out across the manicured expanse of Pleasant Valley. He glanced up, unusual in itself, and a flicker of recognition crossed his worn face. He reached out a hand to Vanda in the first sign of recognition he had exhibited in weeks. Evidently, Darren wasn't the only one affected by how much Vanda's smile reminded him of Rita. The Ambassador had been very fond of his daughter-in-law.

"I'm so pleased to see you, Rita," the Ambassador said.

The moment passed quickly. He dropped Vanda's hand and retreated back into himself. But there had been the moment. Darren invited Vanda to the Farm.

"There'll be a memorial ceremony on Tuesday," he explained.

"One of the soldiers?"

"It's a burial for the body of a young woman my son Cassidy brought back. I'm sure you'll hear the story."

"Your sons all sound like wonderful men," Vanda said, a little wistful at the thought of her daughter still being held in jail. She cheered immediately, however, melancholia not being a long part of her makeup, especially since Jennifer was at least safe. She squeezed Darren's hand and laughed. "I'd love to go on one condition, that being we stop by the Pig Out café for breakfast on our way out of town to pick up our parents."

And so the Pig Out was at the top of the day's itinerary.

Cassidy with his broken leg, now recast, and Brandon were already on their way to Tennessee from Fort Bragg with Margo and Brandon's more-pregnant-than-ever wife Summer. Cameron couldn't make it. He had been promoted to overseeing chaplains and worship services throughout the U.S. armed forces in Iraq. But Kelli Rule, the former AFSOC's Southern-bred niece and, the General thought, a prospective daughter-in-law, asked to be invited after talking long-distance with Cameron. She flew up from Florida to South Carolina to motor the rest of the way to the Farm with Brown Sugar Mama and her husband Raymond.

Operation Cold Dawn soldiers would naturally attend, with the conspicuous and sad absence of Steve "Doc Red" Mancino, whose military funeral had been held at Fort Bragg on Saturday. Troop One's gourmet cooks, Sergeants Ice Man Thompson and Diverse Dade, had promised to do the cooking—roast lamb and all the trimmings, Scottish style. Delta Force commander Colonel Buck Thompson and General Paul Etheridge from CENTCOM were coming, along with CIA's Tom Hinds and whoever else might be able to tear himself away from the War on Terror for a couple of days. Claude Thornton couldn't make it. He was still in the hospital waiting to heal sufficiently for Congress to rake him across the corrugated tongues of the Second 9/11 Commission about who knew what and when.

Claude laughed it off. "At least they no longer lynch Southern Negro gentlemen. I can't escape the commission this time, Darren, but I'm giving Della a few days off so she can do the Irish ritual with you Kragles. Don't corrupt her."

"How about a ski trip to Colorado after the elections?" the General said, in a good mood. "To make up for your not getting off now."

"I suppose it depends upon how the elections turn out. None of us may feel like celebrating."

Darren hoped pundits were wrong when they said you didn't have to fool all the people all the time, just enough of them to get elected. He had to put his faith in the common sense of the American people to distinguish the difference between a genuine man of guts like Woodrow Tyler and the empty suit of Lowell Rutherford Harris, who kept proving there was nothing he and his supporters would not stoop to in order to seize power. Wasn't it time for another "Greatest Generation" to step forward to confront all hardships, endure all sacrifices in the long battle for civilization's survival?

Leaving his resignation unsigned, the General got up from the desk, showered, and changed into a Class A Green uniform with ribbons and gold-braided cap. How could he in all good conscience take it off when the nation faced its greatest challenge in more than a half century? He still had a few good years remaining. The fight for freedom was a lonely battle sometimes. But if the United

States didn't lead it, sometimes imperfectly but mostly with honor, then who would?

He looked at his resignation and retirement papers. Then he methodically tore them into shreds, wadded the shredded paper into a hard ball and tossed it into the waste basket on his way out to meet Vanda in the lobby. He looked forward to the drive to Tennessee with her and their parents.

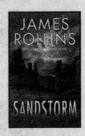